# A
# Promise
# *for* Spring

Books by
# Kim Vogel Sawyer

---

*Waiting for Summer's Return*

*Where Willows Grow*

*My Heart Remembers*

*Where the Heart Leads*

*A Promise for Spring*

# A
# Promise
## _for_ Spring

# Kim Vogel
_A Novel by_
# Sawyer

BETHANY HOUSE PUBLISHERS

_Minneapolis, Minnesota_

*A Promise for Spring*
Copyright © 2009
Kim Vogel Sawyer

Cover design by Brand Navigation
Cover photography by Steve Gardner, PixelWorks Studios, Inc.

Scripture quotations are from the King James Version of the Bible.

Published by Bethany House Publishers
11400 Hampshire Avenue South
Bloomington, Minnesota 55438

Bethany House Publishers is a division of
Baker Publishing Group, Grand Rapids, Michigan.

Printed in the United States of America

ISBN 978-0-7642-0507-1

---

**Library of Congress Cataloging-in-Publication Data**

Sawyer, Kim Vogel.
    A promise for spring / by Kim Vogel Sawyer.
       p.   cm.
    ISBN 978-0-7642-0507-1 (pbk.)
    1. English—United States—Fiction. 2. Ranchers—Fiction. 3. Kansas—Fiction.
4. United States—History—1865–1898—Fiction. I. Title.
    PS3619.A97P76    2009
    813'.6—dc22

                                             2008042960

*For KATHY, of course.*

You were there when the seed blossomed.

"THE LORD IS MY SHEPHERD;

I SHALL NOT WANT.

HE MAKETH ME TO LIE DOWN IN GREEN PASTURES:

HE LEADETH ME BESIDE THE STILL WATERS.

HE RESTORETH MY SOUL."

PSALM 23:1–3A, KJV

# ONE

◡

## May 1874

NEXT STOP—MO-O-O-ORELAND, Kansas . . . Next stop, Moreland!"

Emmaline Bradford's heart pounded in the top of her head. *Moreland . . . My stop . . .* She peeked over her shoulder and watched the conductor move slowly up the aisle, his gait swaying with the motion of the train. When he reached Emmaline's seat, she held out her gloved hand and whispered, "E-excuse me, sir."

The conductor paused, his feet set wide, and peered down at her. The gray hair of the man's bushy eyebrows splayed out in every direction, nearly covering the top half of his round spectacles. It gave him a fierce look.

Emmaline licked her dry lips. "Can you tell me . . . how much longer to Moreland?"

He pulled on a loop of chain hanging across his well-filled brocade vest, freeing a gold pocket watch from its hiding spot. A flick of his broad thumb opened the cover on the gold disk. He squinted at the watch's face for a moment, causing his thick brows to slip briefly behind the circles of his eyeglasses. Then he gave a brisk nod of apparent satisfaction and his face relaxed. "Less'n fifteen minutes, miss." He gave a single, emphatic nod. "Yes, miss,

7

oughtta be pullin' into Moreland right on schedule—three-fifteen on the dot."

Emmaline's stomach turned over, and her palms grew moist within the confines of her cotton gloves. "Th-thank you, sir."

The conductor tipped his hat before moving on.

Less than fifteen minutes and she would step off this train into a new life. For nearly eight weeks she had traveled, dreading this moment, and now it was upon her. The high, white muslin collar of her dress choked her, and she slipped one glove-covered finger beneath its edge and pulled, trying to give herself room to breathe. It didn't help. She gripped her hands together and pressed them into her lap. Tears stung behind her nose, but she set her jaw against them. Crying would accomplish nothing.

Oh, why was she here on this foul-smelling train, covered in coal dust, heading to what was sure to be some cheerless hovel on an empty plain? She looked out the window again, her heart sinking in despair at the sight of the nearly treeless, rolling plains of dry brown grass. No green meadows or fields of daisies or cobblestone streets like at home.

Despite her efforts to refrain from weeping, a tear slipped free of its perch on her lower lid and trailed down her cheek. The strong breeze coursing through the open window dried it before Emmaline had a chance to sweep it away. Oh, how she missed her home.

It hadn't been her idea to leave Yorkshire County in England— it was Father's. Mother hadn't wanted her to go, either. But Father had insisted it was best, and when Father insisted, everyone had to agree or be made to feel miserable.

Well, Emmaline reasoned as she blinked rapidly against more tears gathering in her eyes, she could not possibly be more miserable in England facing Father's disapproval than she was right now, sitting in this uncomfortable berth, facing a bleak future in a bleak land with a man she hadn't seen since she was a child of seventeen. What had Father been thinking to send her here?

In a pocket hidden in the seam of her wide skirt she carried the letter that had started it all. Father had said, "Take it with you, Emmaline, and show it to your Geoffrey in the event he should not recognize you." The way he'd said "your Geoffrey" had sent a knife of terror through her breast. Father must have seen the fear in her eyes, because he added in a surprisingly kind tone, "I do not believe there will be a question, Emmaline. It is merely a safeguard." And she had nodded in unwilling acquiescence, not daring to tell Father what she truly feared. How could she think of this stranger as "her" Geoffrey? She barely remembered the man!

If perchance he should fail to recognize her, would she be allowed to return to her beloved England? Every night since Father had made his announcement that Great-Uncle Hedrick would accompany Emmaline to America to become, at long last, the bride of Geoffrey Garrett, she had prayed fervently. Prayed for release from the arrangement made when she was too young to fully appreciate the consequences. Prayed for understanding from Father. But Father had never wavered in his resolve to send her away.

"A Bradford honors his word," he'd insisted, ignoring Emmaline's tearful pleas. It hadn't seemed to matter that Geoffrey had not honored his word. Hadn't he promised on the day he set sail that he would return in a year's time to exchange wedding vows in the little chapel their families had attended? But five years slipped by, and then instead of returning, he had merely summoned her with the directive that they would wed in Kansas. They would live in Kansas. Away from family and friends.

During each leg of the journey, she had begged God to allow her to turn around and go home again. Still the ship and the trains had moved her relentlessly toward Kansas and her waiting groom. Groom—what a frightening word that was. Better she should say her "waiting stranger," for that is what Geoffrey Garrett was—a complete and utter stranger!

"Prayers are no more effective than tears," she moaned softly, clutching the letter in her pocket with trembling fingers. "Neither prayers nor tears do any good."

She quickly brought up her fingers to swish away the moisture on her cheeks. Taking her hands from her face, she looked at her gloves and wanted to cry again. Dust had changed the once-pristine whiteness to a dingy gray. With dismay, she realized that she must be covered from head to toe in the awful dust emitted from the coal-burning engine. She consoled herself with the thought that at least on her black dress it would be less noticeable than on her gloves.

*What a sight I must be. Perhaps Father was wise to send the letter with me—Geoffrey might indeed have difficulty recognizing me under this covering of soot.*

The conductor weaved his way down the aisle again, calling in a deep tone, "Next stop is Moreland, folks."

Moreland. Where Geoffrey would be waiting.

Pressing her hand to the square of paper in her hip pocket, she closed her eyes and prayed once again for deliverance.

———

Geoffrey Garrett stood in the stiff Kansas breeze, his focus on the parallel lines of track disappearing over the horizon. His heart thrummed rapidly. Each passing minute brought her closer. Emmaline—the daughter of his father's best friend, the sweet girl who had filled his dreams since he left Yorkshire County five years ago, the woman who would be his bride.

The broadcloth of his best suit felt strange after wearing well-worn work trousers and cotton shirts for so long. He fought the temptation to remove the string tie and open the top button of his cambric shirt. But how would Emmaline recognize him if he were dressed as a common ranch hand? She would need to see Geoffrey Garrett, the gentleman. Then she would know she had reached her groom.

Bride . . . Groom . . . He had been anticipating this day—been praying for its arrival—for so long it hardly seemed conceivable that it was truly here. Soon he and Emmaline would stand before Reverend Stanford and recite their vows. And then the sweetest of his dreams would become reality—he would take his Emmaline to the home he had prepared.

"So, Geoff, she's comin' today, huh?"

The greeting pulled Geoffrey's gaze away from the silver trails of track. He glanced over his shoulder, then waved when he spotted Harvey Rawson's thin, friendly face peering out from the depot's window. With firm steps, Geoffrey crossed to the window and shook the depot manager's hand.

"Yes, Harvey, today my Emmaline arrives."

Harvey snorted. "You look ready for a wedding, all right—or a funeral! Those are pretty fancy duds for a rancher."

Geoffrey looked down his length, scowling briefly. "Perhaps not appropriate for herding sheep, but I think I am perfectly attired for meeting my future bride."

Harvey chuckled. "Nervous?"

Geoffrey considered the question. He had known Emmaline since she was a baby—had actually pushed her pram on lengthy walks through their small village with their mothers when he was a young boy. Letters from her father had kept her very much a part of his life during the years he had been in Kansas, getting his ranch started. What he felt was excitement and anticipation, not nervousness.

"No, Harvey, I am not nervous."

Harvey laughed again, leaning his bony elbows on the counter and grinning widely. "Well, you're an uncommon man, then, not nervous on his wedding day."

"I have nothing about which to be nervous," Geoffrey insisted. "Emmaline's family and mine have been friends since well before my birth. We grew up together—her older brother Edward was my best chum." A distant, shrill whistle drifted across the plains. He spun toward the sound. Here she came!

The Union Pacific engine chugged steadily toward the depot, its shiny black stack sending up puffs of gray smoke into the clear blue sky. The ground beneath Geoffrey's feet vibrated as the train neared. When the huge black engine was within several hundred feet of the depot, the brakes screeched loudly enough to make the fine hairs on the back of his neck stand at attention. A pressure built in his chest as the powerful locomotive drew ever nearer. And then, finally, the train squealed to a stop in front of the depot, the engine sputtering and heaving in exhaustion before it quieted with a release of white steam.

The engineer and his fireman hopped down from the tall engine and hollered a greeting to Harvey. Geoffrey's gaze bounced along the lines of square windows on the three boxy passenger cars. At last a blue-suited conductor appeared in the open doorway of the middle car, and Geoffrey moved on unexpectedly shaky legs in that direction.

He pressed his hand against his suddenly jumping stomach. *Perhaps I am a bit nervous.* The conductor hopped out and placed a wooden step on the ground in front of the exit before lifting his hand toward the train car. Geoffrey's breath caught, his footsteps slowing, when a slim, glove-covered hand emerged, stretching daintily to meet the hand of the conductor.

Geoffrey swept the hat from his head and took off at a run.

He should be the one to take her hand and help her down. But he was moments too late. As he came to a stop beside the conductor, Emmaline stepped to the ground with her head lowered. Immediately her hands became lost in the folds of her skirt as she grasped the voluminous black muslin and shook it mightily. The flapping released a cloud of gray dust that swirled around her, and he took one involuntary step backward.

She must have seen his feet, because the swishing abruptly stopped. Her face lifted slowly, and her eyes—the gentle, nut brown eyes he remembered so well—seemed to travel from his boots up the length of his suit until they finally met his welcoming smile.

He sought words that would convey all of the longing and dreaming of the past five years while he had waited for her to grow up and come to him. But something lodged in his throat, and he had to swallow hard before he could speak. When he opened his mouth, only one hopeful word was uttered—one word that held everything his heart felt: "Emmaline . . ."

# TWO

S HE HELD HIS GAZE, her brown eyes as wide and fear-filled as a hunted doe's. Realizing he was panting, Geoffrey pressed his palm to his stomach, trying to calm himself. He stepped forward, uncertain how to proceed. She stood so still and so silent.

"It *is* Emmaline, is it not?" Geoffrey disliked the apprehension he heard in his own voice, but her fearful reaction did not inspire confidence.

So slightly he thought he might have imagined it, she lifted her chin and gave a quick nod. The tip of her tongue sneaked out to lick her lips, and finally she spoke in a whisper-soft voice. "M-Mr. Garrett?"

"That is right. But, Emmaline, you mustn't greet me as if I were a stranger." He smiled in what he hoped was an encouraging manner. Beneath the coating of gray dust, her face looked deathly pale, making her brown eyes appear even larger than they were. Her hands shook, and he was certain he saw tears quivering on her lashes. In fact, those two clean paths down her cheeks must have been created by tears. Perhaps the ride had made her ill.

He coaxed, "Come now, you cannot have forgotten my Christian name."

Again her tongue crept out to moisten her lips. Obediently she recited, "Geoffrey."

He offered his brightest smile, settling his black bowler back on his head. "That's my Emmaline!" At his words, she sucked in a sharp breath and reared back. Geoffrey's brows lowered in puzzlement. What on earth was the matter with her? He looked toward the doorway of the passenger car. "Where is your great-uncle? Your father indicated he would be accompanying you."

Her forehead pinched. "Uncle Hedrick became ill shortly after our arrival in America. He . . . he died, and the engineer said we mustn't dally. A minister assured me he would be given a Christian burial. I was not even allowed to attend the graveside service."

"Oh, Emmaline." Geoffrey's heart lurched in sympathy. "How difficult for you."

"I left him with strangers in a strange town, in a strange land." Her voice quavered, and she blinked rapidly.

The sad story explained her reticence. He said, "I am so sorry for your loss."

She nodded and then fell silent. Determined to turn her thoughts to more cheerful things, he stepped close and offered his elbow. "Come, Emmaline. We must retrieve your trunk from the baggage car, and then I have a little surprise for you."

He hoped that promise might make her eyes light up in happy anticipation, but he saw no change in her expression at all. However, she did place her small hand into the crook of his arm.

They walked beside the train, and she kept her face aimed straight ahead, allowing him the opportunity to give her a thorough perusal. Her uncle's death explained her attire. Dressed all in black—save her collar and gloves, which he assumed had once been white—she looked as if she'd just returned from a funeral. The dress was of the finest quality, but she was truly filthy. When might she have last had an opportunity to wash her face?

The reddish brown hair that emerged from beneath the dusty, feathered hat looked as if it needed combing and rearranging. There was a musty odor emanating from her, clearly discernible even over the odors of coal smoke and animals. What had he been thinking to have planned for their wedding vows to be spoken upon her arrival? Before they could have such a ceremony she would require a bath and a change of clothing. She looked nothing like the bride he had envisioned.

Geoffrey tried to set aside his disappointment. He was being unfair. Traveling by train across country, she would not have had a chance to clean up before meeting him. No doubt she was as uncomfortable with her rumpled, unkempt appearance as he was. Discomfort must certainly add to her timidity. If she looked nothing like the bride he had anticipated, her behavior was far from what he had hoped for, as well.

Eager to put her at ease, he asked, "Did you have a pleasant trip?"

"Y-yes, thank you." She answered primly, still refusing to look at him. The stammer unsettled him. He didn't remember her stuttering as a child.

He tried again. "I trust the accommodations on the S.S. *Wyoming* were satisfactory."

Her chin quivered slightly before she replied. "Oh yes. Qu-quite. Thank you."

"Did the ship's maid assist you as needed?"

"She was quite helpful, thank you."

This conversation was getting him nowhere. He stopped, forcing her to stop, too. He waited until she had turned her uncertain gaze upward. "Emmaline, please tell me what I am doing that

frightens you. I do not wish for you to be afraid of me. I have—"
How could he summarize all of his plans in such a way that he
would not overwhelm her? He had expected a grown woman to
step off of that train, but Emmaline behaved very much like a
child in need of assurance. His voice dropped to nearly a whisper.
"I have been looking forward to your arrival. It has been quite
lonely, all these years away from my family. Your lovely face is an
exceptionally welcome sight."

Emmaline's gaze darted to the side and her cheeks flooded with
color. He noticed her free hand remained pressed tightly against the
hip of her dirty dress. The fingers of that hand convulsed. Finally
her lips parted and she brought her gaze back to his face. He had
to lean forward to catch her airy words.

"I thank you for your kind welcome. I . . . I will be fine once
I become accustomed to things here."

She glanced across the dry, rolling prairie. A hot gust of wind
caught her skirts, wrapping the full folds around her knees. She
released the hold on her hip long enough to straighten the tangled
layers of muslin. Then, again, she cupped her hip and finished
meekly, "It is quite different from home, is it not?"

Geoffrey, encouraged by her lengthy speech, squeezed the
hand resting in the crook of his elbow. "Oh yes, the landscape and
climate are quite different from England's. But I have adjusted, and
I know you will, too." He gave her hand another pat and started
moving again.

They approached the baggage car, and Geoffrey squinted at
the two men unloading goods. One of them climbed into the car,
but the second one turned in their direction and swept his battered
hat from his head. This gesture revealed the familiar tousled mass
of red hair belonging to Max Tolbert.

Max grinned broadly and called out, "Ho, Geoff! So this is
your Emmaline, eh?"

Geoffrey placed a hand on Emmaline's back to propel her forward. "Emmaline, I would like you to meet an acquaintance of mine, Mr. Maxwell Tolbert." They came to a stop before Max, who stood grinning stupidly. "Max, this is Miss Emmaline Bradford from Yorkshire County, England."

Max held his hat against his chest. "How do, miss?" He plunked the hat back on his head and, offering a cheeky smirk, poked Geoffrey with his elbow. "But not 'miss' for long, eh, Geoff?"

Emmaline stiffened, and Geoffrey wished Max had not been so brazen. These men did not understand polite conversation where ladies were concerned. "If you are referring to our wedding plans," Geoffrey said in a formal tone, "then you are correct. I have made arrangements to exchange our vows before we retire to the ranch this evening."

Geoffrey sensed Emmaline's startled gaze swing to him. From within the car a voice boomed, "Max! Stop jawin' an' help me out here!" A crate slid across the wooden floor and nearly sailed through the open doorway.

Max lost his hat as he dove for the opening. He stopped the crate and then bellowed, "Fool crazy nincompoop! Watch what you're doin', Lyle!"

Lyle hollered back, "I am watchin' what I'm doin'! You need to be watchin' 'stead of yammerin'! We got work to do!"

Max continued to mutter but returned to work. Geoffrey led Emmaline well away from the train car and allowed the men space to finish their tasks. He spotted Emmaline's wooden trunk marked clearly on its cover with her name, the name of the ship, and her destination of Moreland. Several other crates of varying sizes were removed, and finally a twelve-foot-long brown-paper-wrapped tube emerged. Geoffrey experienced a rush of delight when he spotted this item—his wedding gift to Emmaline.

"Max, if I bring my wagon round, would you and Lyle load my things for me?" Geoffrey asked as Lyle hopped out of the car.

"Sure, Geoff," Max replied good-naturedly while Lyle scratched his head. "You ain't exactly dressed for haulin', are you?" Max gave Lyle a jab with his elbow. "Ol' Geoff is gettin' married today, Lyle."

"Yeah, yeah, I heard." Lyle shoved Max's elbow away. His tone turned congenial as he offered, " 'Gratulations, Geoff. Wishin' you many years of happy."

"Thank you." Geoffrey took Emmaline by the elbow and steered her back toward the station. He called over his shoulder, "I shall return with the wagon momentarily."

Geoffrey helped Emmaline onto the springed seat, then settled himself beside her. She grasped her skirts and pulled them close to her knees. Not even a whisper of fabric touched Geoffrey. He wondered if she held her skirts close to protect his clothing from the coal dust or to keep herself away from him. With a slight scowl, he released the brake and expertly guided the wagon to the waiting boxes. He and Emmaline watched in silence while Max and Lyle loaded everything into the bed of the wagon.

When the men were finished, Lyle pointed at the long tube that stuck out the end of the wagon. Scratching his head again, he asked, "What is that thing, Geoff? It's heavier'n the crates o' books we delivered to the schoolhouse last week!"

Geoffrey laughed. "That's a surprise for Emmaline." He glanced at Emmaline, hoping to see a spark of curiosity in her eyes. She stared straight ahead, seemingly unaware of the exchange between the men. With a disappointed sigh, Geoffrey issued a halfhearted invitation. "Come out to the ranch in a week or so, Lyle, and you'll see what was in there. Bring Clara with you to meet Emmaline."

Lyle gave him a gap-toothed grin. "Sure thing, Geoffrey.

Me 'n' the missus'd be glad to come out for a hello. Bye now, Miss Emmaline."

Emmaline barely nodded in return. Geoffrey slapped the reins on the horses' rumps, and they obediently lurched forward.

# THREE

As Geoffrey guided the wagon through the center of Moreland, he waved at townspeople and called out greetings. Emmaline only stared straight ahead, her hands clasped in her lap. To fill the awkward silence, Geoffrey told her about the little town. "Moreland was originally a railroad town, but it has grown into a nice community. It already has its own newspaper, called *The Progress*, a post office with rural delivery, and two banks in addition to a school and three flourishing churches."

Although she didn't reply, Emmaline's gaze followed the rows of businesses—everything from a dry goods store to a millinery shop.

"I wish we had time to let you explore a bit before heading to Reverend Stanford's." Even as he spoke the words, he realized she was in no state to be entering any places of business. Her filthy appearance would make the other ladies view her with disdain, and he didn't want that for his Emmaline. He hid his smile as she turned nearly backward in the seat and watched the town disappear behind them.

Of course, he also had to admit she was in no state to be standing before a minister and reciting wedding vows. She needed a bath and a change of clothes. Where could they stop along the way to see to that need?

"Um, Emmaline?"

She brought her wary gaze from over her shoulder and fixed it upon Geoffrey.

"I—" He cleared his throat. "I wondered if you came prepared with . . . appropriate attire . . . for a wedding."

Emmaline tucked her chin and her cheeks blazed with pink. "Mother arranged a bridal trousseau." Her voice sounded hoarse. The Kansas wind tossed a loose strand of hair across her cheek, and she brusquely anchored it behind one ear. "So we are . . . we are to be married . . . today?"

Geoffrey nodded. "Yes. I realize you have only just arrived. But, Emmaline, I . . . I cannot take you to my home without . . . without the benefit of a clergyman's blessing." He intensely disliked his own stammering. He gave her a sideways glance, feeling certain the heat in his face had nothing to do with the warm May sun. He desperately hoped Emmaline would understand his message.

Apparently she did, for the color in her cheeks deepened and she abruptly changed the topic. "Tell . . . tell me about the ranch, please, Geoffrey."

It was the first time she had spoken his name without encouragement. The sound of it on her tongue made Geoffrey's heart rise up in his chest and beat rapidly.

"I have written of the ranch in my letters to your father," he said, noting that her hand once again ventured to her hip. "How much has he shared with you?"

Emmaline shook her head and an odd expression crossed her face—a mix of defiance and helplessness that Geoffrey didn't understand. "Very little," she answered. "Father told me that you had a lucrative business—in wool, on which he has come to depend—and would provide well for me."

Geoffrey wondered why Jonathan Bradford hadn't given Emmaline more information. He had kept the man up-to-date over the years, describing every hardship and triumph in lengthy letters intended to keep Emmaline involved in his life. At Bradford's insistence, he had sent the letters to her father so he could choose what to share and what to withhold. Bradford had always been protective of his only daughter.

Injecting a great deal of enthusiasm into his tone, Geoffrey began his explanation. "Your father was right, Emmaline. You will want for nothing, I can assure you. My ranch is situated on some of the choicest sections of Sheridan County, right on the south fork of the Solomon River. In fact, the river runs less than thirty yards from the north side of the house. The sound of the water is peaceful and it reminds me of Psalm Twenty-three—'He leadeth me beside the still waters'—you know the reference, I'm sure."

Sweat dribbled down his forehead, and he reached inside his jacket to retrieve a handkerchief and wipe the moisture away. He chuckled as he looked skyward and squinted into the sun. "I confess a dip in that water would be refreshing right now. It is unseasonably hot for this time of year." He returned the handkerchief to his pocket. "Several large cottonwoods stand beside the river and offer a welcoming spot of shade when the temperature is high."

Emmaline linked her hands and placed them in her lap. "I saw few trees on the prairie as I traveled. I am pleased to know that your property is not without shade trees."

"Granted, the trees are few in number," Geoffrey felt obligated to clarify. "But I believe you will appreciate the size of those standing. They are truly magnificent."

She gave a small nod. "So your business is in wool?"

"Yes." Geoffrey straightened his shoulders, pride filling him. "I raise Merino sheep. Hardy animals, well suited to the Kansas landscape, with a thick coat. Last year I shipped half a ton of fleece to your father's textile mill—nearly one-quarter of all the fleece from Kansas. In addition, I butcher nearly eighty lambs a year and sell the meat."

"How much land do you own?"

"The Homestead Act allowed me to purchase one hundred sixty acres. Each of the men who accompanied me to Kansas from England also purchased one hundred sixty acres with my money. Then, last year, I bought the claim from a neighboring couple who had need of the money, but I've allowed them to remain on the property. The man is a blacksmith, and he repays me in horseshoes and tools. Altogether, I own six hundred forty acres—a sizable holding."

"Father spoke of wars between cattle and sheep ranchers."

"Your father is correct that battles do take place, but not in Kansas," Geoffrey said. "That is mostly in Texas. Our neighbors who don't raise sheep raise crops. Corn and barley mostly, so we are not in competition with one another." Satisfaction filled him when he envisioned his property—more land than he could ever have hoped to own in England. "It has taken much effort, but it has been well worth the hard labor. Chetwynd Valley is the most successful sheep ranch in all of northwestern Kansas."

"Chetwynd Valley?" She sounded surprised. "You named the ranch for your grandmother?"

"A fitting memorial, I believe." He smiled, remembering the warm, loving grandmother who provided a safe haven during the years his father battled with the demon rum. Grandmother's estate would have been Geoffrey's had Franklin Garrett not gambled it away. "When you witness the serene setting, I believe you will agree that the ranch was aptly named."

"May I ask a question that is s-somewhat personal in nature?"

"You are to become my wife. You may ask me anything you like, Emmaline."

Her cheeks filled with color again, but she continued. "You were so familiar with your father's business of ale making. Why did you not choose to establish a similar business here in America?"

Geoffrey cringed inside. Emmaline had been young when he left England. Obviously she was unaware of the falling-out between him and his father over his father's business. He had no interest in establishing a business that led to men imbibing alcohol and becoming drunkards. Geoffrey still carried the burden of his father's weakness.

He had no interest in dredging up that portion of his past, even with his new bride. So he chose an abbreviated version of the truth. "Emmaline, I am quite isolated here on the prairie. A business in ranching is a much better choice for this land than establishing a brewery. Besides, providing your father with wool for his factory allows me to give something back to him for the . . . help . . . he gave my family."

"I see." Her fine eyebrows pinched together. "How much farther is it to your ranch?"

Geoffrey hoped her question indicated an interest in reaching the ranch soon. "Chetwynd Valley is seven and a half miles west of Moreland, near the town of Stetler. Stetler is much smaller than Moreland, but the citizens are quite friendly and welcoming, so I believe you will find it to be a community in which you will feel at home."

Emmaline took a deep breath, plucking the wind-tossed hair from her face again. "Oh, I would enjoy a place that feels like home."

Geoffrey heard an undercurrent of sadness, and he reached out to place one hand on her clasped fists. "Emmaline, I want you to know that I understand your loneliness. I felt much the same when

I arrived here five years ago. But Chetwynd Valley has now become my home. You will soon feel the same way about it."

He pictured the ranch's little rock house and the nearby spring-house, the indoor pump, and the garden plot all tilled and fenced, ready for Emmaline's attention. He knew it was far smaller than the home in which Emmaline had been raised, yet he'd built it all with Emmaline in mind.

As he'd built his home, stone by stone, he had envisioned the delight on his bride's face when she would see how it resembled the stone cottages of their native England. When he placed his hands beneath the first cold rush of water from the pump in the kitchen, his chest had swelled with pride, knowing he would be able to tell his Emmaline that theirs was the only home in Stetler with running water. Oh, how he hoped she would approve of the little rock house beside the river. He wanted her to feel at home within its sandstone walls.

Beside him, Emmaline suddenly stiffened on the seat and pointed with a trembling finger. A large dust devil, nearly twenty feet high and six feet in diameter, danced along the roadway ahead of them. The horses nickered in protest, and Geoffrey pulled back on the reins, bringing the wagon to a halt. The horses pawed the ground nervously as Geoffrey and Emmaline watched the whirlwind cross the road in its weaving pathway. It skipped across the landscape, tossing bits of dried grass from its moorings until, caught by the tall, waving grasses, it dissipated. Emmaline released a sigh of relief as the dust devil twirled itself out and settled onto the prairie like a tired runner collapsing beside the road.

"Was . . . was that a tornado?" Emmaline's brown eyes were wide, her face pale.

Geoffrey stifled a laugh. Apparently she had been warned of the perils on the American plains. He hastened to assure her. "No, Emmaline. That was what is known as a dust devil, or whirlwind.

They spring up frequently thanks to our flat prairie and end-less blowing winds. Most are much smaller. Dust devils can be a nuisance—I have seen large ones knock a sheep off its feet—but they are not generally dangerous."

Emmaline's shoulders slumped in obvious relief. She kept her eyes turned to where the dust devil had faded away, as if concerned it might bound to life again. Then her gaze narrowed and she pointed again. "Is that smoke?"

Geoffrey perked up at that question. Smoke on the prairie was never a good sign, especially considering the lack of rain the area had received this spring after a dry winter. He shielded his eyes with his hand, scowled, and then sagged in relief. "Yes, that is smoke, Emmaline—smoke from Tildy Senger's cook fire." Sud-denly he knew where Emmaline could prepare for their wedding ceremony. He turned to her with a huge grin. "Would you like to meet some friends of mine?"

Emmaline offered a hesitant nod, and Geoffrey slapped the reins on the horses' rumps again. "Gee up, there," he called cheerfully. "Let's go give a greeting to Ronald and Tildy!"

# FOUR

MMALINE HELD TIGHT to the jouncing wagon seat as Geoffrey left the roadway and turned the horses across the untamed prairie. The land rose gently, leaving a view of only a thatched roof with a thin spiral of smoke rising upward from a rock chimney. As they crested the top of the rise, the entire dwelling came into view, and Emmaline wrinkled her nose in distaste when she got a close-up look at the house belonging to Geoffrey's friends. Why, it appeared to be constructed of blocks of mud and was little more than a shack! The barn behind it seemed more sturdy than the house. A resounding *clang-riiiiiing, clang-riiiiiing* echoed from the depths of the monstrous limestone barn. The blacksmith must be hard at work.

A half dozen scrawny chickens pecked in the dirt in front of the house, but they scattered when Geoffrey drove the wagon onto the grassless yard. Geoffrey wrapped the reins around the brake handle and hopped down, calling cheerfully toward the house, "Is anyone home? Tildy?"

Before Emmaline could alight, the warped plank door of the ramshackle house opened, and a large black woman emerged into the sunshine. At first her hands rested on her beefy hips in a pose of aggravation, but when she spotted Geoffrey, her broad face broke into a huge smile. "Why, Geoffrey Garrett, as I live an' breathe!" She threw her arms open wide. "Git on over here, boy, an' give ol' Tildy a hug!"

Geoffrey obliged while Emmaline remained on the wagon seat, watching in disbelief. *This* was Geoffrey's *friend*? An elderly Negro woman? While the woman continued to hold Geoffrey in her massive embrace, she rolled her chin sideways and bellowed, "Ronald! Ronald Senger, git yo'self out here! We gots comp'ny!"

The clang-and-ring stopped, and a tall, rail-thin man stepped out of the barn. His dark brown face glowed with perspiration, and his white smile stretched as wide as Tildy's. He ambled across the yard, forcing the sleeves of his long johns above his elbows.

Geoffrey disengaged himself from Tildy's hug and lifted a hand to direct her attention to the wagon where Emmaline sat perched. "Tildy, this is Miss Emmaline Bradford, arrived from Yorkshire County just this afternoon." He took two steps toward the wagon, his hand extended to help Emmaline down, but Tildy pushed past him and reached her man-sized hands up to Emmaline.

"Oh, what a purty li'l thang," Tildy gushed in her low-pitched voice. "You come on down from there, honey, an' let Tildy git a good look at you."

Emmaline, her stomach roiling with apprehension, stepped from the wagon while Geoffrey and the man named Ronald shook hands. Tildy grasped Emmaline's wrists and held Emmaline's arms outward. Her gaze roved up and down unabashedly, and she clucked her tongue. "Lawsy, chil', but you's a spindly thang. Don't they got nothin' bigger'n nubbins at that there England country? You don't look hardly half growed!"

Emmaline remained silent, uncertain as to whether or not she should be insulted by the other woman's straightforwardness. Tildy carried the odors of her cook stove—ham and cabbage and bread. The good smells reminded Emmaline that she hadn't eaten since early that morning, and—much to her embarrassment—her stomach growled.

Ronald stepped near, his long, gangly limbs reminding Emmaline of a giraffe she had once seen in a traveling circus. "Let me git a look-see at Geoffrey's Emmaline." He pronounced her name with "lion" at the end. He, too, gave Emmaline a thorough once-over that made her neck feel hot. Nodding in approval, he said, "You chose yo'se'f a right purty li'l gal, Geoffrey."

Where Tildy sounded as if she had a throat full of gravel, Ronald's voice flowed like honey. The pair were opposites in every sense of the word, yet it was clear to Emmaline that they had one thing in common—they both held Geoffrey in high esteem. How, she wondered, had this unlikely trio formed such a friendship?

Turning back to Geoffrey, Ronald added with a lazy smile, "Yup, ever'thang you've said 'bout her 'pears to be true."

Emmaline wondered what Geoffrey had said, but before she could ask, Tildy wrapped a thick arm across her shoulders and herded her toward the sad-looking little house.

"She be purty, awright," Tildy said, "but she's near black as me under all that soot! An' you's fixin' to get hitched yet today? Mm-hmm, gonna need a goin'-over wit' some soap an' watuh 'fore you can stand front o' the preacher-man an' 'cite them vows. You jus' come wit' Tildy, honey, an' we'll git you sparklin' clean."

Emmaline had little choice but to obey.

Tildy glanced over her shoulder. "Ronald, fill the washtub an' haul it in here. Geoffrey, you fetch this li'l lady's trunk. Cain't have a bride what looks like she's been rolled through Ronald's cinders." She gave Emmaline's back such a hearty pat that Emmaline feared it would leave purple marks behind. Then, to Emmaline's horror, Tildy announced, "I's givin' you a bath, Miss Emmalion!"

———

As much as Emmaline hated to admit it, the bath felt heavenly. The washtub only accommodated her if she scrunched her knees beneath her chin, but submerging herself in water after only having cursory rag washes for the past several weeks was a real treat. A rather improper question—how did Tildy bathe in this minuscule tub?—flitted through her mind, but she dared not voice it.

The water was tepid from the start, yet it felt soothing against her sticky skin. The layer of scum that floated on the surface when she had finished appalled her, and she apologized.

Tildy laughed. "Ooh, chil', that ain't nothin' compared to what I clean up after that man o' mine, so jus' don't be gettin' all pink-cheeked on my account!"

Emmaline would have preferred a private bath—her modesty had never allowed a servant into the washroom—but Tildy insisted on washing Emmaline's hair. After Emmaline got over the initial embarrassment, she found that Tildy's strong hands were infinitely gentle, and she relaxed, enjoying the soapy massage on her scalp.

Once the bath was finished, Tildy discreetly disappeared, leaving Emmaline alone behind the hanging canvas that had allowed her to bathe in concealment. She sighed as she rubbed herself dry with a rough length of toweling. It felt so wonderful to be clean! She wrapped the toweling around herself and reached for the clean drawers and camisole lying across a stool next to the washtub. After peeking around the edge of the canvas to be certain she was completely alone, she dropped the protective towel and scrambled rapidly into her underthings.

Her thoughts raced ahead to this evening when she would need to undress and climb into her nightclothes. Would Geoffrey be in the room when she clothed herself for bed? How would she find the courage to allow him to see her clad so scantily?

Standing barefoot in only her lacy cotton underwear, she wondered what Tildy had done with her trunk of clothes. Tiptoeing forward, she pulled back the canvas and peeked out again. Her trunk waited in the corner, near the quilt-draped bed. To her dismay, she realized she would need to come out completely from behind the canvas to reach it.

Panic rose in her breast—she dare not venture forth in such a scandalous state of undress! Where had Tildy gone? In a whisper, she called, "M–Miss Tildy?"

No response.

A bit louder. "Miss Tildy?"

Still no answer.

Taught that a lady should never speak with excessive volume unless in an emergency, she contemplated her present state of undress. Her situation qualified as an emergency, albeit a small one. Drawing a great breath, she called, "Miss Tildy!"

The front door opened and Tildy entered, a huge smile lighting her dark face. She chuckled. "You ready to put on yo' weddin' dress?"

Emmaline nodded and then ducked back behind the canvas. Tildy joined her moments later carrying a creamy yellow dress of lawn. She held the dress at arm's length and looked it over. "Lawsy, chil', you gonna be as purty as a posy in this. You got so many purty thangs in that box."

At Tildy's words, an image filled Emmaline's mind—of her mother carefully folding the new dresses, placing them in the trunk, and then smoothing the fabric the way she used to smooth Emmaline's hair. Tears sprang into her eyes as a longing for dear, quiet Mother overwhelmed her.

Tildy reached out a rough hand to cup Emmaline's cheek. Her sandpapery fingers stroked Emmaline's clean skin. "Here, now, chil', no time for tears. You's too purty to be red-eyed on yo' weddin' day. What would yo' mama think of you bein' unhappy and teary-faced on such a 'portant day?"

Emmaline sniffed, bringing the tears under control. Tildy was right—Phoebe Bradford would want her daughter to be a joyful bride. Joyfulness meant nothing to Father, however; he would merely expect obedience.

Suddenly, Tildy's eyes narrowed, and she said, "Better git that hair outta the way." Very gently she laid the dress on a sideboard. Placing her hands on Emmaline's shoulders, Tildy lowered her onto the stool beside the washtub. With long, steady strokes, she brushed Emmaline's hair away from her face.

"You got a good head o' hair, chil'," Tildy commented in her gravelly voice. "Thick as molasses an' the color o' cinnamon. A crownin' glory to take pride in . . ." Her fingers were amazingly nimble, and Emmaline's scalp tingled pleasantly as Tildy worked the damp lengths of hair into a twist on the back of her head.

Her hair secure, Emmaline stepped into the skirt of the dress, and Tildy buttoned it up the back. Emmaline pressed her hands against the smooth skirt front while Tildy fluffed the layered flounces across the back. Each flounce sported a row of lace, and matching lace ran from the shoulders to the waistline in the front as well as around the wrists of the tight-fitting sleeves. The dress was hopelessly wrinkled from its ride across the ocean in the trunk, but it would have to do.

Tildy circled Emmaline, fingering a bit of lace at Emmaline's shoulder. She released a rueful sigh. "Too bad we don't have no orange blossoms to put in yo' hair."

"Orange blossoms?" Emmaline touched a hand to the heavy twist of damp hair.

"Yup. Symbol o' fertility an' chastity. Most o' the brides in the East put orange blossoms in their hair as a way o' giftin' their grooms."

The words made Emmaline's face blaze. Tildy, apparently unaware of the discomfiture her words had caused, gave Emmaline another once-over and said with a nod, "You's gonna be the purtiest bride ever 'cited vows in the Congregationalist Church."

Emmaline managed a polite "Thank you," but the word "bride" sent her heart into wild thumping.

Tildy balled her fists and rested them on her ample hips. "Now, lemme give you a li'l advice, chil', since your mama ain't here to give you a talk. Bein' married is a good thang when it's to a good man, an' you got a good man out there. Now, he done tol' us how you ain't seen him since you was a young girl, but me 'n' Ronald—we seen him 'most ever' week since he come here from 'cross the ocean, an' we know he be a good man. One o' the best men. So you got no cause for fret.

"Somethin' else . . . You wanna make this marriage work good, you just gotta 'member that marriage takes compermize. When both people is willin' to give a li'l, and both people puts the needs of the other one just a li'l bit higher'n the needs of themselfs, thangs have a way o' fallin' into place. So you 'member that, Emmalion, you hear?"

Emmaline wondered if Ronald was having the same conversation with Geoffrey right now. The thought carried a bubble of humor that erupted into a grin.

Tildy leaned forward, her face only inches from Emmaline's. "You hear?"

Emmaline gave a start and nodded. "Yes, ma'am. I hear."

Tildy's broad face relaxed into a smile. "Good." Her eyes drifted shut as she released a sigh. "This be a good land for buildin' a life. A body's got freedom here—an' this land'll grow you stronger'n you knew you could be." Opening her eyes, she gave Emmaline's cheek another rough caress. "Now, let's feed you." She yanked down the canvas and pointed to the table in the middle of the room.

Emmaline seated herself, glancing around the simple planked house while Tildy dished up a plate of ham, some kind of stewed greens, and a large chunk of yellow, mealy bread dripping with butter.

Emmaline pointed to the yellow square. "What is this?"

Tildy's eyes widened in shock. "Why, that be corn bread, honey. Ain't you never had corn bread?"

Emmaline decided not to inquire about the greens. Instead, she offered a weak smile and carried a bite to her mouth. The flavor was not unpleasant, and she eagerly forked up a second bite. Tildy, apparently satisfied, moved to the stove and hummed to herself.

Emmaline let her gaze rove over the small house as she ate and wondered if the house Geoffrey had constructed was similar to this one. This house had only one room, plus a lean-to that held the iron cook stove. A rope bed lay in one corner, a pine sideboard holding kitchen utensils stood near the lean-to, and a rough-hewn table and chairs dominated the middle of the room. Two trunks squatted along the west wall, and a row of hooks above the trunks held serviceable clothing. The floor was simply hard-packed dirt. Tildy and Ronald owned very little, it seemed, but everything was clean and very well cared for.

As soon as Emmaline finished, Tildy snatched up her plate. "Chil', you scoot outside an' git back in that wagon so's you can go 'cite those vows afore the sun sets."

Emmaline wished she could ask to stay here with Tildy and forget about reciting those vows. Tildy's humble dwelling with its pleasant smells of supper had become a secure haven in the short amount of time she had been there.

She and Tildy stepped from the shadowed house into the May day. The sun still hung brightly in a cloudless sky, but it had inched its way toward the horizon over the course of her time with Tildy. Evening was approaching, and Emmaline had no idea how much farther they needed to travel to reach Stetler and the minister.

Whether it was apprehension about facing the minister or just a reaction to the heat of the day, Emmaline broke out in a sweat. She stretched the snug collar of the dress away from her neck, hoping the breeze might dry some of the moisture from her skin. The lightweight lawn was appropriate for the Kansas heat and humidity, but all the layers and the snugness of the bodice and sleeves left Emmaline feeling stifled. The clean, fresh feeling of the bath departed with the prickle of perspiration.

Tildy used her full-throated voice to locate the men. In moments, Geoffrey was at Emmaline's side. His gaze swept from her toes to her face.

"You look beautiful, Emmaline," he whispered, taking her hand.

Fire filled her face at the approval shining in his eyes. She jerked toward the wagon. Her limbs quivered as she allowed him to assist her into the seat.

Ronald ambled from behind the house. He clutched a thick cluster of lavender flowers heavy with jagged leaves on deep green stems. With a dapper bow that belied his rough appearance, he presented the bouquet to Emmaline. "They's jus' wild flowers, Miss Emmalion—called rose verbena—but they make a right purty li'l nosegay for you to carry."

Her throat tightened as she looked at her wedding bouquet. "Th-thank you." She gave Ronald a wavering smile, her vision suddenly blurred with a spurt of tears. The gesture was so unexpectedly touching, especially from this angular black man in his soot-stained long johns and suspenders.

"I'll git yo' trunk." He headed into the house and returned quickly, the trunk balanced against his lean belly. His biceps bulged and he released a grunt as he swung the box into the back of the wagon. The wagon bounced with the weight.

"We need to be heading on to Stetler now," Geoffrey said. "Thank you, Tildy and Ronald, for your hospitality. We—"

Tildy held up a thick finger. "Wait!" She picked up her skirts and waddled back into the house while Ronald looked after her, his long fingers toying with his suspenders. Tildy came out holding a bulky, folded bundle. She thrust the bundle into Geoffrey's arms. "A weddin' gift for you an' Miss Emmalion. Me an' Ronald is wishin' you nothin' but the very best."

Geoffrey offered the bundle—some sort of heavy fabric—to Emmaline, and she took it gingerly. The wind flipped the top layer over, revealing a variety of patches painstakingly sewn together to create a crazy-quilt pattern. Emmaline recognized the quilt from Tildy's own bed.

"Oh, Miss Tildy—"

Tildy thrust her pink palm in the air. "No arguin'. Come winter, you'll be thankful for that kivver." She chuckled, a low, rumbling sound like the purr of a great cat. "It don't stay hot like this year round, you's gonna learn."

Geoffrey put a hand on the quilt and gave Tildy a smile. "We thank you, Tildy. Emmaline and I will treasure this gift." His voice sounded tight.

"You go on, now," Tildy said as she waved one big hand. " 'Cite them vows. Then you be happy, hear?"

Geoffrey laughed. "Yes, ma'am, we will do our best."

Emmaline twisted in the seat as Geoffrey aimed the horses back toward the road. She watched Tildy lift a corner of her apron to wipe her eyes, then place her face against Ronald's chest. Ronald wrapped his arms around her.

Emmaline glanced at her husband-to-be. Geoffrey held the reins between his fingers and leaned forward, a slight smile tipping up the corners of his lips. He looked so different from the young man who had run in and out of her house all during her growing-up years. The Geoffrey who boarded the ship for America five years ago had been a smooth-faced boy compared to the chiseled, mutton-chop-whiskered man seated beside her.

Tildy's claim that Emmaline had a good man in Geoffrey had raised a desire to find out if Tildy was right. Oddly, she yearned to turn her face to Geoffrey's chest and feel his arms coming around her as Ronald's arms had around Tildy. How had Tildy known Ronald would not push her away? In all the years of her parents' marriage, she had never seen Mother and Father behave in such an intimate manner. She felt certain Father would have reprimanded Mother had she made such an overture of affection in the light of day with others looking on. How would Geoffrey respond if she leaned against his arm?

Geoffrey turned his face toward her and gave her a sympathetic smile. "I would imagine you are quite tired from your travels, are you not, Emmaline? We are less than a mile from Stetler. Reverend Stanford is expecting us, so we will be able to proceed with the ceremony immediately. And then I will take you home to the ranch."

A shudder raced through Emmaline. What would Geoffrey expect of her then?

# FIVE

~

THE SUN HOVERED, huge and radiant orange, above the horizon as Geoffrey brought the wagon to a stop in front of the Congregationalist Church of Stetler. Varying shades of blue, lavender, and pink decorated the sky. Kansas sunsets were worth taking the time to watch, but Geoffrey had more pressing business this evening. His thoughts turned to what would take place within the church walls in mere minutes, and his heart rolled over in his chest.

Geoffrey set the brake, wrapped the reins around the handle, and turned to Emmaline, who sat still and silent on the seat. She leaned forward slightly with her hands clasped in her lap, the wilted cluster of rose verbena drooping over her fists. *She must be anxious to see this finished so she can rest.*

"Emmaline, stay here for a moment." He hopped down from the wagon seat, making the springs *ting*. The gentle sound must have brought her out of her stupor, because she sat upright and blinked rapidly. He pointed to a white clapboard house near the steepled church. "I'm going to alert Reverend Stanford and his wife that we are here. Then we will go into the church and proceed with the ceremony."

Emmaline's face appeared pale in the dusky light. Was it fear or exhaustion that gave her the haunted look? He waited until she gave a quick nod of agreement and then hurried to the reverend's house and knocked on the door. Only a few minutes later, Geoffrey and Emmaline stood side by side in front of the unpretentious wooden altar with the Reverend Stanford smiling down at them.

The soft glow from lanterns located along each wall brought out the red highlights in Emmaline's hair—the same highlights he had observed in her childish braids the day she had stood on the pier with her family and waved farewell to him five years ago. The remembrance brought a tightness to Geoffrey's throat. His moment of claiming Emmaline as his wife had finally arrived. Even if they weren't allowed the luxury of a church full of family and friends, God had answered his prayers.

He repeated his vows with due solemnity as he gazed into her apprehensive, velvety brown eyes. "I, Geoffrey, take you, Emmaline Rose Bradford, to be my lawfully wedded wife . . ." *Look at me fully, my Emmaline, and see that my heart is pure, and my love for you is real. Do not be afraid of me, for I have only your best interests at heart.*

The stutter that had lessened throughout the day reappeared as Emmaline uttered the words the minister instructed her to repeat. "I, E-Emmaline, t-take you, G-Geoffrey Dean Garrett, to be my . . . my . . ." She stopped, her wide-eyed gaze darting to Reverend Stanford.

The minister tipped his head. "My lawfully wedded husband . . ."

Emmaline opened and closed her mouth like a fish gulping air.

"To be my lawfully wedded husband," Reverend Stanford repeated a little louder, his thick brows low.

Geoffrey held tight to Emmaline's gloved hand. She trembled from head to toe.

Concerned, he asked, "Emmaline?"

She jerked her hand from his grasp and took a step backward. "Please, I . . . I cannot . . ." Tears flooded her eyes. One loud sob shattered the sacredness of the ceremony. Dropping the wilted bouquet of rose verbena, she lifted her skirt and raced out of the church.

Geoffrey shot a startled look toward the reverend, who stared at Emmaline with a look of disbelief on his face. The reverend's wife rose from the front pew and gestured toward the open doorway at the head of the aisle. "Shouldn't someone . . . ?" She moved toward the door.

Geoffrey stepped into her path. "I shall go." He forced a confident smile he didn't feel. "She is tired from the long journey, and grief at the loss of her great-uncle has overwhelmed her. I shall allow her a few minutes to collect herself. Please wait." He strode out of the chapel, worry for Emmaline battling with embarrassment for himself. The moment he stepped out of the church, he spotted her leaning against the side of the wagon. She had buried her face in the bend of her elbow, and harsh sobs shook her frame. Worry overrode his embarrassment.

He cleared his throat, warning her of his approach. Her shoulders stiffened, and the sobs abruptly ceased. Yet she didn't turn from the wagon, and when he grazed her arm with his fingertips, she jerked away as if she found his touch painful.

He licked his dry lips. "Emmaline?"

"P-please. Go away."

Stung, he pressed his sweaty palms against his pant legs. His mind skipped backward in time, to when she was fourteen. Her favorite cat had run away, and he had held her in his arms and comforted her. Should he gather her in his arms and soothe away whatever fear held her captive? He frowned at the sky. The sun was disappearing fast. He didn't have time to coddle her. They needed to complete the ceremony and return to the ranch before darkness fell.

Squaring his shoulders, he decided on a no-nonsense approach. "Come now, Emmaline. Reverend Stanford is waiting. Let's go inside and—"

"No!" She spun around, her eyes wild. "I cannot go inside. I cannot do what you expect of me."

Confused, Geoffrey shook his head. "What are you saying?"

She clasped her hands to her lace-covered throat. "I cannot marry you! Please do not force this marriage upon me."

*Force?* He took two stumbling steps backward. He had forced nothing! She had agreed to this union before he left England. She had come to him using the tickets he'd purchased with his hard-earned money. Did she not stand before him in a dress obviously sewn for this very occasion?

"Emmaline, you speak rubbish. I am not forcing you to do anything!"

She shrank against the wooden slats of the wagon bed. Her reaction reminded him of a skittish lamb. She would bolt if he didn't curb his temper. He drew a deep breath, blew it out with puffed cheeks, then spoke in a low, even tone. "No one is forcing marriage upon you. You agreed to marriage before I left England, remember? You came to me knowing we would be wed." He glanced at the rapidly darkening sky. "The time has come for us to exchange our vows. So let us return to the ceremony." He reached for her arm.

She scuttled sideways. "I cannot!" She sounded nearly hysterical.

Geoffrey glanced over his shoulder. The reverend and his wife stood in the chapel doorway, witnessing his humiliation. He turned back to Emmaline and spoke quietly but firmly. "Yes, you can. And you must."

Tears filled her red-rimmed eyes and spilled down her cheeks. Her chin quivered. Sympathy rose in Geoffrey's chest. Gentling his voice, he said, "Emmaline, I realize things have moved rather quickly since your arrival, but you must see the necessity of exchanging vows without delay. Already the hour is late—traveling is treacherous in the dark. We must go back inside and complete the ceremony before we go to the ranch."

"B-but I do not wish to go to the ranch."

He stared at her in bewilderment. "Where else would you go?"

"Back . . . home." She sucked in a shuddering breath. "Can't I please return to England?"

Her petulant query stirred Geoffrey's anger again. "Return to . . . ?" He clamped his jaw and turned his back so he wouldn't see her beseeching gaze. His dreams crumbled before him. All the years of waiting—years of faithfulness and effort—now seemed wasted in light of her childish request.

Spinning back around, he snapped, "And if I agree to this ludicrous appeal, how do you intend to pay for the return passage?"

She blanched, her throat convulsing.

"I haven't the funds to return you to England, Emmaline." He spoke honestly—his expendable funds had been used to bring her to him. But, he acknowledged to himself, even if he did have the money, he wouldn't spend it so recklessly.

"I have the . . . dowry Father sent," she whispered.

A wave of agony surged through him. The dowry was to be *his* wedding gift. He opened his mouth to remind her of the purpose of the dowry, but a hand closed around his elbow. Shifting his gaze, he found Reverend Stanford at his side.

"Is everything all right?"

"No." Geoffrey pushed the word past clenched teeth and chose not to elaborate. How could he explain the problem when he didn't understand it himself?

Reverend Stanford held out one hand toward Emmaline. "Miss Bradford, are you ready to recite your vows?"

Emmaline shrank back. "No, sir, I am not."

The reverend's eyebrows shot high. For a moment he pulled in his lips and looked back and forth from Geoffrey to Emmaline. Then, with a tug on Geoffrey's arm, he drew him aside. "Geoff, it seems your bride is all atwitter."

"Atwitter?" It was a humorous word, but Geoffrey didn't feel like chuckling.

"Yes. It isn't uncommon for someone to suffer an attack of nerves before a wedding. Considering the length of time that has passed since you last saw her, she probably needs a day or two to adjust to the idea."

Geoffrey wanted to shout that she'd had five years to adjust to the idea. Instead, he said, "But I cannot wait. I need to return to the ranch. It's nearly dark already."

Reverend Stanford tapped his lips with one broad finger. "I have a suggestion. Let Emmaline spend the night here with us. A good night's sleep, a chance to look around town tomorrow and see what a nice place it is, and she should be able to set her fears aside."

"Do you believe so?" Geoffrey hoped he didn't sound as unsure as he felt.

"Nervousness passes," the reverend replied with a smile. "If we push her now, she might resent you. Would you not rather start your new life as man and wife on a happier chord?"

Geoffrey considered the minister's words. The disappointment of Emmaline's reaction pressed on his heart like a heavy stone. Yes, he wished for a more joyful start to their married life. He gave the reverend a slow nod.

"Good." Reverend Stanford clapped Geoffrey's back, then strode to Emmaline. "Miss Bradford, come with me. My wife will show you to our guest room. You will stay with us."

Emmaline's gaze skittered to Geoffrey and then back to the minister. "With y-you?"

"That's right."

"And . . . and then . . . ?"

At her hopeful tone, Geoffrey clenched his jaw so tightly his teeth hurt.

"We'll talk more in the morning," Reverend Stanford told her. Looking toward the chapel, he called, "Lorna? Come show Miss Bradford to our guest room, please."

Like a docile lamb, Emmaline followed the reverend's wife into her house. She didn't even look back when Geoffrey swung into the wagon seat, snatched up the reins, and set the horses to trotting.

# SIX

S UNLIGHT SPILLED ACROSS Emmaline's face, teasing her from a restless, dreamless sleep. She scrunched her eyes tight, unwilling to emerge from the cocoon of the musty featherbed. But the bright sun could not be ignored. With a small grunt of displeasure, she tossed aside the light cover and sat on the edge of the bed. After her weeks of travel, of gliding across the open sea or rolling over the landscape, the solid, unmoving floor beneath her feet seemed foreign.

She blinked, clearing the sleep from her eyes, and focused on her surroundings. Immediately, her heart lifted. Last night, with only lantern glow lighting the tiny room tucked beneath the eaves of the attic, she hadn't realized the walls and ceiling were papered in a cheery floral pattern of lavender and green. She let her gaze rove slowly, the previous day's melancholy easing with the sight of delicate morning glories climbing the walls and coiling across the steeply pitched ceiling.

But then, without warning, memories of sweet purple pansies and bright pink heliotrope from the garden in her backyard at home crowded in. Sadness smacked her so hard her shoulders sagged. Oh, she wanted to go home!

A light tap on the door gave her a start. Clasping her cotton nightgown at her throat, she called, "Yes? Who is there?"

The door cracked open, and the minister's wife peeked in, a smile creasing her round, gently lined face. "Good! You're awake. I have breakfast waiting—biscuits, bacon, and coffee. Come downstairs, wash your face, and eat."

"Oh, thank you very much, ma'am, but I am not at all hungry."

"Now, don't be silly," the woman scolded, her smile never wavering. "Put on a dress and come down. The house is small— you will have no trouble at all finding the kitchen. The reverend is waiting to speak with you before he leaves for the church." She closed the door, leaving Emmaline alone.

Emmaline clenched her fists and glared at the door. Must everyone tell her what to do? Father said, "Go to Geoffrey in America." Geoffrey said, "Marry me." Mrs. Stanford said, "Get dressed and come down." The reverend would no doubt also give commands. When might Emmaline be allowed to decide what *she* wanted to do?

Pushing off from the bed, she crossed to the square window that looked out over the town. Geoffrey had said she would feel at home in Stetler, but little about the town resembled an English village. No close-set stone cottages or tall Tudor houses with overflowing window boxes; no narrow cobbled streets. Instead, a wide dirt road separated evenly spaced wood-sided buildings, many of which lacked even a coat of paint.

Yet the morning sunlight bathed the scene in gold, making it appear a cheery place where horses nodded lazily at hitching rails and people moved up and down the wooden boardwalks. The peaceful bustle of the town reminded her that the Stanfords were downstairs waiting.

With a sigh, she turned from the window and looked into

her trunk. The only dresses she could don without the assistance of a maid were the identical traveling dresses of black muslin. She lifted the one she'd worn the day before. Her nose wrinkled at the dust coating the frock, but all three traveling dresses were equally filthy.

Her fingers trembled as they fastened the buttons up the front of the dress. The room had no mirror she could use to do her hair properly, so she combed the long locks straight back into a simple tail at the nape of her neck. Then, drawing in a strengthening breath, she made her way down the narrow, enclosed stairway.

When she reached the bottom of the stairs, she entered a small foyer. A glance to the right showed a meagerly furnished parlor. The doorway on her left revealed the kitchen. Strong scents of fresh coffee, biscuits, and bacon grease made her stomach churn. She pressed her hand to her middle, and her palm brushed the sharp edge of the folded letter still tucked in her dress pocket. Anger swelled, and she spun to race back up the stairs.

"Miss Bradford?" The reverend's voice brought her to a halt. "Please come in and sit down."

For a moment Emmaline considered ignoring him, but she had been taught to respect her elders, and especially members of the clergy. Lifting her chin, she turned a slow circle and entered the kitchen.

Mrs. Stanford rose from the table, gesturing toward an open chair. "Sit here, Miss Bradford, and I'll get you a plate."

"Oh no, please, I—"

"It's no trouble." The woman smiled and moved toward the stove. "Just sit."

Emmaline slid into the chair opposite the minister, who beamed at her over the rim of his tin coffee cup.

"Did you rest well?" The man took a deep draw of the coffee.

"Um, yes. Thank you." Emmaline chose not to tell the minister how she had lain awake far into the night, worrying about what today might hold.

"Here you are, dear." Mrs. Stanford set a plate heaping with fluffy biscuits and thick slices of bacon on the table in front of Emmaline.

Emmaline swallowed a wave of nausea at the sight of the food. When the woman handed her a cup of steaming, aromatic coffee, Emmaline feared she would be sick. Yet looking into the friendly faces of her benefactors, she knew she must at least make an attempt to eat.

The biscuits seemed the most innocuous of the offerings, so she broke off a small piece, dabbed it with butter from a misshapen pat in the middle of the table, and carried it to her mouth. Too late she realized she hadn't blessed her food. And right under the watchful eyes of a man of God! Shame struck hard, and the bit of bread turned to sawdust in her mouth. She yanked up the cup of coffee to chase the offending bite down her throat. The hot liquid scorched her tongue.

Gasping, she smacked the cup onto the table. Coffee sloshed from the cup and spattered the tabletop. Embarrassed beyond endurance, Emmaline shot out of the chair and ran upstairs. She slammed the door and threw herself facedown onto the unmade bed. The springs hadn't even stopped twanging before a firm knock sounded on the door.

She raised her face a few inches and called, "I prefer to be alone." Holding her breath, she waited for a reply. Footsteps retreated down the stairs. With a sigh of relief, she allowed her head to collapse onto the bed. For several minutes she lay with her face pressed to the rumpled sheets. Finally she rolled over and sat up. As she did, the letter in her pocket crinkled.

Frowning, she yanked it out and held it at arm's length, as if it were a snake that might strike. Words from the page flitted through her memory, each phrase as piercing as fangs. *Dear Mr. Bradford* . . . Couldn't Geoffrey have written to her? *Enclosed are tickets for Emmaline's transport to America.* He had promised to come for her himself! *Be certain she brings her wedding dress, as we will have our ceremony at the Stetler Congregationalist Church immediately upon her arrival.* And what of the promised wedding in England? *She will want for nothing here.*

Emmaline snorted aloud. Rising, she dropped the letter, crossed to the window, and looked out on the dusty street, blinking rapidly to hold back tears of despair. Want for nothing? Why, he and his land called Kansas could provide nothing that compared with England!

Stomping back to the bed, she snatched up the letter, tore it into bits, and scattered the pieces across the floor. Then she planted the toe of her shoe against the largest piece and ground it into the unfinished wooden floor. Although she knew it was a childish action, she couldn't deny the rush of satisfaction it brought. But when Emmaline shifted her foot aside to reveal the shredded scrap, she realized the tantrum had done nothing to ease her loneliness. Sinking back onto the bed, she stared at the remains of the letter. The scattered pieces painted a picture of her shattered dreams.

Dropping to her knees, she gathered up the remnants and held them in her lap. She couldn't put the letter back together again, but she could put her life back together—if she returned home. Father would be cross, without a doubt, but Mother would welcome her. Even if Father cast her out, she could find a job—perhaps sorting books at the newly constructed library or clerking in one of the shops. Menial jobs, to be certain, but respectable. In time, she could put this ordeal behind her and move forward as if Geoffrey Garrett and his ridiculous scheme to build a life in Kansas had never included her.

Geoffrey swallowed the last bite of beans, wiped his mouth, and pushed away from the table. He glanced at the plates in front of his ranch hands—nearly empty, too. Carrying his plate to the washbasin, he said, "Jim, I believe it's your turn to do the dishes."

Jim Cotler made a face. "Mr. Garrett, I'll be awful pleased when this wife of yours finally arrives and takes over the household chores."

Jim's brother, Chris, cuffed the younger boy on the back of the head. "Don't be insolent."

The youngster picked up his plate and dragged his heels against the floor as he walked to the washbasin. "I apologize, Mr. Garrett. But I have washed dishes so many times, my hands are as soft as a nursemaid's!"

Chris rose from the table, chuckling. "You could wash dishes from now until the turn of the century, and they would never be that soft."

"Well . . ." The boy scowled, cranking the pump handle up and down. "I still don't like to wash dishes."

"One more time, Jim," Geoffrey said, "and then Emmaline will take up those chores." He had allowed Chris and Jim to assume Emmaline's train was delayed rather than admit she'd refused to accompany him to the ranch. The deceit pricked his conscience, yet he couldn't bring himself to confide the truth even to those who had labored with him to build this home for her.

Chris said, "If you like, I'll do the dishwashing today, and you can see to my chore."

Jim's face lit with hopeful interest. "What's your chore?"

Geoffrey and Chris exchanged a smirk. Geoffrey answered, "Chris is going to de-worm the ewes today." De-worming consisted of forcing the animal to ingest a mixture of ground charcoal, oil, vinegar, and cloves. Geoffrey hadn't yet encountered a sheep that willingly surrendered to the treatment.

Jim elbowed Chris away from the washbasin. "No, sir! I'll wash dishes!"

Geoffrey and Chris laughed, and Geoffrey gave Jim's narrow shoulder a light smack. "Very well, Jim. Dishes for you. But when you have completed the job, you will need to join Chris in the barn." A band of trepidation constricted his chest. "I am . . . going to town."

Both of the Cotler brothers nodded in reply, but neither asked any questions, for which Geoffrey was grateful. Heading to the horse barn, he reflected on his restless night. He had battled with himself, alternately cross with and concerned for Emmaline. Finally, on his knees, he had laid the situation at Jesus' feet, and with that release he had discovered a tenuous peace.

He loved Emmaline. Even as a boy in knickers, he had loved her. Memories of her pretty face had carried him through the long, lonely days in Kansas. Desire to provide for her had motivated him to make his ranch a successful one. Even though they had resided thousands of miles apart, in his heart they had been a team. They were meant to carve a life together here on the plains.

*I pray Emmaline spent her night remembering the dreams we shared before I left her to build this ranch.*

———

When Emmaline awakened again, sunshine no longer streamed through the little window, although the room was still light. She presumed the time to be midafternoon. Crossing on tiptoe to the door, she pressed her ear to the hard surface and listened. No sounds came from below, and her heart lifted in hope. If the Stanfords were gone, she would be able to slip out of the house unnoticed.

A plan formed quickly in her mind. Locate a local farmer or a community member and offer him a small token for transportation to the Moreland train station. Use the dowry money to purchase a ticket to the coast and then book passage on a ship. A daring plan, but it was her only option. She could not marry a man she no longer knew, no matter how adamant Father was.

The decision made, she spent a few precious minutes straightening the covers on the bed and disposing of the shredded letter. She grabbed the leather handle of her trunk and tugged the cumbersome box across the floor to the stairway. She couldn't lift it by herself, so she continued dragging it, cringing with each hard thud as it bounced down the stairs.

At the bottom, she rubbed her lower back and panted from the exertion. Could she drag the trunk all the way to town? Resolve brought her upright. She had to.

Taking hold of the handle once more, she yanked the trunk across the floor of the foyer to the front door. She reached for the doorknob, but to her surprise, it turned on its own and the door swung wide open. Reverend Stanford stood on the stoop. Geoffrey was right behind him.

# SEVEN

WHEN GEOFFREY SPOTTED Emmaline's trunk beside the front door, his spirits lifted. Obviously she had brought it down in readiness for her drive to the ranch. He smiled and stepped past the reverend to take her hand.

"Emmaline. How good to see you looking well rested. Shall we—" His enthusiasm faltered when he realized she wore the same black, dusty frock she had worn yesterday. "Why have you not put on your wedding dress?"

She jerked her hand free of his grasp and buried it in the folds of her skirt. Without a word she blinked up at him, her lips pursed.

Reverend Stanford cleared his throat. "Perhaps we should sit for a chat. Miss Bradford, you may leave the trunk there." He gestured to the small room that served as a parlor. "Make yourselves comfortable."

Geoffrey waited until Emmaline moved stiffly into the room and perched on one end of the sofa. He followed and sat at the opposite end. Reverend Stanford chose the wooden rocking chair in the corner.

The reverend bounced a smile toward both of them. "My wife will return from the schoolhouse in an hour or so. At that time we can go over to the chapel and complete your wedding service."

"An hour?" Geoffrey repeated. "That should give Emmaline time to change." He looked at her, expecting her to rise and retrieve the yellow dress from her trunk.

But Emmaline lowered her gaze to her lap. She linked her fingers together with such force it appeared the knuckles might snap. "I shall not change."

"You intend to be married in . . . *that*?"

Emmaline's jawline tensed for a moment. Then, in a barely audible voice, she said, "I do not intend to be married."

The quietly phrased statement of rebellion brought Geoffrey from his seat. "What?"

Reverend Stanford put out a quieting hand. "Geoffrey, sit down, please."

Drawing a lengthy breath through his nose, Geoffrey slowly lowered himself to the sofa. He cupped his hands over his knees and sat ramrod straight, biting down on the tip of his tongue to hold back the words of protest that fought for release.

"Miss Bradford." Reverend Stanford waited until Emmaline lifted her head. "Did you not travel to America for the purpose of marrying Geoffrey?"

Her chin quivered. "My father sent me for that purpose, yes."

"But you—" Geoffrey started.

"Did you not agree to this union?" Reverend Stanford asked.

Emmaline's gaze flitted briefly to Geoffrey before jerking back toward the minister. She licked her lips. "Y-yes, sir. When I was a mere girl. But now . . ."

Geoffrey's chest ached so fiercely he feared his heart would be torn in two. "Emmaline—" The word croaked out. He swallowed hard and started again. "Emmaline, have you found someone else?"

She gaped at him. "No!"

"Then what—"

"I do not *know* you!"

At her hysterical exclamation, Geoffrey slumped against the stiff back of the sofa. The ridiculousness of the comment should have made him laugh. But instead fury bound his chest.

Reverend Stanford leaned forward and rested his elbows on his knees. "Miss Bradford, please help me understand. My impression from Geoffrey is that your families are well acquainted—that you and he grew up together."

Emmaline turned her face to peer at Geoffrey. He sat still under her scrutiny, but it felt as if her gaze left behind a fiery trail as it ventured from his hair to his whiskered cheeks and all the way to his worn brown boots. He should have changed into his polished black boots before coming to town.

Her appraisal complete, she looked at the minister and blinked in innocence. "So much time has passed. . . . When he left, he claimed we would wait a year—two at most—to be wed." A hint of defiance colored her tone. "And he never wrote to me—not once. He sent me sporadic messages through my father. How can I know him? Over the years, he slipped away from me. . . ."

Geoffrey stared at her sweet profile, silently railing against her words. He hadn't wanted to wait so long. But the land had resisted his efforts to tame it. The government had insisted on five years of occupancy. When he wrote to Jonathan Bradford, the man had assured Geoffrey the delay would merely increase Emmaline's desire for him and would give her an opportunity to mature into the kind of wife who would embrace life on the Kansas prairie. All these years, he had envisioned her eagerly anticipating the moment their hearts would join as one. How could he have been so wrong?

Emmaline lifted her chin and said, "I do not wish to hurt you, but I cannot marry you. I should never have come."

Geoffrey sat in stunned silence. Wouldn't the town gossips enjoy discussing this indignity? Everyone knew how excited he had been to bring Emmaline to America. Everyone knew of his plans to be wed. He had built a reputation in the area as a man of honor—a man of his word. What would they think of him now that the woman he claimed to love had jilted him? People would disdain him the way they had his father when his mother left their family.

"You will marry me, as we planned," he growled. The words contained a menacing note that surprised even him. He never spoke so forcefully, not even to the ranch hands who served under his leadership. But he had never experienced such rebellion from his ranch hands.

Reverend Stanford cringed. "Geoffrey, I think it might be best if we—"

"No, sir." Geoffrey realized his response was less than respectful, but the tension in his middle made polite exchange impossible. "She is to be my wife. For five years, I have waited for her to come. She pledged herself to me, and she will honor her word."

Emmaline's face, devoid of emotion, paled once again. Her white skin against the harsh black of her gown gave her a ghostly appearance. It occurred to Geoffrey that his words were draining the life from her, yet he continued, speaking to Reverend Stanford, even though the message was meant for his intended bride.

"When we speak our vows, she will promise to honor me. It is best she begin by honoring me now. Her survival on the plains depends on her willingness to listen and follow my directions."

Turning to Emmaline, he said, "Please retrieve your wedding dress from the trunk and change for our ceremony. I am going to the chapel, and I will wait for you there."

He rose and stomped out the door.

---

Geoffrey's command carried Emmaline back to England, to her childhood and the authoritative father who had raised her. Having been taught unthinking obedience, she stood abruptly. For a moment she wavered, her shaky legs threatening to collapse, but she managed to remain upright. She turned toward her trunk.

"Miss Bradford?"

The minister's tender voice halted her in her tracks.

"I can assure you Geoffrey Garrett is a good man. He will be an upstanding husband to you and an honorable father for your children."

Emmaline swallowed the bile that rose in her throat. "Yes. I have been told he is a good man." Tildy had spoken highly of Geoffrey, too. Yet Emmaline's thoughts raged. *If he is such a man of honor, why did he not keep his promises to me?*

With resignation, Emmaline lifted the lid of her trunk, removed the dress of yellow lawn, and draped it over her arm. Then she faced Reverend Stanford. "When your wife returns, might she assist me in dressing?"

"Of course."

Emmaline went upstairs to wait.

---

Mrs. Stanford insisted on running an iron over the yellow lawn to remove the travel wrinkles before helping Emmaline dress.

She also combed out Emmaline's hair, braided the long tresses, and coiled the braid into a figure eight on the back of her head. Since the little bouquet of rose verbena had long since wilted, the woman plucked a handful of bachelor buttons from the wild plot between the house and the chapel and tied the stems with a length of yellow ribbon.

Beaming, she said, "Emmaline, you look lovely." She stroked Emmaline's cheek and added, "But a smile would add much to your appearance."

Emmaline tried, but her lips refused to curve upward. Her chest felt weighted, as though her trunk rested upon it, and her leaden legs resisted movement. But somehow she followed Mrs. Stanford out of the house and across the yard to the chapel. When they entered, they found the reverend and Geoffrey seated together on a bench near the front. Both men jumped to their feet, and Geoffrey's face lit—with pleasure or satisfaction, Emmaline wasn't sure.

Mrs. Stanford's hand on her back propelled Emmaline forward, and Geoffrey stepped into the aisle to meet her.

"You are very beautiful, my bride," he whispered.

The words should have delighted her, yet somehow they created a feeling of foreboding. *My* bride . . . *His* to own. *His* to make demands upon. *His* . . . Emmaline reeled.

Geoffrey placed his arm around her waist and guided her to the front of the chapel, where they faced the reverend. The clergyman sent a concerned look over the pair, but he opened his little Bible and began to read. " 'My beloved spake, and said unto me, Rise up, my love, my fair one, and come away. For lo, the winter is past, the rain is over and gone. The flowers appear on the earth; the time of the singing of birds is come. . . . Arise, my love, my fair one, and come away.' "

*Come away . . . Come away . . .* The words reverberated through

Emmaline's mind. Geoffrey had asked her, years ago, to come away with him. In the foolish impetuosity of youth, she had agreed. Now the words compelled her to turn and run away, to make her escape as she had planned. But Geoffrey's firm hand on her back held her captive as surely as if a sturdy rope were tied around her middle.

Reverend Stanford looked at Geoffrey. "Geoffrey, repeat after me: I, Geoffrey Dean Garrett, take thee, Emmaline Rose Bradford, to be my lawfully wedded wife."

Geoffrey peered into Emmaline's eyes. He opened his mouth, but no words came forth. His eyebrows pulled down and his lips twisted into a grimace. He jerked his head to face the minister. "I . . . cannot."

Emmaline released her held breath in a mighty whoosh. She stared at Geoffrey's profile, certain she had misunderstood. Had her prayer for deliverance been answered? Might Geoffrey release her from her previous commitment?

Geoffrey's gaze swept over the reverend and his wife. "Could Emmaline and I have a few moments of privacy, please?"

The reverend stepped past them, took his wife's elbow, and led her from the chapel.

Geoffrey guided Emmaline to the nearest bench and sat, tugging her down next to him. "Emmaline, I find that I cannot proceed as planned."

Her breath escaped in little spurts. Sweet words of liberation!

"Yet I love you, and I cannot simply let you go."

"But—"

"Please, Emmaline. I believe I have a compromise that will benefit us both. Will you listen?"

Miss Tildy had mentioned compromise. The remembrance lured Emmaline into nodding in agreement.

"You said you don't know me any longer. As much as I regret

it, my agreement with your father—to write to him rather than to you—has added to the distance between us." He made a rueful expression, giving a slight shake of his head. "I should have shared the past years with you, but your father was convinced the difficulty of establishing my ranch would frighten you. It would seem too harsh a landscape for you. So I yielded to his request to write to him and allowed him to share whatever information he deemed acceptable. In so doing, I alienated you. For that, I am truly sorry."

Emmaline knew her father well enough to know Geoffrey spoke the truth. Father had maintained control of everything. "I understand."

A quick smile graced his face before he continued in a serious tone. "As for the amount of time that has transpired between my leaving England and now . . ." He sighed, looking to the side for a moment. What was he reliving in those seconds of introspection?

"My immaturity and inexperience misled me. The task was larger than I expected." His gaze bored into hers once more. "Years slipped by quickly in the midst of hard work, but I never lost my desire to be your husband. I never stopped loving you, Emmaline."

Deep emotion blazed in his hazel eyes. Mesmerized, Emmaline nodded.

"But you . . . you stopped loving me."

For the first time, Emmaline experienced a stab of remorse. Until that moment, her thoughts had centered on herself—her sorrow at leaving England, her fear of this new place, and her resentment over Geoffrey's broken promises. But now she saw what the years had cost him, and although she fought against it, compassion filled her.

She searched for a gentle way to make him understand. "The

change in my feelings toward you did not come intentionally. When we were growing up, you were always there, an extension of my own family. It was only natural that I would love you, as I loved the others who spent much of their time with me."

He ducked his head, his brow furrowed. "Did . . . did you ever really love me . . . as a woman loves a man?"

Emmaline considered the question. How many nights had she sat in the window seat of her bedroom, peering out at the stars and dreaming of how it would feel to be held in his arms? Many fine young men had crossed her path at school, and her brother had frequently brought home friends, but none of the boys had captured her attention and affection the way Geoffrey had.

His first year away, she had yearned for him with such fierceness, the desire for food had fled and she had cried herself to sleep at night. She had loved him as wholeheartedly as a moonstruck girl could. She answered honestly, "Yes, Geoffrey, I did love you."

His head shot up, eagerness lighting his expression. "Then . . . then it is possible that you could love me again?"

Did love ebb like a tide, retreating and returning? "I do not know."

She read displeasure in the downthrust of his eyebrows. But then he wiped his hand over his face, and the frown vanished. "Would you be willing to try?"

Emmaline licked her lips. "W-what do you mean?"

"Will you give me ten months, Emmaline? Ten months to win your love and dedication. If, at the end of that time, you still desire to return to England, I shall book passage and return you to your father's house myself. I shall take full responsibility for the breach in the relationship, and I shall do all I can to mend any disagreements between you and your family before returning to my ranch."

Emmaline stared at him. "Why not just send me back now?" Surely it would be less painful, and much less expensive, to end things now and send her back alone.

"I have neither the time nor the money to pay for another trip right now. I will not have either until I have butchered and sold the fall lambs. By then it will be winter, and winter is not a good time for traveling."

"But I could use the dow—"

"The dowry money belongs to your father until which time we are wed."

Emmaline knew Geoffrey could demand the dowry now as payment for their betrothal. His decision to wait to claim the money until they were legally wed pleased her.

Geoffrey went on, "And I love you. I want to share my life with you." The sweet words of devotion sent a coil of something pleasant through Emmaline's frame. He took her hands. "I am willing to allow you time to decide if you want a life with me. You carry resentment from past wrongs, and it influences how you look at me right now. I understand your feelings, but I also wish to earn your forgiveness and trust. Will you give me that chance, Emmaline?"

His calloused fingertips pressed into her knuckles. "If you choose to stay, the months will be a time of learning for you. Being a rancher's wife is far different from the life you had in Yorkshire County. We will discover if you have the strength of will to meet the challenges of this land. You can serve as my housekeeper until which time you decide to become my wife, if you so choose. So . . . will you stay, Emmaline? Will you stay until next spring?"

Emmaline became aware of his thumbs tracing a circle on the back of her hand. The touch ignited a fire beneath her skin, and she jerked her hands free. "B-but what will my parents say? They sent me here to be your wife, not your housekeeper."

He pinched his lips together. "It might be best to simply allow them to believe we have wed."

Emmaline drew back. "I cannot tell a fabrication to my parents, Geoffrey."

He raised one shoulder. "It would be an omission of truth rather than a bold lie."

Emmaline considered this. "Where would I live during this time?"

"You will live in the ranch house."

She pressed her hand to her bodice. Her heart pounded beneath her palm.

Geoffrey shook his head. "We would not share a . . . sleeping room." Defensiveness colored his tone. "I would make use of the sofa in the parlor or sleep on a shakedown in the spare room."

"My mother would be appalled should I live under the same roof with a man who is not my legally wed husband." Emmaline tried to sound forceful, but her uneven breathing made the statement quaver.

Geoffrey looked to the side for a few moments, his face wrinkled in thought. "Then I shall live in the bunkhouse with my hands. It is a two-room bunkhouse, and one half is now empty because—" He jolted. Facing her, he continued, "One half is empty. The bunkhouse is well away from the house, so propriety would be observed. When I come to the house for meals or evening visits, the ranch hands will be nearby, so no ill conjecture will mar your reputation while we become reacquainted."

"I am uncertain, Geoffrey. . . ."

He snatched up her hands, pinning them between his broad palms. "We need the opportunity to become acquainted again. In order to do that, we need time together. To have time, we must both be at the ranch."

Emmaline carefully extracted her hands and scooted farther away on the bench. "Let me think, please." Turning away from his pleading gaze, she focused on a cobweb in the corner of the church and tried to make sense of the confusing situation.

She could still use the dowry money and return to England. Father would be furious, but at least she would be in familiar territory. But, she realized, living under Father's roof only meant following his dictates again. He would no doubt set out to find her another husband—she was, after all, twenty-two years of age. Perhaps his selection would not meet her approval, and she would have little choice in the matter.

She turned abruptly and fixed her gaze on Geoffrey. "You will allow me to decide if I become your wife? You will not pressure me?"

He raised one hand, as if making a pledge. "I shall not ask you again until the winter has passed. At that time, if you choose not to marry me, I shall escort you back to England, just as I promised."

A troubling thought struck her, and Emmaline lifted her chin. "How do I know I can trust you? You did not keep past promises."

He grimaced, hanging his head for a moment. "I cannot change the past. I can only work to earn your trust again. You will decide what our relationship will be—husband and wife, or . . ."

Emmaline quietly offered, "Friends?"

A wistful expression flitted across his features. "Yes. I pray that we should at least part as friends."

Emmaline's heart twisted at his words. A longing to turn back the years washed over her, to regain the fondness she had once held for Geoffrey Garrett. Perhaps she would never grow to love him as she once had, but at least they could part with no animosity between them.

She drew a deep breath and made her decision. "All right, Geoffrey. I will stay. Until the winter is past."

His shoulders dropped in relief, and he grinned at her. "Thank you, Emmaline. Now, let us retrieve your trunk and I will take you home."

# EIGHT

E VENING DUSK HAMPERED Emmaline's view of her new home. Long shadows fell across the yard, giving the surrounding landscape an eerie appearance. Even the trees—the massive cottonwoods Geoffrey had promised—appeared to send out tentacles of danger. But a lantern burning inside the rock house highlighted an oval stained-glass window, the bright reds and blues incongruous against the black and gray shadows. The window seemed to shine a welcome, and she focused on the colored glass as Geoffrey brought the wagon to a stop inside the iron fence surrounding the front yard.

"Welcome to Chetwynd Valley, Emmaline." Geoffrey's voice, whisper soft, held a hint of melancholy. She knew it wasn't the homecoming he had envisioned.

Turning her gaze from Geoffrey, she examined the house. Small and L-shaped, it was built of rough, oblong stone blocks identical to those used to construct Ronald Senger's barn. A porch sporting gingerbread trim that resembled a row of triangles on point ran the full width of the house. A bay window jutted from the shorter side of the L.

Geoffrey pointed to the trio of tall windows. "That room is

your parlor, Emmaline. I planned it so you would have plenty of light."

Emmaline managed to give him a small smile. A parlor was nice, but whom would she entertain on this barren prairie? Her gaze lifted to the sod roof of the little dwelling, then across the empty yard. Her heart fell as she realized there was nothing growing in the yard—no bushes or flowers or grass. Just dirt. Brown, dismal dirt. She straightened her spine. As temporary mistress of this house, that would be the first change she would make. She would plant grass and flowers immediately. She would not accept the forlorn prairie landscape creeping right up to her doorstep.

The front door opened and a splash of light fell across the wide wood planks of the porch floor. A tall man, his face as heavily whiskered as Geoffrey's, stepped into the bright rectangle of light and raised a hand in greeting. "Mr. Garrett, welcome back!" He turned a broad smile in Emmaline's direction as he moved easily across the ground toward the wagon.

Emmaline observed he wore tan trousers and a shirt with its top buttons unfastened. She turned her gaze from the tanned wedge of exposed skin beneath his taut neck.

"And this must be Mrs. Garrett. I am pleased to make your acquaintance, ma'am."

Emmaline waited for Geoffrey to explain she was Miss Bradford and not Mrs. Garrett, but Geoffrey simply climbed past her and leaped to the ground. He reached to assist her from the wagon. Her hips felt stiff from the bouncing journey, and for a moment she feared her legs would give way. Geoffrey must have sensed her debility, for he kept hold of her arm until she was steady. Then he placed his hand on the small of her back. The familiar gesture sent a shiver up her spine.

"Emmaline, this is Chris Cotler. He serves as foreman of the ranch."

Emmaline moved away from Geoffrey's touch. "It is very nice to meet you, Mr. Cotler."

Cotler gave her another nod and turned to Geoffrey. "Mr. Garrett, I left lanterns burning for you and a supper in the hob. It's nothing fancy—just a maw stew—but if you are hungry, it will fill you."

The foreman's rough appearance did not extend to his speech. His voice was well modulated and proper. Remembering the railroad workers' and Tildy and Ronald Senger's rough talk, Mr. Cotler's formality was welcome to her ears.

"Thank you, Chris," Geoffrey returned. He pointed into the back of the wagon. "I will prevail upon you to carry Emmaline's trunk into the house. The horses will need caring for, and then you may turn in for the evening."

A prickle of trepidation crept over Emmaline's scalp as she listened to Geoffrey's orders. His ease in delivering commands sounded too much like Father—too much like the man who had ordered her to don her wedding dress earlier that day. Might he turn into that man again and deliver more orders to her?

"Certainly, Mr. Garrett," Chris agreed amiably. But first he put two fingers in his mouth and blew a shrill whistle.

Another man came around the corner of the house at a trot. This man, too, was casually attired in tan dungarees and a plaid shirt, but he bore no whiskers on his face. As he neared, Emmaline realized he was a boy of perhaps fourteen. When he spotted Geoffrey and Emmaline, he grinned and came to a stumbling halt directly in front of Emmaline. "Welcome to Chetwynd Valley, Mrs. Garrett! It's very good to have you here! It seemed as though you would never arrive, but now here you are. Did you have a good trip?"

Emmaline pressed a hand to her throat. How should she respond to the affable lad?

Geoffrey cleared his throat, his cheeks twitching with silent laughter. "Emmaline, please meet Jim Cotler. Jim is Chris's younger brother, and also one of my hands. Although he still has some growing to do, he's the best shearer around. And, as you have no doubt already realized, he is not timid."

Jim remained close to Emmaline, his face split with a friendly grin.

Chris released a low-toned chuckle. "Now, Mr. Garrett, you know after all the talking you've done, we feel as if we already know Mrs. Garrett." He smiled broadly at Emmaline, his teeth a flash of white in the waning light.

Heat suffused Emmaline's cheeks. She hoped the sun was low enough that it would hide her embarrassment.

Chris moved to the tail of the wagon. "Come over here, Jim, and help me carry in Mrs. Garrett's travel box. Then we must leave these newlyweds alone."

Newlyweds! Emmaline's heart clamored at that word. "Oh, please, Mr. Cotler and . . ." How should she address the youngster who was also a ranch hand? "Jim—"

"Come along, Emmaline." Geoffrey hurried Emmaline toward the house with his hand at the small of her back.

The pressure of his warm palm rendered her speechless once more. She stood uncertainly in the middle of the planked floor and watched the two ranch hands carry her trunk over the threshold. They dropped the big box with a thud, and then each gave a nod of good-bye.

Geoffrey turned to face Emmaline with an unreadable expression. Why hadn't he explained their arrangement to the Cotler brothers? Suddenly, she realized she was miles from any town, at the mercy of whatever Geoffrey chose to do to her. What if he chose not to honor their agreement? What if he began issuing commands?

On shaky legs, she moved to her trunk and pressed her knees against the solid wood. She wished she could open the lid and cower beneath her folded clothing. Geoffrey cleared his throat, and she held her breath waiting for him to speak.

"Would you like to see the house?"

Her jaw dropped at this unexpected, gently toned question. Slowly she turned to face him. He stood near the door, his hat in his hands, his face hopeful. Instantly, a long-buried memory surfaced. In her mind's eye, she saw Geoffrey and her brother, Edward, walking down the stone-lined pathway toward her home while she sat on the stoop, her skirts exposing her slippered feet and thin legs. As the boys entered through the open gate, Geoffrey's gaze lit upon her. His laughter stopped. He paused, an odd expression flitting through his eyes before he smiled. He then moved briskly toward her, leaving Edward smirking at the gate. Holding out a small brown cone of paper, he asked, "Would you like a sweet?" Emmaline wrapped her arms around her knees and shook her head so adamantly her braids flopped. Geoffrey's face had fallen in disappointment.

Now, looking at his hopeful expression, she was twelve years old again with the power to please or disappoint. For reasons she could not fathom, she did not want to disappoint. She gave a small nod and licked her dry lips. "Yes, please."

A smile broke across his face, bringing a lift to her heart. He swept his arm to indicate the room in which they stood. "This is, of course, the sitting room." Moving past a pair of matching, straight-backed chairs, which fit snugly against the wall, he walked to the fireplace. He ran his hand across the smooth top of the mantel. "I ordered the marble and oak mantel from the Montgomery Ward catalog a year ago. I have not placed bric-a-brac atop it. You will have that privilege."

She wondered if she would order the bric-a-brac from the

catalog, as well. He looked at her expectantly, obviously awaiting a response. "It is quite pretty. Smaller, of course, than the fireplaces at home, but I'm sure it is sufficient for heating this room."

A brief scowl marred his brow, and Emmaline wondered what she had said to upset him. But then his expression smoothed and he nodded. "Yes, it is quite sufficient." He held out his arm to indicate a doorway. "In here is the kitchen."

Emmaline stepped through the opening, her heels clicking softly against the wood floor. The kitchen was rectangular in shape, half the size of the sitting room, with one wall of built-in cabinets. A huge iron stove filled the near corner, and an unfamiliar yet pleasant aroma—no doubt left over from supper—teased her nostrils. The wall opposite the stove held a built-in, hip-height cupboard with a square, four-paned window above it. A red iron pump stood on the counter next to a deep enamel sink. Geoffrey rounded a scarred table in the center of the room to take hold of the pump's handle, his eyes as bright as a child's on Christmas morning.

"Look, Emmaline." He worked the handle vigorously. A stream of water gushed forth, splashing into the sink and spattering the surrounding wood countertop. "Running water, right in the house."

That was impressive, Emmaline had to admit. She had presumed she would carry buckets from a well, the way Miss Tildy and Mrs. Stanford did. The pump was a welcome surprise.

"Tomorrow I shall show you the springhouse," Geoffrey continued, plucking a sheet of toweling from a nearby peg and drying the countertop. "It is just outside the kitchen." He pointed to a door that presumably led outside. Then, cupping his hand over the pump, he said, "We have a spring that runs right under the house, so we are never without water." His face clouded for a moment. "God certainly provided for me with the spring, since we have had no rain this season at all. Others depend on the Solomon for their water supply."

"No rain?" Emmaline found a spring season without rain hard to believe.

Geoffrey nodded seriously. "We need to pray for that provision." He gestured back toward the sitting room. "The house has three more rooms. Let us go to your parlor, shall we?"

Emmaline followed Geoffrey through the sitting room to a pair of paneled pocket doors. He slid one open, revealing a small, plain room. "This will be a sleeping room one day, but it serves as a storage space for now."

The room held everything from tools to a funny-looking bench holding an upended boot on a peg. Obviously Geoffrey did his own cobbling. Once more she was struck by the isolation of this ranch.

Geoffrey didn't pause to allow her to explore but passed directly through the room to a single pocket door across from the double doors. This, too, he opened, and then turned a huge smile in her direction. "Your parlor."

Emmaline sensed his pride as she stepped past him to enter the room. The bay windows, devoid of curtains, looked out on the front yard. Two tall, narrow side windows, their sashes high to allow in the night breeze, faced the Solomon River. In the gloaming, Emmaline could not see the river, but she could hear the gentle sound of water moving. A peaceful sound.

She moved deeper into the room. A large secretary stood between the side windows. Emmaline crossed to it and touched the fold-down desktop. The attached china cupboard held no ornaments, but paper and envelopes filled the cubbies of the desk. A pen and a fat jar of ink awaited use. Her fingers itched to make use of the pen and paper. Tomorrow she could write a letter to Mother and tell her she had safely arrived. But she must word her letter carefully lest she let slip this unusual arrangement, which would certainly displease her parents.

She turned away from the secretary and spotted a spindled rocking chair in the corner beside a square parlor table that held an oil lamp. A perfect place to sit and embroider—if Geoffrey allowed her to purchase muslin and floss.

"I am certain you will want other furnishings eventually." Geoffrey remained in the doorway, his eyes following her as she investigated the room. "But I felt you would like to choose those yourself. We will go to Moreland one day soon and allow you to order things from the catalog."

Emmaline clasped her hands behind her back and turned to Geoffrey. He had tried so hard to make this house her home, and his expression seemed to beseech her to offer assurances for the future. Yet uncertainty sat like a rock in her belly. She blinked back tears. "I-it is a v-very nice parlor, Geoffrey. Thank you."

He nodded silently, biting down on his lower lip. Then he turned to another raised panel door, this one on hinges. He cleared his throat, and the nervous sound caused the fine hairs on the back of Emmaline's neck to prickle.

"And here," Geoffrey said, swinging the door wide, "is our— your sleeping room."

# NINE

❧

EMMALINE WAS AS skittish as a canary in a room full of cats, her brown eyes huge in her colorless face. Geoffrey felt his pulse beating in his neck, and he hoped it didn't show. He forced himself to breathe shallowly when Emmaline entered their sleeping room. As she passed him, she tucked her skirts close to her legs and pressed against the opposite side of the doorframe.

He couldn't deny a feeling of deep disappointment. In his dreams, he had carried her through the doorway, placed her gently on the bed, and pressed his lips to hers. He shook his head to dispel the idea. They were not wed. They might never be wed. Until the end of the getting-reacquainted period, he must curtail such thoughts or go mad.

He watched her move to the center of the room and stop with her back to him. Her arms remained pressed to her sides, and she did not turn her head to peer around in curiosity as she had done in the parlor. The muscles in her back quivered, and he longed to reach out and curl his hands around her narrow shoulders, to assure her that he meant her no harm. But fearful of what might happen if he touched her, he plunged his hands into his pockets instead.

Silent seconds ticked by while she stood motionless beside

the bed and he hovered in the doorway. Then, deciding someone must take action, he cleared his throat. She jumped at the sound and spun to face him. Her cheeks wore two bright banners, and he was certain his own face blazed red, too. "Before I retire for the evening," he said, "I will bring your trunk in here so you will be able to put away your clothing."

She finally looked around the room. "Where is the wardrobe?"

"No wardrobe. Rather, you have a closet." He moved past her to the corner and opened a door.

Tentatively, she stepped toward the open doorway and peered in. She swung her startled gaze to his face. "Why, it is so large! It is like another room!"

Geoffrey smiled. English closets were narrow cubbies since large closets were taxed like a room. But in America a person could have as large a closet as he wanted. He looked down at Emmaline, admiring the golden flecks in her brown eyes. "Will it be large enough to hold your clothing? If not, I can purchase a wardrobe for you."

She moved backward a few feet, putting more space between them. "The . . . the closet is sufficient. You needn't bother with a wardrobe."

He nodded and closed the door. He toyed with the middle button of his jacket as silence filled the room once more. "Well . . . I will . . . retrieve your baggage so you may . . . prepare yourself for bed."

At the word "bed," Emmaline stumbled sideways to lean against the bedpost. Then, as if the wooden post burned, she jerked away from it, covering her mouth with trembling fingers.

Was there any way he could assure her that she needn't fear him? "Emmaline, I—"

"Why did you not tell Mr. Cotler and Mr. . . . . Jim that we are yet unwed?"

Could her skin be any whiter? Surely no blood remained in her face.

He stepped forward. "I thought to spare you the embarrassment of sharing something so personal in front of strangers. I shall go to their bunkhouse and tell them tonight."

No rosy hue lit her cheeks, but she no longer appeared ready to crumple. When she didn't respond, Geoffrey ventured, "You do understand, Emmaline, that I will honor my word to keep my distance until you make your decision?"

She licked her lips, then gave a little nod. Clasping her hands at her waist, she whispered, "I . . . I understand. Thank you."

There was one more issue to discuss before he allowed her to turn in for the night, one that would cause discomfort. But he was also certain she was in need of this particular knowledge. So he swallowed once more, squared his shoulders, and said, "Emmaline, I will now show you . . . the washroom."

———

Emmaline hung the last dress on a hook in the closet. Geoffrey's clothes hung there also, although she assumed he would remove them in the morning. She stood for a moment, transfixed by the sight of their clothes side by side. An intimate image. An uncomfortable image. Quickly, she stepped back. Her nightgown—the one her mother had sewn as part of her bridal trousseau—rested across the bed in an inviting tumble of ruffles, ribbons, and lace. A great lump of sorrow filled Emmaline's throat as she gazed at the white cotton gown.

"Oh, Mama, how you labored over this gown." She lifted the

beautifully embellished gown and crushed it to her chest. "Your tears stained the fabric as you stitched. So much love went into this piece of clothing—so much hope for my happiness. But now . . ." Sighing, Emmaline peered around the large room; the blank walls and empty space mocked her. "Now I am alone."

She couldn't wear this nightgown tonight. She might never wear it, and that thought saddened her. Almost with reverence, Emmaline folded the gown and returned it to her trunk. As she did, her knuckles grazed the remaining item in the bottom of the trunk. A smile toyed at the corners of her lips.

With both hands, she lifted out a smooth gray rock. Slightly smaller than a loaf of bread, the rock was heavy in her hands and felt cool to the touch. She held it up toward the lantern's glow. Two striated lines of tan formed an uneven pathway all the way around the roughly oval shape. Emmaline closed her eyes, remembering her mother plucking this rock from their garden at home.

"Take this with you, daughter," Mother said, "and let it serve as a reminder of your homeland." Mother's eyes had shimmered with tears as she'd said the words, much the way the rock shimmered with tiny bits of minerals.

Emmaline stood for long moments, looking at the rock but seeing Mother's face. When she couldn't bear the loneliness a moment longer, she started to put the rock back in the trunk. But then, instead, she carried it to the front room where the fireplace mantel waited, empty of ornamentation. She placed the rock in the center of the highly polished mantel and stepped back to examine her handiwork. The rock seemed an appropriate adornment for the surroundings.

She drew in a satisfied breath. "A tiny touch of home in this new, rugged land."

As she inhaled, the same aroma that had caught her attention in the kitchen earlier filled her nostrils. Her stomach gave an answering lurch, reminding Emmaline how little she had eaten that day. She followed the enticing scent and discovered a green-striped crock bowl covered with a square, blue-checked cloth in the warming hob of the stove.

She lifted a corner of the cloth and peered into the bowl. Chunks of some sort of dark meat swam in a thin gravy. Curious, she grasped a piece of meat between her fingers and carried it to her mouth. She chewed, her forehead pinched in thought as she tried to recognize the flavor. The closest comparison she could find was chicken, yet the chunks did not resemble a chicken's pale meat. She pressed her memory—what had Mr. Cotler called the dish? A maw stew? The name had no meaning for her.

Perhaps, she reasoned as she located a fork in a tray in one of the cabinets, the meat from prairie chickens had a different appearance than domesticated fowl. She would ask Geoffrey in the morning. Regardless, the meat was tasty, and hunger encouraged her to devour the contents of the bowl. When she finished, she rinsed the bowl with water from the pump, washed her hands, and extinguished the wick on the lantern.

Her stomach full, she moved through the heavily shadowed house to the sleeping room. The echo of her feet against the wood floor sent a shiver of unease down her spine. Inside the sleeping room, she closed the door and then stood in the middle of the floor, hugging herself to ward off the chill of fear. She gave herself a little shake. Hadn't she traveled across the ocean and then on to Kansas without benefit of a chaperone or companion? Why was she so fearful now, in this sturdy rock home with Geoffrey and his ranch hands nearby?

Yet as she traveled, there had always been others around. On the ship, she had shared a suite with Uncle Hedrick; on the train, even after her uncle's death, other passengers filled the berths. Here, she was truly and completely at the mercy of the three young men sleeping in the bunkhouse.

"Stop being a ninny," she scolded herself, speaking aloud to cover the unfamiliar sounds the wind carried through the open windows. "Get into your nightclothes and go to bed."

But following her own directive proved more difficult than she'd expected. At home, and even while traveling, there had always been a willing pair of hands to assist with dressing and undressing. She certainly couldn't ask Geoffrey to unbutton her frock! Finally, by twisting her arms in directions she didn't know they could go, she managed to unfasten enough of the multitude of buttons up the back of her dress to wriggle out of it.

As she hung the dress of summery lawn on a peg in the closet, a question flitted through her mind: How different might this night have been had she not refused to exchange marriage vows?

Her heart skipped a beat. She understood little of the intimacies between men and women. Stepping forward, she touched the bright patchwork quilt that lay across the foot of the bed—the one Miss Tildy had given to her and Geoffrey.

Emmaline pressed her trembling fingers to her lips. Would she and Geoffrey be happy as a married couple? Flinging herself away from the bed, she wished she had shared a long chat with Mother before departing for America. Then she would have some idea of what to expect when . . . or if . . . she finally decided to become a wife.

She crossed to the lantern and extinguished the wick, plunging the room into darkness. Then, dressed in her undergarments, she wiggled between the sheets—sheets that had previously cradled Geoffrey's body. The thought brought a rush of embarrassment, and she scrambled out of bed again.

For a moment she stood beside the bed, contemplating changing the sheets. But where would she find clean ones? Miss Tildy's advice echoed through her mind: "*Compermize . . .*" With a decisive nod, she lay down on top of the covers. Even though the room was dark and she was without an audience, she felt exposed with no covering. She reached down and tugged the quilt across her body. The weight was too much for the warm weather, but Emmaline found comfort in the soft fabric and the remembrance of the kind woman who had sewn the patches together.

Closing her eyes, she listened to the lullaby of the whispering wind combined with the gentle gurgle of flowing water. "The song of the Solomon," she murmured, finding the thought soothing. A smile formed on her lips as she awaited blessed sleep.

———

In the darkness, Geoffrey stood beside the small porch that fronted the rock bunkhouse and explained the arrangement he had made with Emmaline. His words faltered occasionally, testament to the mixed emotions that swept through him, but he concluded, "Next March she and I will either be wed, or I shall accompany her back to England. But until then, we will treat her as if she were the hired housekeeper on the ranch."

Jim dropped his feet from the top edge of the porch railing, his boot heels thudding against the planked porch floor. He stared at his boss with his mouth open. It seemed the garrulous boy had, for once, been rendered speechless.

Chris remained in a relaxed pose with his ankle propped on his opposite knee, his hand curled around the bowl of his pipe. "So you have postponed your wedding, and you are going to be staying in the bunkhouse . . . for almost a *year*?" His tone clearly displayed confusion.

Geoffrey clamped his hands over the railing that fronted the porch. The sweet-smelling smoke from Chris's pipe drifted past his nostrils and made him cough. He would never understand the pleasure some men took in pulling smoke into their lungs.

"That is correct." He grimaced and turned his head to avoid the next lingering puff of smoke. "I assure you, I understand your consternation."

The bunkhouse, divided down the middle into equal portions, had been built to accommodate four people. Jim, who roomed with his brother, had begged to be allowed to move into the second half now that Ben Mackey was no longer with them. Chris had also made the request in a bid for privacy. Geoffrey had given permission for Jim to make the change on his fifteenth birthday, which was only a few weeks away. But now with Geoffrey moving into Ben's former half, the Cotler brothers would be forced to continue to bunk together for nearly another year.

Geoffrey waited for either Chris or Jim to complain about his going back on his promise. If either of them expressed a great deal of displeasure, he would reside in the dugout, but he hoped it wouldn't be necessary. The four of them, including Ben, had shared the primitive dwelling for the first three years on the ranch. His memories of that time—the cramped space, the earthy odors, the uncleanliness—were far from pleasant. He preferred to use the dugout as a storm shelter rather than a residence, but he also wanted contented workers.

He examined each man's face carefully, searching for signs of rebellion. "The time will go quickly," Geoffrey said to assure himself as much as them. "Can you manage to share a room for another few months?"

Chris and Jim exchanged looks. A silent message seemed to pass between the brothers. Chris pulled the pipe from between his lips. "Of course, boss. As you said, time goes quickly." He flashed a crooked grin. "The past five years rushed by, didn't they?"

Geoffrey raised his face to the star-speckled sky. Their first years in America had disappeared swiftly, filled with hard work and dreams for the future. All of those dreams had centered around Emmaline and how this ranch would eventually become her home. Now she was here, but his dream still remained as distant and unreachable as one of the bright stars overhead.

Chris mused, "It seems a strange agreement to me, having her here but not marrying her."

Geoffrey sucked in a calming breath, once more filling his senses with the odor of Chris's pipe. The smell transported him back to evenings spent in his father's study while the man drilled him on his schoolwork. Perfection—Father had always demanded perfection. Yet the man had not exercised that standard himself.

Geoffrey coughed again. "I admit, the situation is less than ideal. Of course I would prefer to have married Emmaline immediately. But a gentleman does not force himself on a lady."

He stared up at the sky. "She needs time to reacquaint herself with me and to become accustomed to this new land. She waited five years for me; I can now wait for her."

Chris stepped off the porch, turned his pipe upside down, and tapped it on the railing. Bright embers fell to the ground and scattered. He stomped out the glowing coals. "Will you need us to move anything from the house out to the bunkhouse for you?"

Geoffrey thought of his large bed and feather mattress. He would leave that for Emmaline. "I shall make use of Ben's bed and dresser."

Jim stood, shaking his head. "I sure looked forward to getting my own room. . . ."

"Hush, Jim," Chris snapped. "You just mind the boss."

The boy fell silent, but he jutted his chin sullenly. He stomped through the open doorway to his side of the bunkhouse.

Geoffrey, watching him, frowned. The boy was obviously annoyed. He didn't like the arrangement either, but there wasn't much he could do about it. Eventually Jim would accept the situation, just as Geoffrey had. They would do it for Emmaline.

# TEN

～

J IM COTLER FLOPPED onto his lumpy rope bed but left one bare
foot dangling on the floor. After almost two years of sleeping
on the straw-stuffed mattress, it fit his frame like his worn,
broken-in boots fit his feet. Across the room, Chris broke into a
rattling snore. Jim stared at the ceiling and let out a huff.

Mr. Garrett had promised him his own room. He did a man's
work, but he earned a boy's wage. Having his own room would
have made earning less money a little more tolerable. He should
have argued. He should have said, "Mr. Garrett, you promised me
my own room and, by thunder, I'm going to have my own room!"
He punched the air with his fist, finding release in the fierce jab.
But as quickly as it rose, the rebellion dissolved. He lowered his
arm to the crackly mattress and sighed.

Jim knew better than to argue. His father—God rest his soul—
had taught him and Chris that a wise man respected authority.
Whatever the boss commanded, Jim obeyed. Geoffrey Garrett was
a fair man, but he was also a man who didn't mince words when
it came to giving orders.

Mr. Garrett made pretty good decisions. In his five years of
living with the man, Jim couldn't remember a time Mr. Garrett had

given an order that turned out to be a mistake. Even though Mr. Garrett didn't have any experience with sheep ranching when he came to America, he had prospered at it. Jim didn't know anybody smarter than Geoffrey Garrett.

Even before the first fifty head from Spain arrived on the train, Mr. Garrett could tell a person anything he wanted to know about the Merino breed. At night in the dugout, while they wove fibers into rope or built furniture to pass the time, Mr. Garrett had filled his, Chris's, and Ben's heads with information about the breed of sheep that would make his ranch the best in all of Kansas. Thick wool! Easy lambing! Flavorful meat! Jim smiled as he remembered how much his boss had praised the Merinos. Yep, Mr. Garrett knew a lot about sheep, there was no doubt about that.

But it sure seemed like Mr. Garrett didn't know much about women. Jim's heart thudded as he pictured Emmaline Bradford's heart-shaped face and big brown eyes. After all of Mr. Garrett's descriptions, Jim had expected Emmaline Bradford to be pretty. But now that he'd seen her himself, "pretty" didn't seem like a good enough word to describe her. She was tiny, like a sparrow, and the minute he saw her up close something inside him had wanted to protect her. He'd never experienced such a feeling toward a girl before. Mr. Garrett was a fool not to have married her the moment she stepped off the train. What was he thinking, waiting until next spring?

Jim rolled fully onto the mattress and faced the wall. He shouldn't be thinking like this about Miss Bradford. She belonged to Geoffrey Garrett, and the Bible was pretty clear that a fellow shouldn't harbor possessive thoughts about another man's intended bride.

He stared at the shadowed wall. But what if Emmaline didn't become Mr. Garrett's bride? A lot could happen in ten months. Maybe Miss Bradford would decide she didn't want to marry Mr.

Garrett. Maybe she'd want to marry somebody else. He sucked in a lungful of air as another thought flitted through his mind. He was growing like a weed these days. Chris complained about having to buy him new britches every other month. Maybe if he were man-sized, Miss Bradford would see him as a man and—

He shouldn't think such things! Miss Bradford belonged to Jim's boss, and a man respected his boss. Slamming his eyes closed, Jim focused on the rhythmic wheeze-rattle of his brother's snoring. But somehow images of Emmaline Bradford's big brown eyes and pretty face still crept through.

———

Emmaline sneaked back into the house after visiting the washroom. Although it was very early—the sun a mere slit on the horizon—she was wide awake. After examining the selection of frocks in the closet, she chose one of her black traveling dresses. The other items in her wardrobe buttoned up the back, making it impossible for her to dress herself without assistance or contortions.

Tying her own corset proved challenging, and the strings were not as tight as a maid would fasten them, but it would have to do. The looser corset layered with pantaloons and petticoats made the dress fit more snugly than was comfortable, but she refused to ask any of the men for help.

Fully clothed, she wound her hair into a braid and twisted it to form a bun on the back of her head. She smoothed her fingers over the coil of hair, assuring herself that it was secure. She must speak with Geoffrey about purchasing a small mirror for her use. In the kitchen, she splashed water from the pump on her face, completing her morning ablutions. Then she stood in the middle of the dusky kitchen with her hands clasped in front of her, wondering what she should do next.

Geoffrey had indicated she would serve as housekeeper. She assumed this included cooking duties, but what did the men prefer to eat for breakfast? And more importantly, would she be able to prepare it? Her cooking skills were woefully limited. The family cook prepared meals at home, and the woman had been territorial concerning the kitchen. Emmaline could boil eggs and butter bread. Did Geoffrey have eggs and bread available?

Moving to the built-in cupboards, she opened each door in turn, seeking the needed ingredients to put breakfast on the table. Many of the cupboards were empty, but in one she found a variety of dry goods, including corn meal, flour, sugar, and tea leaves. Pulling out the tin of tea, she opened it and sniffed the dried leaves. The rich aroma enticed her into taking a deeper draw. Her stomach rumbled with desire. She placed the tin on the table so she could steep a pot of strong tea.

In another cupboard she located a sparse assortment of canned goods—mostly beans. She found nothing that would serve as breakfast fare. Frowning, she turned a slow circle, searching for clues. Where might Geoffrey keep eggs, bread, or meat?

Suddenly the kitchen door burst open, and Emmaline let out a squawk of surprise when someone rushed into the room. Then she recognized one of Geoffrey's hands—Jim, the young boy who was the good shearer—and she nearly collapsed in relief. "Oh my, you startled me."

A wide, friendly grin broke across his face. "Oh. You are awake. I came to light the stove. It's one of my chores."

She grimaced. "Certainly it is my task now. . . ."

The boy shrugged. His movements were jerky, as if he had more energy than he could contain. "I can do it for you. I don't mind. Not at all."

Emmaline stepped aside. "Please do. I shall watch and learn."

With wide strides, Jim crossed to the stove, giving her another big smile as he passed her. Crouching down, he used a small shovel to transfer black lumps of coal from a bucket on the floor into the stove's combustion chamber. Then he straightened and removed a wooden match from a jar on a shelf near the stove, swished it against the sole of his boot, and placed it on top of the coal.

Emmaline leaned sideways and watched each step carefully. "That doesn't appear too difficult. I shall manage it tomorrow."

The boy rose to his feet and whisked his hands together. Long and lanky, he stood at least five inches taller than she. "You have to keep adding coal as it's burnt up." His gaze bounced from the empty tabletop, to the stove, and then back to Emmaline. "Do you want me to help with breakfast?"

"Might you show me where to find eggs or some breakfast meat?"

The boy charged out the kitchen door, and Emmaline followed. He led her to a mound of dirt behind the house. A wood-planked door lay snug against the gentle hill. Grasping a knotted rope attached to the door, he gave a tug. "We keep milk, cheese, and butter in the springhouse, but the eggs, meat, and vegetables are in the cellar. I like going into the cellar. It reminds me of a cave, and it stays nice and cool down here even in the summer." His grin twitched. "Sometimes, when it's very hot outside, I like to go down and just sit. It's a good thinkin' place."

Emmaline stared into the dark hole. A musty smell rose from the cavern, and she wrinkled her nose. Despite the warmth of the morning, she had no desire to enter that black hollow. "Food is stored down there?"

"Yes, miss. Stay here. I'll go get some eggs and salt pork." He turned and hurried down the dirt steps, disappearing below ground. After a few moments, he emerged with four speckled eggs cradled in one hand and a lumpy cloth-wrapped item tucked beneath his elbow.

Emmaline glanced around the yard. She saw no chickens. "From where did the eggs come? Do you hunt for prairie chicken eggs?"

The boy laughed. "Prairie chickens? No, miss." Jim headed for the kitchen with a rapid gait, and Emmaline was forced to trot to keep up. "Mr. Garrett barters for things we need. We get eggs and milk from the Sorensons and pork from the Martins. Sometimes we trade for vegetables, too." They entered the kitchen, and Jim placed the eggs and pork on the counter. "But now that you're here, Mr. Garrett says you'll do the gardening and we'll have our own vegetables."

Emmaline gave the boy a dubious look. She enjoyed gardening, but she preferred to raise roses and nasturtiums. What did she know of carrots and potatoes? "Do you *eat* prairie chickens?"

Jim cocked one hip and slipped his hand into his front pocket. "We never have. Chris brings down geese whenever he can, and he shot some quail one time—they were real good with rice." The boy smacked his lips. "But mostly we eat mutton and pork and deer meat. Why?"

She pointed to the crock bowl in the sink. "There was some sort of dark, flavorful meat in this bowl. I ate it for supper last night. I thought it was chicken."

Jim shook his head. "No, that was maw stew. You chop up the organs of a sheep—the heart, lungs, and liver—and cook them in the sheep's stomach."

Emmaline's stomach rolled. "The . . . the organs of a—"

"Of a sheep," Jim repeated, his cheerful voice a direct contrast to the vile feeling his words conjured. With a short laugh, he added, "We use every part of the sheep except the *baa*, Mr. Garrett says."

The room seemed to tilt. She clutched her belly.

"Miss Emmaline, are you all right?" Jim grabbed her shoulders and held her upright.

"Jim!"

Jim released her so quickly she nearly fell. She grabbed the edge of the sink as Geoffrey came toward them, a fierce scowl on his face. He stopped beside Emmaline and grasped her elbow. "Is he bothering you?"

She wrenched free, glaring up at him. He had let her eat the *lungs* of a sheep! She lowered her gaze slightly and her eyes collided with his chest. The top two buttons of his plaid shirt were unfastened, as if he were half dressed. Dark, curling hair peeped from the opening.

She jerked her chin upward, drawing on fury to chase away the odd feelings that assailed her. "No, he is not bothering me. He is assisting me. He started a fire in the stove and then retrieved breakfast items since *you* did not advise me."

Geoffrey's gaze dropped to the eggs and meat on the counter. He turned his attention to Jim. "I believe you have tasks to complete before breakfast. Miss Bradford will ring the bell when the food is ready to be served."

Jim scurried outside without a backward glance.

Geoffrey wheeled on Emmaline. "Why were his hands on you?"

"I . . . I felt sick. I thought about . . ." If she allowed herself to dwell on what she had consumed last night, she might embarrass herself by regurgitating on the kitchen floor. "It isn't important. He was not doing anything improper."

Geoffrey stared at her in silence for several long seconds. Then he folded his arms over his chest and gave her a stern look.

"Emmaline, I must ask that you not spend time alone with either of the hands. Chris is trustworthy, and Jim is still quite young, but they are *men* and susceptible to temptation."

"I did not deliberately set out to spend time alone with Jim." Emmaline's chest tightened as she defended herself, but she maintained an even tone. "He came to the kitchen and assisted in making the needed preparations to begin cooking breakfast."

Geoffrey's stern expression did not soften. "All the same, kindly exercise caution in the future. It would not bode well for you to—"

"To entice them? I assure you, that is not in *my* nature, and I resent your implication."

Geoffrey's shoulders rose and fell with his great intake of breath. "I was not accusing you, Emmaline, but merely—"

Emmaline picked up one egg and threw it forcefully into the sink. The shell shattered, the contents exploding against the enameled sides of the basin. "While residing here, I will by necessity come in contact with the ranch hands. If you are concerned about the situation, perhaps you should arrange different living accommodations for me." She spun to leave but then turned back and added, "And kindly button your shirt in the presence of a lady!"

Anger propelled her through the house to the sleeping room. Geoffrey called her name, but she ignored him and slammed the door behind her. She stared at the door. There was no lock. Would he enter uninvited?

A knock sounded. "Emmaline?"

Although he did not raise his voice, she recognized an undercurrent of frustration. She scuttled into the corner, refusing to answer.

"Are you going to prepare our breakfast?"

She gaped at the door. "Not until you have apologized to me for your ridiculous accusation." The words burst out, and she held her breath afterward, certain he would break down the door and take her to task. Her father would have never accepted such behavior. But all she heard was her own pounding heartbeat. At long last, the sound of retreating footsteps told her he had departed.

Standing erect in the corner of the room, she waited for her fury to drain. But it held her captive. Goeffrey claimed to love her, but apparently he didn't trust her. How could she remain at a place where her movements would be evaluated, always fearful of his jealous reactions?

Filled with righteous indignation, she grabbed her carpet bag from the floor of the closet and threw it on the bed. She wadded up a dress and jammed it into the bag's belly. As soon as Geoffrey and the others were away from the house, she would walk all the way to Moreland, if she had to, and board an eastbound train. She would use her dowry money and go home no matter what Geoffrey thought.

# ELEVEN

EMMALINE PAUSED ALONG the roadway to swipe her hand over her sweaty face. Anger had carried her this far, but the heat of the shimmering sun had melted her icy fury to a puddle of nagging frustration. Looking down the road, she wondered how much farther to Moreland. Her feet ached, and surely her arm would disconnect from her shoulder if she had to carry the carpet bag another foot.

She had only packed her travel dresses and personal items, reasoning Geoffrey could ship her other belongings to her. But just before stepping out the door she had removed the stone from the mantel and placed it atop the dresses. Its weight slowed her considerably, but she would not discard it. That stone represented *home*, and it would return to the garden in England—just as she would return to her home in England.

Resolutely, she took a few stumbling forward steps. A cramp caught between her shoulder blades. Hissing through her teeth, she released the bag. Dust rose when it hit the ground, drifting across the already grimy toes of her shoes. She stared at the bag, willing herself to lift it and continue her trek. Her weary muscles refused to cooperate.

"Perhaps a short rest." Using the bag as a makeshift seat, she sank down, folding her legs to the side. She closed her eyes and let her head drift back. The breeze rustled the tall grass alongside the road and dried the sweat on her neck. A bird called, its song sweetly mournful. Emmaline relaxed, allowing herself to absorb the peaceful sounds of the countryside.

But the rumble of wagon wheels on hard-packed earth floated toward her. Geoffrey? She bolted to her feet, ready for flight. A ramshackle wagon, pulled by gray-muzzled mules, rolled toward her. It wasn't Geoffrey on the high seat. The relief collapsed her once more.

Atop the wagon seat, Ronald Senger held the reins, his brown face wreathed in a friendly yet curious grin. He tugged back on the reins, drawing the mules to a stop next to Emmaline's bag. "Why, if it ain't Miss Emmalion. What you doin' out here by yo'self?" He hopped down from the seat, his wiry body graceful in the dismount, and glanced at her bag. "You goin' somewheres?"

Emmaline nodded, licking her lips. "Yes. I . . . I am going to Moreland."

The man's eyebrows shot high. "Morelan'? Why, that be a far piece on foot, Miss Emmalion. Geoffrey tell you to walk it?"

Emmaline set her jaw. Although an affable man, Ronald Senger was Geoffrey's friend. He would surely return her to the ranch immediately if he knew she had defied Geoffrey.

Ronald stared at her, his jaw working back and forth. Finally another grin twitched his cheeks. "You look full ready to melt clean away. A drink sound good?"

Emmaline licked her lips again, aware of her parched throat. Hesitantly, she offered a nod and pushed to her feet.

Ronald reached into his wagon and withdrew a tan jug. He popped the cork from the narrow mouth and held out the jug to her.

Emmaline stared at the homey vessel. Desire to quench her thirst battled with distaste at placing her lips on a spout that had previously been used by someone else. She pressed her palms to her stomach.

He bounced the jug and gave an encouraging nod. "Go ahead, Miss Emmalion. It be ginger watuh. You can drink much as you wan' an' no matter how hot ya been, yore tummy'll hold it down jus' fine. No need for worries."

But she sucked in her lower lip and locked her fingers together.

Understanding dawned across his face. He drew himself upright and spoke with great dignity. "I's sorry, Miss Emmalion, that I gots no cup to pour the watuh in." His wiry brows formed a brief V before smoothing out. "Reckon a lady like yo'self couldn't be drinkin' from no jug."

He replaced the cork and thumped the jug back under the wagon seat. Turning, he said, "But if you's still needin' a drink, I could tote you on to our place. Tildy'll fix you up with a cool cup o' watuh, an' you could rest a spell outta the sun."

Shamed yet uncertain why, Emmaline nodded. "That . . . that would be quite nice, thank you." She allowed Ronald to assist her onto the wagon seat. He tossed her bag in the back as if it weighed nothing, then climbed up beside her. She scooted to the opposite side of the rough-hewn bench seat, giving him plenty of space.

Flicking a diffident grin in her direction, he slapped the reins down on the mules' glistening backs. "Git up now, Fern 'n' Frank." After several more brisk whacks with the reins, the mules finally leaned against the rigging, and the wagon rolled forward.

———

Tildy slung the bucket of wash water across the soft mounds of soil that made up her garden plot. It sure felt good to have all the seeds in the ground. She smacked her lips, anticipating the first tomatoes and green beans stewed together in an iron skillet and seasoned with chunks of squirrel or rabbit. The prairie could be harsh, but it lent its bounty, too, and Tildy appreciated every offering.

She glanced toward the road and frowned. Where was that Ronald? He'd promised to restring her clothesline as soon as he got back from delivering the repaired plow to the Sorensons' place. She shook her head, glaring at the sky. "Lawd, I hates to be complainin', 'cause I knows You meant the wind for good, but it sure can cause us troubles, too . . ."

She needed to get the sheets hung before they dried in a rumpled mess in the basket. Plucking the line from the ground where it lay like a lazy snake, she shook the dust from it. Should she fetch a stool, climb up, and reattach it herself? Heaven only knew when that slow-moving man of hers would return. She lifted her apron to wipe her brow, and when she lowered it she spotted a rise of dust from the road. Finally!

Dropping the line, she trotted forward to meet the wagon. "You git to jawin' wit' the Sorensons an' forget where you live?" Then she spotted Emmaline, and her aggravation with Ronald fled. "Why, you brung Miss Emmalion for a visit! Git on down here, honey!"

Ronald assisted Emmaline to the ground, and immediately Tildy wrapped her in a hug. "Mm-mm-mmm, you look as bedraggled as a tomcat at sunrise." She gave the younger woman a gentle nudge toward the house. "Git in the shade, chil', an' splash yo' face wit' watuh from that barrel."

Emmaline eagerly scooped water from the barrel that sat next to the front door and doused her face and neck. Water spattered the front of the girl's dress, leaving dark splotches behind.

Tildy shook her head. Foolish English girl, wearing dark material in this heat. "You cain't be wearin' black in the summertime. That sun'll plumb roast you to nothin'."

Emmaline shot her a sharp look, but she didn't argue.

Clucking her tongue, Tildy pointed to the open doorway of the house. "Now let's git some watuh inside ya."

Tildy refilled the tin cup three times before Emmaline stopped reaching for more. Once the girl's thirst was slaked, Tildy pushed her into a chair at the table and plunked herself down across from her. "Well, Miss Emmalion, it be mighty nice to have some comp'ny. But I gotta say, I's surprised to see you. You ain't even had time to hardly settle in at yo' new home, an' here you is a-visitin'."

Emmaline opened her mouth as if to speak, but then she clamped her jaw closed again.

Tildy scowled. "Somethin' eatin' at you, chil'? You can tell me. Ol' Tildy's got some good listenin' ears."

The girl's gaze darted to the doorway. Ronald stood in the opening. An unfamiliar carpet bag dangled from his hand. He hefted it, his eyes on Emmaline. "What you want me to do wit' your bag, Miss Emmalion?"

*So that's the way the wind blows.* Tildy fixed Emmaline with a knowing stare. "You come to stay, did ya?"

Emmaline shook her head wildly and jumped up from the table. "No!" Spinning to face Ronald, she tangled her hands together. "Just put it down. I . . . I shall . . ."

"Ronal'—" Tildy sent her husband an "I's-meanin'-it" look— "drop the bag an' go hang that line foh me. Toss them sheets over it once you got it hung, too. Emmalion an' me'll sort things out."

His dark face puckered as though he'd bit down on a sour pickle. "When we gonn' eat our dinner?"

Tildy huffed. "We eat when I says we eat! You just go on an' do what I tells ya."

With a shrug, Ronald thumped the bag onto the floor and left.

Tildy pointed to the chair. "Sit, Miss Emmalion. Reckon you an' me is gonna have us a talk."

Stubbornness flared in the girl's dark eyes. "I have nothing about which to speak."

Tildy chuckled at her bravado. "Even wit'out you speakin', that bag ovuh there says plenty." She nodded toward the chair. "Sit down."

The girl remained upright, staring at the bag.

Tildy smacked the tabletop. "I says, sit down, Miss Emma-lion."

With a startled look, Emmaline quickly sat.

Tildy reached across the table and patted Emmaline's hand. "Good. Now, let's hear it."

Emmaline stared, wide-eyed but silent.

Giving the girl's slim hand another pat, Tildy said, "Had you a disagreement, did you?"

Tears welled in Emmaline's eyes. She offered a slow nod.

"Uh-huh, them men . . . always doin' somethin' to upset us womenfolks." Tildy made sure her voice carried sympathy. She clucked her tongue. "So what was it, chil'?" She leaned forward, tucking her chin low. "He give you a whack? 'Cause ain't no woman gots to put up wit' a man like dat."

Emmaline reared back. "Certainly not! But—but he let me eat something deplorable, and he said I was not to speak to the hands on the ranch. He behaved as though he expected me to . . . to flirt with them."

"So you packed up an' plan on leavin'?"

The girl stuck out her chin. "Yes."

"Well . . ." Tildy traced a circle on the tabletop with her finger, gathering her thoughts. Youngsters could be brash, and it appeared this one was as headstrong as the man who'd fetched her from across the ocean. *I sho' could use some help here, Lawd.* "I reckon he acted foolish 'cause he was jealous. You's a plumb purty little gal, an' it'd be hard-pressed for them workers on the ranch not to notice. An' that Geoffrey, he's been waitin' a long time to have you here. Reckon he's a-wantin' you all to his own self."

Emmaline protested, "The ranch hand in question is a mere boy."

Tildy raised her hand. "Now, I's not defendin' him, mind you, just tryin' to help you see his side o' thangs. You bein' young like you is, an' newly married"—Emmaline's face turned bright pink—"it's gonn' take some time to learn ever'thang 'bout each othuh. You jus' keep assurin' him, an' he'll soon see you got eyes for nobody but him."

The color in the girl's cheeks deepened to a scalding red. She turned her gaze to her lap.

Tildy sighed. "Men is jealous creatures, chil', so we'uns just do what we can not to worry 'em. Things'll get better by an' by."

Emmaline whispered something.

Tildy couldn't hear the words. "What you say, chil'?"

Emmaline raised her head. "I said . . . we're not married."

Tildy jerked backward, her spine connecting sharply with the back of the chair. "You ain't married? But—" Hadn't she given those young'uns a wedding gift? Why, the girl had drove off holding on to a wedding bouquet!

"After all the time that has passed, I feel as though he is a stranger to me! How could I marry a stranger?" The girl planted her palms on the table and leaned forward. "So we made an agreement for me to stay in Kansas until winter's end so I can learn how to be a rancher's wife and to try to rediscover the love I once held for him. I agreed in the hopes that things would go well, but . . ."

Shaking her head wildly, Emmaline exclaimed, "I cannot honor the agreement! Not if meals consist of the organs of an animal cooked in that very animal's stomach. Not if it means being told to whom I can and cannot speak. Why, he treated me as though I were nothing more than his property!" She clamped her hand over her mouth, her eyes wide. "Oh! I did not mean—"

Tildy flapped her hand. "Now, no need for apologizin'. Truth is, me an' Ronal' *was* property, an' it ain't a pleasurable thang. So's I understan' better'n most what you's sayin'."

Emmaline's shoulders slumped. Her face slowly returned to its normal color. She licked her lips and sent a hopeful look across the table. "Since you understand, will you and Ronald help me? Will you take me to Moreland so I can purchase a train ticket and go home?"

Tildy rose and paced the length of the house. "Now, chil', I understan' how you's feelin', but that don' mean I's gonna help you run off."

Emmaline's face fell. "But why?"

" 'Cause a person's word's gotta mean somethin'." Tildy crossed to the table and took hold of Emmaline's hands. "If you an' Geoffrey made an agreement, then you gotta stick to it."

"But how can I live with a stranger who—"

Tildy gave the girl's hands a shake. "You think you're the only woman ever married a stranger?" She tilted her head toward the doorway. "That man out there—Ronal'? Him an' me was strangers when we jumped de broom. Massuh bought him from a plantation in North Carolina an' brought him to me. Says he's to be my man." Remembrances—some good, some bad—tugged at Tildy, but she pushed them aside to stay focused on Emmaline and Geoffrey.

"I took one look at him an' thought, 'Mm-hmm, Massuh be thinkin' a tall man an' a wide woman make some sturdy field hands.' But I say nothin', just jump dat broom an' take Ronal' to my cabin like I's told. Didn't feel nothin' for him at first, but jumpin' dat broom meant I was his an' he was mine. We was *committed* to each othuh. No ma'am, didn't feel nothin' at first, but after a heap o' prayin' an' the Lawd answerin' . . ."

Tildy closed her eyes for a moment. Then, looking at Emmaline again, she placed her hands over her heart. "Over time, that man become my whole world." She touched Emmaline's pale cheek. "That kind o' feelin' don't come on right away, Miss Emmalion, but it do come on when you look to the good Lawd to help you honor a commitment."

Emmaline pulled back and rose from the chair. Turning her back on Tildy, she said, "So you will not assist me in reaching Moreland?"

Tildy sighed. Hadn't the girl listened to anything she'd said? "No, Miss Emmalion, neither Ronal' nor me is gonna help you break a vow . . . even if it ain't a weddin' vow."

"Very well, then. I shall walk." Emmaline strode purposefully to the door. She bent over to grasp the handle on the carpet bag, but then she jerked straight up, looking outside. Geoffrey Garrett's wagon pulled into the yard. Emmaline jumped behind the doorjamb. "Please! I will not ask anything else of you ever, but please do not tell him I am here!"

Her desperate whisper pierced Tildy's heart. *Lawd, what do I do?*

# TWELVE

GEOFFREY SET THE brake and hopped over the side of his wagon. The sheets flapping on the clothesline meant Tildy was home, and the wagon beside the barn indicated Ronald's presence. He cupped his hands around his mouth and called, "Ronald? Tildy?"

Ronald stepped from the barn, and a moment later Tildy emerged from the house. Neither wore their usual welcoming smiles, but that suited Geoffrey today. He didn't have time for chitchat. The worry that struck when he had returned to the ranch house at noonday and found Emmaline missing still held him in its grasp. He had to find Emmaline.

She must have gone for a walk and gotten lost. He could think of no other explanation. While hitching the team to the wagon and scanning the countryside on his way to his friends' house, he had prayed constantly for her safety.

Geoffrey strode forward to meet Tildy. "Emmaline's gone. I looked everywhere on the ranch, but I couldn't find her. I hoped you might agree to—"

Tildy and Ronald exchanged an uncomfortable look that made

Geoffrey's mouth go dry. He reached out and grasped Ronald's forearm. "You know something. Tell me."

Ronald extracted his arm and scratched his head, glancing at his wife. "You tell 'im, Tildy."

"What?" Geoffrey barked the word, fear honing a sharp edge to his tone.

Without speaking, Tildy waved her thick palm toward the house. Geoffrey looked past her shoulder. A shadow moved inside the door. Emmaline! Dashing past Tildy, he charged through the door and swept Emmaline into his arms.

"Oh, thank the Lord . . ." He pressed his face to her hair and inhaled. The sweaty smell from her hair spoke of hours in the sun. She must have wandered aimlessly before stumbling upon the Senger homestead. Sympathy rolled through him. "I feared you were lost. . . ."

She squirmed in his arms. He released her but then caught her shoulders and peered into her face. "In the village of Wortley you had the freedom to venture wherever you pleased, but you are no longer in Yorkshire County." His voice rose as he considered all the things that could have happened to her as she roamed across the prairie. "From now on you will remain at the house unless I accompany you off the property."

Emmaline jerked free of his hold and moved away, stepping over a carpet bag. The carpet bag from the closet at the ranch. The buttoned collar beneath his chin seemed to tighten. He jammed a finger toward the bag. "What is the meaning of this?"

Emmaline folded her arms across her chest and looked to the side. The stubborn set of her jaw stirred Geoffrey's ire. Before he could insist she answer him, Tildy and Ronald entered the house.

"Tildy and Ronald, please leave Emmaline and me alone."

"Uh–uh."

Tildy's refusal reminded him of Emmaline's defiance. Geoffrey spun to face Tildy.

She caught his arm and tugged. Her gravelly voice rasped directly into his ear. "You go easy on Miss Emmalion. She didn't come to harm, an' you needs to be grateful 'stead o' raisin' Cain."

"Tildy . . ." Geoffrey groaned the name.

"You be 'memberin' what the Good Book says 'bout how we is to love. Seems to me there be a verse 'bout a man lovin' his woman the way Jesus loves the church. Would Jesus be a-hollerin' right now or would He be tender?"

Tildy's admonition pricked Geoffrey's conscience, but it didn't remove his determination to understand why Emmaline had packed a bag and set out. He gave Tildy's hand a pat and moved to Emmaline's side. Aware of his audience, he tempered his voice.

"Emmaline, please explain why you left the ranch this morning."

Emmaline sent Tildy a pleading look, and Tildy stepped to Emmaline's side and slipped her thick arm around the younger woman's waist. "Now, now, you know sometimes we do thangs afore thinkin' 'em all the way through," she said to Geoffrey. "Reckon Miss Emmalion's moseyin' off today was just one o' them thangs."

Geoffrey waited for Emmaline to substantiate or refute Tildy's statement, but she remained stubbornly silent.

"You take her on back to Chetwyn' Valley now an' let her rest up from her wanderin' in the sun. Then this evenin' "—she gave Geoffrey's arm an emphatic pat—"you two have a nice talk. Pray together. Things'll come out right in the end."

Geoffrey gritted his teeth. "Oh yes. We shall certainly have a talk this evening." He held out one hand toward his errant bride-to-be. "Come along, Emmaline."

She stepped past his hand, hefted the bag, and walked out to the wagon without a word or a glance in his direction. He clamped his jaw and followed.

Emmaline sat stiffly upright on the wagon seat, clutching the bag in her lap as if it might give her strength to face whatever waited when they reached the ranch. Geoffrey's firmly set jaw and stiff shoulders told her how upset he was with her. She tried to tell herself she didn't care—why should it matter if he were upset? It was his foolish action that had precipitated her desire to leave. She was the innocent victim.

Yet, deep down, guilt pricked. The image of his relieved face when he had spotted her in the Sengers' house played through her mind. Her skin tingled when she recalled the warmth of his embrace. His emotionally voiced gratitude to the Lord rang in her ears and stirred something inside of her. In that moment when Geoffrey had swept her into his arms, she had regretted her hasty departure. Now, the remembrance of those fleeting snippets of time kept her from giving full vent to indignation.

She risked a quick sidelong glance at his stern profile. She saw little of the young man she remembered in the firm line of his jaw and tanned skin. Lines fanned the corners of his eyes, making him seem older than his twenty-seven years, and an etched V between his eyebrows gave him the appearance of one who had weathered much and emerged stronger and able to conquer whatever difficulties came his way. Even his hands, clenched around the reins so tightly his tendons stood out like rope, had a chiseled hardness alien to the hands of the average English gentleman.

She stared at her own hands wrapped around the handle of the bag. Mother had always admonished her to protect her skin—to keep it white and smooth, as a lady should. Would time in this country make the same changes in her skin that she witnessed in Geoffrey's? Would time here build in her an inner strength?

Geoffrey pulled the reins, guiding the horses to turn the wagon in at their lane. "Whoa..." He drew the horses to a halt, wrapped the reins around the brake handle, and finally turned to face her. Despite the bright sun overhead, his steely gaze chilled her to her toes. "Please go into the house, Emmaline, and prepare a decent supper. The men and I did not have lunch since we were seeking you. After supper, we will discuss today's . . . activities."

Although the words were uttered in an insipid tone, they rode on an ominous current. A flash of rebellion lifted her chin. "Yes, we shall discuss today's . . . activities." She carefully emulated his tone. His accusation from the morning still stung, and she expected an apology. She shifted the bag to the seat before climbing over the side of the wagon. She tugged her skirt free of the rough wood and then reached for the bag. Geoffrey handed it to her. She stumbled backward with its weight when he released it.

Through clenched teeth, he said, "Are you all right?"

In spite of the situation, Emmaline nearly laughed. As angry as he was, he still attempted the role of considerate suitor. She offered a brusque nod.

"Very well. I shall see you at suppertime." He slapped the reins down on the horses' backs, and the wagon rolled around the house.

———

"Thank you for the meal, Miss Emmaline." Chris wiped his mouth with his napkin and dropped it over his plate.

Emmaline glanced up from her own plate. Her best efforts had produced a charred-on-the-outside-but-raw-in-the-middle pork roast, soggy potatoes, and half-cooked carrots. From the lumps beneath the napkin, she knew Chris had eaten little of the meal. His polite statement shamed her.

"I am sorry it was not more . . . palatable." She dabbed her mouth with her napkin, flicking her gaze around the table to include all three men in her apology. "I was not given many opportunities to cook at home." Certainly this dismal meal proved how ill-equipped she was for this place. Why couldn't Geoffrey just allow her to go home? With a sigh, she added, "It may be necessary for Geoffrey to hire a cook lest we all starve."

Geoffrey scowled. "And who might you suggest?"

Emmaline offered a one-armed shrug. "Perhaps Tildy?"

The V between his eyebrows deepened. "Tildy is our friend, not our servant."

Chastened, Emmaline lowered her head. A movement caught her eye, and she peeked to witness Jim Cotler scooping another serving of potatoes onto his plate. With a bold grin, he carried a forkful of the deplorable mess to his mouth, chewed, and swallowed. Then he patted his stomach, waggling his eyebrows. Emmaline's lips twitched as she fought the urge to bestow a big smile of thanks on the young ranch hand. His impish behavior reminded her of a colt frolicking through a meadow. With a light giggle, she said, "I appreciate your enthusiasm, Jim, but you will surely get a stomach-ache from consuming so much of this sorry meal."

Jim raised his shoulders in a shrug and continued eating. When he finished, he and Chris carried their plates to the sink. Jim glanced over his shoulder at Geoffrey and then Emmaline. "Would you like me to help with the dishes, Miss Emmaline?"

Chris gawked at the boy. "You never wanted to wash—" Then a knowing look crossed his face. He grabbed the back of Jim's neck and tugged him toward the kitchen door. "Come on. We have chores waiting in the barn."

With their departure, Emmaline and Geoffrey were alone. She jumped up and began clearing the table.

Geoffrey sat back in his chair, his coffee cup hooked on one finger. His eyes followed her every movement. She found his silent observation unnerving. Her ineptitude in cooking equaled her lack of skill in housekeeping. She wished he would leave her to struggle through the tasks without an audience, but she couldn't find the courage to ask him to leave. She stacked all of the dirty dishes on the counter beside the sink, then reached for the pump.

In seconds, Geoffrey was at her side. "You must use hot water or the dishes will not be clean." He directed her to the reservoir on the side of the stove. Using a dipper, he ladled several scoops of water into the sink. Steam rose from the tin basin.

Emmaline hesitated at putting her hands into that steamy water, yet the dishes must be done. She lifted a stack of plates and started to place them in the sink.

Once more, Geoffrey intervened. "You need *soap*, Emmaline."

The impatience in his tone raised her defenses. Plunking the plates onto the counter with a noisy clatter, she spun to face him. "As I said at suppertime, I have not been given the opportunity to learn housekeeping. At home, I did not cook. I did not clean. I did not sew or sweep or . . . or wash dishes. If you want these tasks done to your satisfaction, then do them yourself or hire someone. But do not expect perfection from me!"

They glared at each other, their noses only inches apart. Emmaline saw her own angry reflection in Geoffrey's pupils. She marveled at her behavior—she had never so boldly rebelled against anyone. Perhaps this unforgiving land was already molding her into someone new.

Geoffrey lifted his face to the ceiling and drew a long breath. When he looked at her, the irritation in his expression was gone. "I do not wish to fight with you, Emmaline."

Gathering her newfound courage, Emmaline drew her shoulders back. "Then kindly do not find fault with everything I do.

As you told me before bringing me here, I have much to learn to become a rancher's"—her throat went dry—"wife." She swallowed hard and crossed her arms. "I now see that you have much to learn about being a husband." The downthrust of his eyebrows gave her pause, but she finished her thought. "You cannot claim to love me and then distrust me. Love and trust are inseparable, Geoffrey. Your accusation this morning . . ." She paused, the remembrance of his harsh words stinging anew. Lifting her chin, she said, "I am not a trollop."

"I did not say you were a trollop."

"You insinuated as much."

Geoffrey caught her elbow and guided her to the table. "Sit down, Emmaline. Please."

The final word compelled her to pull out a chair and seat herself stiffly on its edge.

Geoffrey sat across from her and folded his hands on the crumb-laden tabletop. "I apologize for my words this morning. The sight of Jim's hands on your shoulders . . ." His thumbs twitched. "I didn't like it."

Apparently Miss Tildy had been accurate in her assessment of Geoffrey's jealousy.

Fixing her with a steady gaze, he said, "You must understand that you are a very attractive woman, Emmaline. Having you here could create . . . temptation."

His declaration of her attractiveness pleased her, yet his warning raised a note of anxiety. "Do you think either Jim or Chris would . . . would . . ." She couldn't bring herself to complete the thought aloud.

"I believe they are human enough to respond to an invitation, whether real or imagined. And since we are not yet wed . . ."

"But Jim is just a boy. Why, he doesn't yet shave!"

"A boy can have feelings like a man." Geoffrey's serious tone

silenced any further protest. "We must all reside here together,
so . . . be careful. It would be best if you weren't alone with either
of the hands any more than necessary. I will make sure Jim and
Chris understand the boundaries. But you must do your part, as
well."

Before she could respond, he stood and waved toward the sink
as he made his way across the room. "There is lye soap there on
the counter beside the sink. Scrape some into the basin and stir
briskly to create foam. Then wash the dishes."

That man! Must he always issue orders? The desire to flee this
place gripped her once more.

# THIRTEEN

〜

I BEEN THINKIN' . . ." TILDY waited until Ronald lifted his attention from his plate. When that man was focused on food, no words got past his ears to his brain. "Miss Emmalion, she bein' raised in a fine house over there across the Big Watuh, prob'ly don't know much 'bout livin' the hard life."

Ronald's brow puckered in thought. "You's prob'ly right at that." He picked up the remaining half biscuit on his speckled plate and sopped up gravy. "Now, we'uns, we knows 'bout the hard life, don' we?"

Tildy tucked her chin low. "Mm-hmm, yes we do. Troubles a-plenty." She pointed at him. "But blessin's, too. Lots o' blessin's. The Lawd has been good to us."

"Yup." Ronald popped the biscuit in his mouth and chewed slowly, a look of pure pleasure on his face.

One thing Tildy had always liked about Ronald was how he enjoyed his food. She might not put anything more than corn pone and wild greens on his plate, but he savored every morsel. Sometimes she wondered if his open appreciation for a meal stemmed from a time of being denied food, but she'd never asked him about it. There were some things a body just didn't want to know.

"Seein' as how the Lawd's been so good to us an' we learned how to make this hard land a place of good livin'," she said, "I's thinkin' maybe I could do somethin' to help out that little gal o' Geoffrey's."

Ronald's eyebrows rose. "You gonn' give her some lessons on livin' hard?"

Tildy chuckled. "Reckon nobody needs lessons in that. Life takes care o' that on its own. No sir, I's thinkin' I gonn' give her some lessons on *survivin'* the hard life. 'Cause sure as God made the sky blue, she's gonn' face some real trials in this place o' dust an' wind."

"You think that li'l gal's gonn' listen to an old colored woman? You just gonn' git yo'self hurt."

Tildy's temper flared. She liked the idea of her man trying to protect her, but his getting in her way when she had something she wanted to do was another thing altogether. "The good Lawd done placed that gal on my heart an' I be obliged to answer His call. So's I gonn' help her."

Ronald reached across the table and put his leathery hand over hers. "You a good woman, Tildy Senger."

"Well, you oughtta know, hmm?"

They shared a soft laugh. Tildy gave his hand a squeeze and then rose to start clearing their table. "Don't know 'xactly what all Miss Emmalion needs, but I do know for sure she could use a friend. Looked like a li'l lost lamb when she turn up here today. Mm-hmm, just a li'l lost lamb."

When she tried to take his plate, Ronald held on to it. "Cain't I have another piece o' that sweet 'tater pie?"

Tildy reared back, one eyebrow high. "You done already had two pieces."

"I knows it, but there be some law say a man cain't have three pieces o' pie?"

Tildy shook her head. "I gits you another piece, but you cain't have the last one. I's takin' that over tomorrow mornin' as a treat for Miss Emmalion. That gal could use some fattenin' up."

———

"Now *that's* a pie!"

Emmaline couldn't resist beaming at Tildy's ecstatic exclamation. Choosing to ignore the three ruined pies that rested in the bottom of the slop bucket beneath the counter, she focused solely on her success—a perfect, beautiful sweet potato pie.

"Thank you for teaching me, Miss Tildy." Emmaline leaned over the pie and sniffed. The mingled aromas of cinnamon and nutmeg made her stomach rumble in eagerness to sample a bite. But she would save this for tonight's dinner. How surprised the men would be!

"It's purely pleasure to share some o' my recipes with you, honey," Tildy said, her walnut brown eyes glowing. "You's givin' me a gift by listenin' to what I got to say."

Tears pricked Emmaline's eyes. Over the past two weeks, the colored woman had spent part of each day at Chetwynd Valley in patient tutelage. Emmaline could now start her own stove and adjust the heat by turning the damper. She knew to keep the reservoir filled so she would have hot water available whenever she needed it. She understood the importance of burying the contents of her slop bucket lest she invite coyotes or raccoons to her back door. There were moments when she felt like a true Kansas pioneer.

Even her cooking had improved. Last night's roast, while tougher than Emmaline would have preferred, was neither charred nor raw. The potatoes and carrots were boiled to perfection since she had learned to poke them with a fork to determine their doneness.

She could fry eggs, bake corn bread, and make a stew—but not a maw stew.

As for cleaning, Tildy had woven stiff bristles together to make a broom and taught Emmaline how to sweep without filling the air with dust. Surely many of Tildy's own chores went unfinished during the time she spent with Emmaline, yet she never voiced a single word of complaint. She also never, never made Emmaline feel dim-witted for her lack of knowledge. She merely explained the steps and then praised Emmaline's fledgling efforts. Tildy had announced that next week she intended to teach Emmaline how to bake bread. After today's success with pie baking, Emmaline felt ready to tackle the challenge of a perfectly browned loaf of bread.

"I never realized how much effort went into the running of a household." Emmaline touched the delicate crust on the pie with one finger. "Something as simple as baking a pie takes so many steps! When someone else does all the work, I don't believe you can fully appreciate the endeavor." Tilting her head to the side, she fixed Tildy with a pensive look. "Do you find that to be true?"

"Well, now, chil', since I always been a worker, I don' know I fully unnerstand what you's sayin', but somewhere in the Good Book . . ." She tapped her full lips. "I believes it's in 'Clesiastes, but I cain't be recallin' 'xactly where. Somethin' like 'there ain't nothin' better for a man . . . that he should make his soul enjoy good in his labor.' "

"Do you read the Bible every day?" Emmaline asked. In their time together, Tildy had often quoted Scripture.

A crooked smile curved Tildy's round cheeks. "Oh, now, I don' do no readin' myself. But ol' massuh's wife spoke o' the Good Book to us slaves. Said it be her Christian duty. An' she liked that'un about labor a whole lot. Prob'ly as a means o' gettin' her workers to take satisfaction in their toil 'stead o' slackin' off."

Emmaline found it impressive that Tildy had memorized so much Scripture just from hearing it read aloud. Perhaps she hadn't paid enough attention to sermons while growing up, because she couldn't quote any verses. "While it is satisfying to complete tasks assigned to me, I cannot honestly say I enjoy spending my entire day working." Thoughts of home flitted through her mind—the hours spent arranging flowers in lovely vases, reading books, taking slow walks through the daisy-filled cemetery, or embroidering delicate butterflies and pansies on crisp white cotton. Those activities, though not taxing, had held their share of pleasure.

"We gits rewarded when we works hard," Tildy insisted. She propped her fists on her hips. "When my Ronal' leaves the table wit' a big ol' smile on his face, does my heart good to know I satisfied him. Don't it pleasure you to see Geoffrey sit back an' pat his belly aftuh a good meal?"

Emmaline gave a little start. Was she learning all of these things to please Goeffrey, or to prove to herself she could meet the challenges of the prairie?

"An'—" Tildy gestured toward the pie—"ain't you proud o' what you done learned today? Now you can invite peoples over to sit in dat parlor wit' you, an' you can serve 'em a pie you made wit' yo' own two hands."

"But I don't know anyone except you." Emmaline tried to imagine herself and Tildy sitting in the parlor, sipping tea and eating pie, but the image eluded her.

"Ain't you met nobody when you go to church on Sunday?"

Emmaline shrugged. "Certainly. But seeing them so briefly does not lend itself to forming friendships."

"Well, you knows Geoffrey." Tildy frowned. "Do the two o' you sit together of an evenin' an' reflect on the day? Mebbe read some Scripture from the Good Book an' pray for each othuh?"

Emmaline shook her head. "We do sit together on the porch—it is cooler there—but he does most of the talking. He tells me what he did with his day, and he instructs me on what I should have done differently." Defensiveness climbed her spine. How she tired of Geoffrey pointing out her inadequacies. She glanced again at the pie and her chin lifted in pride. He would find no fault with that pie!

She added, "Geoffrey spends all day tending to the sheep and the land. And between the household chores and keeping up with the garden, my days are quite full."

An odd expression came over Tildy's face—a combination of irritation and sorrow. She squeezed Emmaline's shoulder. "Summertime is work time—storin' up so's you can survive the winter months. Geoffrey's got work on his mind right now, but you wait . . . come winter, when things slow down, you'll have that chance to sit an' talk the way you wants to."

Emmaline didn't answer. Winter seemed far away, and loneliness was her present companion. She felt no closer to Geoffrey now than she had when an ocean separated them. Winter was just another season to bear before she could return to England.

The sound of wagon wheels on hard-packed earth carried through the open window. Tildy looked toward the front of the house, her face lighting. "That be Ronal', comin' to fetch me home foh my own chores." She gave Emmaline a quick hug, bouncing her thick palm up and down on Emmaline's back. "You put that pie under a cloth when it's cool an' bring it out as a su'prise after supper. Yo' man'll bust his buttons in pride over what you done today."

Emmaline returned Tildy's hug. "Thank you again for your help. I shall see you tomorrow."

Tildy headed out the door, her skirt held as high as the tops of her battered brown shoes. Emmaline slipped to the window and watched as Ronald jumped down from the wagon and offered his hand to his wife. She took it with a giggle and clambered aboard. Ronald climbed up beside her, taking a moment to nudge his shoulder against hers. They exchanged a smile—a smile that spoke of enjoyment at being together again—and then he slapped down the reins. The wagon jolted down the lane, with Tildy snug up against Ronald's side and her bandana-covered head resting on his shoulder.

A stab of jealousy propelled Emmaline from the window. She returned to the stove and stared down at the sweet potato pie. Tears blurred the image. It would take more than learning to bake a pie to restore her relationship with Geoffrey.

She moved to the open kitchen door and peered across the expanse of open prairie. If only one could turn back time. How lovely it would be to spend one more day in England with Geoffrey. To walk the streets of their little village side by side, with his knuckles occasionally brushing hers, their gazes colliding and then skittering away, their lips curved into permanent smiles of contentment.

Back then, her heart had thrummed with joy every time he was near. Now, whenever he approached, apprehension sped her pulse. Would she ever stop mourning England and all she had left behind? She spun toward the broom in the corner, her skirts swirling around her ankles. Her black dress fit her perpetually somber mood. She began to sweep but then threw the broom aside. Many times back in England, she and Geoffrey had walked through the garden, sharing their innermost hopes and dreams, and often, Geoffrey had gifted her with a bouquet of fresh-picked daisies. Her soul hungered for the sight of daisies. Or pansies or morning glories. If she could pick a cluster of something bright and cheerful and place it on the table, surely her spirits would lift. Maybe the flowers would even provide a small reminder of England—of those wonderfully carefree days of kinship she shared with Geoffrey. And maybe he would remember, too.

The decision made, she tied a bonnet over her hair and headed for the door.

# FOURTEEN

GEOFFREY STOPPED AT the pump house to wash up before entering the house for the evening meal. He'd spent much of his day digging a ditch to channel water from the Solomon to a reservoir between two feeding pastures. His muscles were sore and tired, but he'd made sure the depth and width of the drainage would create a flow that soothed rather than frightened the sheep.

If the water ran too quickly, the nervous sheep would refuse to come near and drink; but if it stood motionless, it could stagnate and be dangerous for them to drink. He found the responsibility of caring for the sheep both invigorating and exhausting, but he eagerly met the needs of his flock. His favorite Bible verse ran through his mind: "The Lord is my shepherd; I shall not want . . ." Caring for the sheep reminded him of the care he received from his Shepherd. Yes indeed, the Lord had blessed him abundantly in this new land. He only wished Emmaline could embrace this life as enthusiastically as he had.

He pushed his shirt sleeves above his elbows and plunged his arms into the water, the shock of the icy liquid on his hot skin making him shudder. Within minutes, his tiredness lifted, and he felt refreshed despite the day's hard labor. He glanced toward the house, where a thin line of smoke rose from the stovepipe—silent proof that Emmaline had supper cooking.

Had she burned tonight's meal? In the two weeks that he and his men had eaten Emmaline's cooking, all of them had dropped a few pounds. He hated to be critical, but wasting food created concern beyond indigestion. They would need every precious morsel when winter arrived.

Tildy's assistance had brought an improvement, for which Geoffrey was grateful, and he harbored hope that Emmaline could indeed gain the required skills for surviving as a rancher's wife. However, he would need to speak to her about cooking something besides roasts for the evening meal. The meat in the cellar would need to carry them until the next butchering, which was still months away. He rolled his sleeves back into place, reminding himself to suggest she ask Tildy to share more recipes with her.

He turned toward the house and then stopped, his thoughts freezing his feet. When had his thoughts of Emmaline become limited to recipes? What had happened to the other images that once filled his mind—stepping behind her at the stove and kissing her neck, holding her hand at the table while he prayed, chatting together on the porch while they watched the blazing sunset before retiring to bed?

With a groan, he ran his hand through his still-damp hair. *Lord, this is not what I wanted when I brought Emmaline here! But how can I have anything more while she is not my wedded bride?* No, as difficult as it was, he must maintain his role as employer to employee. He must continue to advise and direct her, keeping his emotions firmly in check. Then, when she had adequately acquired the necessary skills, his attention could turn to wooing her. But everything in due time.

He drew in a deep breath of hot air and strode purposefully

to the kitchen door. It stood open, but as had become his custom, he rapped his knuckles on the doorjamb to alert Emmaline of his presence. "Emmaline?"

She bustled through the sitting room doorway. Her hands overflowed with a huge cluster of wild flowers trailing dirty stems. "Oh! Is it dinnertime already? I'll have it on the table shortly." She scurried to the sink and placed the flowers in the basin. Giving the pump handle a vigorous downward yank, she said, "I want to get these flowers into water before they wilt. It is so hot in the sun! I nearly wilted myself."

He stepped next to the sink, scowling down at the assortment of flowers. "Where did you find these?"

"All over the place. I had no idea so many different flowers grew here! Look." She lifted one thick stem holding a dome of small bluish-purple flowers. "Does this not resemble a lilac's bloom? It is quite fragrant, too." She shoved the flower beneath Geoffrey's nose.

He sneezed and pushed it aside.

She giggled. "I'm sorry." She went back to washing stems.

"Emmaline, I asked where you found these flowers. I do not recall them growing on the property."

"Oh, they don't." She set aside a few long stems bearing tiny white flowers. "I had to climb over a fence and walk the prairie to find them. But aren't they lovely?"

She had climbed a fence and trekked across the prairie? He caught her arm, stilling her busy hands. "Emmaline, I thought I told you not to leave the area around the ranch house."

She looked up at him. "But I didn't run off. I only wished to make our dinner table more festive."

"Our dinner table will be festive enough when you learn to cook meals that please the palate!"

Jerking her arm loose from his grasp, she took several backward steps. Tears filled her eyes, but she blinked rapidly and the moisture disappeared. She opened her mouth, but then without speaking a word, she spun and stormed out of the room. The front door slammed, and he pounded after her. He yanked the door open, expecting to see her fleeing across the yard. But instead she stood on the edge of the porch. She pressed her hand to one stacked stone pillar, her gaze aimed across the rolling prairie.

The breeze ruffled the hem of her black dress. If she yearned for something festive, she could dress in something other than the black frock she insisted on wearing every day. "Emmaline?"

Her fingers contracted against the pale stone of pillar.

"I'm sorry I got upset with you. But the flowers . . ." He gritted his teeth. "Collecting them was a foolhardy activity. I need you to promise me you will stay near the ranch for your own safety."

Emmaline stood still for long moments, staring straight ahead. Geoffrey was on the verge of marching forward and turning her to face him when finally she shifted. But she only turned partway, giving him a view of her profile. Her chin quivered when she spoke. "I shall put your supper on the table." She pushed past him and entered the house.

Clamping his jaw, Geoffrey strode to the same pillar where Emmaline had stood. The worry her admission about wandering the prairie had created rose again, making his pulse pound in his temple. He had worry enough in caring for the sheep; Emmaline would be expected to make better choices.

When Geoffrey went back inside, the kitchen was empty, the table neatly set for three. Three, not four. A beautifully baked pie waited in the center of the table. A sniff told him the pie was sweet potato with lots of cinnamon.

Pounding footsteps warned him of the approach of the hands before Chris and Jim stepped through the open kitchen door.

Chris crossed directly to the table, leaned over the pie, and inhaled deeply.

"Mmmmm. Looks like Tildy brought us a treat."

Geoffrey nodded but didn't reply.

Jim held out a bedraggled mess of wilting flowers. "These were scattered all over the ground outside the door."

Geoffrey heaved a sigh. "Would you put them in a jar of water, please, and place them on the table? I must fetch Emmaline, and then we shall eat."

He crossed through the sitting room and spare bedroom into Emmaline's parlor. He looked at the wide, smoothly sanded plank floor, imagining the wedding gift he had purchased spread out across the white wood. Right now, the rug of cabbage roses, which he had ordered from the East, stretched across the rafters in his half of the bunkhouse, still wrapped in its paper tube. He had chosen it because it reminded him of the rose garden in the narrow side yard of Emmaline's home in England. Would he ever get a chance to give it to her?

A slight shuffling sound came from the bedroom. He moved to the closed door and tapped lightly. "Emmaline, do you intend to eat?" He waited, his ear pressed to the wooden door.

Finally her voice came, pinched and somber. "I am not hungry. Go ahead and eat. I shall clean up after you have returned to the bunkhouse."

Geoffrey's chest constricted as he battled frustration. Why must she be so childish? "Would you not care to sit on the porch and visit this evening?"

"I know what chores await me tomorrow, and Tildy has already offered adequate instruction. You needn't worry about my incompetence for the tasks."

"Emmaline, I—"

"Go and eat, Geoffrey, before the dinner grows cold."

Geoffrey stomped back to the kitchen. Chris and Jim sat at the table, silent but watchful. "Go ahead and eat," he barked. Then he stormed out the back door.

He intended to go to his room at the bunkhouse, but at the last minute he swerved and headed, instead, behind the barn. His feet stirred dust and flattened the dry grass. He should have Jim trim the weeds close to the house lest a snake creep up unnoticed. Snakes were one of the many dangers that existed on the prairie. Why could Emmaline not see the peril she put herself in when she wandered away from the land near the house?

Rounding the barn, where the sheep were settled down for the evening, he approached the tiny plot that served as the ranch's cemetery. Only two wooden crosses stood in the square of earth— one large and one small. He passed the small one, the marker for a stray pup Jim had taken in during their second year on the ranch. The boy had insisted on a decent burial when the dog had chased a wagon and gotten caught beneath the wheels. Geoffrey had thought it foolish to give a dog a burial, but now he was glad there was some company for Ben on this lonely spot of ground.

He stood before the larger cross and read the carved name: BEN MACKEY. Although more than a year had passed since Ben's death, pain still stabbed Geoffrey's heart. Ben had been a good man—a good friend. The day he died was permanently etched in Geoffrey's memory: Ben heading out to the north range, his back straight in the saddle. Lunchtime coming and going with no sign of Ben. Geoffrey saddling a horse to go look for him. Finding Ben's horse first, then the man himself lying in the midst of the confused sheep, unconscious.

Not until he'd brought Ben back to the ranch had he seen the puncture marks on his leg. He'd died without ever regaining consciousness. After Ben's death, people from town had told Geoffrey story after story of other ways the prairie had claimed lives—falls into ravines, flash floods, attacks from rabid animals, heatstroke, broken bones.

Suddenly, in place of Ben's cross, Geoffrey envisioned Emmaline lying crumpled on the ground, puncture marks on her leg. He shook his head to send the image away. He could not bear it if something happened to Emmaline. Somehow he must make her understand the hazards of wandering across the plains.

Then her father's voice filled his memory: "She is a fragile girl, Geoffrey. We must use discernment in sharing information with her or she shall wither in fear."

Geoffrey had allowed Jonathan Bradford to determine what Emmaline should be told and what should be kept from her when he sent letters outlining his experiences in Kansas. What advice might Jonathan give now to keep his daughter from harm? The truth might frighten her, but it could also save her life.

Geoffrey turned from the grave and headed to his room in the bunkhouse. Somehow she must be made to understand. . . .

# FIFTEEN

⌒

From the bedroom window, Emmaline watched Geoffrey stomp across the backyard. She cringed with every dust puff that rose from the firm tromp of his foot against the ground. When he moved out of sight, she turned from the window and sat on the edge of the bed. She tried to hang on to her anger, but it melted away, leaving behind a deep hurt.

Collecting that bouquet of flowers had given her more joy than anything else since she'd arrived in this country. For the first time, she had felt truly at one with the land. Holding those graceful stems had filled her mind with pleasant remembrances. She had returned to the house with a light heart and eager step. But Geoffrey had taken one look at the flowers and seen nothing but an act of disobedience. Had his time in Kansas wiped away all vestiges of their shared moments in England?

She could not please Geoffrey any more than she had been able to please her father. But at least her father had never made any pretense of loving her. He had little use for a daughter except to groom her into a desirable wife for some young man who would offer the family an improved situation.

The union between herself and Geoffrey benefited her

father—he received a dependable source of wool to keep his mill running. His son was his business partner, and his daughter was his pawn. Even as a child Emmaline had recognized her inferiority in her father's eyes. Her attempts to earn his approval had ended when she left her girlhood behind, but the silent compliance that had carried her through childhood remained a part of her character until this last act of obedience: coming to Geoffrey.

Yes, she had come. Across an ocean and over mountains, rivers, and plains—all the way to Kansas. A good portion of the journey she traveled alone after Uncle Hedrick had died. And she could make the journey alone again. She *would* do it again.

If Geoffrey held no memories of their time in England, then she wanted nothing from him now. She would leave. And this time, she would make it all the way back to England. Father would be shocked to see her on the doorstep, and she smiled a little, imagining it. It would be worth the tirade he would deliver to see the look on his face when he realized that she—a mere woman—had managed to devise and survive such a lengthy trip.

She pushed off the bed and headed to the kitchen to clean up whatever Jim and Chris had left behind after the evening meal. As she crossed through the sitting room, she heard someone whistling.

Pausing, she tilted her head. She had never heard Geoffrey whistle, so it must be one of the Cotler brothers. She entered the room and found Jim at the wash basin.

She hurried to his side. "Oh, Jim, I should be the one washing the dishes."

Jim gave her a lopsided grin. "I don't mind. It doesn't take long. Especially when only two of us ate. Weren't you hungry?"

Smells from supper lingered in the room, and Emmaline's stomach clenched with hunger, but she said, "Not particularly. You have your own chores. I shall do mine."

Jim shrugged and moved away from the sink. He dried his hands slowly, watching her push her sleeves to her elbows and plunge her hands into the water. He hung the length of toweling on its hook but then loitered beside the counter.

Emmaline glanced at him. "Do you not have evening chores?"

"None that can't keep." He crossed his arms and leaned his hip against the counter, settling in. "Is Miss Tildy coming again tomorrow?"

Emmaline couldn't define why she didn't send him away. She only knew having someone to talk to was preferable to being alone. Geoffrey would be upset, but Jim was only a harmless boy. "She and I have plans to bake bread." It occurred to Emmaline that when she left, Tildy would arrive to bake bread and find the house empty.

Jim nodded eagerly. "Oh, good. The pie she baked was very good." He patted his stomach.

Pride filled Emmaline as she told him, "I baked the pie."

Jim jolted straight up, his eyes wide. "You did? Will you bake another one tomorrow?"

His boyish excitement made Emmaline giggle. "Did you finish this one so soon?"

"Chris and I had two pieces each." Jim puffed out his cheeks and then laughed. "I like pie. My mum baked apple pie—my very favorite. Miss Tildy brings us sweets—egg pie, and shoofly pie, and sweet potato pie like you baked. One time Reverend Stanford's wife gave us a peach pie, but it was too mushy." The boy made a sour face. "Your sweet potato pie was just as good as Miss Tildy's. I would have eaten more if Chris had let me."

"You may have another piece if you like," Emmaline said.

"Will you have one, too?"

She looked into his hopeful face. Her stomach growled,

reminding her of her hunger. Slowly she removed her hands from the dishwater. "I would like to taste it, I suppose."

Jim charged to the cabinet and removed two saucers. Emmaline fetched forks, and she put one piece of pie on each plate. They sat across from each other, and Jim dove into his piece with an enthusiastic stab of his fork. Emmaline lifted a smaller bite, but at the first explosion of flavor on her tongue, she raised her eyebrows in pleased surprise.

Jim grinned. "Good, huh?"

"It is." Emmaline wiped crumbs from her mouth with her thumb. "I hope it isn't arrogant to praise my own cooking."

"Not when it's the truth." Jim shoved another sizable bite into his mouth and then spoke around it. "When Geoffrey or Chris cooked, they never made sweet stuff." He swallowed. "Will you learn to make cakes, too? I like spice cake with whipped cream on top. My mum used to bake that."

Emmaline paused in eating. "Is your mother gone?"

Jim nodded, carrying the last bite to his mouth. "Mum and Dad died of measles when I was six. But Chris took good care of me, and then Mr. Garrett brought us here to America. We have a grand life here."

His blithe recital made Emmaline's chest constrict. How much heartache must lurk beneath the simple words? "Do you not miss England at all?"

"Why should I?" The boy pushed his empty plate aside. "It's just Chris and me, nobody there for us anymore. We have a better job here in Chetwynd Valley than anything Chris could have found in England. Except . . ."

Emmaline tipped her head. "Except?"

"Except since we left England, I haven't gone to school. I wish I could go to the schoolhouse in Stetler. Mr. Garrett let me go part of the year when we first arrived, but since Ben—" He stopped, his startled expression telling Emmaline he had nearly said something he shouldn't.

"Who is Ben?"

"Nobody." Jim stood up. "I mean, just somebody who isn't here anymore." He backed toward the door. "I better see to my chores now, Miss Emmaline. Thank you for the pie." He dashed out.

Emmaline stared after him, wondering at his strange behavior. Why couldn't the boy speak of this mysterious Ben? What had the man done?

She carried the two plates and forks to the sink and quickly finished the dishes. After returning the pans, plates, and utensils to their places in the cabinets, she went to the bedroom. The carpet bag waited in the closet, still holding her English rock and some of her clothes. As soon as night fell, she would set out.

At that moment, the distant howl of a coyote carried through the window. She shivered at the mournful sound. Did she dare set out at night, when animals prowled? She pushed that fear aside. She must reach Moreland, and if she left during the day, Geoffrey would notice. She must leave at night.

"I can do this," she told herself firmly. "I *can*." She sat down on the edge of the bed to wait for darkness to fall.

———

A banging roused Geoffrey from a sound sleep. He sat up in a rush, his feet flying from the mattress.

"Mr. Garrett?" Chris called through the door.

Geoffrey rubbed his eyes. "What is it?"

The door cracked open. A slice of sunlight spilled across the floor. "I wanted to check on you."

"What time is it?"

"Almost seven."

Seven? Geoffrey bolted from the bed and reached for his pants. He skimmed them over his long johns, berating himself for sleeping so long. He had lain awake last night, praying for wisdom in dealing with Emmaline, but he hadn't realized how tired he was. Never had he slept so long past sunrise. "Have you and Jim had breakfast?"

"We ate some canned beans and the last of the pie."

Geoffrey paused in tucking in his shirt. "Canned beans and pie? Is that what Emmaline put on the table?"

Chris pinched at the whiskers on the side of his face. "Miss Emmaline wasn't around, either."

A sick feeling rose in Geoffrey's middle. He shoved his feet into his boots, dancing a bit as he tried to hurry. "Get the sheep out to pasture," he ordered as he charged past Chris. "I'll be working on the ditch again today."

"Yes, sir."

Chris trotted in one direction and Geoffrey headed toward the house. She wouldn't leave. Not again. Not at night. He didn't knock on the door but charged directly through the house to the bedroom. Maybe she, too, had overslept after a restless night. But the bedroom door stood open, the bed neatly made. And empty. With fear making his mouth dry, he crossed to the closet and looked inside. The carpet bag was missing.

Geoffrey spun on his heel and thudded through the house. Just as he reached the kitchen, Ronald Senger's wagon rolled into the yard. Tildy climbed down, and Geoffrey hurried to meet her.

"She's gone. Took off during the night," he grated out in lieu of a greeting.

Tildy grasped his arm.

"I must go find her," he said.

Ronald called, "I can look, too."

"Thank you." Geoffrey pointed. "You go west; I'll go east."

Tildy's fingers tightened on his arm. "I'll be a-prayin' you find her safe an' sound."

Geoffrey gave Tildy's hand a pat, then headed for the horse barn. He hitched the team to the wagon by rote, his mind filled with unpleasant pictures. Determinedly, he set the ugly images aside. He would find her before anything bad happened.

He raced the team at an unsafe pace down the road. Dust billowed from the horses' hooves and the wagon's wheels, obscuring his vision. Clenching his teeth, he slowed the team. His eyes scanned the horizon in both directions. Surely she would have kept to the road. At night, with only the moonlight to guide her, she wouldn't have dared leave the relative safety of the road.

The early-morning sun, huge in the eastern sky, burned his eyes, but he blinked as little as possible, fearful he might miss seeing her. *Let me find her. Please let me find her.* Within a mile of Stetler, his eyes spotted an odd black lump at the side of the road. He leaned forward, straining to see more clearly.

His heart launched into his throat when he realized the lump was Emmaline in her black dress.

"Yah!" He whipped the reins, and the horses lurched into a full run. In seconds the wagon reached her, and he jerked back on the reins so abruptly the horses nearly sat down. He leaped from the wagon and raced to her. Falling to his knees, he cupped her face in his hands. "Emmaline?"

She roused, twisting her face into a grimace. Opening her eyes, she looked around blearily. Then her gaze met his, and she bolted away from his touch, scooting backward on her bottom. When she was out of his reach, she struggled to her feet. Without a word, she grabbed the handles of the carpet bag and staggered off.

For a moment Geoffrey sat on his heels, disbelief sealing him in place. Then he jumped to his feet and trotted up alongside her. "What do you think you're doing?"

With a determined set to her jaw, she kept walking, her gaze straight ahead. "Now that I'm rested, I am going on to Moreland."

"And what are you going to do in Moreland?"

"I am going to purchase a train ticket and return to England."

Geoffrey grabbed her arm, bringing her to a stop. "You will do nothing of the kind!"

"Geoffrey, release my arm."

The defiance in her eyes raised Geoffrey's anger another notch. "I will not! You will turn around, get into the wagon, and return to the ranch."

She glared up at him for several seconds, her lips pursed tightly. Dropping the bag, she pried his fingers from her arm, then scooped up the bag and walked on as if he hadn't spoken.

Geoffrey clutched his hair. He lowered his head for a moment, fighting for control. After several calming breaths, he stomped after her once more, but this time he stepped directly into her pathway.

She tried to step around him. He blocked her. She tried to go the opposite way. He blocked her again. She huffed, "Geoffrey! Get out of my way!"

But he set his feet wide and balled his hands on his hips. "Emmaline, if you do not get into the wagon I shall put you there myself."

Her dark eyes narrowed. "Do not threaten me, Geoffrey."

"It is not a threat. Will you turn around on your own?"

"No!"

"Very well." He bent forward, planting his shoulder in her

middle and grasping the backs of her knees. When he stood, she fell across his shoulder like a sack of feed.

She dropped the carpet bag and began pounding on his back as he carried her across the ground. "Unhand me at once!"

"If you behave like a spoiled child, you can expect to be treated like one." He plunked her none too gently onto the wagon seat and then swung up beside her. Taking up the reins, he directed the horses up even with the discarded carpet bag. "Whoa." Pointing a finger under her nose, he ordered, "Stay put."

He hopped over the side of the wagon and snatched up the bag. The weight nearly dislocated his shoulder. "What do you have in here?"

From atop the seat, she folded her arms and looked across the prairie, her lips clamped in a sullen line.

He tossed the bag into the back of the wagon and climbed back aboard. He said nothing to her as he turned the team and aimed the wagon toward the ranch. She sat in silence beneath the morning sun, but a constant stream of tears ran down her pale cheeks and fell onto her lap, splotching the fabric of her black dress.

Although he was angrier than he could ever remember being, he was still moved by her tears. *Can I make her stay when she is so miserable?* He set his jaw. *I waited so long for her. I cannot let her go.*

# SIXTEEN

WHAT WAS YOU thinkin', girl, takin' off like that? You give us quite a scare." Tildy wanted to take hold of Emmaline and shake her, but the tears that slid down Emmaline's cheeks softened her anger. Both women watched Geoffrey drive down the lane toward the barn. He'd unceremoniously brought Emmaline home, assisted her from the wagon, and handed her over to Tildy.

"You gots to think, chil'," Tildy told the girl.

"I did think, Tildy!" She covered her face with her hands. "I thought very carefully. Oh, why did I fall asleep? If I'd only kept going, I would be to Moreland by now."

Tildy grabbed Emmaline's wrists and pulled her hands down. She wanted to coddle her, but Kansas was a hard land, and if Emmaline didn't learn to let the good Lord give her strength, she'd be conquered by the will of the prairie. "Come on ovah here." She led Emmaline to the porch and sat next to her on a bench beneath the window. "You gots to stop this runnin' away from your problems. Runnin' don't fix nothin'."

Emmaline's chin jutted. "Well, staying will not fix anything, either."

"So what's broke? You tell me an' let's see if we can find a way to fix it."

The girl stared at Tildy. "There is no fix for this situation! Geoffrey claims to love me, yet all he does is tell me what to do, or that I am doing something wrong. He is not the same man I knew in England. That man talked to me tenderly. He picked me daisies. This Geoffrey reprimands me for gathering flowers." She folded her arms over her chest. "I want to go back to England."

Tildy sighed. "I knows you do. But we don't always git what we want. Sometimes we gots to be content wit' what the Good Lawd gives us."

Emmaline gave her a surprised look.

"You think you's the only one's evuh had disappointments? Life's full o' disappointments and unhappiness, chil'. But you gotta look for the good in it."

"Good? In unhappiness?"

"Why, yes. The Lawd don't bring nothin' into our lives that He can't use for good. Even unhappiness. Why, if we nevah had a sad moment, we wouldn't get to 'preciate the good times."

"But—"

"Growin's a good thang, girl." Tildy threw her arms wide. "Why, if a body nevuh overcomes a bad time, we don't gets to show how God gives us strength."

Emmaline turned away. "God has nothing to do with my relationship with Geoffrey."

Tildy nodded at that. "An' that's jus' the trouble. You need God smack-dab in the middle o' your relationship with Geoffrey." She cupped Emmaline's chin and looked into her eyes. "Honey, Geoffrey's jus' a stubborn man who needs to do some growin' hisself. But if you take off, you'll nevuh know how God can grow you's together."

"I don't know, Miss Tildy."

"Well, then, you close your eyes an' let's do some talkin' to God." She clasped Emmaline's hand, bowed her head, and scrunched her eyes tight. "Lawd, I knows you gots somethin' special in mind for Emmalion an' Geoffrey. Right now things ain't goin' as they want, but I trust You'll turn it aroun' in time. Give us patience while we waits, an' give us strength to do the right thangs while we waits. We love You, Lawd. Amen." Giving Emmaline's hand a squeeze, she opened her eyes and stood up. "Now, let's go bake that bread. Nothin' like the smell of fresh bread bakin' to put a man in a good mood."

———

After putting away the team and wagon, Geoffrey saddled another horse and rode to the river. Stripping down to his cotton underdrawers, he made a shallow dive and skimmed beneath the surface of the water. The cold, clear water rushing across his body cooled his temperature . . . and his temper. He rolled to his back and floated, staring up at the cloudless sky.

The sky in England had been blue-gray in the spring, the color of the bottom of an iron bucket. The vibrant blue of the Kansas sky never ceased to amaze him. He wished Kansas had a few of England's clouds, however; they needed rain. His pastures were dry, and if the grasses didn't replenish, he would have to buy feed for the sheep. Maybe he should let the section Ronald rented go to hay and harvest it. The sheep had to eat.

His stomach growled, reminding him he hadn't eaten breakfast. Noon would come soon, but despite his hunger, he wasn't sure he would go to the house for lunch. He wasn't ready to face Emmaline. Her leave-taking carried the sting of betrayal. He had never expected, when he brought Emmaline here, that she would abandon him. Like his mother had. And his father, too, for all practical purposes.

Geoffrey flipped to his stomach and swam upstream several yards, pumping his arms and kicking as hard as he could, but the frenetic burst of energy didn't expend the hurt in his heart. He could swim to the ocean and never escape the feelings of worthlessness that plagued him. Would anyone ever choose to remain permanently in his life?

Water spewed in all directions as he shook himself off on the riverbank. On bare feet, he walked to his clothes. He scanned the land around him. At least he would always have the ranch and his sheep. If everyone left him, this land would remain. He was not unworthy on this piece of land. He was successful. Respected. Several mills—including the one owned by Jonathan Bradford—depended on him. He would not disappoint them.

A thought struck him as he reached to pick up his shirt. Jonathan Bradford depended on fleece from Geoffrey's sheep. The man would suffer if Geoffrey suddenly decided to ship his wool to another mill. If Jonathan Bradford suffered, his family would suffer. Emmaline would never intentionally cause her mother distress. If he were to give Emmaline an ultimatum, perhaps she would be more willing to remain on the ranch where she was safe.

It may not be ethical, he decided as he swung onto his horse's back to ride to the site of his half-completed ditch, but it would be effective. And right now effective would be enough to keep her from harm.

Geoffrey carried the carpet bag into the house when he came in for supper. He had peeked in it, and he marveled that she had made it so far with that big rock in the bottom of the bag. It was a foolish decision to carry a rock for protection, but he was grateful she had done it. No doubt it had slowed her enough for him to catch up to her.

When he stepped through the door, the aroma of fresh-baked bread nearly turned his stomach inside out with desire. Saliva pooled in his mouth, and he swallowed twice. The loaves—three of them, nicely browned—sat in a straight row across the stovetop. A fourth one, sliced, waited in the center of the table, which was set with four place settings. He tossed the bag into the corner and crossed to the table. Picking up the crusty heel, he bit into it with fervor. He nearly groaned with pleasure.

A pot bubbled on the stove, the lid gently bouncing. Still chewing, he lifted the lid and sniffed. The mingled odors of cabbage, onion, carrots, and tomatoes greeted his nose. He took another long draw and could almost taste the soup on the back of his tongue. As he straightened, Emmaline entered the kitchen from the outside door. She used her apron as a pouch to carry something lumpy. When she saw him her brown eyes widened and she jerked the fabric higher, as if hiding its contents.

After a moment's pause, she shifted her gaze away from him and advanced into the room. She lifted a wedge of cheese and lump of butter from her apron and placed them on saucers that waited on the counter. She said nothing.

Geoffrey cleared his throat. "Is supper ready?"

She carried the plates of cheese and butter to the table. As soon as she set them down, she nodded.

"Then I shall ring the dinner bell." Geoffrey's zealous tug of the bell brought Chris and Jim running.

Despite Geoffrey's hunger, he had difficulty swallowing the well-seasoned soup and fresh bread. Emmaline ate silently, her eyes downcast. Chris, apparently sensing the animosity between Geoffrey and Emmaline, ate quickly and excused himself on the pretext of fixing some loose shingles on the sheep barn roof. Even Jim abandoned his attempts at chatter when no one responded.

"You want help with the dishes?" Jim asked Emmaline after he'd slurped the last of his soup.

"No," Geoffrey and Emmaline said at the same time. They looked at each other, and Geoffrey saw a flash of irritation in her eyes. He added, "Thank you, Jim, but I shall assist Emmaline this evening."

The boy shrugged, carried his dishes to the sink, and then slipped out the back door.

Emmaline lifted her chin. "I do not require assistance with the dishes."

"I am aware you are capable of handling the chore alone," Geoffrey said, "but we can talk while we put the kitchen in order."

Emmaline cast a furtive glance in his direction, but she didn't argue. He waited until they had cleared the table and she had filled the sink with soapy water before speaking again.

"Emmaline, we must talk about last night."

Her hands paused momentarily in the water, and then she began scrubbing with earnest.

"Leaving in the middle of the night was a very foolish thing to do. We have wild animals—coyotes, bobcats, even a rare panther or bear. You could have encountered any of them, and you would have been powerless to protect yourself . . . even with that big rock."

Her chin jerked in his direction, but she quickly focused on the dishes again.

"Animals aren't the only danger. What if you had wandered off the road in the dark? You could have stepped in a hole and broken your leg, or maybe even fallen into a ravine."

She set a dripping bowl on the counter, her hand trembling as she released it.

"When I asked you not to leave the ranch, it was for your own protection. Yet you chose to ignore my warnings. Your imprudent decision put you in peril, so now I must decide how to keep you from harm."

Her shoulders rose as she drew in a deep breath. "I—"

"I am not finished." Geoffrey took hold of her shoulders and turned her to face him. One of her hands still rested in the dishwater and the other curled around the lip of the sink. He peered directly into her eyes. "It pains me to do this, but you've left me no choice. If you do not remain on the ranch, I will contact your father and tell him my wool is no longer available to his mill."

Emmaline's eyes grew round. Color drained from her face. "You would blackmail me?"

"It is not blackmail. It is a consequence." He let his hands slip from her shoulders, and she spun to face the sink. "You must decide whether or not you will honor your commitment to remain here until winter's end. If you choose not to honor it, then *all* agreements between our families will end."

Emmaline's chin quivered, but she remained silent.

Geoffrey sighed. "I didn't want to resort to this, Emmaline. You forced my hand." He waited, but she still did not respond. He pushed away from the counter. "Will you attempt to leave the ranch again?"

Very slowly she shook her head left then right. Her eyes shot fiery darts of fury.

"Good. Would you like me to carry your bag to the sleeping room?"

Thrusting both hands into the water, she said stiffly, "I can do it myself."

"Very well." He started to leave the kitchen, but before stepping out the door, he turned back. "Did you truly expect to be able to protect yourself with the rock in the bag?"

She didn't answer for so long that he thought she had ignored his question. But at last she replied, "It is an English rock."

An English rock? "You brought it from England?"

"Yes." She smacked a bowl onto the counter. "Mother sent it with me to serve as a reminder of my homeland."

"But why carry it with you?"

She dipped her chin toward her shoulder. "I did not believe it should remain here in Kansas."

She so hated this land—*his* land—that she would not even leave a rock from England behind?

"But do not worry, Geoffrey," Emmaline continued, her voice low and even. "My rock and I will not leave your property. Your threat will keep me here." She lifted another bowl from the water and placed it with the others. Turning her head to meet his gaze, she finished in a steely tone, "At least until winter's end."

———

Emmaline stood at the window of her sleeping room. She had extinguished the lantern, cloaking the room in darkness. She stared at the bunkhouse windows, her lower lip caught between her teeth. When would the men finally go to bed?

The nighttime stars were bright in the black sky, and the moon cast a whitish path across the ground. As soon as the glow in the bunkhouse windows was gone, she would perform her task. She knew exactly where she wanted to hide the dowry money sent by her father to give to Geoffrey. As a child, playing hide-and-seek with her brother, Edward had always managed to elude her. Once when she had complained loudly about the length of time she'd spent searching, he had laughed at her. "I was under your bed the entire time," he'd said. "You never once searched your own room, because you did not expect to find me in such an obvious place." His chuckle had infuriated her. "To be successful at hide-and-seek, Emmaline, you must think like the seeker and do the opposite of the expected."

Remembering her brother's statement, Emmaline had heeded his advice. If Geoffrey were to look for the money, he would expect her to hide it in her sleeping room or the parlor or kitchen—places of familiarity for her. Never would he suspect she would choose one of *his* areas of familiarity.

So as soon as the men were asleep, she would sneak to the barn and hide the tin box of money. Then, when spring came, if Geoffrey refused to honor his promise to send her back to England, she would have her own money to use.

The window on Geoffrey's side of the bunkhouse finally went dark. She blew out a breath of relief. Tucking the tin box against her ribs, she headed on tiptoe to the front door and crept out beneath the moonlight.

# SEVENTEEN

~

By August, Emmaline had fallen into a housekeeping routine that offered a predictable structure but little joy. She adopted Tildy's pattern of washing on Monday, ironing on Tuesday, mending on Wednesday, baking on Thursday, and housecleaning on Friday. On Saturday she prepared additional food for Sunday's use, ensuring that Sunday would remain a day of rest.

On Sunday afternoons she wrote long, newsy letters to her mother. At times Emmaline saw herself as noble, sparing Mother the truth of her aching loneliness and cheerless life; other times she berated herself for her dishonesty. A part of her longed to pour her heartache onto the page, yet given the distance between England and Kansas—and Mother's inability to fix any of the problems—she couldn't bear to cause Mother anxiety. So she wrote of the land, the sheep, the many duties . . . but nothing of her heart.

Every day included garden chores—watering, weeding, picking. Her crooked rows of beans, tomatoes, carrots, peas, corn, turnips, and beets grew fruitful in spite of the withering sun and dry, blowing wind.

She chose to work in the garden first thing in the morning, before the sun got too high. Even in the early-morning hours, sweat would dampen her hair and make her black dress stick to her chest. She had resorted to wearing her dress over a simple, Tildy-made cotton shift and pantaloons. Her mother would be mortified to know Emmaline had discarded her corset and layers of petticoats, but her mother had never lived on the prairie.

Afternoons were hot enough to fry an egg on the tin roof of the springhouse—as Jim had proven. He thought it a clever trick, but Emmaline had been appalled. Ever since she had watched the egg bubble and pop on the roof, the heat had seemed even less bearable.

On this morning, Emmaline collected new potatoes to boil with green beans and ham for lunch. She pushed her hand through the soft mound of dirt beneath a potato plant and blindly sought potatoes. Tildy had taught her she shouldn't uproot the plant, but merely borrow a few small potatoes from each root. Then other potatoes were left to grow. Those would carry them through the winter months.

Emmaline pulled two or three egg-sized potatoes from beneath each plant, placing them in her basket on top of the tumble of fresh green beans. She had a difficult time keeping up with the green beans—she picked the plants clean each day, but always the next morning, more would be ready to pick. She disliked the sticky feel of the leaves against her hands.

She plopped the last potato in the basket, and her gaze fell on her hand. Holding it up, she examined it front and back. Her nails were chipped and rimmed with dirt, and her skin was brown from its exposure to the sun. She barely recognized the hand as her own. Touching her cheek, she wondered if her face was equally as tanned.

Pushing to her feet, she lifted the basket and scuffed her way to the house. She blamed her sluggish movements on the heat, but she realized there was a deeper reason. Everywhere she looked, all that greeted her eyes was brown grass, brown dirt, brown rock. The sky was as blue as a bluejay's wing, but she couldn't pluck a piece of the sky and carry it with her. Her soul longed for color.

She entered the kitchen and dumped the vegetables into the sink. She splashed water over the beans and potatoes and began to scrub them clean of dirt. As she worked, in her mind's eye, the potatoes became colorful rocks from the garden at home and the beans flower stems heavy with fragrant blooms.

Sitting at the table, she began snapping the beans, discarding the tops and throwing the edible portion into a large pot that already held the clean potatoes. She watched the growing mound in the pot, thinking of the picked vegetables stored in the springhouse and cellar. Tildy had promised to teach her to preserve the vegetables so they would keep through the winter months, but first Geoffrey would have to purchase jars for her. When he came in for lunch, perhaps she would ask if she might accompany him to town when he made the purchase.

She thought back to the day he had retrieved her from the train. He had promised she could order items from a catalog or go into Moreland to buy some bric-a-brac to make the house more cheerful. But that promise remained unfulfilled. She'd spent every day on this dry, brown ranch.

She snapped the last bean, carried the heavy pot to the stove, and ladled water over the vegetables. Automatically, she added salt, pepper, dried onion, and a ham hock and gave the mixture a quick stir with a wooden spoon. With a satisfied nod, she placed the lid over the pot and looked around the kitchen. Amazingly, nothing else required her attention.

As she stepped to the doorway to catch a bit of the breeze, the sound of moving water captured her attention. The gentle song of the Solomon River. How wonderful it would feel to immerse herself in the cool water. She didn't have time for a swim, but perhaps she could soak her feet. Quickly, before some chore tugged her thoughts elsewhere, she skipped out the front door and headed for the river.

———

Jim rounded the corner of the main house and swept his gaze past the garden plot that filled the side yard. Each day, Emmaline labored under the morning sun, clearing the weeds from the squiggly rows of vegetables. He'd grown fond of the sight of her neatly coiled hair shimmering nigh red in the sun. Red, he'd decided, was his favorite color.

He smacked his hat against his thigh in disappointment when he found the garden empty. But then he noticed a spot of black along the edge of the Solomon. She sat with her back to him. Her shoes lay side by side next to her hip.

Indecision held Jim in place for a moment. Mr. Garrett had instructed him to swing by the house and make sure Emmaline was all right. Ever since the night she had wandered off—sending Mr. Garrett down the road in a state of panic—the boss had kept a watchful eye on Emmaline. Jim thought it foolish, but he did what he was told without asking questions. He should go back to the north pasture and let Mr. Garrett know she was safe and soaking her toes in the water. The boss's instructions hadn't included talking to her—but neither had they prohibited it.

Adjusting his hat, he strode across the hard ground. Eagerness sped his footsteps, and when he arrived at her side, he was panting. As he stepped into her line of vision, he smiled broadly, tipping his hat as he'd seen a gentleman in Moreland do toward a lady. But then he realized her eyes were closed.

She slept with her head tipped to the side. Her hands rested, palms up, in her lap. Against the black fabric of her rumpled skirt, her skin seemed pale. Jim crouched beside her, and his boot heel came down on a small twig. At the snap, her head swiveled and her eyes flew wide. When their gazes collided, her face flooded with pink.

"Jim!" She yanked her feet from the water, turned her back on him, snatched up her shoes in one hand, and stumbled to her feet. "I . . . I'm so sorry." She looked around, as if expecting someone to jump out of the bushes at her. "Is it lunchtime? I had better go in."

Jim held up both hands, shaking his head. "It's not lunchtime yet. Another hour probably."

She sighed, her shoulders slumping. "Good. I have some time, then. . . ." Suddenly she jerked her shoulders back and lifted her chin high. "But I suppose you came to check on me."

Jim frowned. The harsh undertone in her voice didn't match her soft appearance.

"Well." She thumped her leg with her shoes. "You may return to Geoffrey and tell him I have obeyed his orders to remain close to the house."

Uncertain how to respond, Jim gave a hesitant nod.

Emmaline's expression turned penitent. "Please forgive me. I'm not angry with you, Jim."

"That's all right, Miss Emmaline." Jim wished he could hold her hand. She was the prettiest thing he'd ever seen—softer and sweeter than a baby lamb. "Sometimes I don't like being told what to do, either. But my brother says that as long as I'm drawing a wage, I do what the boss says." He added in a conspiratorial whisper, "Even checking up on you."

Her brow crinkled. "I suppose I should understand why he sends you. He does not trust me after I . . ." She looked across the river, the muscles in her jaw twitching. "I should not be speaking to you this way. It is far from proper."

Jim reached out and allowed his fingertips to brush her sleeve. "It's all right. I won't tell. Who else would you talk to?"

For long moments she stared into his face, her full lips pursed into a scowl of uncertainty. "You're right. There is no one else with whom I can share my thoughts now that Tildy doesn't come each day."

"You miss Tildy?"

"Oh yes. I enjoyed her company very much."

"Well . . ." Jim scratched his head. "This afternoon I'll be taking the wagon over to the Sengers' place to pick up the shears Ronald sharpened for us. Maybe Mr. Garrett would let you go along."

A smile curved her lips, making Jim's heart patter wildly. "Maybe he would," she said.

"Do you want me to ask him?"

"No, I shall ask. Then, if he grows surly, you will be spared."

Jim clasped his hands together. She wanted to protect his feelings. Did that mean she liked him? "All right. You can tell me after lunch."

"Very well. But I have dawdled beside the water long enough. I have a lunch to complete. Do you prefer corn bread or biscuits?"

Jim licked his lips. "Biscuits. With butter and honey."

She smiled. "Very well, then. Biscuits. I shall see you in less than an hour." She turned and ran to the house, her bare feet flashing beneath the hem of her full skirts.

---

Sitting atop the wagon seat next to Jim and heading down

the road, Emmaline couldn't deny a sense of freedom. Never had Geoffrey allowed her to leave the ranch with anyone but him. Maybe—she hardly dared allow the thought—this meant he was beginning to trust her. If he trusted her, perhaps he would allow her to venture out on her own one day. How she longed to roam unheeded, filling her arms with wild flowers and maybe even making a trip into town.

Jim jabbered away, his hands wrapped around the reins and his elbows resting on his bony knees. She listened with half an ear, nodding on occasion, but oblivious to the meaning behind his words. She had decided over her months of listening to his prattle that he enjoyed hearing himself talk and needed no encouragement to continue his endless flow of words.

From atop the wagon seat, she glimpsed a splash of yellow amidst the dry grasses. She pressed her hands against the seat to raise herself higher. Her eyes feasted upon a veritable sea of bright yellow flowers with round, brown centers, and she gasped in surprise.

Jim stopped mid-story. "What?"

Emmaline eagerly turned to him. "May we stop? I should like to pick some of those flowers."

Jim drew the team to a halt and squinted across the landscape. "You want those sunflowers?"

"Sunflowers . . ." Indeed, their color and their round faces were as bright and cheerful as the sun that blazed overhead.

"Why do you want them?" His tone reflected disgust. "They're weeds—a real nuisance. They'll take over a field if you let them."

Emmaline turned to him in shock. "But they are lovely! They are like a large yellow daisy. I must have a cluster." Before he could voice an argument, she leaped over the side of the wagon and dashed into the field.

"Miss Emmaline! Miss Emmaline, wait!"

Jim's panicked voice slowed her for a moment, but then she resumed her pell-mell race across the ground, her skirts held high so they wouldn't get caught up in the stiff grass. She reached the flowers, wrapped her hands around one tough stem, and tugged as hard as she could.

Jim pounded to her side. "Miss Emmaline, you should never run out into a field like that!"

The stem broke loose, and she stumbled backward slightly as the hard ground released the plant. "Oh?" She traced one brightly hued petal with her finger, smiling.

"No, ma'am. There are snakes in the pastures, and they don't like to be surprised. If you frighten a snake, it strikes."

The boy's obvious fear penetrated Emmaline's senses, and a bit of trepidation leaked in. "Have you been bitten?"

He gulped and turned away from her. "I know someone who got bit. He . . . died."

Emmaline had never seen the affable youth so jittery. She battled between worry about snakes and the desire to collect more sunflowers. The stem she had plucked held half a dozen blooms. If she cut them loose from the main stem, she would have a small but pleasant bouquet. She could be satisfied with that. "All right. If you're concerned, we can go back to the road."

"Stay behind me," Jim ordered, his voice cracking on the last word. He set off at a slow pace, setting his feet down with deliberation. Not until they reached the road did his shoulders relax. He helped her into the wagon, and for the next few minutes they rode in silence.

She clutched her hard-won flowers. How cheerful they looked! To draw Jim out of his silence, she said, "Thank you for letting me pick these. I plan to save the blooms and let them go to seed. Then I can plant them at the corner of the house, right in front of the porch. Having their happy faces on the property will be almost be like having a garden of daisies."

Jim sent her a low-browed look. "Mr. Garrett won't let you plant weeds in front of the porch."

"Oh yes, he will." Emmaline crushed the flowers to her chest. Geoffrey would not deny her the pleasure of adding color to the barren yard, would he? Her heart lifted as she looked again at the cluster. Their odor was not pleasant, but their cheery appearance more than compensated for the pungent smell.

She lifted her attention from the flowers and peered down the road, but her attention slid to something billowing on the eastern horizon. A cloud—churning and rolling, changing from black to the green of a frog's underbelly and then black again. Might rain fall today?

Pointing, she said, "Jim, look. I believe we may get rain."

Jim looked, but his face didn't light with pleasure. Instead, his brow furrowed. "That's a cloud, all right, but I've never seen one like it. I don't like the looks of it, either."

"Do . . . do you think it might be a terrible storm?" Emmaline had remembered the stories about tornadoes that ripped apart houses and carried people from one county to the next.

"It's not a tornado, but . . ." Jim shook his head. "I don't know for sure, but we better get to the Sengers'. Yah!" He cracked the reins twice, and the horses began to run.

# EIGHTEEN

❧

GEOFFREY CUT HIS horse gently to the left, smiling as the flock turned with him and headed for the watering ditch. Their curly coats were growing back following the early-summer shearing. He counted a number of bulging bellies, grateful for the promise of new life in another few weeks. Lambing season was the busiest time of the year and, to Geoffrey, the most rewarding. He gloried in each lamb bleating for its mother because it represented profit and the continued success of his ranch.

The sheep nosed the air, their baas becoming more insistent as they neared the water. After a morning of feeding, they were ready for a long drink and then a rest before a second feeding. Part of the Twenty-third Psalm played through Geoffrey's mind: "He maketh me to lie down in green pastures." He only wished the pastures were more green than brown. Yet the sheep were willing to eat.

As he watched the woolly backs that resembled a sea of cotton, he let his thoughts wander. Should he have allowed Emmaline to accompany Jim to the Sengers'? The boy was smitten with her—that was obvious. Surely Emmaline realized it. Would she use his affection to convince him to take her past the Sengers' and on to Moreland and the train station?

He pushed the thought aside. Jim would never go against him that way. Besides, Emmaline knew he would follow through on his threat to sell the wool elsewhere.

On the opposite side of the flock, Chris turned backward in his saddle. "Boss?" He kept his voice low in deference to the sheep's penchant for being easily startled. "What is that?"

Geoffrey shifted, his saddle creaking with the movement. A thick cloud of . . . something . . . advanced upon them. As he stared, an unfamiliar sound carried over the whistling wind—a hum that reminded him of the song of cicadas yet was lower-pitched. He squinted, trying to make sense of the undulating mass, and something hit him. Hard. Before he could register what it was, the cloud descended, filling the air with flapping, buzzing, whirring insects.

The sheep disappeared from view under the deluge, but their frightened bawls filled the air, adding to the confusion. Geoffrey's horse snorted and bucked, and he nearly lost his position. Ducking low over the beast's neck, he urged the horse to spin and gallop away from the flock. The insects—grasshoppers, he now realized—rained from the sky. Some pelted him and bounced off, but others took hold, their sticky feet attaching to his clothes.

Had the Old Testament come to life right here in Kansas? His scalp prickled; his skin crawled. Using his hat, he slapped at himself, but the bugs landed on his head, tugging his hair. He shook his head wildly and then smacked the hat back in place. "Yah! Yah!" he urged his horse onward, hoping the animal wouldn't step in a hole and break a leg or throw him from the saddle.

He finally cleared the whirring horde and slowed to look back. The sight baffled and horrified him. Sheep, their coats covered with green shimmering insects, milled in noisy confusion. The ground appeared to move and shift on its own, buried an inch thick by the insects. The hoppers coated every bush, tree, and fence post, their continual buzz drowning out all other sounds. More stirred the air, their wings flashing under the sun.

Chris broke free of the melee and joined Geoffrey. He panted as if he'd just run a mile-long race. "What do you make of it?" he yelled over the deafening whirr of wings.

"I don't know. I've heard of such a thing, but I never believed I'd see it." Geoffrey plucked more bugs from his clothes and tossed them as far as he could. He gaped at the plaid fabric covering his arms. "They ate holes in my shirt!"

"What do we do about the sheep?"

Geoffrey's heart ached at the fear the poor, dumb animals were experiencing. "We can't do anything until the hoppers clear."

"When do you think they'll go?"

Through gritted teeth, Geoffrey said, "When they've eaten their fill." Suddenly he remembered Emmaline and Jim taking off toward the Sengers'. He spun toward Chris. "Stay here. As soon as you can, start rounding the sheep back to the barn. I've got to see to Emmaline."

He raced down the road at a reckless pace. Evidence of the grasshoppers' devastation greeted his eyes everywhere he looked. Fields of grass, knee-high and waving only that morning, were gone. Trees appeared denuded, patches of bark eaten away. Dust clouds rose over the ground, unhindered now with the loss of vegetation. Geoffrey's chest tightened. What about the farmers' crops? Their garden? And the fields he'd allowed to go to hay so he could harvest it for winter feed? Could anything be salvaged?

When he reached the Sengers' he found Tildy sitting on the

ground, cradling a dead chicken in her lap. He reined in beside her
and hopped down, dropping to one knee. She lifted her sorrowful eyes to him.

"Fool hens. Thought a feast came from heaven. They was
eatin' as fast as they could. Done ate themselfs to death." Pointing
toward the barn, she said, "Ronal' was out here a-smackin' at 'em
with the shovel. He scooped up as many of the hoppers as he could.
He's gonn' set 'em afire an' hope the smoke keeps more bugs from
comin'." She set the chicken tenderly on the ground, shaking her
head. "Won't do nothin' to help my poor cluckers. . . . Gonna miss
seein' them peckin' out here of a mornin'."

Geoffrey put his hand on her shoulder. "We'll find you some
more chickens."

"Oh, law, I knows it. Just seems sad, that's all." She pushed
to her feet and jerked her chin toward the soddy. "Be easier to
get chickens than a new roof. They plumb ate the top off my
house."

Geoffrey turned and discovered Tildy was right. The roof of
the soddy, held together by the roots of dried grass, had collapsed
inward. "Oh, Tildy . . ."

Tildy's chin quivered for a moment; then she set her jaw. "If I
can get to my stove, we'll have us stewed chicken tonight. Ronal'
always liked stewed chicken an' dumplin's. He'll be right happy
for the treat. You take one o' my clucks home, too, for Emmalion
to fix for your supper."

Geoffrey looked sharply right and left. "Where is Emmaline?"

"In the root cellar. Ronal' sent her an' young Jim down soon
as they pulled in. When we saw the cloud, we thought it was a
storm brewin'. Had no idea . . ."

Geoffrey trotted to the door of the root cellar and yanked it
open. "Emmaline? Jim?"

Jim emerged first, his eyes huge. "Did you see them, Mr. Garrett? I'd never have believed it if I hadn't seen it. Such noise! The horses didn't like it at all. I almost couldn't control them when those bugs started landing on them. Ronald put the team in the barn."

Emmaline came out of the cellar with one hand holding her skirts and the other grasping a green stalk only a few inches long. She held it up. "They ate the flowers right off the stem. While I held it." Her hair was in disarray, and her black dress bore several holes. Her wide eyes and pale skin spoke of shock. "They followed us right under the ground." She shivered. "Are they gone now?"

He longed to embrace and comfort her, but his arms remained stiffly at his sides. "They're moving on, and I don't think they'll come back. They've eaten everything—there's no reason to stay."

She dropped the little stem and hugged herself. "It was awful. They attacked us. Just fell out of the sky and attacked us."

Tildy waddled over and wrapped her plump arms around Emmaline. She rocked gently while glowering at Geoffrey. "They's all gone now, Emmalion. You's gonn' be fine now. You jus' go on home an' get some rest. Come mornin', you'll be feelin' bettuh."

Geoffrey turned to Jim. "Take Emmaline home, then go to the north pasture. Chris will need some help rounding up the sheep—they scattered when the hoppers landed."

"Sure, boss." Jim took a step, then turned back. "Are you coming, too?"

Smoke coiled from behind the barn. A foul odor filled the air. Geoffrey looked at Emmaline, who stared straight ahead as if unaware of his presence. "I'll give Ronald some assistance and then come home. Hurry now."

"Yes, sir. Come along, Miss Emmaline." Jim caught Emmaline's elbow and propelled her toward the barn.

As soon as Jim and Emmaline were out of earshot, Tildy propped her hands on her hips. "What be the mattuh wit' you, Geoffrey Garrett? Don't you know a woman needs some consolin' when she's had a scare? An' Emmalion just had a good scare."

"Not now, Tildy." Geoffrey marched past her as the wagon emerged from the barn. The horses still looked wild-eyed. They tossed their heads and flared their nostrils. He caught the harness chin strap on the closest horse and held tight. He dared not let Jim try to drive the team when they were still so agitated. "Jim, I've changed my mind. You stay here and help Ronald. I'll go see to the sheep."

"Yes, sir." The boy leaped down and trotted behind the barn.

Geoffrey climbed up beside Emmaline. She sat with her arms wrapped around herself, shivering despite the blistering heat of the day.

Tildy stood on the ground, looking up at him with a scowl on her face. She hissed through clenched teeth, "You see to Miss Emmalion afore you see to the sheep, you hear me, Geoffrey?"

———

Emmaline could scarce believe this was the same expanse of land she and Jim had traveled less than two hours ago. The waving grasses and sunflowers had disappeared, leaving behind only bare ground. Not so much as a single leaf remained on the bushes or trees.

They pulled into the yard at Chetwynd Valley, and she nearly cried when she saw the huge cottonwoods leafless and with gaping holes in their bark. She ran to the river's edge to examine the trees; then she shrank back in horror at the sight of grasshoppers floating in the river, their green bellies shimmering. Covering her mouth, she held back a cry.

Hands descended on her shoulders. "Emmaline," Geoffrey's husky voice whispered into her ear. "I need to see to the sheep. Will you be all right?"

The sheep . . . always the sheep. "I . . . I shall be fine. You go."

His fingers pressed tighter. "Are you sure?"

Oh, if only she could turn and bury her face against his shoulder. If only she could cry and feel his arms surround her, soothing the revulsion of the past hours away. But she shrugged, dislodging his hands. "I am quite sure. I shall see if there is anything left of the garden." She feared all of her carefully tended plants were gone. For the first time, she was glad she'd had no flower garden. At least she needn't mourn its obliteration.

"All right, then. I don't know if we'll be back by suppertime. Just . . . hold something for us, please."

His decorous bearing was the opposite of what she needed. But she responded with equal formality. "Of course. I'll keep something warm on the stove."

"Thank you." He strode away.

Jim arrived almost two hours later astride Geoffrey's horse. He tethered the horse at the gate and ambled to the garden where Emmaline raked dead grasshoppers into a pile.

"Is there anything left?"

Emmaline pushed her hair out of her eyes with her elbow and kept raking. "Not much. The carrots, turnips, beets, and potatoes are safe below the ground, but if I did not have little sticks to let me know that beans, peas, and tomatoes once grew here, I would not know. They ate everything, including the paper signs off the sticks." She released a humorless chuckle. "To think that only this morning I rued having to pick green beans every day."

Jim scratched his head. "Will we have enough food for winter?"

Emmaline had no answer for that. She had never lived through a Kansas winter. How much food was needed? "The grasshoppers were unable to enter the springhouse, so that food was spared. I haven't yet been in the cellar."

"They couldn't get in there. The door is too thick."

Emmaline sighed. "Thank the Lord." Maybe they wouldn't starve. She hoped others in the area hadn't lost everything.

"Do you need help burning those?" He pointed to the repulsive pile of insects.

She had no desire to be involved in the burning. The smell from Ronald's fire still lingered in the back of her nose. "I'll ask Geoffrey to do it. You go on and see if he needs help with the sheep."

Jim nodded and jogged back to Geoffrey's horse. In moments he disappeared around the house. Emmaline walked to the shed to put away the rake. The day's trauma slowed her steps, tiredness slumping her shoulders. She hung the rake upside down from a wooden peg and then stepped back outside. The unchanged sun, hanging high and bright in a blue sky, seemed incongruous against the ravaged landscape.

Unwilling to return to the house alone, she decided to take a walk and examine the ranch. Had any vegetation survived the grasshoppers' assault? The sheep must have grass to survive.

She walked into the empty sheep barn. Its rock construction kept it reasonably cool, and she slowed her steps to better enjoy the respite from the sun's heat. Musky odors greeted her, and she crinkled her nose. She rarely ventured in this direction. As she passed through the long barn, her eyes drifted across each of the vacant stalls and the loops of rope hanging from the ceiling beams.

The first time she had entered the barn, she'd questioned the lack of doors and the purpose for the ropes. Geoffrey explained how the men leaned into the ropes to support themselves while they sheared the sheep rather than bending over. She couldn't imagine that having a rope cut into one's stomach was more comfortable than bending forward, but she didn't question it. The reason for the open doors—allowing air to flow through and keep the barn dry for the health of the flock—made more sense. But had grasshoppers come in through the openings? She could see no evidence.

The sun made her squint when she left the protective shade of the building. She turned to the right, and something caught her attention. Two crosses stood side by side within a hip-high iron fence. Curious, she crossed the ground and opened the gate. She crouched before the crosses. The smaller one had no writing on it, but the second was carved with a name: Ben Mackey.

A little warning sounded in the back of her head. Where had she heard that name before? She scrunched her forehead, thinking, and finally she remembered. Jim had mentioned the name and then had immediately fallen silent. She stared at the cross, puzzlement tilting her head. Why would the boy try to hide the fact that a man named Ben had died at the ranch? Was something sinister involved in his death? Why didn't Geoffrey ever speak of Ben?

"Emmaline."

At the sound of her name, she jumped and clutched her bodice. She spun around and found Geoffrey standing outside the iron fence.

"What are you doing?" He looked as tired as she felt. Dark circles rimmed his eyes, and lines pulled his mouth into a frown.

"I went for a walk and—" She bit her lip. Heading for the gate, she said, "I need to return to the house and fix supper."

"No need. It will be well past dark when we come in, and I'm sure we'll be too tired to eat. Is our garden destroyed?"

She nodded, sorrow striking anew. "All except what grows far under the ground. Are the sheep all right?"

He glanced across the pasture. "They've scattered, and they're so frightened they don't come when they hear my voice. They have always responded to my voice before. I feel as though I've failed them."

The sadness in his eyes made her heart ache. She had no words of comfort, but she could meet a need. "In case you change your mind about supper, I will prepare something. You shouldn't go to bed hungry." She started to hurry past him, but he caught her arm.

He heaved a deep sigh, his gaze still aimed across the prairie. "Before you go, I must . . ."

Very slowly he turned, still holding her arm. As he moved, he pulled gently, shifting her to face him. Her hands rose automatically and rested flat against his chest. An odd look flitted across his face—desire coupled with helplessness. Then his arms slipped around her, pulling her snug against his length.

He smelled of sweat and sheep and smoke, and she inhaled, closing her eyes to memorize the unique potpourri of odors. They stood unmoving beneath the Kansas sun, his arms holding her tight with hers trapped between them. It felt good to finally be in his embrace, but she wanted to wrap her arms around his middle and burrow closer. So she wriggled to free her arms. But at her movement, he released her and stepped back.

She peered into his somber face, her heart pounding, wondering what had precipitated the hug and what she could do to entice him to repeat it. She leaned toward him. He raised his hand, but instead of reaching for her he ran it over his face. When he looked at her again, the strange longing she had seen earlier had disappeared.

"If you want to prepare something, you may." He spoke as if the hug had never occurred.

"A-all right, Geoffrey." She battled tears. She would never understand the man he had become here in Kansas.

"If we haven't come in by nightfall, go on to bed. I will see you in the morning." He turned and headed toward the ravaged pasture.

# NINETEEN

～

EOFFREY LEANED ON the railing of the bunkhouse's porch and gazed across the ground that separated the bunkhouse from the ranch house. The sheep, safe in their barn, muttered nighttime bleats as they settled down for a night's sleep. Chris and Jim had already gone to bed. But despite the hour, Geoffrey was not ready to turn in.

The first two days following the grasshopper plague, neighbors stopped by to compare losses. It pained Geoffrey to admit how much of his pastureland had been destroyed by the insects. His water supply was also severely compromised with the presence of dead grasshoppers—the sheep refused to go where the scent of decaying bugs remained, and he had already lost two expecting ewes to dehydration. Despite his and the Cotler brothers' best efforts, they had been unable to locate the entire flock. Sixteen head were missing, and he surmised the sheep had either been devoured by animals or adopted by neighbors who needed the meat.

But he realized it could have been worse. The grasshoppers literally ate the wool off the backs of the sheep. Had the infestation come one month earlier, his entire year's profit would have been lost. Many of his neighbors were left with nothing of their crops.

He still had the promise of lambs to butcher and sell, and the wool would grow back—he would survive better than most. If he could find feed for his flock . . .

Yesterday at church, a local farmer shared the rumor that the bordering territory of Colorado planned to send hay and other food supplies to help the Kansans who had lost their money crops, but Geoffrey wasn't willing to wait and see if the rumor proved true. His sheep needed food now. But that meant leaving the ranch for a period of time.

A light flickered in the window of the sleeping room, where Emmaline, no doubt, was preparing for bed. He stared at the glowing window, envisioning what was taking place behind the muslin curtain she had hung for privacy. Ever since he'd enfolded her in his arms three days ago, he had battled the desire to hold her again. To do more than hold her.

She'd pushed him away. Maybe in that moment she had recognized that the hug was more about his receiving comfort than giving it—something he'd realized himself much later. He had needed that hug desperately. He had needed someone to hold on to, and he had wanted her to be that someone. But she had squirmed, and he had been forced to relinquish his hold. The next time he hugged her, it would be at her invitation. He wouldn't open himself to rejection again.

They hadn't sat on the porch this evening. She had spent the entire evening snapping beans and flicking peas from their pods. Tildy planned to come early next week and help Emmaline preserve the vegetables that hadn't been destroyed by the grasshoppers. He feared the amount would be less than what was needed to sustain them through the winter, but at least they would have something set aside.

The light still glowed in the window. Perhaps she wasn't able to sleep, either. And if she couldn't sleep, they might as well talk.

Before he could convince himself to stay away, he stepped off the porch and moved briskly across the shadowed ground. The gentle song of the Solomon drifted on the night breeze. He loved the sound of the water. He loved the sound of the wind racing through the grass. He loved this land. And he loved Emmaline.

If only Emmaline loved him . . .

He knocked softly on the front door of the house, then stood listening. After a few seconds, he heard footsteps, and a lantern's glow lit the door's round window from within. "Yes?"

"It's me—Geoffrey. May I come in?" How odd to ask permission to enter his own house.

"Of course."

He opened the door to find Emmaline clutching a robe closed at her chin with one hand and holding the lantern aloft with the other. Her hair spilled over her shoulders in a mass of reddish brown waves. Her eyes, wide and questioning, seemed huge in her heart-shaped face.

His heart caught at the innocent picture she painted, and he swallowed hard. "I saw the light on, so I knew you were awake."

"Yes. Sleep eludes me tonight for some reason . . ."

Did she want him to ask why? He cleared his throat. "I need to speak with you about a trip I must take."

She crossed to the straight-backed chairs that sat against the far wall and seated herself. Placing the lantern on the small table between the chairs, she tipped her head in invitation. "Please sit down. You needn't stand in the doorway."

After a moment's hesitation, Geoffrey crossed the room and sat in the opposite chair. The dark room, and she in her night attire, lent an intimacy to their conversation.

"The grasshoppers destroyed much of my pasture. Without rains, the grasses will not grow back. I do have some land undamaged, but not enough. I need to purchase feed."

Her brown eyes, soft and velvety, remained pinned on his face. "I suppose none of your neighbors can spare feed."

"No. Some have lost their entire crops to the grasshoppers." He sighed, shaking his head. "Who would think mere bugs could create such devastation?" He drew a deep breath. "I am sure the grasshoppers did not affect the entire region. Somewhere, there will be a farmer or rancher willing to share his bounty with my sheep. So tomorrow I plan to set out in search of feed."

"Can you not send telegrams to neighboring communities to inquire?"

Genuine concern underscored her soft voice. Was she worried about the sheep, or about him? "I must see about the feed myself," he said. "There are unscrupulous men who would try to benefit from our desperation. I dare not purchase feed sight unseen."

Her head bobbed in a slow nod. "I see." She sucked in her lips for a moment. "How long will you be gone?"

"I am not sure. Maybe a week . . . or two. I hope not much longer than that since it means Chris and Jim will carry much responsibility. But it depends on how far the grasshoppers reached, and who has an abundance to share."

She tucked her hair behind her ear. "Do not worry about the ranch. Chris and Jim are capable of caring for the sheep. And I shall do what I can. With my garden gone, I shall have time free each day."

It occurred to Geoffrey that he and Emmaline were having a real conversation with each other, the way he'd always wanted. He actually felt as though she shared his burden and, in doing so, lightened it.

"Thank you, Emmaline. I . . . appreciate your support."

Her expression was so very, very tender. A sense of comfort, of well-being, of homecoming enfolded Geoffrey. His hands ached to reach across the little table, take hold of her, and draw her into his arms.

He bolted to his feet. "I must let you rest."

She stood, too. Her face, lit by the soft glow of the lantern, registered a disappointment that confused him.

"I plan to make an early start."

"Then I shall rise early and prepare you a hearty breakfast."

He headed for the door, not daring to look at her.

"I shall pack some food for you to take with you. Raisin biscuits and dried venison, and perhaps crackers and cheese."

He turned the doorknob.

"I do hope you find adequate feed for the sheep."

Geoffrey swung the door wide and darted for the bunkhouse before he forgot she was not yet his wife.

---

"Have a safe trip, Geoffrey." Emmaline stood beside Geoffrey's horse, her hand cupped over her eyes.

"Thank you, Emmaline. I wish I knew when to tell you to expect me. . . ."

"You just take care of yourself." She forced a cheerful tone. "I shall be fine."

She watched Geoffrey leave, remembering their last farewell in England, right before the ship carried him away. That time, he had bestowed a long hug and pressed a lengthy kiss on the top of her head. That time, she had sobbed against his chest, then stood waving, waving, waving, until she could no longer make out his form at the ship's railing. That time, she had mourned for days.

This time, she turned and headed to the house to clean her kitchen. She had prepared a massive breakfast—eggs, Geoffrey's favorite raisin biscuits, fried potatoes with onions, and thick slices of salt pork. Somehow, filling Geoffrey's stomach reduced her inability to fix the greater problems.

She spent the morning taking care of the week's laundry. It was an arduous chore, requiring filling tubs with water, scrubbing a bar of soap on the dirty clothing, then rinsing in another tub before hanging the items to dry in the breeze. The rote activity allowed too much time for thought. Where might Geoffrey be now? Would someone be willing to sell him feed? What if he had to go as far as Nebraska or the Dakotas?

Affixing a pair of men's long johns to the line, she said out loud, "I shall drive myself mad if I continue asking myself questions! Now get busy!" In short order, the sheets, trousers, shirts, and long johns snapped in the wind in a satisfying line. She lifted the basket and turned toward the storage shed, but the rattle of a wagon captured her attention.

She looked to the road, delighted to see Ronald and Tildy turn in at the lane. She lifted her hand in a happy wave. Dropping the basket, she skipped to meet them. "I thought you weren't planning to come until next week. I haven't removed the beets from the ground yet, but I can—"

Then she noticed the canvas-covered lumps in the back of the wagon. "Tildy?"

Ronald sat facing forward, his jaw jutted out, but Tildy looked down at Emmaline. Her chin quivered. "Miss Emmalion, we's come to tell you good-bye."

Emmaline grabbed the edge of the seat. "Good-bye? But—but—"

Tildy put her big hand over hers. The warm, rough palm offered a caress. "Our house caved in, Miss Emmalion. Roof collapsed after the hoppers did their damage, an' then last night's wind took the north wall."

"Oh, Tildy!"

"Still got the barn, still can work, but people is short o' cash now that they got no crops to sell. How're me an' Ronal' gonn' make it here? So he says we gotta git on down the road where the hoppers ain't been an' start anew." Her eyes begged Emmaline to understand.

Emmaline clutched at some excuse to keep them near. "But Geoffrey will want to say good-bye to you, and he's gone on a trip. Can't you—"

Ronald said, "Seen Geoffrey this mornin' when he rode by." The man fixed his lips into a somber line. "We says our fare-thee-wells to him."

"Then won't you come in for lunch? Or tea?" Tildy was the best friend Emmaline had ever had, yet not once had they sat in the parlor and shared a cup of tea. What had her thoughtlessness meant to Tildy? She had to rectify the situation before she could say good-bye. "You can at least have a cup of tea with me first, can't you?"

Ronald worked his jaw back and forth. Tildy peered at him, silently waiting. Emmaline clutched her hands beneath her chin. "Please?"

Finally he gave a single nod. "Yup. I reckon we can do that." He set the brake and climbed over the side.

Emmaline nearly collapsed with relief. She embraced Tildy the moment she stepped down; then she scurried toward the house. "Ronald, you just sit on the porch and relax. Tildy, come in and talk to me while I brew the tea."

Emmaline took her time preparing the tea and placing wedges of gingerbread on plates. She longed to talk, to fill the time with chatter, but a lump in her throat made talking difficult. Tildy, too, sat in uncommon silence, but her large eyes reflected her sadness.

Only one chair sat in the parlor—the rocking chair—so Emmaline asked Ronald to carry in the pair of straight-backed chairs from the sitting room. Then they sat in a circle around the little piecrust table, sipped their tea, and ate gingerbread. Tildy's large, chapped hands on the fragile cup painted a heartbreaking picture, and Emmaline could barely swallow for the tears that filled her throat.

Tildy smacked her lips. "This be right flavorful, Miss Emmalion. Even better'n the tea brewed from chamomile I growed behind my soddy." Her face drooped.

"I don't believe I've sampled chamomile." Emmaline managed a bright tone. "Geoffrey purchased this orange pekoe in Stetler. I do enjoy its full flavor."

Several long, quiet minutes ticked by while the Solomon sang its melody outside the window. Ronald set his cup and saucer on the table and slapped his knees, rising. "Well, I 'preciate the tea an' the treat, Miss Emmalion, but I reckon—"

Tildy sat straight up. "Ronal', you go on outside. I needs some time wit' Miss Emmalion."

Ronald scowled. "We gots to git movin', woman."

"An' we'll git movin' soon as I's talked wit' Miss Emmalion." Her glare dared him to argue.

With an exaggerated sigh, Ronald rolled his eyes toward the ceiling. "Aw right, but you don' dally. We gots a long ways to go." He then turned to Emmaline, and his expression gentled. "It's been right nice knowin' you, Miss Emmalion. You take care o' yo'self now, y'hear?"

Emmaline swallowed hard. "Y-yes, Ronald. Thank you. I wish you well."

He ambled out the door with his long-legged gait.

Tildy watched him go, her chin tucked low. "Mm-mm-mmm, all these years togethuh, that man move slow as molasses in January, but now he's in a hurry." She shook her head, her full lips pursed. "An' I reckon I shouldn't make him fractious, so I's gotta talk fast."

She captured Emmaline's hands in hers. "You's a good girl, Miss Emmalion, but I's concerned for yo' soul. We ain't taken time to talk deep about God an' knowin' Him. Seems we done too much workin' together, but you learned good on ever'thang I showed you. I be right proud o' you."

"Oh, Miss Tildy . . ." Emmaline bit down on her lower lip to keep from sobbing.

"No time for caterwaulin' now, Miss Emmalion. You jus' listen careful."

Holding tight to Tildy's hands, Emmaline blinked several times. "Yes, ma'am."

"You been doin' a right good job here, an' I don' wanna take nothin' away from all you done. But there's somethin' more you gotta do. You gotta learn to lean on God. If'n you don't, you's gonna come across a day when yo' strength ain't enough. An' you'll just go all to pieces. But if you got God's strength, chil', then you'll always have the strength you need, no matter how hard thangs git."

Emmaline thought about the grasshoppers, the wind, the ruined food, and the separation from Geoffrey. The combination weighed on her. She moaned, "But how do I do it, Tildy?"

Tildy grabbed Emmaline's wrists and raised her hands. "See how you's got your hands all balled into fists?"

Emmaline looked at her own hands. She held them so tightly closed her fingernails bit into her palms.

"You gotta open up them fists and lay it all at the feet o' Jesus. Lay yo'self there first, then every burden you got. He done promised there ain't no burden He won't carry for us. Lawd knows He's taken a-plenty from me." Tildy seemed to drift away for a moment, her gaze dreamy. "Wanted more'n anything to be a mama, even though I knows any babies I birth would be the massuh's property. But I begged God to let me have 'em, an' He answered. Give me three babies . . ." One plump tear formed in each of her eyes. "But none of 'em lived past the sucklin' age. Mighty hard for me to put my babies in the ground. But then I see other babies, when they's full-grown, tore from their mama's arms an' bein' sold to other massuhs. Their mamas never see 'em again. An' I's grateful God spared me that. I could go sit at those little graves an' know my babies was safe in His arms."

The tears rolled down Tildy's round cheeks. "I didn't have the strength to face losin' my babies all on my own, Miss Emmalion. But I had Jesus in my heart, an' I could call on God to give me the strength I needed to carry on. An' if He can make me strong enough to give my babies back to Him, then He can give you strength for whatevuh you face, too."

Emmaline threw herself against Tildy's chest. "I'm so sorry, Tildy."

"Now, don' be sorrowin' over me." Tildy patted Emmaline's back, holding her close. "The Lawd gives an' the Lawd takes away, an' we just praise Him for knowin' what's best." She pulled back and cupped Emmaline's cheeks. "But I cain't leave without knowin' you'll rest in Him, chil'. I . . . I love you like you was my own, an' I cain't bear goin' 'less I know I's leavin' you in His arms."

A longing rose up from Emmaline's heart, nearly strangling her with desire. She deliberately opened her fists and held her hands flat, palms up. "I want His strength, Tildy. Will you help me?"

At once Tildy dropped from the chair and knelt on the hard floor. Without hesitation, Emmaline joined her. "You jus' talk to your Maker, chil', an' tell Him you want His fillin'. He never denies a request from one o' His own. Jus' ask."

Emmaline squeezed her eyes tight. She licked her lips and began to speak in a faltering voice. "God, I need you. I cannot face things alone. Please come to me. Let Jesus fill my heart, as Tildy said, and give me strength." A warmth flooded Emmaline's body. "Oh, thank you, God. Thank you for coming to me. . . ."

She opened her eyes to find Tildy beaming at her. "You ain't never gonn' be alone now, chil'. An' if'n we don' see one another again on this earth, we'll meet up in the Lawd's house by-an'-by."

# TWENTY

J IM COAXED HIS horse into its stall by dumping a bucketful of oats into the feeding trough. He ducked when Horace blew air down the back of his shirt. "Here now, you behave yourself." While the horse munched, Jim stroked its sheeny neck.

"Jim?" Chris called from outside the barn.

Jim trotted to the opening. "Yeah?"

"Did you check to be sure the sluice gate is open on the water-way? The reservoir needs refilling."

Jim let out a huff. "No. I thought you were going to do it."

Chris propped one fist on his hip. "I told you to do it. Weren't you listening?"

Jim let his scowl provide the answer.

"Make sure you ride out there and get it done before supper."

"But I just unsaddled Horace! I—"

"No excuses, Jim." His brother's stern bark stopped Jim's protests. "The sheep will need the water tomorrow afternoon." Chris turned and strode away without waiting for a word of agreement.

Jim stomped back into the barn, muttering. Chris had wasted no time assuming the role of "boss" in Mr. Garrett's absence. Jim couldn't wait until he was old enough to decide what he wanted to do instead of always having to follow orders.

He headed for Horace's stall, scuffing his feet against the hay-strewn floor. Bending over to pick up his saddle, his eye caught the brief flash of something shiny. Was there a coin tangled in the hay? His mouth watering at the thought of buying sourballs with his find, he dropped to one knee and brushed aside hay and dirt to investigate.

Rather than a coin, the corner of a small tin box emerged. Jim glanced over his shoulder. Chris was gone, so he scooped the protective dirt away with his fingers and pulled the box free. He set it on his knee. It felt heavy, which excited him all the more. What was inside? He tugged at the latch, but it wouldn't give. Grunting in disgust, he gave the box a shake. A solid *thunk* sounded from within.

He poked his finger in the lock. Could he pry the box open? Digging into his pocket, he fetched his pocketknife. A few twists with the blade released the lock. He lifted the lid, cringing when the hinges squeaked. When he glimpsed the contents, he slammed the box shut and hugged it to his chest, breathing hard. He leaped up and spun toward the door. On tiptoe, he crept to the opening and looked right and left. Seeing no one, he scurried back inside and hunkered in the corner of Horace's stall. He opened the box again, slowly. There were three stacks of bound bills! He didn't even need to count the money to know he had found a small fortune.

Who might have left this here? It couldn't belong to Chris— Chris always spent his paycheck. Mr. Garrett used a safe in the spare room of the ranch house. Maybe this box had been here when Mr. Garrett bought the land and they had built the barn right over the top of it without knowing. Think of all the things he could buy with this money!

He jumped up and shoved the box under his horse's nose. "Horace, look here. I can get you all the oats you want with this!"

The horse went on chewing, unimpressed. Jim paced back and forth, the box held tightly between his hands. He needed to hide it. Should he put it back where he'd found it? Nah, both Chris and Mr. Garrett spent a lot of time in the barn—they might stumble upon it just like he had. He needed a better hiding spot. Since he shared a room with Chris, he couldn't put it in there. If only he had his own private room where no one could go through his things . . .

Then an idea struck. He could put it in the cemetery next to Pup's grave. No one would think to look there.

He tucked the box inside his shirt and lifted his saddle. "Come on, Horace. I need to go open the gate before Chris has my hide, and then we've got some digging to do."

———

A distinct heaviness weighed on Emmaline as she placed the last plate on the shelf. How strange it had felt to sit at the table today with only Chris and Jim. Geoffrey's empty chair seemed to mock her. Where was he now? Might he drop her a letter while he traveled? Maybe he would send her father word as to his whereabouts, she thought with a small smile. Then she wondered how she could find amusement in something that had so frustrated her before. Yet laughing felt better than being angry.

She examined the kitchen to make sure nothing required her attention; then she lifted the lantern from its bracket and headed for her bedroom. But as she crossed through the sitting room, she realized she wasn't yet ready to turn in. Sinking down on the sofa, she wished she had someone else in the house with whom she could visit.

Her thoughts drifted to Geoffrey. Although at times she had resented their nightly ritual of sitting on the porch together, she now discovered she missed it. She missed *him*. That night before he left, when he had knocked on the door and they had talked in the parlor, she had felt as though she was visiting with the young man who had courted her under her parents' watchful gazes. It had given her heart a lift to hear him sharing his thoughts and concerns rather than taking her to task for her inadequacies.

She closed her eyes for a moment, allowing herself to remember England and the days when Geoffrey had sent her heart aflutter with words of devotion and declarations of love. She had expected him to woo her again when she arrived in Kansas, but they spoke of nothing personal and spent very little time together; the easy camaraderie they had shared in England had vanished.

But how to fix things? Tildy had told her everything was possible with God's help. Perhaps she and God together could find a way to bring back the Geoffrey of long ago. . . .

Opening her eyes, Emmaline glanced around the room. The furnishings, though stylish, lined the walls as if they were soldiers on parade. The sitting room in her parents' home in England had been an inviting place, with groupings that encouraged one to sit, relax, and indulge in lengthy conversation. Might she and Geoffrey find a way to breach the extensive gap between them if this room were more welcoming?

She must find out. She set the lantern on the nearest table and tried to move the sofa in front of the fireplace. The heavy, carved-wood furniture refused to budge. With a grunt of displeasure, she put her hands on her hips and glared at it. She needed help. She hurried through the kitchen and stepped outside to give one quick tug on the dinner bell. In a few minutes, Jim loped from the direction of the sheep barn.

"Did you need something, Miss Emmaline?"

"Yes." She spun and headed back inside, knowing he would follow. "I want to arrange the sitting room more attractively, but I cannot move the furniture myself. Will you help me?"

"Sure, I will." Jim held out his hands as he inquired, "Where do you want things?"

For the next several minutes, Emmaline pointed and Jim worked to create two groupings. When he had finished, the sofa and two matching chairs sat in a half circle facing the fireplace. The straight-backed chairs and small table from the parlor fit neatly in front of the window. She stood with her hands on her hips and surveyed their handiwork, smiling brightly. "This is much more pleasant to the eyes, and much more inviting."

Jim glanced around the room. "It does look nice. But . . ." He scratched his head. "Shouldn't there be something on the mantel? At our cottage in England, Pa had a clock on the mantel, and Mum had a little china doll. She was very proud of that doll." He scrunched his face. "I wonder what happened to it. . . ."

Emmaline sighed. "Oh, it would be nice to set something lovely on the mantel. But I brought nothing from England except a rock."

Jim's gaze swerved in her direction. "A rock?"

With a soft laugh, Emmaline nodded. "Yes. It came from my mother's flower garden. My rock is a small piece of England in Kansas."

Jim fixed her with a pensive look. "Will you stay, Miss Emmaline? Or . . . will you go back to England?"

She had no answer for that yet. Much depended on whether she and Geoffrey were able to work out their differences. . . . Could God repair their broken relationship?

"If you go—" The boy swallowed, his Adam's apple bobbing in his skinny neck. "I could go, too."

A tingle of awareness crept across her scalp. "That . . . that's very kind of you, Jim, but why would you want to leave Kansas? You said there is nothing left for you in England."

A look of devotion came into the lad's eyes. "But if you were there, then I should have a reason to be there, too."

Had her attentiveness reminded Jim of his mother's care? The thought should have been heartwarming, but it carried an element of responsibility that gave her pause.

Forcing a glib tone, she said, "I shan't be going anywhere tonight—of that I am certain." She swished her palms together. "Thank you again for your assistance. Now that the room is finished, you may retire for the evening. The leftover raisin biscuits are in a pail on the counter. Help yourself to some before you leave."

Jim stared at her for a moment. He looked hurt, but she didn't know why. "Sure, Miss Emmaline," he said. "Good night."

She remained in the sitting room when Jim left. She heard the lid on the tin pail clank, and then a click signaled the door closing. With a satisfied glance at the newly arranged sitting room, she hustled through the kitchen and locked the back door.

———

Geoffrey tossed water over the campfire, listening to the sizzle as the flames died out. The warmth of the evening hadn't required a fire, but having a blaze pierce the night had made him feel less lonely.

He leaned against his saddle and sighed, patting his belly. He'd eaten the last of Emmaline's biscuits and the dried venison for supper. The only thing remaining in his pack was a hard lump of cheese. Tomorrow, when he reached a town, he'd need to make some purchases—and he hoped one of the purchases would be feed for his flock.

In his three days of travel, he had made his way out of Kansas and into Nebraska, but he still hadn't found a farmer willing to part with some of his precious feed. The stories were the same—lack of rain and destruction from grasshoppers had left people hoarding their harvests. Should he have gone to Oklahoma or Texas? Unfortunately, the cattlemen hated sheepherders—he likely would have found no sympathy in Texas.

Maybe Wyoming? Although he hated to venture so far from home, he knew there were sheep in Wyoming. Maybe Wyoming had been spared the drought and the hoppers. If he didn't find anyone willing to sell him some hay or barley tomorrow, he'd put himself and his horse on a train and ride into Wyoming. Traveling on horseback was taking too much time—he needed to find feed and get home.

Home to his sheep.

Home to his ranch.

Home to Emmaline.

———

The wagon wheels hit a rut, and Jim cringed as the jars in the back of the wagon clinked together. "Whoa . . . slow down there," he called as he pulled lightly on the reins. As eager as he was to get back to the ranch, it wouldn't bode well to arrive with broken canning jars. Or a broken figurine.

That's what the lady at the general store had called the little item he'd purchased: a *bisque figurine*. It looked like a doll to Jim, but he liked the sound of the word. "Figurine," he said aloud, letting the word roll off his tongue.

When he'd asked about china dolls, the clerk had first shown him children's toys. It took some doing before she understood what he wanted, but it had been worth the time of explaining. Emmaline would be so surprised and happy when he gave it to her! Three figurines had waited in a glass case in the corner of the store. Since Emmaline had liked those sunflowers so much, Jim had chosen the one wearing a yellow dress. The figurine's hair was brown and all wavy, the way Emmaline's hair probably looked when she took it out of her braided twist. The face of the doll, the clerk had said, was hand-painted, and Jim had duly admired the perfectly shaped eyebrows and delicate lips. Still, it couldn't compete with Emmaline's beauty.

The little painted-faced girl in the flowing yellow dress would look perfect on the mantel. Much better than a rock. Even though it had cost him dear, he wasn't worried—if his month's pay ran out, he still had the tin box full of money. But he wouldn't use it unless he really needed it. Chris would get suspicious if he suddenly started sporting new clothes or showed up with a new gun or saddle. There was a proverb that said a fool and his money were soon parted, but Jim didn't intend to be a fool!

"Gee," he called, giving the reins a flick. The horses obediently turned right. The wagon rolled up the lane to the front of the house. "Whoa!" Jim set the brake and hopped down, calling, "Miss Emmaline! Your jars are here!"

She came out the kitchen door, wiping her hands on her apron as Jim lowered the hatch on the back of the wagon. Her face lit when he lifted one of the crates of quart jars from the back. "Oh, good! Did you fill my whole list?"

"It's all back there." They only ventured into town for shopping once a month, so he'd been given a lengthy list of items.

Somewhere in one of the crates, the figurine nestled in a brown paper wrapping, cushioned with cotton batting. He'd have to find that little package before Emmaline started going through things. Then he'd need to find the perfect time to give it to her—when they were alone.

Emmaline rested her fingertips on the edge of the wagon and peered into the bed. "Oh my, there are so many jars! I am eager to get those vegetables preserved before they spoil." Her face clouded. "I wish Tildy were here to help me."

Jim balanced a crate against his stomach. "Maybe Mrs. Stanford or one of the other church ladies could help you."

Emmaline licked her lips, her expression uncertain. "Perhaps. I shall ask when we go to church on Sunday." Then she flapped her hands. "But don't stand out here with those heavy jars! Put them on the table."

Jim set the crate down carefully, cringing when another round of soft tings sounded. "I sure hope I didn't break any of them. The road has a lot of holes, and I didn't miss them all."

"I shan't complain if one or two are broken." Emmaline pulled at the lid of the crate with her fingers. "I appreciate your going to town for them."

"Here." Jim pulled the pocketknife from his pocket and stepped in front of her. "Let me get that." In a matter of seconds, he had the top slats loose enough to lift.

"Thank you, Jim. What would I do without you?"

He didn't intend to let her explore the answer to that question. He pointed to the door. "I'll go get the other crates. The lady at the store said I should bring you four dozen quart and two dozen pint jars. If you need more, I can always go back."

By the time Jim had carried in all the crates, the kitchen table and the counter were buried beneath the wooden boxes. Emmaline put her hands on her hips and gave a mock scowl. "Well! How am I to serve dinner tonight?"

Jim smirked. "Maybe we could have a picnic on the porch."

To his surprise, she clapped her hands in delight. "What a marvelous idea! We shall have a picnic. It will be cooler there, away from the cook stove. And then I needn't rush to put everything away. What should we have? Oh, wait. I will surprise you."

Catching his arm, she escorted him to the door. "Go on with you. Put the wagon away and then go find Chris. I have work to do. I shall ring the bell when supper is ready."

Jim scuttled out the door. She had just been very bossy, but somehow he didn't mind. He didn't mind a bit.

# TWENTY-ONE

⁓

**I**S GOOD FEED. Dry—not green. I vould not sell second best."

Geoffrey pulled a straw from the closest bale and nipped the end with his teeth. He chewed, spat, and then nodded at the stocky German rancher. "It will do. How much can you spare?"

Just over the border between Nebraska and Wyoming Territory, he had discovered a community that hadn't suffered the effects of the grasshoppers. Even so, most homesteaders were unwilling to sell any of their baled hay, claiming that, when winter arrived, they would need it for their stock. But one man had lost half of his herd to hoof-and-mouth disease and needed money to rebuild in the spring.

"Six dozen bales," the man answered. "That vill meet your need?"

Geoffrey had hoped for more, but he wouldn't beg. "For now, I suppose."

"Vell, if you discover you need more, you send me word by telegram to Cheyenne. If I can spare, I vill send more on train for you. If I have none to spare, I check with neighbors and try to make help for you."

Geoffrey chewed the inside of his lip. He disliked purchasing anything sight unseen, but this was better than nothing.

"Vill be same hay—all good feed," the man said as if reading Geoffrey's thoughts. "The *gut* Lord frowns at cheaters. I vill not cheat you, Mr. Garrett."

Geoffrey looked into Mr. Wagner's sunburnt face and saw honesty in the deep blue eyes. He gave a decisive nod and stuck out his hand. "I thank you."

"I thank *you*." The man pumped Geoffrey's hand and smiled brightly. "With the money you pay me, new cows I buy. Healthy cows. Is *gut* deal for both of us."

Once the man had Geoffrey's payment tucked in his pocket, he cupped his hands around his mouth and bellowed, "Bernard! Konrad! Dietrich!" Three yellow-haired, strapping boys came running. The man fired off a volley of words in German, accompanied by broad hand gestures, and the boys spun and took off for the barn.

Geoffrey swung into the saddle. "Thank you again, Mr. Wagner." With a tug on the reins, he prompted the horse to head out. Eagerness to get home—to check on his flock, to reassess the damage done by the hoppers, and to see Emmaline—tempted him to dig his heels into the horse's side and gallop all the way back to Kansas. Had Emmaline missed him?

He patted the horse's neck. "Should I ride you home and save the train fare, or should we board the Union Pacific train in Cheyenne and get there faster?"

Faster sounded better. A train ticket took money, but supplies for the trail also took money. "It's a trade-off," he informed the horse, "and the train would get us there in less than half the time." The horse nodded its head and nickered as if agreeing. Geoffrey laughed. "All right. A train ride home."

———

Emmaline hummed as she carried the plates, silverware, and cups to the porch. The kitchen was unbearably hot, the result of her day of preserving vegetables. She thought about the rows of jars containing beans and peas now cooling on the table, and she smiled. Geoffrey would be so surprised when he returned and discovered the outcome of her labors!

She hadn't done the work alone—two ladies from town had assisted—but it gave her great pleasure to see the end result. And now that she knew how to blanch the vegetables, boil the jars, and check the seal, she would be able to continue on her own tomorrow. Which meant, of course, another day in a heated kitchen—but she wouldn't complain. She had a nice big porch where a breeze teased her hair and the song of the river provided a soothing backdrop. Jim especially enjoyed eating outside, and his youthful enthusiasm made the evening meal pass pleasantly despite Geoffrey's absence. Somehow she felt less uncomfortable eating with Jim and Chris out in the open, where she needn't look at an empty chair across the table and wonder where Geoffrey was and what he was doing.

She spread a quilt on the porch floor and laid out the plates and cutlery as precisely as if she were preparing the dining room at home. Certainly the men didn't care if she followed protocol, but her surroundings were largely austere; she felt the need to have *something* reflect civility.

If only she had a bouquet of flowers for the center of the table. Back home, Mother always insisted on decorating the center of the dining room table with fresh flowers. Emmaline glanced around, wishing she could make flowers magically appear, but the same dry, dismal landscape greeted her. With a sigh, she turned toward the house.

"Miss Emmaline?"

The whisper so closely matched the gentle wheeze of the wind that Emmaline wasn't certain she had heard her name called. But she paused, cocking her head.

"Miss Emmaline, over here."

She looked over her shoulder and spotted Jim at the corner of the house, near the parlor windows. He peered at her with wide, excited eyes. A grin dimpled his cheeks. Crooking a finger, he beckoned her near.

"What are you doing?"

"Shh!" He pressed his index finger to his lips. "I don't want Chris to hear."

Puzzled, Emmaline crept near, looking right and left. "But why?"

From behind his back, Jim brought out a brown-paper-wrapped package and plopped it in her hands. "I got you a present. Chris will rib me something awful if he sees, so don't tell him it's from me, all right?" The boy's face glowed bright red.

"A . . . a present? But what for? It isn't my birthday or . . . or . . ."

"It's for the mantel," Jim said. Then he spun and darted around the house, leaving Emmaline alone with the package in her hands.

She stepped back up onto the porch and crossed to the bench below the stained-glass window. Sitting, she placed the package in her lap. Mixed feelings assaulted her, vying for precedence.

Should she accept a gift from Jim? Surely she would crush the boy's feelings if she refused it. With trembling fingers, she loosened the string holding the paper in place and peeled the layers away. She lifted a wad of cotton and then gasped when a beautifully painted figure of a lady fell into her hands. By the shiny glaze and the light weight of the doll, Emmaline knew it was crafted of porcelain bisque. Mother had similar figures of bisque in her built-in china cabinets in the parlor at home.

She held it at arm's length, admiring the sweetly curled hair, the uptilted red lips, and the gown of sunshiny yellow with ripples of white lace. The figure was truly exquisite, and looking at it gave Emmaline a rush of pleasure that was purely feminine. She lowered the figure to her lap as her mind raced. The gift must have taken a sizable portion of Jim's monthly pay. Why would he buy something like this for her?

He had said it was for the mantel. She remembered him mentioning a doll that rested on the mantel of his mother's cottage in England. Her heart melted for Jim—in so many ways, he was still a boy in need of a mother's care.

She rose, cradling the figurine in her palms. How well she understood wishing for a mother's attentive care—her heart still ached with loneliness for her own mother. She would reach out to Jim in a motherly way.

She carried the little figure into the house and put it in the center of the mantel, where Jim would be able to see it if he peeked through the window during their evening meal. And she would do something kind for him in return.

———

Jim brought the bushel basket of apples from the cellar, as Emmaline had requested. She'd been depending on him more and more since Mr. Garrett left. And he liked it. If he could, he'd spend his whole day seeing to her needs, but Chris kept him busy. Jim set down the basket and let the cellar door slam. Seemed like somebody was always telling him what to do.

But Emmaline asked kindly. She didn't order him around like

he was just a kid. His affection for Emmaline grew deeper day by day. The longer Mr. Garrett stayed away, the more he would be needed. Maybe Mr. Garrett would stay away forever.

He scooped up the basket. One of the neighbors had traded Emmaline four pumpkins for the bushel of apples. Emmaline wanted apples so she could bake pies—his favorite kind of pie. She planned to slice up the apples and dry them, so she could bake apple pies during the winter, too. They were just crab apples—small and bitter. But if Emmaline wanted to dry them, he wouldn't argue. Even if the pies tasted terrible and gave him a bellyache, he would eat three pieces without a word of complaint.

He entered the kitchen and stood in the doorway, watching her bustle around as she cleaned up after lunch. She hummed as she worked, her skirts swirling around her ankles. What would she look like in a party dress? Her black dresses looked old and tattered, but she didn't seem to mind. And—he gulped—even in a worn-out black dress she was too pretty for words.

He cleared his throat to get her attention. "Where do you want the basket?"

She spun from the cabinet. "Oh, good! Just put it on the table, Jim. Thank you."

He thumped it down, then wiped his hands on his thighs. She'd already said it would be his job to lay out the slices on the tin roof of the springhouse and storage shed. In years past, he had scattered wild grape clusters over the roofs and let the sun shrivel them into sweet raisins. This year there wouldn't be raisins—the grasshoppers had destroyed the grape vines. No doubt it would take longer for apples to dry than it did grapes, but the late-August sun still burned hot enough to do the job. He wondered if the crows would leave any slices at all. Birds were hungry, and they weren't bashful.

"You might want to dry your apples in the house," he said, "or the birds might gobble them up."

She laughed softly. "Oh, I don't begrudge the birds a few bites. But I can dry some in the house and some outside. That way I make sure we have enough for your pies."

*His* pies? She came right out and said she was making them for him! He took a step backward, nearly tripping. "Well, if that's all you need, I better go get to work. Chris expects me."

She opened a cabinet and retrieved a knife. "Go right ahead. I have lots of peeling to do. Enjoy your afternoon."

Jim scurried out the door, his face hot. Emmaline was making the pies especially for him! He wished he could get her another gift. He couldn't get to town to buy her another figurine, but she liked flowers so much. The grasshoppers had eaten most of the wild flowers, but maybe there were still some growing somewhere.

He headed for the pasture, his stride long and his arms swinging. His gaze searched far into the distance in both directions as he walked. His boots stirred dust. Two small grouse exploded from some scraggly bush just ahead. He stopped to watch them disappear before setting out again, a happy whistle on his lips.

Too late he heard the warning rattle. He froze, fear making his mouth go instantly dry. His heart pounded so hard he thought it might leave his chest. The rattle came again, from his left. What should he do? His brain raced to retrieve the instructions Mr. Garrett and Chris had given him about what to do if he ever encountered a rattler. But he couldn't remember. He couldn't remember!

With a cry of distress, Jim braced to run, but before he could take a step, the snake lunged. Jim screamed when the fangs connected with his boot, right on the arch of his foot. Just as quickly as it had struck, the snake turned and slithered away. Jim grabbed his foot, the spot burning like a red hot coal pressed to his skin. He screamed again.

Finally he remembered what his brother had told him: *hold still.* Dropping to the ground, Jim grasped his leg and screamed as loud as he could.

# TWENTY-TWO

EMMALINE CIRCLED THE apple with her knife, and the peel fell away into the slop bucket. She dropped the apple into a pan on the table and reached for another, but as her fingers closed around the red fruit, a screech of anguish reached her ears. Was it an animal? One of the sheep?

She crossed to the door, peering across the yard and listening intently. The scream came again. A chill slid down her frame. The sound was human—not animal. Grabbing her skirts, she began to run. Ahead, past the barn but not quite to the sheep enclosure, she saw something rolling on the ground. Then she recognized the plaid shirt—Jim!

"Jim! Jim!" She puffed with the effort of running while battling her skirts. When she reached him, she dropped to her knees and grabbed his arms. He held on to his foot and moaned. "Jim, what happened? Did you fall and hurt yourself?"

"Snake!" The boy's terror-filled eyes bore into hers. "A snake! Oh, please, Emmaline, I don't want to die like Ben!"

Ben . . . She gulped as realization washed over her. How she wished Geoffrey were here! She cradled the boy in her arms. A feeling of helplessness made her want to collapse into wild sobs, but the remembrance of a voice whisked through her mind: *"Lean on God's strength, chil' . . ."* She cried out to the blue sky, "God, help me!"

Steely resolve poured through her. She looked directly into Jim's white face. "I will not let you die." A vision of the cross behind the barn flitted through her mind, but she pushed the image away. "I know Tildy told me what to do in case of snakebite. . . ." She pressed her memory. "Stop the poison from spreading!"

Grabbing the hem of her skirt, she ripped the fabric. "Where is the bite?"

Jim pointed to the top of his foot, his face contorted in pain. "Here. Right here."

Emmaline yanked off Jim's boot and thick sock. Two angry red dots marked the place where the snake had bitten him. The flesh swelled, forcing his toes to splay. She tied the strip of cloth above the bite but below his ankle. "Now lie still. I've got to get help. Where is Chris?"

"No! Don't leave me!" Although man-sized, Jim proved his youth with his tearful plea and his grasp on her arms.

Emmaline pressed him gently backward. He fought against her hands. "Jim, you must lie still! The poison will spread if you don't!" She yanked off her apron and wadded it into a ball. "Use this as a pillow, but please—lie down."

Jim slumped back and dropped one arm over his eyes. His body shook with sobs. "Please, Emmaline, I don't want to die."

Emmaline took his hand in hers. "You shan't die. But I must get you some help. I shall bring Chris."

The boy continued to moan, "Don't leave me." No matter how many times she asked, he wouldn't tell her where to find Chris. Finally, she stood, her frantic gaze searching in all directions. He could be anywhere on the ranch. Clenching her fists in frustration, she cried out, "I don't know where to look, God!"

Emmaline dropped again to her knees. Opening her hands, she held them outward and prayed, "We need help, God. Please, please send help for Jim."

As she prayed, an idea formed in her mind. She jumped up. "Jim, I shall be right back. Lie very still and pray!" Running as fast as she could, she covered the ground between the barn and the house. She came to a panting halt beside the dinner bell. She grasped the rope and pulled. And pulled. And pulled.

The clang made her ears ring and her head pound, but she continued to yank, all the while scanning the grounds. Geoffrey had said no matter where he was on the ranch, he would always hear the dinner bell. Surely Chris would hear it, too. "Let Chris hear the bell, God!"

Just as she had hoped, a horse pounded toward the house with Chris in the saddle. "Emmaline—what's wrong?"

Emmaline raced to his side. "It's Jim—a snake bit him."

Chris went pale. He held out his hand. "Take me to him."

She placed her hand in his and he swung her behind him. Emmaline directed him to the area behind the barn. Without taking time for questions, Chris lifted Jim onto the saddle then climbed up behind him. He supported the boy by wrapping one arm around his middle. Jim slumped against his brother's chest.

"I'm taking him to the doctor in Stetler, Emmaline. Can you see to the sheep?"

Emmaline had never cared for the sheep before, but she had no other choice. She stared at Jim's pale face and nodded. "Go quickly!"

Chris whipped the reins against the horse's neck, and the horse shot off toward the road.

Emmaline found Jim's horse ground-tethered beside the sheep barn, still saddled from his day's work. Seeing that saddle slumped her shoulders in relief—she didn't know how to saddle a horse. She would ask Geoffrey to teach her when he returned. After leading the horse to the fence, she managed to clamber aboard. Her feet didn't reach the stirrups, so she clamped her legs against the horse's warm belly, grasped the saddle horn with one hand, and held the reins with the other.

Her head spun when she looked down—the ground seemed so far away! The horse whickered, tossing his head. She presumed her skirts upset him, and she released the saddle horn to tuck them in as best she could. Then, as she'd seen the men do, she tugged on the reins and bounced her heels on the horse's tawny hide.

With a slight snort, the horse trotted forward. "Please go to the sheep," she commanded. Emmaline held tight to the saddle horn, wincing with every jolt of the horse's hooves against the ground, but to her relief the horse headed for the open pasture. By the time she reached the grazing flock in the far northern pasture where the grasshoppers had left a few blades of grass behind, her thighs ached from the effort of remaining in the saddle. But she hadn't yet begun to work.

"What do I do?" she asked aloud. A few sheep lifted their heads, eyeing her with curiosity, their jaws working in circular motions. Emmaline sat high in the saddle and surveyed the contented flock. Despite her worry for Jim, despite her concerns about bringing the sheep safely home, a feeling of peacefulness washed over her. In that moment, she understood why Geoffrey liked being out in the pasture with the sheep.

But she couldn't leave them out here. Geoffrey always brought the sheep to the barn at night. Once more, she voiced the question, "What do I do?" The horse pawed the ground, softly blowing air. Emmaline wished he could understand her and answer, and then the thought of a horse replying made her giggle. At her laughter, several sheep gave a start. One leaped forward, three others following.

"Oh!" Emmaline waved her hands. "No, do not leave!"

But it was as if a silent message had been passed through the flock. Like a rolling tide, the sheep began to move, heading in the opposite direction of the sheep barn. And Emmaline sat, helpless to stop them.

Suddenly, to her surprise, the horse bounded into action. She grabbed the saddle horn with both hands and bounced in the smooth leather seat as the horse galloped along the outer edge of the moving throng of wooly creatures. When it reached the front of the flock, it angled sharply left, and the sheep turned with it. Her mouth open in amazement, Emmaline simply held on as the horse turned the entire flock and prodded them toward the barn.

With a series of bleats and quavering baas, the sheep made their progress across the pasture. The horse trotted back and forth at the rear, nosing at the occasional straggler and preventing any from leaving the group. The sheep barn waited ahead, its doors open. Emmaline stared in amazement when the sheep fell into line and entered the structure without any prompting.

When all of the sheep were safely inside, the horse stopped outside the doors and tossed his head. Emmaline slid from his back, her aching legs nearly collapsing when her feet met the ground. She held to the horse's reins until her quivering muscles stilled enough to support her weight, then she gave the beast several pats on his glossy neck. "Good job, boy. Thank you. You did a good job." The horse turned his head, snuffling against her neck, and she laughed. "I shall give you a treat after I figure out a way to make sure the sheep stay in the barn."

Leaving the horse standing along the fence, she tugged a few empty barrels into the doorway as a makeshift barrier. She felt certain the barrels would do little to prevent the entrance of marauding animals, yet she had no idea what Geoffrey did to ensure the sheep's safety at night. The barrels would have to do until Chris returned.

With the thought of Chris, a pang of worry shot through her. Had Chris been able to locate the doctor? Might Jim lose his foot . . . or his life? She shook her head. Worrying would accomplish nothing. *"Lay it all at Jesus' feet. . . ."* Tildy's reminder rang through Emmaline's memory. Grasping the horse's reins, Emmaline closed her eyes and whispered a prayer for Jim's well-being.

The prayer complete, she gave the reins a tug. "Come with me. I have something special for you." She fed the horse two crab apples, laughing at his obvious enjoyment of the fruit. He nosed her hands, searching for more. "Now, do not be greedy. We must leave some of these apples for Jim. I'm to bake him pies, you know."

Baking would be the perfect way to keep herself occupied, she decided. She wished she knew how to remove the saddle from the horse, but that task would have to wait until Chris returned. She spent the next hour slicing apples, preparing a crust, and putting together two well-filled apple pies with extra cinnamon and sugar. That boy had such a sweet tooth.

While the pies baked, filling the room with the aroma of apples, Emmaline chopped vegetables for a stew. She could keep a pot simmering, and Chris and Jim could eat whenever they returned.

The evening stretched endlessly while she waited, alone. She filled the time by peeling the remainder of the apples, slicing them, and hanging the slices on twine that she stretched across the parlor. Jim had planned to dry the slices on the roof of the springhouse, but she didn't know when he might be well enough to do that. Thinking of Jim made tears prick behind her eyes. Lowering her head, she began to pray once more.

———

Geoffrey jolted awake when someone tapped his shoulder. He blinked, clearing his vision, and peered into the face of the conductor.

"You asked me to wake you when we were within a half hour of Moreland." The man tapped his watch. "We'll pull in at five-oh-five—twenty-five more minutes."

Geoffrey sat up and rubbed his eyes. "Thank you."

The conductor waddled off.

Geoffrey glanced out the window. The familiar rolling landscape filled him with pleasure—home was so close now! He removed his hat, dropped it on the empty seat beside him, and ran his hand through his hair. His weeks on the trail hadn't allowed time for bathing or shaving. Emmaline might turn up her nose at him when he arrived. His heart rate quickened at the thought of seeing her soon. How he had missed her over the past two weeks.

Often, alone beneath the stars, he had thought of that last night, sitting next to her, talking quietly. She had listened, and her expression had been serene, not scared or defensive. They might have been in her parents' sitting room in England, sharing their thoughts with each other. That evening had given him hope that they could recapture what they'd shared while living in the little village of Wortley—a deep friendship, a tender love. . . .

He drew in a deep breath, and the packets in his shirt pocket crinkled. He slipped the packets free and counted them. Three packs of flower seeds—bachelor buttons, daisies, and black-eyed Susans. The merchant in Nebraska had assured him they would last until spring if he kept them in a warm place.

These were wild flowers—not the roses that grew in her mother's garden back home—but they would survive on the plains where roses would surely wither and die. Besides, Geoffrey knew Emmaline loved any kind of flower. If it would make her feel more at home, he would harvest wild flowers for her. And if they were growing near the house, she would have no reason to venture out onto the prairie in search of flowers. She would be safe.

Slipping the packets of seeds back into his pocket, he closed his eyes and pictured Emmaline's face beaming with pleasure at the unexpected gift. He could hardly wait to get to the ranch.

———

The sun was a mere thumbnail on the horizon beneath a dusky pink-and-purple sky when Emmaline finally heard the clop of horse hooves. She stepped outside, pausing beside Jim's horse, which still stood in the side yard with its saddle in place. A tall bay, carrying Chris, entered the yard and stopped in front of Emmaline.

Chris swung down, meeting her gaze. His unsmiling face sent a chill of unease down her spine. She moved forward, her hands tangled in her apron. "Jim—is he . . . ?"

"He's alive." Chris swiped his hand beneath his nose. "Let's go to the house. I could use something to eat."

"I have the soup pot waiting."

He gave a somber nod, and then he headed for the house. His slumped shoulders and plodding steps spoke of a heavy burden. Emmaline winged a silent prayer heavenward for his aching heart.

She dished up a bowl of stew while Chris plopped tiredly into one of the kitchen chairs. He picked up his spoon, but instead of digging into the bowl, he fixed Emmaline with a serious look. "The doc says there's a good chance Jim will make it."

"Oh, thank the Lord . . ." Emmaline sank into the chair across from him.

"The snake didn't bite deep—probably because Jim's boot leather took some of the force. Your wrapping that bandage prevented the poison from going up his leg." Chris ran a hand down his face and sighed. "The doc sucked out what poison he could, and he put a raw liver poultice over the bite. But it sure looks ugly. Jim's foot is twice its normal size, and he's thrashing around like he's not in his right mind. The doc gave him something to make him sleep and sent me home. He said there's nothing more we can do except . . . wait." The torment in Chris's eyes pierced her heart. "Emmaline, if he dies . . ." Chris swallowed. "After we lost our mum and dad, I figured it would always be Jim and me. I get aggravated with him sometimes, but he—he's all I've got. I can hardly think of—"

"Don't." Emmaline grabbed his hand. "Don't even allow yourself to have such thoughts."

"But you didn't see him—rolling his head back and forth like someone was torturing him." Chris clamped his hand over his eyes, and his chin quivered.

Emmaline rounded the table and wrapped her arms around Chris's shaking shoulders. "Shh, now. You needn't distress yourself. Jim is with the doctor. He's being cared for. Now we need to pray that he will be all right. Do you want me to pray?"

Chris nodded.

Emmaline lowered her head, pressing her cheek to his hair. She closed her eyes and opened her mouth to petition God on Jim's behalf.

"This is a pretty picture."

At the harsh exclamation, Emmaline bolted upright and Chris jerked around in his chair. Geoffrey stood framed in the kitchen doorway. A saddlebag dangled from his hand and his eyes flashed with fury.

# TWENTY-THREE

ALL OF THE air had been sucked from the room. Drawing a breath was torture. Geoffrey could scarcely believe what he was seeing—his Emmaline with her arms around Chris Cotler!

"Excuse me for interrupting. I shall go to the bunkhouse and allow you two your privacy." Geoffrey pounded toward his horse.

"Geoffrey, wait!" Emmaline caught up to him and grabbed his elbow.

Chris stood slightly behind her, his face blanched. "Mr. Garrett, let me explain."

With a furious glance at both of them, Geoffrey yanked free of Emmaline's grasp. Her pleading expression brought a wave of revulsion in his gut. He faced Chris rather than view her stricken face. "Emmaline and I aren't wed. If, in my absence, you've found one another pleasing then I shall not stand in your way." He flung his arms wide. "Go back and continue . . . courting."

Emmaline's jaw dropped, and then her eyes narrowed. She clenched her fists. "C-courting? You think we were—?"

"But before you return to your own selfish needs, Chris, you might take care of those poor horses." He pointed to the pair ground-tied in the side yard, still wearing their saddles. "A man takes care of his mount." He turned again to leave.

Chris's insistent voice followed him. "Mr. Garrett, wait, please."

A small hand captured his shirt sleeve, pulling him to a stop. He looked into Emmaline's flushed, furious face.

"You and your petty accusations—you are the most insufferable man I know!"

Someone needed to explain the meaning of "apology" to her.

"After what Chris and I have been through, you dare to—Oh!" Emmaline released his arm and whirled around. "I shall not waste one precious breath defending myself to you." Pushing past Chris, she stomped back toward the house and called over her shoulder, "There is stew on the stove if you're hungry, but do not expect me to serve it to you!"

Geoffrey refrained from firing back his unwillingness to take anything from her, including stew.

"Mr. Garrett—"

Holding up his hand, he stilled Chris's words. "There is nothing more to say. I must see to my horse. Make certain you and Jim care for your mounts before you retire for the evening." He grabbed his horse's reins and headed for the barn. He hoped to have his horse put away before Chris or Jim showed up or there might be a fistfight. Geoffrey had never been prone to fighting, but he'd never before had anything worth fighting for.

He took the packets of seeds from his pocket and tossed them in the yard. The wind tumbled them away into the evening shadows. Good riddance. He swallowed his temper as he curried his horse and gave it fresh feed and water. He groomed the animal as quickly as possible so he could be out of the barn before one of the other men showed up.

Although he was curious how the sheep had fared in his absence, he decided it would be best to go directly to the bunkhouse and check on the sheep in the morning. But as he passed the sheep barn, the strange sight of barrels—some upright, some on their side—lined up in the doorway captured his attention.

He walked slowly along the row. "What on earth?" The sheep offered no explanation, and he looked toward the house. What all had gone on here while he was away? Leaving the barrels, he strode to the bunkhouse. Both halves of the building were dark, signifying Jim must already be asleep. Just as well—the boy didn't need to be exposed to his brother's improper behavior, especially when he harbored feelings for Emmaline, too. The woman collected beaus the way some collected handkerchiefs!

Geoffrey sat on the edge of his bed, his shoulders slumped. He had hoped Emmaline would be the one person who would not forsake him. All those years he had clung to memories of her sweetness, her attentiveness, her trustworthiness. Over and over, Jonathan Bradford had assured him she remained loyal to Geoffrey. But it was not true.

When Geoffrey stretched out on his bed and closed his eyes, the picture of Emmaline and Chris embracing in the kitchen continued to haunt him. Once more, someone he loved had tossed him aside.

Geoffrey awakened well before dawn and headed to the river with a bar of soap. The moon hung high and bright, illuminating his path. Although not overly cool, the air felt crisp, heavy with dew. He made noisy progress, hard earth crunching beneath his feet. Would the rains ever come back to Kansas?

An owl hooted and then took flight, the sound of its flapping wings almost harsh against the gentle rush of water and whispering breeze. He reached the water and quickly stripped down to his underdrawers. When he first stepped into the river, goose flesh broke out over his arms, and he shuddered. But after a few splashes, his body adjusted to the cool temperature. He lathered and scrubbed himself clean, relishing the release of sweat, grime, and oil. If only he could wash away his feelings of inadequacy . . .

In his dreams, an image of Emmaline had faded in and out with images of his mother. He had forgiven his mother a long time ago. Despite the heartache she'd caused when she abandoned her son, she had left for good reason—no woman should be forced to remain with a drunkard. But he wasn't sure he would ever be able to forgive Emmaline. He had built this ranch for her. Had pledged his life to her. And still she had chosen Chris.

Clean again, he stepped out of the water and picked up his discarded shirt. He stood for a moment, watching the eastern sky turn pink and orange, signaling the start to a new day. Sunrises had once filled him with joyful anticipation. But this morning's show left him cold and empty.

Using his shirt as a towel, he rubbed himself dry before slipping into his pants. He sat and put on his socks and boots. With his wadded shirt in his hand, he rose to walk back to the bunkhouse. But the sight of Emmaline slipping across the yard between the washroom and the ranch house stopped him. Her flowing robe gave her the appearance of an apparition in the early-morning light. Her hair tumbled down her back, free from restraints. Even from this distance, he could make out the sweet curve of her jaw. Lord help him, he still loved her.

He stood as if nailed in place, riveted by the sight of her, and suddenly she turned her head. He knew the instant she spotted him. Her body froze midstep; only her gown moved, gently swaying in the light breeze. For long seconds they both stood still, their gazes pinned to each other. And when she began moving again, Geoffrey's heart fired into his throat. Because she walked toward him.

A part of him wanted to walk away from her, but that would be the coward's way out. It was best they settle things now, early, without Jim and Chris looking on. So he squared his shoulders and waited until she stood less than six feet from him. With her hair loose around her shoulders, she looked very young and innocent, and he tightened his fists around his crumpled shirt to keep from reaching for her.

"Geoffrey." The single word served as both greeting and query.

He made no reply.

"You were wrong last night."

The image of her with Chris filled his mind. He drew a deep breath through his nose and clenched his jaw. "I know what I saw."

"What you saw," she said, her voice low but intense, "was me offering comfort to Chris. He was distraught, and I was trying to calm him."

"Distraught." Geoffrey barked the word. It described his feelings last night, as well.

"Jim was bitten by a rattlesnake."

Geoffrey drew back as if it were he who had been bitten.

"Chris took him into Stetler and left him in the doctor's care. But he was worried about losing his brother. When you came in, I was praying with him."

Geoffrey's knees nearly buckled as several thoughts flooded his mind. *Jim hurt . . . Chris in need of comfort . . . Emmaline innocent, praying . . .*

Emmaline continued, "I realize I have given you reason to distrust me after I ran away. But I have tried to set things right. I have remained on the ranch. I have learned to perform the duties you required of me. Yet you still do not trust me. And, Geoffrey—"

Her voice broke. "I cannot stay in a place where I am not trusted. I cannot stay with a person whom I do not trust. . . ."

Her pained admission cut deeper than last night's angry outburst. He wished she would call him names, accuse him of being unfeeling, anything that might absolve him of the shame that now sat firmly on his shoulders. "Emmaline, I—"

"I will stay until spring because—as my father has so often preached—a Bradford honors his word, and I dare not break our commitment lest you choose to discontinue your business relationship with my father. But then I must leave, Geoffrey. I will not allow you to hurt me like this again."

Without giving him a chance to respond, she turned and fled, her long hair rippling like a banner behind her. The sun, creeping over the horizon, lit the fiery strands of red in her flowing locks. Geoffrey closed his eyes against the sight before it caused his heart to break.

———

Emmaline sealed herself in the house and leaned against the sturdy door, breathing hard. Had she really just told Geoffrey she unequivocally would not be staying? How had she found the strength?

When she spotted him standing, shirtless, in the dawn's soft light, the taut muscles in his chest had seemed to invite her to press her palms to his uncovered flesh. The feelings that swept over her in those moments had nearly dissolved her into a puddle on the ground. For brief seconds she had forgotten his harsh words, forgotten the pain he had caused, forgotten everything except . . . desire to be held in his arms.

The intense reaction had both frightened and thrilled her.

And convinced her that she did, indeed, love Geoffrey. Why else would she be willing to toss aside her indignation in return for his embrace? She must protect her heart from further pain. She must hold herself aloof from Geoffrey. If she did not, she would never be able to leave him in the spring.

"God, help me . . ." She closed her eyes, her chin trembling. "Help me do what's right."

The brief prayer stilled her racing heart, and she returned to her room to dress for the day. She lifted one of her familiar black dresses from a hook and then paused, holding it at arm's length. How she wished to wear something other than these dreary black dresses. But there was no other choice unless she asked for assistance. With a sigh, she slipped the dress over her head and fastened the buttons.

After fashioning her hair into its familiar knot, she made her way to the kitchen and lit a fire in the stove. As she reached to lift a skillet from the shelf, a light knock sounded on the door. Nervous trepidation trickled through her at the thought of facing Geoffrey again so soon. She drew a deep breath and opened the door, then nearly sagged with relief. Chris stood on the stoop, a sheepish expression on his face.

"Chris . . ." As the name left her lips, discomfort assailed her. She hoped her face didn't reflect the awkwardness she now felt in his presence. It angered her that Geoffrey's unjust accusations could so adversely affect her reaction to this faultless man. "Please, come in."

"I had better wait for Mr. Garrett." He held his hat against his middle with one hand, but he extended the other hand toward her. A square paper packet rested on his open palm. "I found this out in the yard. Is it yours?"

Emmaline stepped forward and took the packet. When she saw what was printed on it, she gasped. "Flower seeds—daisies!

Oh, how bright and cheerful their faces look!" Tears pricked her eyes. "Thank you!"

He tipped his head, pointing with his chin. "I found it lying out alongside the fence. There was a second one, too, but it had broken open and the seeds were gone. I threw it away."

Emmaline clutched the seed packet to her chest. "I shall so enjoy seeing these bloom next spring!" Immediately, her heart fell. She wouldn't be here next spring. . . .

Chris cleared his throat and shuffled in place. "I plan to go into town this morning and check on Jim. I know Jim went to the general store not long ago and brought back supplies, but I thought to check if there was anything you need."

Emmaline fingered her skirt. She had adequate food stores, canning jars, and even a beautiful porcelain figurine for the mantel. And now flower seeds! The only things she truly needed were dresses that buttoned up the front. Preferably in a color other than black. She sucked her lower lip, wondering if she dared ask Chris to choose something for her. But how else would she add to her wardrobe?

"Do you know . . . are there ready-made dresses available in Stetler?"

Chris scratched his head. "There are work trousers and shirts at the dry goods store. I've never had reason to look for dresses"— a grimace twisted his lips—"but if they have other ready-made clothes, it seems possible that they would have dresses, too."

Emmaline started to ask if he would take one of her dresses from the closet with him and try to find something similar in size only with buttons up the front, but she caught a movement from the corner of her eye. Geoffrey, now fully clothed with his shirt buttoned properly to the neck, strode toward them. She clamped her lips shut, and Chris took a step backward, putting at least four feet between them.

Geoffrey's steps slowed as he approached, his shoulders tensing. His gaze flitted sideways, across the ravaged garden, and then returned. The air seemed to crackle with tension when he stopped at the edge of the stoop. "Good morning, Emmaline . . . Chris."

Chris nodded, his eyes downcast.

Emmaline tilted her head in reply.

"I presume . . ." Geoffrey's voice cracked, and he cleared his throat. "I presume you will want to go to town and see Jim this morning."

Chris peered sideways at his boss. "Yes, sir, I would." His respectful words conflicted with the resentful undertone.

Geoffrey stared at Chris for a long moment, his brow puckered. "Would you take Emmaline with you?"

Emmaline's chin jerked upward, her eyes flying wide at this unexpected query.

"I am sure she would like to assure herself that Jim is being well cared for."

His willingness to let her leave the ranch with Chris was surely meant to serve as an apology. But she could not forgive him. She could not risk her heart again. Swallowing the lump of regret that choked her, she said, "I would like to check on Jim, and I would also like to . . . to make a purchase, if I may."

It occurred to her that she had no money. She would not use the dowry money, hidden safely in the barn. If she were to make any purchases, Geoffrey would need to make the payment. But would he?

Geoffrey looked into her face, his expression unreadable, while Chris dug his toe in the dirt and two birds scolded each other from the roof of the springhouse. At last a sigh heaved from his chest, and he raised his head in a single nod. "You may purchase whatever you need and add it to my account."

A thank-you formed on her tongue, but she held it back.

Expressing gratitude would bind her to him once more. As his housekeeper, she deserved something more than room and board. She would accept the dress in lieu of a salary. Turning to Chris, she said, "Would you like to leave immediately, or would you like to eat breakfast first?"

Chris shrugged. "I'm not hungry. And the earlier we leave, the sooner I can return to work." His gaze skipped briefly to Geoffrey. "It isn't easy taking care of everything alone, so I will come back and help."

Geoffrey stepped forward. "Go ahead, Chris. I can handle things for as long as I need to. You take care of your brother—and tell him I . . ." He blew out a breath, shaking his head. "I'm sorry he was hurt."

Chris gave a formal nod. "I'll tell him, Mr. Garrett." He turned to Emmaline. "After I hitch the team, I'll collect you."

"I shall be ready."

# TWENTY-FOUR

⁓

E MMALINE STOOD BEFORE the free-standing oval mirror in the corner of the mercantile and examined her reflection. Although it might be considered prideful to scrutinize oneself, she had a difficult time tearing her gaze away.

She hadn't glimpsed her own reflection in so long. The person peering back at her from the glass seemed a stranger in many ways. Her once-creamy skin now bore a brown tint; her always slender frame had become trimmed and toned, no doubt the result of hard work. The simple hairstyle, coupled with the unadorned dress of yellow cotton scattered with lavender pansies, added years to her appearance. Had she imagined looking so homely after only a few months on the prairie, she might have fought harder to remain in England. But now, she realized, her outward appearance mattered much less than it had in previous years. Meeting her own steady gaze, she saw a maturity, a strength of will, and a confidence that had been sorely lacking when she looked in the mirror before she came to Kansas. Surely those attributes would serve a useful purpose in the future . . . even if that future took her back to England.

"Does the dress fit?" The storekeeper peeked through the curtain that served as a barrier between the main part of the store and the dressing area. Her thin lips pursed as she moved behind Emmaline and tugged at the shoulders and waist of the frock. "It isn't snug-fitting, but that's best for a work dress. You need freedom of movement." Her eyes met Emmaline's in the mirror. "Will this one do?"

Emmaline nodded. "This one, and that." She pointed to a dress of deep green with tiny pink roses, which lay over the arm of a chair. The dresses possessed identical, simple styling with straight sleeves, a smooth bodice with a row of utilitarian white buttons marching from the waist to the rounded neckline, and a full skirt. They would serve nicely as work dresses.

Reaching to unfasten the buttons on the yellow dress, she added, "But I should also like a dress appropriate for Sunday service. Do you have something with a bit of lace, or with a puffed sleeve?"

The woman pressed her finger to her chin for a moment. Then she brightened. "Wait right here." The curtains swished as she dashed between the panels.

Emmaline slipped out of the dress and stood in her cotton chemise and bloomers. The storekeeper returned with a large box in her broomstick arms. She beamed as she set the box on the chair and lifted the lid. "This arrived in a shipment from the East. I considered sending it back—most of the women here prefer simpler styles—but it was so pretty . . . I hoped the right buyer might come along."

She pushed aside tissue paper and removed a gown of deep brown bearing half-dollar-sized flowers the color of a mushroom. Each flower petal was edged with gold, giving the dress elegance. Emmaline gasped at the sight of it.

Giving the dress a shake by the shoulders, the shopkeeper held it toward Emmaline. "It *is* lovely, isn't it?"

"Oh my, yes . . ." Emmaline fingered one sleeve as she took

in the delicate creamy lace at the neckline and wrists, and the ruffled skirt. How often she had bemoaned the dismal brown of the landscape—brown dirt, brown grass, brown buildings—and longed for color. Yet, this gown made the color seem refined rather than austere.

The woman flipped the dress around. "It is actually a skirt and blouse, but the waistband of the skirt buttons to the underside of the blouse, giving it the appearance of one piece as well as an hourglass shape." Another quick flip showed the back. "And the blouse has an attached bustle. With the double row of ruffles at the bottom of the skirt, this dress is meant to garner attention." Smiling, she asked, "Would you like to try it on?"

"Oh yes!" To Emmaline's delight, the blouse, which hung several inches below the hips, buttoned from the high, lace-graced neckline to the waist in the front, making it possible for her to dress herself with ease. When she fastened the last carved wooden button, she clasped her hands beneath her chin and beamed at her reflection.

The shopkeeper nodded, her eyes wide. "Why, it seems to have been tailored for you! You *must* have this dress, Miss Bradford."

Emmaline completely approved of the idea. "What is the price?"

The amount made Emmaline cringe. In England, she would have given no thought to spending such an extravagant sum on a single gown. But somehow, in Kansas, it seemed foolhardy. She bit her lower lip, vacillating. What would Geoffrey say?

The shopkeeper folded her arms over her chest and raised one eyebrow. "I may regret this, but I shall sell the dress to you at my cost. As I said, I considered sending it back, and that would cost me shipping expenses. If I let you have it at my cost, at least I haven't lost any money."

Emmaline gaped in amazement. "Are you quite sure?"

A soft smile formed on the older woman's face. "I am very sure, my dear. As I said, it's as if it were made for you. And with a new hat—I have the perfect felt sailor hat in deep brown with a cream-colored ribbon around the crown—you'll be the talk of the town!"

Emmaline was not sure she wanted to be the talk of the town. Besides, a hat was not a necessity. Dresses were. Pushing aside the desire to complete the outfit with the felt sailor hat, she said, "I shall take the dress, but I will make do with my straw bonnet. Thank you."

The woman's face fell for a moment, but then she shrugged. "Very well. If you change your mind, and the hat sells to someone else, I can always order another. I'll leave you to change."

"I believe," Emmaline said with a grin twitching her cheeks, "I shall remain in this garment." She wrinkled her nose as she looked at the discarded black dress. "I have no desire to wear that again."

The woman laughed and picked up the two work dresses. "I will put the total on Mr. Garrett's account."

"Thank you."

When Emmaline stepped out from behind the curtain, her gaze drifted around the store. A row of books on one shelf captured her attention. Although an avid reader at home, she'd had little time to read since arriving in Kansas. But with winter coming, perhaps she would have more free time. Curious as to what books were available, she crossed to the shelf. A surprisingly intriguing assortment awaited purchase.

She ran her finger along the spines, reading the titles. *The Earthly Paradise* by William Morris; Jules Verne's *Twenty Thousand Leagues Under the Sea*; several of Dickens' works; *The Holy Bible* . . . Her heart gave a leap. As a child, she'd had a Bible she carried to chapel, but she'd left it back in England. Slipping the Bible from the shelf, she laid it in her palms. It fell open where a slim red ribbon served as a bookmark. She read, "The Lord is my shepherd; I shall not want . . ."

How appropriate the words were, considering she lived on a sheep ranch. Hurrying to the counter, she handed the Bible to the saleswoman. "Please add this to Mr. Garrett's tab, as well."

Emmaline left the store with a sizable box under her arm and a bounce in her step. Chris had indicated he would remain at the doctor's office until she had completed her shopping, so she crossed the street to the square, two-story building that housed the doctor's office and his living quarters.

When she entered, she found Chris sitting on a short bench in the waiting room. His elbows rested on his knees, and his head hung low. At the click of the door latch, he looked up, and immediately he bolted to his feet.

"Miss Emmaline!" He rose, snatching his hat from his head. "You . . . you found a new dress."

Emmaline didn't need to ask to know that Chris found the new frock fetching. She touched the lacy collar with her fingertips and released a self-conscious laugh. "Yes. Actually, I found *three*. Geoffrey may not allow me to go to town untended again."

Chris chuckled but then sobered. "I have been watching for you. Jim asked for you."

She stepped forward and dropped the box on the bench. "Where is he?"

"Upstairs, in the doc's back bedroom. I'll show you." He waved to indicate the direction, then he followed her up an enclosed staircase that opened into a hallway. "The second room on the right."

A heavy, medicinal smell hung in the air when Emmaline entered Jim's room, and she battled the desire to cover her nose. She crossed to the tall, narrow bed where Jim lay uncovered.

His bare, hairy legs and feet stuck out from beneath the hem of a cotton nightshirt. The swelling from the bite had not dissipated. His left foot was twice its normal size, the skin raw and blistered. Repulsed by the sight, she turned quickly away and touched his cheek. "Jim?"

His dry lips parted, and his eyes opened. A lopsided grin climbed one cheek when he saw her. "Miss Emmaline . . . you came."

The rasped, simple sentence was so different from his normal exuberance. She could scarcely believe she'd once found his incessant chatter tiresome. From now on, she would cheerfully listen to every lengthy discourse. "Of course I came," she replied. "How are you?"

He grimaced, his eyes scrunching shut. "Hurt . . . all over."

Emmaline scowled at Chris. "Is that normal? Should the pain not be limited to the extremity that was bitten?"

Chris shook his head. "The poison gets into the blood, and that's what has made him sick."

"Can the doctor not remedy this?" Jim's suffering brought tears to her eyes. She stroked his hot, dry cheek. "There must be something more that can be done. . . ."

Jim caught Emmaline's wrist with a weak grip. "Miss Emmaline . . . the figurine—is it still on the mantel?"

Leaning down, Emmaline pressed her cheek briefly to his. "Of course it is. That is why you bought it, did you not? So it is there—and it looks beautiful."

"So you like it?"

"I treasure it."

"Then . . . that means you like me?"

Tears flooded her eyes. Emmaline cupped her hand over his. "Yes, I like you, Jim. Very much."

"So . . . will you be . . . my girl?"

She sent Chris a startled look. Chris raised his shoulders in a helpless shrug. Turning back to Jim, she sought words that would be forthright but sensitive. "I . . . I think you should concentrate on getting well. Let us save that topic for another day."

"No-ooo." His fingers clutched her wrist. "Tell me, Miss Emmaline. I . . . I have money. I can buy you . . . figurines . . . and more fancy dresses." His fever-brightened eyes widened. "You look . . . so pretty. I knew you would . . ."

Gently, Emmaline peeled his fingers from her wrist and placed his hand on the mattress. "You must rest, Jim."

The boy thrashed in agitation for a few moments, mumbling, but then, to Emmaline's relief, he lapsed into sleep. She gazed down at his inert form, regret bowing her shoulders. How long had Jim viewed her as a potential sweetheart? Maybe she should have heeded Geoffrey's warnings and not spent so much time with Jim.

With a sigh, she turned to Chris. "I . . . I did not know what to say to him."

Chris offered a sad smile. "Lying to him won't do him any good." He crossed to the bed and gazed down at Jim, sympathy in his eyes. "Poor bloke—he's so smitten he can't see you only have eyes for Mr. Garrett."

Emmaline drew back, her fingers flying to her neck. She could feel her pulse beneath her fingertips. "I . . . I . . ."

"You don't need to deny it for Jim's sake, Miss Emmaline." Chris tugged a blanket up over his brother's frame. "Everything you've done at the ranch? I can't think of another fine lady from England who would have been willing to take over the tasks you have." Facing her, he crossed his arms over his chest. "Mr. Garrett said you were different. Special. Worth waiting for. And he was right." He lowered his head and chuckled as if remembering a private joke. "I have to admit, had it been me separated from my intended for five years, I would have moved on to someone else. Most every man I know would have moved on. And it isn't as though a few ladies from town didn't encourage him to."

Fixing his gaze on Emmaline, he finished softly. "But I guess you aren't the only one who is different. Mr. Garrett is different, too. He held on to you—he is still holding on."

From downstairs, a clock chimed, its resounding bong counting out the hour. Chris scowled. "It's late. We need to get back to the ranch."

Emmaline followed him out the door, but her mind was on the words he'd just spoken.

# TWENTY-FIVE

⁓

A S SOON AS Chris helped Emmaline down from the wagon, she headed to her sleeping room and changed out of the fancy brown dress into the yellow work dress. The eleven o'clock hour had passed, and the men would be in soon for lunch. Given the time constraints, she chose to fry slices of salt pork and open some canned beans. If she also baked a pan of corn bread, the men would have enough to fill their stomachs.

As she set the plates at three chairs, she thought about the pleasant picnics she had shared with Jim and Chris on the porch. Maybe she should carry the dishes outside . . . but no, it wouldn't be the same without Jim's chatter. Besides, picnicking had been Jim's idea; picnicking without him seemed cruel in a way she couldn't define.

A scuffling sound at the door let her know the men had arrived for lunch. Lifting the skillet from the stove, she glanced toward the doorway. "I prepared a simple lunch, but—"

Geoffrey entered the kitchen. Alone.

Her lips trembled. "W-where is Chris?"

"I asked Chris to stay with the sheep while I ate. I do not like leaving them in the far pasture untended. When I go back, he can come in."

"Oh. Well . . ." With shaking hands, she set the skillet in the center of the table and reached for the bean pot. If only Chris were here, too! Why did Geoffrey's presence make her want to flee? The next months would be agony if she could not set aside the self-conscious prickles that assaulted her whenever he was around. "J-just sit down," she told him. "I . . . I neglected to get butter from the springhouse. I shall be right back."

Lifting her skirts, she walked toward the door. But Geoffrey didn't step aside, and she came to an abrupt halt. She stared at the top button of his shirt and waited for him to move. His Adam's apple bobbed in a swallow, shifting the button slightly.

"I like your dress."

She fussed with the skirt. "Th-thank you."

"I am glad to see you have recovered from the loss of your uncle."

What did he mean by that? Had he thought she was wearing the black dresses as a sign of mourning? Truthfully, after the initial shock of Uncle Hedrick's unexpected passing, she hadn't thought much about her great-uncle. They had never been close.

Geoffrey's approving gaze swept from her neckline to her toes and back again. "Your mother understood the necessity for simple attire on the plains. It is an excellent choice."

She had more than one misconception to clarify. Pressing her hands to her stomach, she said, "Mother did not send this dress. I bought it today in the Stetler mercantile."

Geoffrey's brows dipped slightly.

"Actually, I bought three. Two work dresses and one for Sunday. I . . . I needed them." But how to explain why they were needed when he had seen her trunk full of frocks? "I also bought a Bible.

I hope you find that satisfactory." Heat seared her face while she awaited his response.

"If you wanted to read the Bible, you could have borrowed mine."

Was he upset with her for making the purchase or was he merely offering to share with her? She could not tell by his tone or expression. "If I take yours, you will not have one to read. I believe it is better to have my own. But if you feel it is an unnecessary expense, you may return it."

Instead of replying, he slipped his fingers into his shirt pocket. When he withdrew his hand, he held a wilted lavender bloom. "I found this in the pasture. It matches the flowers on your dress."

Tears sprang into Emmaline's eyes. Blinking rapidly, she pointed to the counter. "P-please lay it there. I must get the butter." She dashed past him before he could speak another word.

In the springhouse, she pressed her palms to her hot cheeks and closed her eyes. A fervent prayer rose from the depths of her soul. *Not now. Please don't let him give me flowers now. Not when I'm determined to leave in the spring!*

But it was too late. The image of that sweet little bloom, cradled in the palm of his hand, was permanently etched in her mind.

———

Geoffrey walked amongst the sheep, having sent Chris to the house for lunch, but Emmaline filled his thoughts. If he'd previously managed to squelch any of his feelings for her, they'd been immediately reignited by her appearance in that pretty yellow dress—the color of sunshine.

The contented bleats uttered by the sheep at rest, normally soothing no matter what troubled his mind, did little to settle his rambling thoughts. Her mention of needing her own Bible so she wouldn't take his had provoked an odd feeling. Emptiness, maybe it was. When had he last opened his Bible and sought peace and guidance from God's Word? In most of his years building this ranch, he had rarely gone more than a day without reading Scripture. Sometimes it was only a verse or two, but reading the Bible had been as much a part of his day as eating, sleeping, working. . . . But the habit had slipped away. And he didn't know why.

Straightening from rubbing the nubby head of a young ewe, he looked past the sheep to the barren landscape. As summer gave way to fall, he saw little change on the prairie. Their hot, dry summer had given the land the brown, brittle appearance of late autumn long before the calendar indicated it was so. The devastation of the grasshoppers, which had robbed the trees of their green leaves, had brought the appearance of winter. It was enough to make a man feel hopeless.

"When are you going to send rain, Lord?" he asked the sky. There was a recalcitrance in his tone, but he decided to be honest with God and not apologize. Rain had been too long denied; prayers had gone unheeded. Perhaps that was part of the reason he had separated himself from God over the past months. God, apparently, had turned a blind eye to Geoffrey Garrett, and maybe even all of Kansas. The desolate vista proved it.

Once more, the image of Emmaline danced in front of his eyes. Why had her arrival created such a sense of loss rather than fulfillment? So many hopes had rested upon her coming to him—hopes that remained unfulfilled.

"Mr. Garrett?"

Geoffrey jumped at the sound of Chris's quiet voice. He hadn't even heard the approach of the horse.

"I finished lunch. I'll take the flock to water if you need to do something else."

Biting his bottom lip, Geoffrey considered his waiting tasks. The most pressing was balancing his account book after his trip to purchase feed. One thing he'd learned from his father was the importance of keeping accurate financial records. But how often had Franklin Garrett juggled the figures to cover up the vast sums lost in unscrupulous habits such as the consumption of his company's product?

Pushing thoughts of his father aside, he turned his focus to Chris. "I do have some paperwork requiring attention." He moved slowly between the resting sheep, careful not to disturb them with sudden movements. When he reached his horse, he paused. "Chris, did the doctor give you any indication when Jim might be released from his care?"

Chris's suntanned face pinched into a worried scowl. "He didn't know. He said he would send a messenger if Jim took a turn for the worse. I just hoped . . . well . . ." He rubbed a finger under his nose. "I hoped I might drive in every day and check on him."

Although this meant leaving the ranch short-handed, Geoffrey would not deny Chris the privilege of time with his ailing brother. "Of course. You may go each morning for as long as it is needed." Then something else occurred to him. "Tomorrow when you go, have the telegrapher send a message to Moreland inquiring about the feed I purchased. It will arrive by train, and I will need to arrange transport from the station to the ranch. When you send the message, instruct the railroad workers to cover the bales with a tarp or canvas to keep them somewhat protected from insects and wind."

"Very well."

Geoffrey rode to the bunkhouse and settled at the desk in the corner by the window. He opened his ledger and carefully penned the amount spent on food, train fare for himself and his horse, and the bales of hay. After balancing the figures, he glared at the amount at the bottom of the column.

Paying for Emmaline's first-class accommodations on the S.S. *Wyoming* and ensuring she would have maid service had taken a sizable portion of his ready cash. He couldn't imagine why she'd needed new dresses, unless the ones in the trunk were inappropriate for work. The three dresses and the Bible she added to his account at the mercantile this morning had unquestionably increased his debt.

There had been too many unexpected purchases of late: Jim's doctor bills, the hay and the travel expenses, Emmaline's dresses . . . And if he had to buy food to compensate for the grasshopper-damaged garden—not to mention the wasted food from Emmaline's early cooking disasters—there might not be enough money to carry them through to the next sale of wool and lambs.

When he had come to America, he had made a promise to himself not to accumulate debt. Debt was his father's downfall—debt brought on by gambling and drinking, two things Geoffrey Garrett would *never* do. But looking at that paltry amount of dollars and cents printed in his neat penmanship, he wondered if he would be able to keep his promise to avoid debt.

Closing his eyes, he pressed his thumbs to his eye sockets. Stars exploded behind his lids, but they couldn't erase the image of the amount at the bottom of the ledger page. Releasing a grumble, he slammed the leather-bound book closed.

But then he remembered something. He had access to a substantial sum of money: Emmaline's dowry. He had vowed not to ask her for the money until they were legally wed, but no one would think ill of him if he used it now. Even if she broke their betrothal and returned to England, ethically the money would be his compensation. A big part of him resisted touching it, but if it came down to keeping the ranch going or being forced off his land, he would use it. But there could be no more "unexpected expenses."

He rose from the desk and headed outside. By now the sheep were enjoying their afternoon drink, and soon Chris would bring them in for the evening. At supper, he would visit with Emmaline and Chris about the importance of frugality. And maybe he or Chris could take a hunting trip. A deer—or even better, a bear, although sightings were rare—would stretch their food sources.

Ordinarily he kept several lambs after butchering, but that wouldn't be an option this year. With fewer ewes, he would have fewer lambs. That meant less money coming from the sale of meat. His stomach twisted with worry.

Tapping his fingers against his thigh, he decided it would be wise to take an inventory of their current food stores. He crossed the yard with a wide stride and went directly to the cellar. As he made his way down the stairs, the cooler air washed over him and sent a welcome shiver down his spine. He reached the bottom and stood still, inhaling deeply. The familiar odors of earth, vegetables, and smoked meats were pleasing.

When his eyes adjusted to the dim underground interior, he moved to the bushel baskets lining the west wall. Three were brimful of dirt-encrusted potatoes; two more overflowed with turnips and beets. A peek in the raisin basket showed last year's supply was nearly depleted, but he found a basket of some sort of wrinkled, dried fruit sitting nearby on top of an overturned crate. He plucked out a piece and bit off a little. Apple? It carried a bit of a tang, yet the flavor wasn't unpleasant. He put the remainder of the piece in his mouth. Where had they gotten dried apples?

He turned, still chewing, and his jaw dropped at the sight waiting on shelves built into the opposite wall. Dozens of jars bearing beans, peas, carrots, and tomatoes sat in neat, organized rows. He lifted one jar of sliced carrots and bounced it in his palm. There was more here than he'd expected. Perhaps he needn't worry about winter food, after all.

Suddenly his heart began to pound. He spun around, once more taking in the abundance spilling out of baskets and filling the shelves. All of this food—it must have been purchased. How else could their cellar be so well stocked? What kind of debt must he owe by now?

He charged out of the cellar. He needed to speak with Chris and Emmaline immediately.

# TWENTY-SIX

E MMALINE STEPPED ONTO the stoop outside the kitchen door and braced to toss the pan of murky wash water across the dry yard. But when she saw Geoffrey emerge from the cellar, she balanced the pan against her hip and waited for him to approach.

"Where did you purchase those vegetables in the cellar?"

The harsh note in Geoffrey's voice made her take a step backward. Without waiting for an answer, he railed, "You can't spend money like this, Emmaline. We have to stretch every penny. I realize this morning I gave you permission to purchase whatever you needed, but I must retract that statement. If you believe you have need of something—food, clothing, books—come and ask me for approval before you buy it."

What had happened to the man who, earlier that day, had tried to slip a little purple flower into her hand? Once more she faced a demanding, impatient stranger. Angry, defensive words formed on her tongue. But before the words spewed forth, snatches of a conversation she'd had with Tildy flitted through her mind: "*We was committed to each othuh. . . .Over time, that man become my whole world. That kind o' feelin' don't come on right away, Miss Emmalion, but it do come on when you look to the good Lawd to help you honor a commitment.*"

Emmaline had committed to staying and serving as Geoffrey's housekeeper until spring. *Help me honor my commitment, Lord, and help me not harbor anger with Geoffrey.*

Squaring her shoulders, she met Geoffrey's stormy gaze. "Very well, Geoffrey. If you deem it necessary to return the Bible"—her heart twisted with desire to keep it, but she could always ask to borrow Geoffrey's—"then I shall accept your decision. However, I do need the dresses. All of my dresses from England, with the exception of the black travel dresses, were designed with the idea of a maid offering assistance in dressing."

"Oh." The simple statement, coupled with the bob of his Adam's apple, spoke volumes.

She drew in a deep breath, striving to keep an even, unruffled tone. "As for the vegetables in the cellar, they are the fruit of our own garden. The grasshoppers were unable to destroy what was already in the springhouse or what was under the ground. While you were away, I learned how to preserve them for the winter."

He stared at her, his left eyebrow arching high.

"So there was no expense in accumulating the vegetables. I did, however, ask Jim to purchase the jars from the mercantile."

Clearing his throat, Geoffrey briefly ducked his head. "I . . . I just assumed . . . I'm sorry."

Emmaline nearly gasped. Had he truly apologized to her?

His forehead wrinkled, but it was more in puzzlement than frustration. "You have learned a great deal, Emmaline."

She nodded, but she wondered how he'd react if she told him the most important thing she had learned: to lean on God's strength rather than on her own.

Suddenly a gust of wind whisked around the house, lifting Geoffrey's hair and twisting Emmaline's apron into a knot. They both looked skyward. In the north, the expanse of blue wore a billowing puff of white. Their gazes collided.

"Clouds," Emmaline said.

Geoffrey's eyes lit with hope. "Perhaps rain is finally on its way."

"That would be good news."

Another gust, stronger and cooler than the one before, pulled the pan from Emmaline's hands. It clattered against the ground, spewing water on her skirt and Geoffrey's pant legs. She clapped her hands to her cheeks. "Oh! I am so sorry!"

Geoffrey picked up the pan and handed it to her. "No harm done." His lips quirked into a boyish smile. "But you might want to collect whatever supper items you need and close the kitchen door behind you." He sniffed the air. "I smell moisture."

Emmaline effortlessly returned his smile. "Then our prayers are going to be answered?"

"I hope so." Turning, he jogged toward the barn.

———

Geoffrey pulled the blanket across his legs and lay back on the straw mattress, his ears keenly attuned to the sounds outside the sturdy rock walls of the bunkhouse.

The wind howled and thunder rumbled. All afternoon, he had watched clouds build in the north. When he saw a flash of lightning illuminate the giant puffballs, he tipped his head in anticipation of the first roll of thunder. Not until the fourth or fifth bright flash had the sound finally reached him.

But now it growled repeatedly, following on the heels of jagged bursts of light. Those rumbling clouds would surely bring needed moisture. If the wind didn't blow them away . . .

He hoped Chris was already safe at the doctor's residence. After supper, Geoffrey had sent Chris to town to spend time with Jim. By the looks of the sky and the restless behavior of the sheep, the rain would hit during the early-morning hours.

Now, at not quite eight o'clock, full dark provided a vivid backdrop for the flashes of lightning that shot from the heavy clouds. "Rain, Lord," he murmured. "Send the rain." Another rumble of thunder rattled the windows of the bunkhouse.

Geoffrey had left the horses in their harnesses with the reins attached. With the strange sounds and the lightning, they would spook easily. But their reins, tied securely to the stall rails, would keep them from dashing out into the night even if they were frightened. He hoped Emmaline wasn't frightened. Over supper when the thunder rolled, she had merely smiled and commented on how it sounded like home. Thunderstorms were not unusual in England, but she had not yet experienced a storm on the plains. And she was all alone in the house.

He scowled as he remembered her response when he'd asked if she would like him to stay with her. "No, thank you," she had said with a demure tilt of her head. "I shall be quite fine, and I am hardly *alone*."

He wished now he had questioned her about what she meant, but she had begun dishing dessert—a beautifully baked brown sugar pie, fresh from the oven—and his attention had shifted. Now, replaying her reply, he wondered again at the confidence she'd expressed.

A resounding *crack!* brought him to his feet. He stubbed his toe on a loose floorboard while rushing to the window. Standing on one foot, he rubbed his throbbing toe and peered out into the shadows. The wind had picked up, and blowing dust obscured even the stars. He could see nothing.

Geoffrey shivered as thunder crashed again. The lightning must be close for it to rattle the walls. His heart pounded. If he were this affected by the storm, surely Emmaline must be nervous, as well. Despite her claim that she would be all right, he would not be able to rest unless he checked on her. He sat down and tugged on his boots.

He would check the sheep, too, and draw the gates across the broad openings at either end of the barn. If the storm frightened them too badly, they might try to leave the protection of the barn, and he couldn't tether them the way he had the horses. Keeping them safely inside the structure was imperative—he couldn't afford to lose another head.

Slipping his arms into a sturdy twill jacket, he looked out the window and shivered again. Did he really want to venture out? Another *boom!* propelled him to action. He must see to his flock— and to Emmaline.

----

Emmaline placed another piece of wood in the stove. The sudden drop in temperature both thrilled and troubled her. Surely it indicated the coming of rain, but the abrupt change from hot to cold left her somewhat unsettled. Not since her arrival in Kansas had she used the stove as a source of heat. Yet the chill in the air penetrated the walls. If the wind would stop blowing, perhaps it wouldn't seem as cold.

Over her months in Kansas, she believed she had grown accustomed to the wind. But tonight it howled more loudly than it ever had before, making the windowpanes shake. When combined with the resounding crash of thunder, nature's cacophony was nearly deafening.

Sitting back down at the table, she pulled the lamp closer to the Bible. Geoffrey hadn't declared an intent to return the book to the mercantile, so she felt safe in opening it and reading a few passages. The attached red satin ribbon divided the book at the Twenty-third Psalm, so she began reading at that spot.

She especially liked the beginning of verse three: "He restoreth my soul. . . ." Closing her eyes, she let the words fill her. For a moment, the raging winds and powerful crashes of thunder seemed to slip away as a feeling of peace washed over her.

Even though she missed her mother, missed England, and missed Tildy, she still experienced contentedness that defied explanation. Somehow, God had restored her soul, and although she felt distant from Geoffrey and all of the other people she loved, she was still . . . whole.

She drew in a satisfied breath, and the smell of smoke at the back of her throat made her cough. Turning toward the stove, she frowned. Had she not set the damper to allow the smoke to escape? A quick perusal assured her the damper was open. From where was the smoke smell coming?

*Bang-bang-bang-bang-bang!* She jerked as someone pounded hard on the front door. Her hip slammed against the table, and the lamp tilted. Emmaline quickly grabbed the lamp to keep it from falling. With one hand wrapped firmly around the lamp's stem, she hurried to the front door. A shadowy figure stood outside, and she recognized Geoffrey. She swung the door wide. The smell of smoke was even stronger outside.

"Emmaline! Lightning struck the horse barn! I need your help—come!"

Without hesitation, she placed the lamp on the table near the door. His hand captured hers, and together they ran across the dark yard. Wind tore at her hair, pulling the pins loose. Her skirt tried to wrap around her legs, and she yanked free of Geoffrey's grasp to lift it above her knees.

The distressed neigh of horses carried over the howl of the wind, chilling Emmaline even more than the fierce wind. Ahead, a glow lit the night sky, and smoke coiled like a wild, dancing snake.

They reached the barn, and Geoffrey pointed. "There are buckets in the lean-to. Fill them at the Solomon. I've got to get the horses."

Emmaline grasped his arm with both hands. "You can't go in there!" Flames licked along the eaves of the wooden roof. "The roof could fall on you!"

"I cannot let them burn to death!" Geoffrey broke free of her grasp and ran directly into the barn.

Emmaline stood for one moment in silent horror, but then she leapt into action. She retrieved two buckets from the lean-to, the heat from the barn scorching her skin. Stumbling—blinded by smoke, dust, and her wind-tossed hair—she made her way to the edge of the river and filled the buckets. One horse raced by her, his dangling reins slapping her hard on the side of the face and nearly sending her headfirst into the water.

She regained her footing and lifted the buckets. Her cheek stung, but she ignored the pain. *I must help Geoffrey! God, help me help Geoffrey!* Slopping water as she ran, she returned to the barn and flung the water from one bucket as high as she could. The wind caught most of it and blew it back on her.

Sputtering, she reached for the second bucket. Suddenly Geoffrey was at her side. He slapped the flanks of a wild-eyed horse. "Yah! Get out of there!" It pounded away. He held his arms outward. "Throw the water on me!"

"W-what?"

"Throw it on me!"

Emmaline lifted the bucket and tossed its contents on Geoffrey. Behind him, flames rose into the air. The crackling roar of the fire added to the awful sounds of the storm. He wiped his face and turned back toward the barn.

"Geoffrey! No!"

But he ignored her cry and dashed into the barn. Although she knew she should be retrieving water, her feet refused to move. She stood transfixed, her watering eyes pinned to the wide opening of the barn. With her hands clenched beneath her chin, she counted the seconds and waited for Geoffrey's return.

Two horses ran out, their necks arched and their eyes rolling with terror. One came straight at her, and she ducked aside as it raced past. She stared at the barn. Geoffrey . . . where was Geoffrey?

Then she saw him, hunched forward, his face buried in his elbow. With his other hand, he pulled at the reins of Jim's horse. The frightened horse fought, yanking its head against the reins and neighing horribly. When Geoffrey nearly fell, Emmaline ran forward and grabbed the reins, too. Together they managed to pull the horse to safety. But it continued to scream, shaking its head wildly and pawing the ground.

"Keep it here," Geoffrey demanded, releasing the trailing reins into her hands. "I've got to get the wagon." He turned again toward the barn.

Emmaline dropped the reins and the horse dashed away. She wrapped her arms around Geoffrey's waist from behind. "No! Let it burn!"

"I cannot replace it!" He tried to tear loose of her grip, but she held tight.

"I cannot replace *you*! Please, Geoffrey!"

"Emmaline, let go!"

"No!"

At that moment a roar filled the air, followed by an explosion of flames. He spun and ducked, enclosing her in his embrace as he did so. Smoke billowed, making both of them cough horribly.

Still bent forward, they scuttled toward the Solomon and splashed directly into the water.

Huddled in each other's arms, they watched the barn's roof collapse and sparks fill the air. Tears rolled down Emmaline's face only to be washed away by a sudden downpour. The clouds opened up, and huge drops descended, as hard as pebbles. Rain hammered the barn, extinguishing the flames, but it had come too late. She clung to Geoffrey, her cheek against his chest, his arms trembling on her back.

"Why?" he groaned into her tangled hair. "Why did God hold the rain so long?"

She tightened her grip, burying her face against his shirt front. She had no answer.

# TWENTY-SEVEN

*⁓*

JIM STOOD AT the window of the doc's office and looked out over the street. The crutches bit into his armpits, but he let them hold his weight anyway. His legs—even his good one—felt shaky after five days in bed. But Doc had said he could get up and move around. No matter how weak his body, he wanted to look outside.

There had been times since the afternoon Chris delivered him to the doctor's care when he wondered if he'd ever glimpse the Kansas landscape again—or if his next view would be the streets of gold the preacher talked about. His last day at the ranch, the yellow sun had glowed in a sky as clear and blue as the ocean. But while he lay on the bed, battling the effects of the snake's venom, the sky had clouded, and rain had pounded the roof.

The rain of the past three days was now gone, but evidence of the downpour remained. The sky looked pale gray, like a shirt washed too many times in the cloudy river. Even the sun was faded to half its normal glow. Mud splashed midway up the sides of Stetler's buildings, and the dirt streets were shiny and slick looking. Two wagons, minus their horses, sat axle-deep in muck in the middle of Main Street.

Men draped in rain slickers and women holding their skirts above their ankles high-stepped through the mud on their way to Sunday service, the usual smiles and friendly chatter absent. But in contrast to the somber people, two birds with speckled yellow bellies sat side by side and sang a tune on a windowsill across the street.

The birds' cheerful chirping reminded Jim of singing hymns at the Stetler church. Was Emmaline there now? Or had Mr. Garrett decided the roads were too muddy to travel? He pressed his forehead against the closed window, straining to see down the block to the churchyard. If she was there, would she stop by the doctor's office and visit him before returning to the ranch?

The ache in his armpits became a stabbing pain, so with a grunt of frustration, he turned and stumped his way back to the bed. He dropped the wooden crutches on the floor with a clatter and flopped backward, resting his head on the pillow.

Staring at the ceiling, he let his mind click through memories: riding the range on Horace's broad back; listening to Chris snore at night; seeing Miss Emmaline's smile from across the picnic quilt. He hungered for a slice of Emmaline's apple pie and the smell of the sheep barn and even the lingering tang of Chris's pipe smoke. He'd tasted death and now little things seemed to have an importance they'd never carried before. From now on he would appreciate the pleasures his life in America afforded.

He would also pay attention when walking through the pastures. . . .

A light tap on the door sent him scrambling to throw the sheet over his legs. When he was covered, he called, "Come in."

The door squeaked open, and the doc's daughter, Alice, came in. She carried a tray containing a tin plate of fluffy scrambled eggs and biscuits and a tall glass of frothy milk.

Jim licked his lips and sat up. "Mmm, breakfast. It looks good."

Her rosy cheeks curved with a smile. "Ma put extra salt and pepper on your eggs, just like you like 'em." When she leaned forward to place the tray in his lap, her long braids swung forward and grazed the edge of the mattress. She grabbed the braids and threw them over her shoulders as she straightened. "Ma says when you're done, put the tray on the bedside table—she'll fetch it after church."

Jim picked up the fork and stabbed the eggs. "You going to service?" Maybe he could ask her to tell Emmaline to come by.

She nodded, her eyes bright. "Mm-hmm. Soon as Ma gets the twins dressed." Her shoulders shook as she giggled. "When I came up, she was chasing 'em around the kitchen table."

Jim grinned, imagining the doctor's portly wife puffing behind the energetic three-year-olds.

"But I'm dressed and ready." Alice smoothed her fingers over the collar of her brown calico dress.

Alice's dress reminded him of the one Emmaline had worn when she came to see him. The fever made the memory fuzzy, but he recalled a lacy-necked dress strewn with flowers. The worry in her eyes had let him know she cared. Cared a lot.

Suddenly Alice's face flooded with pink. "I better go help Mama with the twins. I'll see you after service, Jim." She dashed out of the room, slamming the door behind her.

Jim set the tray aside and huffed in aggravation. She'd taken off before he could ask her to deliver the message to Emmaline. He wished he could jump off the bed, get dressed, and go to the chapel, too. He sighed. He shouldn't complain—Chris and the doctor had repeatedly told him he was lucky to be alive—but he was so tired of being stuck in this room.

Tossing the covers off his legs, he lifted his foot and glared at the ugly wound. The skin around the bite had died and peeled away, leaving a gaping sore. Even if he went home tomorrow, it would be at least another week before he could wear a boot—and how would he navigate that mucky ground on crutches?

He flopped back on the bed and tossed his right forearm over his eyes. When he returned to the ranch, he might end up holed up in another room, in another bed. Of course, it would be *his* room and *his* bed. He smiled. And maybe Miss Emmaline would visit him a lot if he were only a few yards away. . . .

A thought struck him, and he sat bolt upright. All that rain and mud and washed-away dirt—had the gravesite survived the onslaught? Was his money box still buried safely at Pup's grave? Could the rain have penetrated the box and ruined the paper money inside?

He had to go home. He had to go home now!

———

Emmaline closed the Bible and lowered her head. Geoffrey had refused to take her to the little chapel in Stetler this morning, because, as he'd said, they had no wagon, it wouldn't be fitting for a lady to ride in on horseback, and the road was too muddy for travel. She suspected, however, that even if the roads had been dry and they still had the wagon, he would have made an excuse.

Folding her hands on top of the leather cover, she turned to God in prayer. She began with gratitude for the return of all the horses, though Horace was badly burned. Then she laid her many concerns before God: Geoffrey's worries; Jim's health; Tildy and Ronald's needs, whatever they might be; her family in England; even the poor cooped-up sheep.

She reveled in the feeling of peace that came over her as she prayed. How had she gone so many years without realizing what she needed to feel complete? She had sought fulfillment through gardening, by being a respectful and obedient daughter to her parents, and then by learning the skills necessary to survive on this ranch. But those activities—although good and proper—had never brought her true joy.

Having God in her life brought an element of joy to each and every day, despite the difficulties she faced. If asked to explain how her soul could be at peace in the midst of these trials, she could never put it into words, yet it was true. What a gift Tildy had given her when she shared the truth of God's love! She offered one last expression of gratitude for Tildy's friendship and for the strength God had given her before whispering, "Amen."

Opening her eyes, she rose and moved to the window. Her heart ached for the devastated land, but mostly it ached for Geoffrey. Over the past few days, she had watched bitter resentment take control of him. The eager bounce in his step as he headed for the sheep barn or the pasture no longer existed, nor did happiness light his eyes. The difficulties of the past weeks were, apparently, more than he could bear.

She had tried to encourage him at the dinner table last night by reading her favorite Scripture from Psalm Twenty-three, but he'd chastised her with harsh words: *"My soul will be restored only when this ranch is restored,"* he'd said. Pacing beside the table, he had run his hand through his hair and scowled fiercely. *"All of my years of hard work, of being an honest businessman, of avoiding the evils of drunken, raucous living . . . and how does God reward me for my efforts? He sends a plague of grasshoppers, withholds blessed moisture, and then tries to wash the land away! Do not speak to me of some Good Shepherd, Emmaline. My father was right: God is a fabrication."*

She'd jumped to her feet, eager to provide words of solace, but the firm upthrust of his palm stilled her words. The tense set of his shoulders and the anger on his face had filled her with a feeling of helplessness. If only Tildy were here, she could make Geoffrey see the truth. . . .

"Help Geoffrey, Lord," Emmaline whispered. "Let him find his way back to You." She experienced blessed release when she handed her troubles over to Him.

She prepared a simple lunch of cold meat and cheese, bread, and leftover vegetable stew. As she stirred the stew, she considered the stores in the cellar. If only she had dug up the last of the carrots and sweet potatoes before the rains hit. Those vegetables were probably now rotting in the sodden ground. Maybe this afternoon she would put on one of the black dresses—it wouldn't matter if she ruined it—and try to salvage the remainder of the garden produce.

Close to noon, both Chris and Geoffrey knocked on the kitchen door. Before coming into the room, they removed their mud-encrusted boots. She hid a smile at the sight of Chris's big toe peeking from his sock. Pointing to it, she said, "I have some darning of my own to do. Would you like me to fix the hole in your sock, Chris?"

The man glanced at his foot and shrugged, then grinned. "Sure, Miss Emmaline, if you don't mind."

Geoffrey's low brows sent a private message, but he didn't say anything. After they'd all seated themselves at the table, Emmaline looked at him, waiting for him to say grace for the meal. But he simply jabbed a slice of bread with his fork and carried it to his plate.

Emmaline cleared her throat. "Chris, would you bless the food, please?" He had willingly prayed for their meals in Geoffrey's absence.

Chris shot Geoffrey a quick look before he said, "Of course."

Emmaline bowed her head and listened as Chris recited a simple blessing. When she raised her gaze, Geoffrey glowered at her from across the table. Choosing to ignore his look of disapproval, she picked up the soup ladle. "Stew, Geoffrey?"

For the next several minutes they ate in silence, the clink of spoons against the soup bowls and the crunch of crusty bread providing the only sounds in the still kitchen. At last Geoffrey leaned back in his chair, wiped his mouth with the cloth napkin, and turned to Chris. "By now my bales of hay have been delivered to Moreland. I'll need to ride one of the horses into Stetler tomorrow and borrow a team and wagon from the livery." His dull, tired tone—so different from his former exuberance when discussing ranch business—saddened Emmaline.

Chris nodded. "I can see to the sheep tomorrow."

"Before I can bring the bales here, we must have a place out of the weather to store them."

Chris lifted a piece of cheese and munched. "There isn't room in the sheep barn—not with the horses in there, too. Where are you thinking we should put them?"

Geoffrey's gaze flicked to Emmaline briefly. "We haven't much choice right now. The only building, besides the sheep barn, that is large enough to accommodate the bales is the bunkhouse. I plan to use my half of the bunkhouse as storage space for the bales until we can repair the horse barn."

"Then where will you sleep?" Chris asked the question that hovered in Emmaline's mind.

Geoffrey looked at Emmaline as he answered. "I shall bunk with you, Chris. I'm putting Jim in the house, in the spare sleeping room. He will not be able to work with the animals until he is free of the crutches, so he can assist Emmaline around the house."

Emmaline's heart clamored nervously. Would time with Jim deepen the boy's affection for her? She certainly didn't wish to encourage him in his belief that she would be his sweetheart. "Do you think that is wise?"

Geoffrey scowled. "I haven't any other choice, Emmaline."

Although she wanted to remind him of his previous warning concerning Jim's feelings toward her, she swallowed any further protest.

Chris asked, "How long do you think it will take to get the barn rebuilt?"

"I don't know," Geoffrey said with a sigh. "Lambing season is nearly upon us. Our yield will be less this year with the loss of those ewes, but without Jim's help, we will be very busy. I don't think we'll have time to repair the barn until after all of the ewes have delivered and the lambs have been shipped to market."

Chris nodded. "Perhaps you should consider hiring—"

"No!"

At the forceful word, both Chris and Emmaline jumped.

Geoffrey's jaw clenched so firmly a muscle bulged in his cheek. "Hiring workers means *paying* workers. I . . . cannot . . . pay anyone. Not now."

Chris stared off to the side, silent.

Emmaline's thoughts traveled forward to spring. Geoffrey had promised to purchase tickets and return her to England. Would the sale of lambs earn enough money to cover the fares? Or would this become another neglected promise?

But then she shook her head, relief flooding her. She still had the dowry money. She could rescue it from the barn and give the money to Geoffrey so he could buy tickets—despite the fire, the money should have stayed safe in its metal box, shouldn't it? Oddly, the thought of leaving Kansas—leaving Geoffrey—brought no pleasure. She would go because she could not stay with a man who did not value her or trust her, but she feared her heart would break when she tore herself from this place.

Geoffrey lifted his cup and drained the last of his tea. "I'm going to start clearing the rubble from the barn."

Emmaline looked at him in surprise. "It is Sunday!"

He raised one eyebrow in silent query.

"It is a day of rest," she reminded him. In all of their growing-up years, he had respected the Sabbath. More often than not, he had come to her home following the Sunday service and sat in the parlor with her family, reading poetry or napping with his hands linked on his stomach. Would he set aside that habit now out of spite and frustration with God?

"It is a *day*." Geoffrey's tone was more resigned than harsh. "And I cannot waste it. There is much work to be done." Turning from Emmaline, he addressed Chris. "If you prefer to rest, you may do so."

Chris sent an apologetic look to Emmaline, but he rose. "I'll help you, boss."

Geoffrey nodded, and the two tugged their boots back on. Before stepping out the door, Geoffrey said, "If you have need of me, Emmaline, ring the bell. I shall return."

With a heavy heart, Emmaline cleaned up the dishes and then moved to the sitting room—the inviting little sitting room where she had hoped she and Geoffrey might sit and chat and rediscover their affection for each other. But why bother now? She would return to England soon, and Geoffrey was no longer the man with whom she had fallen in love.

After all these months, she still didn't know this man he had become.

# TWENTY-EIGHT

〜

A WEEK AFTER THE barn burned, the ground had finally dried enough for Geoffrey to ride into Stetler and rent a freight wagon from the livery stable. It took four horses to pull the long, boxy wagon, and they seemed to find every newly carved rut in the road that led to Moreland. But he didn't complain. At long last, he would be retrieving his purchased bales of feed for his sheep. What were a few bumps when compared to meeting the needs of his flock?

On the high, springed seat beside him, Jim sat with his face toward the sun and his bandaged foot propped on the footboard. The pose indicated contentment, but Geoffrey knew the boy fought tears. His happy chatter had stopped after Geoffrey told him about the barn's burning and Horace's injuries. To alleviate the horse's suffering, Geoffrey had been forced to put the animal down.

Geoffrey wondered if he should have waited until they returned to the ranch before he told Jim about the loss of his horse, but the first statement out of Jim's mouth had been about setting aside his crutches, climbing onto Horace's back, and riding out to the pasture. Wasn't it less unkind to end the fantasy quickly rather than allowing him to indulge it, knowing he would be crushed when the truth came out?

Geoffrey's father had never believed in pampering. Straight-up facts presented in a firm, emotionless tone were what he'd preferred. When Geoffrey's mother had left, his father had said, "Your mother is gone, and no amount of sniveling will bring her back. So dry up and be a man." At nine years of age, Geoffrey had learned that being a man meant swallowing one's sorrow.

He nudged Jim with his elbow. "When we reach Moreland, let's ask if there are any sheepdogs for sale."

Jim blinked rapidly. "You never wanted a dog on the property. You said they dig holes and make mischief." He swiped his hand beneath his nose.

Geoffrey recalled his reaction to the mongrel pup Jim had dragged home. There hadn't been time to deal with a dog due to all of the other responsibilities of getting the ranch running. "We've not had the time to train a dog in the past, but now with you off your feet, you have the time. Do you think you could train a dog to be a good herder?"

The boy's face brightened. "Certainly I could, Mr. Garrett."

"Well, then," Geoffrey said, "we shall ask about. If we can purchase one for less than a dollar, we'll bring home a dog."

The promised dog opened Jim's voice box again. He chattered all the way to Moreland, and despite his worries, Geoffrey found himself responding. The lad's enthusiasm was infectious.

They rolled into Moreland and went directly to the train depot. The message Geoffrey had received indicated the bales were waiting behind the water tower, stacked on a pile of railroad ties and covered with an oilcloth, just as he'd requested. He guided the horses over the tracks and around the depot, bringing them to a stop behind the water tower. An oilcloth-covered mound waited, and his heart leapt in anticipation. But when he yanked the cloth away, confusion smote him.

Had he not ordered and paid for six dozen bales? A little more than half of that number waited. To Jim, he barked, "Stay here." He stomped to the depot window and thumped the counter with his fist. "Harvey!"

The stationmaster immediately scuttled from a small desk in the corner to the window. "What is it?"

"I came to retrieve the bales of hay sent from Wyoming." He sucked in a breath, trying to rein in his temper. "There should be seventy-two bales. Did the entire order not arrive?"

"No, no, we unloaded six dozen bales, just like you said." Suddenly the man made a face, his thin lips nearly disappearing. "I think I might know what happened. . . ." He opened a door to the right of the window and scurried around the building. Geoffrey followed.

The man stood, hands on his hips, and looked at the pile. "Y'see, Geoff, what with all the rain we had, folks was having trouble with flooding. They needed something laid out to hold the ground in place, so . . ." He scratched his head, then held out his hands in supplication. "I reckon they made use of your bales in a time of need."

Geoffrey gritted his teeth. Their need couldn't possibly have been greater than his need for these bales! "Since they were stolen from Union Pacific property, will the railroad be accountable for my loss?"

Again, Harvey's face twisted into a pained grimace. "Once the items leave the freight car, the railroad's responsibility ends. We stacked it an' saved it for you, just as you asked, but . . ."

"Fine." Geoffrey grated out the word. "Then kindly send a telegram to Mr. Johann Wagner in Cheyenne, Wyoming. Tell him I need more bales—as many as he can send."

Harvey started to turn away, but Geoffrey caught his arm. "Harvey, I'm normally a patient man, but I cannot tolerate thievery. Will my next order be here for me when I come to retrieve it?"

Harvey scowled. "We'll keep a close eye on it. That's all I can promise you."

Geoffrey released Harvey's arm and stepped back. "Send the telegram, Harvey."

For the next half hour, while Jim watched, Geoffrey hefted fifty-pound hay bales into the back of the wagon. The physical exertion drained much of his fury. Finally, he folded the oilcloth into a bulky square and carried it to the depot window. "Harvey?"

Harvey turned around, his eyes wary.

Geoffrey held up the cloth. "Where do you want this?"

"Just leave it on the timbers out there. I reckon it'll be put to use again another day."

Stifling a sigh, Geoffrey nodded. He started to leave but then paused. "Do you know of anyone in the area who might part with a dog? I am looking for one to train as a sheepdog."

Harvey twisted his mouth to the side, his brows puckering. "Seems to me the Hiltons out west of town have some dogs. You might check with them."

"Thanks." Geoffrey climbed back into the wagon and released the brake. "All right, Jim. Let's go see if we can find your dog."

As they headed out of town, a ruckus on the boardwalk captured their attention. Two men, apparently inebriated, performed a foot-thumping dance while others looked on and laughed. The watching crowd milled in the street, and Geoffrey was forced to draw the team to a halt. One of the dancers crowed, "Rich, rich, rich! I'm rich as Midas!"

"How'd you do it, Ted?" a man called. "Did you strike gold?"

"Not gold—silver!" One man spun in a circle and made an

awkward bow. "Found my fortune at the Abilene gambling halls! They've got it all—bluff tables, faro, roulette—and purty ladies and music, to boot!" Grabbing his partner's hands, he broke into another wild dance. "A feller can turn two bits into two hundred dollars in the blink of an eye! I'm rich, rich, rich!"

The crowd, still laughing and calling ribald comments, slowly dispersed, allowing Geoffrey passage. Jim cranked his head around to gawk at the men as the wagon rolled past them.

"Think that's true, Mr. Garrett?"

Geoffrey glanced at Jim. The boy's eyes were wide with wonder. "What's true?"

"That you can turn two bits into two hundred dollars in the blink of an eye?"

Geoffrey snorted. "You're more likely to turn two hundred dollars into two bits in a gambling hall."

Jim waved toward the men, who continued their happy revelry. "But he said—"

"He might have gotten lucky." Geoffrey tightened his hands around the reins as memories surfaced. "But luck is fleeting. More times than not, a gambling hall will leave you penniless. It isn't worth the risk."

Shifting in the seat, Jim asked, "Have you ever gambled, Mr. Garrett?"

Coming to Kansas was a gamble. Carving a sheep ranch out of hard, unrelenting land was a gamble. Battling nature, Geoffrey had learned all too well in the past weeks, was a gamble. But he had never gambled in a hall. He'd left that to his father. "No, Jim. I've never gambled."

The boy shook his head, his eyes bright. "But ladies, and music, and all those games . . . Seems as though it could be a fine time."

Yes, Franklin Garrett had thought gambling halls provided a fine time, too. How much money had he squandered in such places?

There was no way to know for sure, since he'd hidden his addiction, but Geoffrey knew how many times his father's good friend, Jonathan Bradford, had come to their aid, paying off the debts and keeping his father from being thrown in jail. But not even Bradford had been able to prevent the loss of Grandmother's estate.

*"A feller can turn two bits into two hundred dollars in the blink of an eye!"* Geoffrey gritted his teeth as ideas tossed around in his brain like dice in a Chuck-Luck birdcage. Franklin Garrett had had very little luck when it came to gambling, but must that be true of his son, as well?

———

Emmaline wiped her face with her apron. After spending the entire afternoon digging through what remained of the garden, she had managed to salvage half a bushel of sweet potatoes and a small pile of carrots. As she had feared, much of the produce had been ruined by the standing water. But some was better than none. Staunchly, she announced aloud, "I choose to be thankful for this bounty, no matter how small."

She carried the baskets to the cellar and put them away, then headed to the house. The late September breeze lifted her apron and tugged at her hair. The wind carried the strong scent of rotted fish, and she wrinkled her nose. The Solomon River still hovered above its banks, but it no longer posed a threat, for which Emmaline was grateful. Now if only the odors would recede like the water line.

She washed a tubful of clothes and then pinned the garments to the line outside with wooden pegs. As she turned to return to the house, someone shouted her name. She shielded her eyes with one hand and peered down the road. A wagon with two people on the seat headed for their ranch. Stacks of hay bales filled the back of the wagon. Geoffrey was back, she realized, and he had called for her. Her heart gave a funny flutter.

She dropped the empty basket and dashed to the end of the lane. The shout came again, but then she realized it was Jim's voice, not Geoffrey's. She pushed aside the feeling of disappointment that accompanied the recognition and forced her lips into a smile.

Raising her hand, she waved. "Welcome home, Jim!"

"Thank you, Miss Emmaline! It's good to be home." The boy grabbed the edge of the seat and leaned toward her as the wagon rolled past.

She trotted alongside it, stopping when Geoffrey drew the team to a halt in front of the house. Jim handed her his crutches and climbed down cautiously. "Be careful," she admonished, feeling like a mother hen.

The boy grinned as he placed the crutches under his arms. "I'm all right."

Emmaline dashed to the edge of the wagon and pressed her hand to one scratchy bale. "You got the hay!" At that moment, a high-pitched bark erupted from the back of the wagon, making Emmaline jump.

Jim burst out laughing. "That's just Miney."

Emmaline shot the boy a startled look. "It's what?"

Jim clomped to the back of the wagon and put his hand in the bed. He lifted out a wriggling body of brown-and-white fur. "Miney." He cradled the half-grown pup under one arm. "There were four pups in the litter, and I did eenie-meenie-miney-moe to choose one. I picked Miney." Sadness flashed briefly in the boy's eyes. "He's to be a sheepdog, just like Horace was a sheep horse. I'm going to train him."

Emmaline stuck out her hand, and the puppy sniffed it before giving her a lick. She giggled. "Silly little dog. You certainly sounded much more fierce than you look."

Geoffrey, still perched on the wagon seat, called, "Step away from the wagon now so I can get these bales put away."

Emmaline took Miney, and she and Jim moved toward the porch.

"I must return the wagon to Stetler before nightfall," Geoffrey said, his unsmiling gaze on Emmaline, "so don't hold supper for me." Without another word, he tugged the reins, urging the team to turn around.

Emmaline held tight to the squirming puppy until the wagon rolled around the house. When she put him down, he bounced around their feet and barked at a twig. She laughed at his clumsy antics, but when she looked up, Jim's fervent gaze immediately stilled her laughter.

"Mr. Garrett says I'm to stay in the house until my leg heals."

Emmaline swallowed. "That's right. Chris brought in a bed-frame and mattress, as well as your clothing. Everything is set up in the spare sleeping room."

A discomforting thought struck. She had to pass through the spare sleeping room to get to her own room. If her own child had resided in the spare room, it would not be a problem, but the thought of intruding upon Jim's space left her feeling unsettled.

Jim seemed to have no apprehensions about sharing the house with her. "Can I see?"

She nodded. "Go ahead."

He swung past her, his movements ungainly as he balanced on the crutches. She followed, watching as he sat on the edge of the bed and peered around the room. Chris had pushed all of Geoffrey's items to one side and put the bed and dresser on the opposite side, leaving the center of the floor open. If she asked Chris or Geoffrey to hang a blanket to partition off Jim's part of the room, then he would have privacy. Perhaps this would work, after all.

Jim sighed loud enough that the sound carried clearly to her ears. She looked at him, and once more the adoration in his eyes made trepidation wriggle down her spine.

"I sure am happy to be home again, Miss Emmaline."

Emmaline allowed him a hesitant nod. "You should sit on the porch and play with Miney while I see to supper."

Jim pushed to his feet and took up the crutches again. "All right, Miss Emmaline. I'll be right outside if you need anything."

She watched him stump out the front door, then nearly collapsed with an expulsion of breath. While greatly relieved Jim had survived the rattlesnake bite and was home again, the change in living accommodations created a sense of apprehension.

*Lord, help me be friendly to Jim without giving him any wrong ideas.*

# TWENTY-NINE

HE EWE'S LABOR had gone on far too long. Geoffrey knelt
by the sheep and checked the notch in the ewe's ear
against the notation in the journal in his lap. Yes, this
ewe had suffered trouble before. He would only use her for wool
from now on.

One of the reasons he had chosen Merinos was their propensity
for problem-free birthing. Seldom did a ewe need assistance in
bringing forth a lamb, but once in a while the birthing was difficult. Thus, he never left the ewes unattended during the lambing
season.

He sighed, flexing his shoulders. He and Chris had kept round-
the-clock vigils since the onset of lambing season. With only two
of them overseeing the sheep, neither of them got as much sleep as
they needed. Two weeks had passed since Jim returned from the
doctor, but the boy still spent most of his time at the house with
Emmaline or training the pup in the front yard. Sometimes Geoffrey suspected Jim's limp was exaggerated—a means of escaping
work—but he hesitated to push too hard. The doctor had cautioned
them to let the boy get plenty of rest.

"Geoffrey?"

He gave a start at the softly spoken word. Emmaline stood in the wide opening at the south end of the barn. She held a napkin-covered plate, and her face wore an apprehensive expression that had become all too common.

"Come in," he greeted.

She approached slowly, her gaze roving past the stalls where sheep rested. "I brought you some supper since you didn't come in to eat."

Geoffrey took the plate and lifted the cloth. Biscuits, fried potatoes, and two chunky links of sausage. He inhaled, and the pleasing aromas made his stomach twist with desire. "Thank you." But instead of eating, he set the plate aside and turned his attention back to the ewe.

Emmaline squatted next to him, her full yellow skirt forming a pouf. She trailed her fingertips through the wool on the sheep's back. "How many born today?"

"Chris reported five females this morning, including two sets of twins. Then two more this afternoon—one male and one female. The male is black—an uncommon sight. It will be butchered, but we'll probably keep the others."

Emmaline tilted her head. "Butchered because it's black?"

"In this case, yes. Black wool is worthless. But we butcher almost all of the male lambs."

"Seems rather harsh."

Geoffrey shook his head. "The males can't reproduce. We've got our rams for mating. Eventually I'll keep the male offspring of an older ewe—one we know won't be producing much longer—and it will become a mating ram. But we can't keep them all."

"I suppose not." Emmaline plucked up a clean piece of hay and twirled it between her fingers.

Geoffrey wondered why she didn't return to the house. He had done his best to keep his distance from her lately. There was no sense in renewing their relationship if she was going to leave in a few months. Having her so near made him feel as though his stomach was tied into a knot.

She shifted, and he let out a breath of relief that she was leaving. But instead of getting up, she sat cross-legged and rested her hands in the nest of her skirt. "October seems an odd time for lambs to be born. Don't they usually come in the spring?"

Geoffrey closed the journal on the pencil and set it aside. "Yes, for most breeds. But these are Merinos. Merinos can birth three times in two years, which makes the lambing season a bit different."

Emmaline gave a thoughtful nod. "I see. So the female lambs are kept for wool and to produce more lambs, and the male lambs are butchered for their meat."

"That is correct, although some females are also butchered. This season, however, I plan to keep as many female lambs as I can to replace those I lost after the grasshopper plague." He turned his attention back to the ewe lying on the straw. "And this one won't be producing anymore. I'll keep her separate during the next mating. She's had trouble before."

Emmaline reached out and stroked the ewe. "Poor thing. Can we help her?"

Why was Emmaline suddenly so interested in the workings of the ranch? Might she be considering staying? His heart did a funny flip-flop at the thought, but he steeled himself against it. "I want to give it a little more time and see if she'll manage on her own. So . . . I wait."

"I shall wait with you."

He frowned. "Why?"

She lifted one shoulder in a shrug. "I suppose because I have never watched a lamb be born. It will be a learning experience. I am quite sure it is different from seeing kittens birthed."

Geoffrey shook his head. Whatever game she was playing needed to come to a close. "Emmaline, you won't ever need this knowledge again. You won't be here for the next lambing season. It will be eight months from now, well past winter, and you'll have returned to England by then."

Emmaline ducked her head, toying with the piece of straw. "Yes. I suppose . . ."

She sounded so dismayed, Geoffrey's heart twisted with pity. But at that moment the ewe began a wild thrashing that captured his attention. He leaned forward, placing a soothing hand on its neck.

Emmaline shifted to her knees, tossing aside the piece of hay. "What can I do to help?"

Geoffrey stood. "Come over here and hold her head. She can't get up if you're holding her head. I'm going to check the position of the lamb. She won't like it, so hold tight." While he spoke, he strode to a bench, picked up a bottle of carbolic solution, and poured the liquid over his hands. He could feel Emmaline's curious eyes on him as he knelt behind the animal, made a dart of his fingers, and reached inside the ewe's canal.

"Ah, there it is." He unconsciously spoke aloud. "But its rump is down, not its head, so its back feet must be underneath it instead of angled into the canal. It won't come out like that. I've got to grab its feet, and then I should be able to bring him out."

Geoffrey briefly saw Emmaline's slender hands holding gently yet firmly to the ewe's head, then he closed his eyes and tried to imagine the lamb inside the womb. He worked his fingers around and found the lamb's feet. Carefully he brought them downward and drew them through the birth canal.

Emmaline must have seen the tiny hoofs appear because she said, "Oh! Now pull!"

Geoffrey shook his head, his focus on those little feet. "No. She can do it now. Just watch."

In a few minutes, a natural contraction forced the entire backside of the lamb through the opening, and the next contraction expelled a small, wet, woolly bundle.

"Let her go," Geoffrey commanded, backing up on his heels. Emmaline did as she was told, scrambling around to kneel beside Geoffrey. They watched as the weak ewe turned her head to nose the newborn, then began licking it. The lamb responded, twisting its head toward its mother. To Geoffrey's relief, the baby struggled to its feet as the ewe rose, and without any guidance, the lamb found the milk sack. It began sucking noisily.

"Oh my. That was quite something."

Geoffrey smiled down at Emmaline, who watched the lamb nurse and the mother gently lick it. Her wide-eyed look of wonder gave her an innocence that sent a jolt of reaction clear through his middle. The longing to draw her close, to press his face against her hair, nearly overwhelmed him.

Steepling her hands beneath her chin, she peered up at Geoffrey. "Male or female?"

Geoffrey tipped his head to peek. "Female."

Her breath whooshed out. "Oh, I am so glad."

"Why?"

"I helped her be born. I wouldn't want to see her butchered. Now, perhaps, I shall see her grow up. Maybe even have babies of her own." Her eyes lit with a smile. "I like that idea."

Why would she make such a statement after vowing to return to England? He took a backward step. "Emmaline . . ."

But before he could finish, she pranced a few feet away. "I shall leave you to your work. I'll send Jim out for the plate later." She turned and scampered out of the barn.

As Emmaline ran through the evening shadows back to the house, she considered the strange look in Geoffrey's eyes when she spoke of watching the lamb grow up. Her face flamed at her own audacity. She knew she had sent a message, but from his reaction, he hadn't wanted to receive it.

*He doesn't want me here, Lord. Oh, how I wish I could help him. He's become so . . . despondent.*

Hadn't Tildy said that when one honored commitment, love crept in? Well, Emmaline had tried to honor the commitment she'd made to Geoffrey, and love had blossomed in her heart once more. But would Geoffrey's heart respond?

"Miss Emmaline?" Jim stood in the doorway between the kitchen and sitting room. "I've got those boxes finished if you want to see them."

"Oh!" Emmaline straightened from the table and untied her apron. "Yes, of course I'd like to see them."

Keeping Jim occupied and out from underfoot had proven challenging since his return from the doctor. Hindered by his crutches, he couldn't wander the grounds, but his hands were capable of working. So she had assigned him the task of crafting some flower boxes for the windows of the house.

She followed him to the spare sleeping room, where he had pushed aside the quilt that served as a barrier. He pointed proudly to six oblong wooden boxes sitting in a row on his bed.

"Oh, Jim, what a fine job!" Emmaline lifted one box. She had scavenged for usable pieces of wood from the barn. All the wood had borne scorch marks from the fire, but apparently Jim had sanded the pieces clean. The wood appeared fresh and yellow.

She turned the box this way and that, admiring the craftsmanship. The corners fit snugly, neatly notched and nailed, and a series of holes drilled in the bottom would allow moisture to escape. "These are perfect." Emmaline beamed at Jim, who rocked on his heels and grinned. "Now all I need is some rocks and dirt, and I can plant my seeds."

"I can attach them outside now, if you'd like."

"Oh no. Not yet." Emmaline placed the box back on the bed and pressed her palms together. "I am going to keep them in the parlor until the weather is warm again. I plan to have an indoor garden."

Jim's eyebrows pulled down. "An indoor garden?"

Emmaline nodded. "Yes. Our gardener in England had a potting shed where he forced flowers to grow year round. My mother was never without fresh flowers for our dining room table—hydrangea, purple clematis, coreopsis, everlastings . . ." She closed her eyes for a moment, envisioning the lovely bouquets that had brightened the table.

"I have no potting shed, but the area in front of the windows in my parlor, where the boxes will receive the sun, shall do nicely. I have daisy seeds—I adore daisies—and I intend to plant a few now, keeping them in the house where it is warm so they can germinate. Then, in the spring, I shall put the boxes outside and also transplant some of the flowers to the yard. Won't it be lovely?"

Jim gave her a suspicious look. "In the spring? But I thought . . ." He licked his lips. "Aren't you going back to England in the spring?"

Emmaline blinked twice. Her mind raced for an appropriate response. "Flowers . . . will make the house seem more like home . . . whether I am here or away, will they not?"

Jim didn't answer.

Emmaline forced a light laugh. "But, regardless, spring is several months away. We needn't worry about it now. Instead, I must prevail upon you to gather pebbles from the river bottom to put in the base of these boxes, and then I shall fill them with garden soil. Then I shall trust that the heat from the little stove in the parlor's corner, together with the sun's rays, will be enough to bring the seeds to life."

Jim picked up his crutches. "I need to go check on Miney and then put him in the shed for the night."

"Be careful. It is dark already."

His eyes narrowed. "I know."

Emmaline hid her smile as he headed out. Whether he realized it or not, he had just responded to her the way an obstinate child related to his mother, not the way a man treated his sweetheart.

Sweetheart . . . Immediately memories from the past paraded through her mind, all of them involving the days when Geoffrey had courted her as his sweetheart. When he smiled at her in the sheep barn right after the birth of the lamb, she had been reminded of the tender moments they'd shared while growing up together. So many of her favorite childhood memories included Geoffrey. When they exchanged that smile in the barn, had he been transported to earlier days? Would the remembrances soften his heart?

Earlier days . . . Of course! Finally, she had found the key to opening Geoffrey's heart to joy and laughter again. Her pulse raced, her smile growing as she considered the means of reaching him. Certainly they had faced difficult times in England—the loss of his mother, and his father's many illnesses. Yet he had emerged, strong and able, because of his belief in God. If only she could take him back to those times in his memory, he would remember where he needed to find his strength to face today's challenges.

All he needed were a few reminders. And she knew just where to begin.

# THIRTY

GEOFFREY AWAKENED WITH a start, his body drenched with sweat. The dream—the nightmare—still hovered on the fringes of his mind. *"You are a disappointment, Geoffrey. You think you shall find success in Kansas? You are a fool! Failure is imminent. Mark my words!"*

"No!" He rasped the word aloud. He breathed in the scent of Chris's pipe smoke, caught in the wood-planked walls and in the fibers of the quilt draped over his body. Surely that scent—the same one that permeated his father's study—had precipitated the nightmare.

Geoffrey shimmied into his trousers, pushed his feet into his boots, and clomped out onto the porch. Sucking in great breaths of the cold night air, he tried to erase the lingering scent from his nostrils, hoping it would also remove the remaining vestiges of the dream from his memory. But his father's callous words, thrown at him the day he had shared his plans to begin a new life for himself in Kansas, were carved onto his soul as permanently as the Solomon River's path across the prairie.

He curled his hands around the porch rail and lifted his gaze to the night sky. Stars and a pale yellow moon peered back at him.

As a boy, visiting his grandmother's estate in the country, he had often crept outdoors to stare up at the night sky. Back then, the majesty of the velvety sky had filled him with a sense of oneness with the Creator of the heavens. Now, however, the vast sky left him feeling small and insignificant in comparison. From God's viewpoint, he must appear like an ant scurrying here and there, working to store up enough to carry him through another winter. Nothing more than an insect, easily squashed. Why work so hard when in the blink of an eye it could all be washed away?

*The blink of an eye* . . . Where had he heard that expression recently? The drunken cowboy who had struck it rich at the gaming tables in Abilene. Geoffrey's mouth went dry. He needed money badly. But badly enough to risk gambling?

No! He smacked his palms on the railing. There had to be another way. He would not resort to his father's habits. His soul longed to pray for guidance, for help, for relief . . . but he refused to release the petitions. God's answers to prayers had proved worthless. Emmaline had come, but she refused to be his wife. Rains had fallen, but too late and too heavy. The ranch had been built, but grasshoppers and a fire had nearly destroyed the work of his hands. He would not give God the chance to disappoint him again.

He looked across the land to the sheep barn, where the glow of a lantern lit the interior. Chris was there, watching over the few remaining ewes still waiting to deliver. Now wide awake, Geoffrey decided he would relieve Chris, let the hand get some extra hours of sleep.

Entering the sheep barn, he scanned the area for Chris. He spotted the man in a corner stall. Chris sat with his head slung low, and Geoffrey's ire stirred. Was Chris asleep? He tromped up behind him, intending to tap his shoulder, but Chris turned and looked over his shoulder before Geoffrey made contact.

"Mr. Garrett." Chris stumbled to his feet. "I was just thinking I should come get you." His gaze dropped to the floor of the stall.

Geoffrey looked, too, and his heart plummeted. A dead lamb lay in the hay, its distraught mother nosing it.

Chris ran his hands through his tousled hair. "It's the second one born dead tonight."

Geoffrey stared at the perfectly formed, lifeless creature. Another senseless loss. *Failure is imminent.*

Chris retrieved a burlap bag from the corner of the barn, rolled the dead lamb into it, then headed for the door. The ewe nosed the area where the baby had been, bleating pitifully. Geoffrey grabbed a rake and cleaned the area of soiled hay. But even with the scent removed, the sheep refused to calm. She paced, her baas echoing through the barn and raising answering bleats from other ewes. Geoffrey tried stroking the ewe to calm her, but her agitation only increased. If she didn't settle down, her anxiety would rouse the entire flock.

"Hush, sheep," Geoffrey commanded, grasping her around the neck and trying to force her to lie down. The ewe thrashed against him, her bleats more insistent. And then suddenly she relaxed, collapsing onto the barn floor. Geoffrey stared, shocked. The mother, too, had died.

He sank down on one knee beside the now-quiet body and bowed his head. Would the losses never end?

———

Emmaline forced herself to focus on the square of fabric in her hand. Her eyes burned, and she yawned repeatedly, but she refused to give in to sleep. She must finish this project.

It had taken some ingenuity to find the means for needlework.

A pillowcase provided the foundational cloth, and by unraveling a portion of the skirt of one of her worn black dresses, she had gleaned thread. The thin strands were not ideal for embroidery work, but sometimes one must make do.

She held the fabric at arm's length and examined her work thus far. The letters were a bit shaky—the result of having to hold the fabric taut with her fingers rather than tightening the cloth using a wooden hoop—but they were readable. She smiled. Surely this Scripture, taken directly from the Twenty-third Psalm, would bring soothing peace to Geoffrey's heart.

When she finished the verses, she intended to ask Jim to build a frame. The boy had done an admirable job with her flower boxes; surely he had the ability to make a simple frame. Then she would tack the fabric to the frame's back and hang the finished project on the wall of Geoffrey's room.

Picking up the needle, she set to work on the next line: *"My cup runneth over."* Recently, it seemed that troubles filled the cup and spilled over. Yet, somehow, she still clung to the promise of verse three—*"He restoreth my soul."*

"God, work the same miracle of restoration in Geoffrey's soul," she prayed as she stitched. Another yawn widened her mouth, forcing her eyes to squint shut briefly. But then she blinked hard, sat up in the rocking chair, and returned to work.

"Miss Emmaline, didn't you sleep well?"

Jim's concerned voice made Emmaline smile. She gave the cornmeal a quick stir and then placed the lid on the pot. "I slept fine once I went to bed. But I went to bed far too late."

"What were you doing in the parlor last night?"

Emmaline shot him an apologetic look. "Did I keep you up?"

He shrugged, his grin sheepish. "I just noticed the light under the door."

She lifted bowls from the cabinet and placed them on the table. "I was working on a gift for Mr. Garrett. I finished my part, but now I need your help."

Jim frowned. "My help?"

"Yes." Turning to the tray with the silverware, she fiddled with the spoons. "I would like a frame for a piece of stitchery." She sighed, replaying the wonderful words of the psalm in her mind.

"What kind of a gift is it?"

Emmaline chose to ignore the jealous undertone of Jim's words. She answered honestly, "It's a good-bye gift." Hopefully it would be the first step in helping Geoffrey say good-bye to his despondence. She turned to face Jim. "So will you help me?"

The boy flashed a bright smile. "Sure. I can make a frame. I just need to know how big."

"I'll show you after breakfast."

Chris came in as Emmaline placed the pot of steaming cornmeal mush in the center of the table. His long face raised her concerns. "Is something wrong?"

He sighed as he sank into a chair at the table. "We lost three lambs and a ewe during the night. Mr. Garrett is quite upset."

A picture formed in Emmaline's mind of the sweet lamb she had helped deliver and its attentive mother. Tears pooled in her eyes. She wiped her hands on her apron. "Chris, you serve the mush. Jim, pour the water for tea. I must go see Geoffrey." She dashed out the door before either of the Cotler brothers could respond.

The morning air held a bite. Without the protection of her woven shawl, she shivered. Folding her arms across her middle, she walked as quickly as possible to the sheep barn. She found Geoffrey sitting on a barrel and leaning his head back against the wall. His eyes were closed, and exhaustion sagged his features. For a moment, she considered creeping away without disturbing him, but then he opened his eyes and caught her standing a few feet away.

"Are you all right?" she asked without preamble.

He shook his head.

She stepped closer. "Chris said three lambs and a ewe died." Swallowing, she addressed her worry. "The one from . . . ?"

"No." He lifted his hand wearily, as if it weighed more than he could support, and pointed to a corner stall. "That mother and baby are fine."

She looked at the ewe and lamb nestled together on the hay, and relief flooded through her. Why it was so important that the lamb she had watched slip into the world still lived, she couldn't say. She only knew it mattered a great deal. But looking into Geoffrey's face, she witnessed the depth of his sorrow. She took one more forward step.

"It is uncommon, then, to lose some lambs during the lambing time?"

"Not uncommon, but never welcome. And especially not this year, when I have no reserve on which to draw."

Emmaline's chest ached at the pain etched into his face. She opened her mouth to offer solace, but he suddenly rose and drew in a deep breath.

Staring somewhere beyond her shoulder, he spoke through clenched teeth. "Emmaline, I fear it may be necessary for me to make use of the dowry money."

Without a moment's hesitation, she said, "Of course you may use it."

His brows came together, his gaze colliding with hers. "You're quite sure? I cannot be certain I will be able to replace the money in its entirety even after butchering and shearing."

"I am sure." She lifted her skirts and turned toward the barn's opening. "I shall fetch it now from the barn."

"The barn?"

With a self-conscious smile, she peeked at him over her shoulder. "I hid it in the horse barn."

Geoffrey's face drained of color, and he dropped heavily onto the barrel.

"Geoffrey?"

He ran his hand over his face. "Emmaline, if you put it in the barn, it's no longer there."

She turned to face him and offered an assuring smile. "Of course it is. I—"

Shaking his head, he released a growl. He rested his clenched fists in his lap. "I have been through every bit of the rubble in the barn. There was no money box."

The money gone? Her security wavered with this knowledge, but oddly she suffered no despair. She looked at Geoffrey, and the helplessness on his face propelled her forward. Emmaline knelt before him and placed her hands over his fists. "I am so sorry, Geoffrey. What else can I do to help?"

He stared at her, his expression unreadable. His lips parted and then closed. He turned his gaze away. "There is nothing, Emmaline."

"Please?" She kept her voice low, aware of the resting sheep and their need for calm. "There must be something I could do. Sit with you, pray with you . . ."

Geoffrey bolted to his feet, nearly knocking her backward. He stormed to the nearest upright beam and raised his fist as if to strike the beam, but instead he pressed his fist to his own forehead. The gesture of agony made Emmaline's heart turn over in her chest. How hard he sought comfort! If only he would accept a touch from the Comforter . . .

"Do you know, Emmaline, that ever since you arrived, things have gone awry?"

She stared at him, shaken by his accusatory tone.

"All the years I spent building this ranch, readying it for you, were successful years. Difficult years, to be sure, but successful. *Building* years. But now all of the building I did is crumbling."

She rose awkwardly, her skirt tangling around her feet. She straightened her apron before crossing the ground to stand in front of Geoffrey. "And you believe the fault is mine?"

He looked into her face, his lips set in a grim line. Although she quaked on the inside, she refused to cower before him. Several seconds ticked by before he turned his gaze aside. "I don't know what to think."

She caught his arm and tugged. He kept his face angled away, but his eyes shifted to meet hers. Gentling her tone, she said, "Life is hard, Geoffrey. I've learned that well during my time here. On our own we are ill-equipped to triumph over the challenges. But Tildy taught me that we can lean on God's strength." She held her breath, waiting for either an explosion or a submission.

Neither came. With a sigh, Geoffrey lowered his head. "Tell Chris when he has finished breakfast that I want him to take the lambs and mothers to the near pasture for a few hours this morning."

She held out one hand toward him. "Geoffrey, I—"

"Don't preach at me, Emmaline." His hardened tone stilled her words. "Just go."

Obediently, she made her way out of the barn. But she did not slump her shoulders in defeat. She would do as she had instructed Geoffrey. She would lean on God's strength, and she would trust Him to restore joy to Geoffrey's soul and to see the ranch through these difficult times.

# THIRTY-ONE

⸻

A WEEK'S WORTH OF late-night stitching had resulted in six samplers. Emmaline laid them in a row on the bed and smiled down at them. The frames were rough, but so were the stitches—so unlike the meticulously formed letters and flower petals on the embroidery work she'd completed in England. But somehow the rustic appearance suited this land called Kansas.

She traced her finger over the final project. What would Geoffrey think when he saw the verses tacked to the walls of the barn and bunkhouse? She had chosen the verses with care, selecting words that offered hope and encouragement. Aloud, she read, "Blessed is the man that trusteth in the Lord, and whose hope the Lord is."

In England, before Geoffrey left, he'd trusted the Lord. He often expressed sadness at his father's stubborn refusal to believe in God. She knew his grandmother had been a wonderful godly influence for Geoffrey, and he had named this ranch Chetwynd Valley in his grandmother's honor. Somewhere underneath his pained disillusionment, Geoffrey's faith must still exist.

"And God's words shall bring that faith to the fore again," she vowed. She slung her shawl over her shoulders and tied the ends in a knot. After stacking the samplers in her arms, she headed outside. Geoffrey and Chris had taken the flock to the far pasture after breakfast, and Jim was somewhere on the grounds with Miney. The boy had tied a wad of sheepskin to a rope, which he used to train the energetic puppy. Emmaline knew little about sheepdogs, but she recognized determination when she saw it. If Jim had his way, that dog would be the finest sheepdog ever.

The morning sun shone brightly, warm and yellow, illuminating the landscape. Emmaline crossed the ground quickly, her eyes scanning the area. Although in many ways desolate, the land held a bucolic beauty that she'd come to appreciate. Untamed pasture, dotted with wind-carved brush and the occasional surprise of spiky green leaves from a yucca plant, stretched as far as the eye could see. The sky, blue as a robin's egg, created an endless canopy. Never had the sky seemed as large to Emmaline as it did here in Kansas.

As she gazed upward, a flock of geese—their raucous honks filling her ears—flew by. She shielded her eyes and watched, thrilling at the sight of their pounding wings and wild calls. Geoffrey had explained the birds flew in a V formation as a means of supporting one another. The air current of one goose's wings helped uphold another. She glanced at the verses in her hands and smiled. Her samplers would help uphold Geoffrey until which time as his own faith could support him.

In short order, using the hammer and tacks from her apron pocket, she had secured the frames to walls in the sheep barn and the bunkhouse. She had one left, which she intended to hang in the tack shed. As she crossed the ground between buildings, a shrill bark captured her attention. She turned to spot Miney racing toward her.

Before she could react, the dog jumped, planting his front feet against her stomach. She fell backward, and the sampler bounced out of her hand. Miney dove on top of her, alternately barking and licking. "Stop!" She tried to push him aside, but he continued his happy attack. "Jim! Jim!" She managed to get to her feet and, with Miney still bouncing around her, made her way to the tack shed.

With a little shriek, she dashed inside the shed and closed the door. The dog jumped on the door and continued to bark.

"Miney! Bad dog!" Jim's voice carried through the door. She opened it a crack and watched Jim approach in the funny double-hop step he used in place of running.

The boy collared the dog, and his voice was severe as he scolded. "Bad, bad dog! You can't jump on people."

Hesitantly, Emmaline opened the door. Miney leaped at her again, forcing her back into the shed. Something coiled up beneath her skirt and caught her leg, tearing through her bloomers to pierce her skin. With a pained cry, she jerked free. Lifting her skirt aside, she discovered a curling length of barbed wire.

Jim, his arms wrapped around the dog's neck, gave her an apologetic look. "Did it scratch you?"

"Yes." She tossed the wire aside and examined the wound. It hardly bled, but a few red drops stained her torn bloomer leg. "But I will mend with less effort than it will take to clean and repair my clothes." She scowled at the pup, which now sat panting within his master's arms. He almost seemed to smile. "Why is he bothering me?"

Jim pulled his lips to the side. "I think it's your shawl. It's kind of lumpy and white, so it must look like a sheep to him." He giggled. "He's trying to herd you."

Emmaline centered the shawl back over her shoulders. "Well, I do not care to be herded. Kindly take him off so I can return to the house."

"Yes, ma'am. Come along, Miney." The boy and dog departed, Jim limping and Miney bouncing at his side.

With a sigh of relief, Emmaline retrieved the dropped sampler from the ground outside the shed. At the sight of the dust scuffs, she huffed out an aggravated breath, but then she shook her head. The dirt didn't detract from the meaning of the words. She hung the sampler right inside the door, then stepped back to admire her handiwork.

Geoffrey wouldn't be able to miss the messages. Smiling, she returned to the house to begin her morning chores.

———

Geoffrey wrapped the reins loosely over the top rail of the fence and clomped toward the bunkhouse. The wind had picked up since morning, with clouds building in the north. He stared at the sky for a few moments, trying to decide if he should drag the hay out to pasture, as he'd planned, or bring the sheep in to the barn to eat. If it rained, it would ruin the hay. But if he brought the sheep in early, he would need to haul water for them later today.

With a frustrated huff, he stomped onto the porch of the bunkhouse. Indecision—something that had never plagued him in years past—hounded him these days. Indecision showed weakness, an inability to lead. He forced his mind to think. He would drag hay to the pasture, but only enough for one feeding. Then the sheep could eat again this evening in the barn.

The decision made, he entered the bunkhouse and moved toward the bales stacked almost to the ceiling. Something on the narrow slice of wall that wasn't covered by bales caught his eye, and his steps slowed. Someone had hung a crude wooden frame with some sort of stitch work inside it. Puzzled, he moved to the frame and read the words aloud. " 'Why art thou cast down, O my soul? and why art thou disquieted within me? hope thou in God:

for I shall yet praise him, who is the health of my countenance, and my God.' "

An image flashed through his memory of Emmaline sitting on the sofa in her family's parlor with her feet tucked beneath her and an embroidery hoop in her hand. From the time she was a little girl, she had excelled at crafting delicate birds and flowers and poems with colored thread. This particular piece of work was primitive in comparison, yet he knew instantly she had created it and hung it.

Anger pressed upward as he examined the message on the cloth: *hope thou in God . . . praise him . . .* He had no reason to praise God. He started to remove the sampler from the wall, but as his fingers closed on the frame, he found he didn't want to remove it. From the depths of his soul, he wished for hope and peace.

He released the frame abruptly and took a stumbling step backward. For several seconds, he stared at the words; then he blinked and ran his hand over his face. "Get the hay out to the sheep," he admonished himself.

Turning his back on the sampler and its words of wisdom, he returned to work.

At supper that evening, Emmaline cast sidelong glances at him without speaking. He knew she wanted him to mention the little signs she had scattered in the barn and bunkhouse. Five in all, hung in places where he was sure to see. How pleased would she be if he told her he had hung his jacket over one and a coil of rope over another? He carried another bite of pork roast to his mouth. He needed to get away from the ranch, from the samplers, from Emmaline.

Turning to Chris, he asked, "Have you cleaned the rifles recently?"

Chris tore off a piece of bread. "Last week. Why?"

"I thought we might go hunting. Meat from a deer would stretch our food stores considerably."

Chris chewed the bread, one eyebrow high. "I agree."

Jim sat up eagerly. "May I go, too?"

Chris nudged him. "Mr. Garrett wasn't addressing you, Jim."

"But I just—"

"Don't be cheeky."

At his brother's admonition, the boy slumped in his seat and poked at his food with his fork.

Geoffrey caught Emmaline's sympathetic look, and he cleared his throat. "Not this time, Jim. You're still recovering. Besides, Chris is the best marksman. It's best that he go."

Jim muttered something unintelligible, earning another sharp poke from Chris's elbow. He glared at his brother.

Geoffrey drew in a deep breath. "But I'm leaving you and Miney in charge of the sheep and new lambs while we're gone. It will be good practice for Miney, to see if he's got the ability to help."

Immediately Jim sat up, grinning broadly. "You're leaving Miney and me in charge? Yes, sir, we'll take good care of the sheep. You can count on us, Mr. Garrett." He bounced to his feet. "May I be excused so I can go tell him?"

Chris snorted, but Geoffrey waved his hand. "You may be excused."

After the boy rushed out the door, Geoffrey turned to Chris. "I hope to only be gone overnight. Do you think you can scout around over the next few days, find some deer tracks? That will shorten the length of the hunt."

Chris linked his elbow over the back of the chair. "Actually, I saw some deer tracks over the fence in the far pasture. Maybe three or four sets. If we go soon, we could catch them before they get too far away from your property."

"Good. Let's plan on going tomorrow, then, first thing."

Geoffrey scooped the last bit of the pork and rice onto his plate, and Emmaline reached for the empty serving dish. As she rose, she winced, and he shot her a sharp look. "Are you all right?"

She shrugged. "Oh yes. I have a little scratch, and it itches when the skin is pulled. But I'm fine." She moved to the sink and placed the dish in the basin. With a big smile, she asked, "Are you ready for dessert? I baked a gingerbread cake, and I can whip some cream."

Chris swiped his mouth with his napkin. "That sounds good."

"None for me, thank you." Geoffrey finished his last bite and pushed away from the table. Choosing to ignore Emmaline's disappointed look, he said, "I want to check the lambs one more time and make sure none have developed infections from having their tails docked."

He hid his smile when Emmaline grimaced. She had stayed far away from the barn when he and Chris had used a small hatchet to remove all but a stub of each lamb's tail. As he recalled, she'd accused them of being barbaric, but she didn't realize what a health hazard a tail could be when it became a breeding ground for maggots.

"So you are going to the barn?" she asked.

Her wide-eyed look of disinterest didn't fool him one bit. He battled between amusement and aggravation. "Yes, Emmaline. The lambs are in the barn."

At his sardonic response, she colored slightly, but she lifted her chin. "Then I shall bring you a piece of cake with whipped cream later."

He scuttled out the door before he gave in to temptation to deliver a kiss of thanks right on her rosy lips.

# THIRTY-TWO

⌒

ATHROBBING PAIN IN her leg awakened Emmaline early the next morning. She rolled to the edge of the bed and pulled her nightgown up. The place on her leg where the wire had torn her skin glowed bright red. She gingerly touched the area around the scratch with her fingertips. It hurt, and she hissed through her teeth.

Rising, she pushed her arms into her robe and padded through the parlor, past Jim's blanket, and on to the kitchen. She lit a lamp and then ladled water from the stove's reservoir to soak a rag. After rubbing lye soap into the hot, moist rag, she lifted her gown and scrubbed the area around the scratch, biting down on her lower lip to keep from crying out. The pressure created a tremendous amount of pain, but she knew the importance of keeping a wound clean.

When she'd finished, she rinsed the rag and hung it over the edge of the sink. As she ladled water to fill the teakettle, someone tapped lightly on the kitchen door. She limped over and opened it.

Geoffrey stepped into the room, his gaze sweeping from her bare toes to her unconfined hair. His Adam's apple bobbed in a mighty swallow. "I saw the light on and was surprised anyone was up. It's very early. Chris and I are heading out." Behind him, a rosy glow on the horizon promised the sun would soon appear.

"I suppose you'll need a lunch packed for your hunting trip." She kept her voice low to avoid waking Jim. In the boy's excitement at being left in charge of the ranch, he'd had a difficult time settling down to sleep last night—she'd heard him rustling around for at least an hour.

Geoffrey nodded, closing the door behind him. "Just some crackers, cheese, and jerky will do. If all goes well, we'll be back tomorrow before sunset."

"Very well." She removed an empty flour sack from the cupboard and began filling it. "I can put the leftover gingerbread in your sack, too." Turning, she bumped her leg against the edge of the stove and cried out.

Geoffrey stepped forward, reaching for her. "What is it?"

Despite the throbbing in her leg, Emmaline laughed. "Oh, nothing. A little twinge. There." Sweat broke out across her forehead as she tied the sack's opening into a knot and held it out.

Geoffrey caught her wrist. "Are you sick? Because I can stay if you're sick."

She stared at him. Her leg throbbed, and her head spun. She wanted him to stay, but she'd seen their food stores and knew that the deer meat would add greatly to their dwindling supplies.

"Go," she said. "Perhaps this afternoon, while Jim is managing the ranch on his own—" she grinned widely—"I shall take a short nap. I'm sure I'll be fine."

He looked into her eyes for long moments, but finally he nodded. "Very well, then. I'll see you sometime tomorrow." He crossed to the door and then looked back. "Take care, Emmaline."

———

Jim rode at the rear of the flock, one hand holding the horse's reins and the other grasping the end of the rope he had tied around Miney's neck. It was a long rope, but it would keep the dog from venturing too far. Pride swelled his chest as the dog trotted behind the sheep, occasionally nipping a heel or delivering a bark that spurred the wooly animals forward. All of their practice with the stuffed sheepskin had paid off.

"You're doing well, Miney," he praised. "Good dog."

The day had gone smoothly, and he had handled everything himself without mishap. His shoulders square, he anticipated the words of commendation Mr. Garrett would bestow when he returned. How many fifteen-year-olds could manage an entire sheep ranch without supervision? And for two whole days! He had posed the question to Emmaline at lunch, and she had replied, "Not many."

He frowned, remembering how quiet she'd been at lunchtime. Her face had seemed red, too, as if she'd been crying. Chris said women were hard to figure out, and Jim decided maybe Chris spoke the truth. But Jim knew how to make Emmaline happy again. Flowers.

She had been tending the seeds in the flower boxes he'd built. As far as he knew, none had sprouted yet, but surely they would. Then she'd always have flowers close by. Until then, though, it would be nice to find some wild ones for her.

He scrunched his brow, trying to remember if he'd seen anything blooming recently. He gave his forehead a whack when he recalled some tall stems of clover standing in the corner of the far pasture. Why hadn't he thought to pick them when he first saw them? Luckily the flowers grew outside the fence, or the sheep would have had them for a snack. After he put the sheep in the barn with hay for their supper, he would ride back out to the pasture and pick those stems for Emmaline. He would be a little late coming in for the evening meal, but Emmaline would forget about that when she saw the flowers.

———

Emmaline placed a wet rag across the back of her neck. The nausea abated, and she blew out a breath of gratitude. All afternoon, she had battled waves of queasiness followed by bouts of chills. Yet, even while she shivered, perspiration soaked through the front and back of her dress.

How she had wished to rest, but who else would do the week's baking? Five loaves of bread, three pies, and a pan of corn bread now cooled on the counter. As soon as she put supper on the table, she would sit for a spell. Her aching leg turned clumsy as she set out plates, silverware, and mugs for tea. She dragged herself to the stove and gave the pot of beans and pork a stir. The heat from the stove caused sweat to bead on her lip. She needed to cool down.

The rag still dripping on her neck, she stepped onto the stoop outside the kitchen door and let the evening breeze caress her body. Her muscles felt quivery, so she sat down, stretching her legs out in front of her.

The throbbing in her injured leg had given way to a sharp, rhythmic stab that carried from her calf all the way to her hip. After glancing around to be certain she wasn't observed, she raised her skirt and rolled down the stocking. She gasped at the sight of her puffy, flushed skin. It looked worse than it had yesterday. Hadn't the frequent soap-and-water washing done any good at all?

She touched her flesh, cringing at the heat that emanated from her skin. Tilting her leg toward the slanting late-afternoon sunlight, she carefully examined the scratch. Oddly, red streaks seemed to run in both directions from the site of the injury. Puzzled, she traced the lines with her fingertips. The gentle touch sent spasms through her leg.

She must wash it again. Pushing her hand against the stoop, she tried to rise, but her leg gave way beneath her. Sweat broke out all across her body. Bile filled her throat. Black dots swam in front of her eyes.

"I must . . . get inside . . ." With quivering muscles, she pressed both palms to the stoop and attempted to stand. The black dots began a wild dance, and a chill shook her entire body. She collapsed, and blackness engulfed her.

———

"There you are." Jim dumped a pitchfork full of hay in front of the horse, then hung the fork on its peg. "Enjoy your supper."

Smiling, he lifted the stems of the clover blooms. "Come on, Miney." The dog trotted alongside him as he headed for the house. He whistled a cheery tune, anticipating Emmaline's expression of pleasure at the unexpected gift of flowers for the table. He left the sheep barn and picked up his pace a bit, doing a double hop on his good leg as had become his habit, even though the snake-bit foot hardly bothered him anymore.

Miney whined, looking up at Jim with his tongue hanging out.

"What's the matter, boy? You hungry, too? Well, Emmaline will give you some leftovers."

The dog whined again, then dashed ahead, darting beneath the fence rail. Jim called, "Hey! Come back here!" When Miney didn't return, Jim grunted. The dog wouldn't be of much use if he didn't obey.

He rounded the fence and spotted Miney near the kitchen

door to the ranch house. The dog had his nose down, nuzzling something that looked like a pile of wash. He frowned. If Miney had pulled the wash line down again, Chris would have his hide! But then he remembered it was Thursday. Emmaline never did wash on Thursday. Then what . . . ?

Suddenly, he recognized the crumpled figure on the ground. He dashed forward, forgetting to hop-skip. The flowers fell from his hand as he bent over her still frame. "Emmaline? Wake up! What's wrong, Emmaline?"

He rolled her onto her back and touched her cheek. The heat of her flushed skin made him jerk away. She was really sick! "Miney," he ordered, pushing to his feet, "you stay! Stay!"

The dog hunkered down, whimpering, with his nose pressed to Emmaline's neck.

"Stay!" Jim ordered one more time. "I—I've got to get the doctor." He turned and raced to saddle a horse.

# THIRTY-THREE

THE MOON CAST sufficient light to make safe progress toward home, but Geoffrey had no desire to bounce the deer from its position on the litter, so he kept his horse to a walk. Beside him, Chris nodded in his saddle, fighting sleep, and Geoffrey considered striking up a conversation to keep him awake. But in the end, he remained silent. The canopy of stars over a cloak of gray landscape created a feeling of holiness. While he couldn't explain it, it seemed that to speak aloud would be to break the sanctity of their surroundings. So he remained silent, allowing the whispering breeze and the soft thud of hooves to provide music for the outdoor sanctuary.

As he and Chris headed across the countryside, the view slowly changed. Despite himself, Geoffrey marveled at the beauty of this predawn hour. Stars glittered overhead in a sky that had faded from dark gray to steel blue. The lighter the sky, the dimmer the stars, until all but the largest were extinguished with the beginning of yellow, pink, and lavender in the east. He was glad he'd decided to head back to the ranch after dressing out the deer, rather than spending the night on the prairie.

Wispy clouds became flashes of brilliance as the slice of white sun appeared on the horizon, tingeing the clouds' undersides with magenta. This was a time of day he didn't often see, and his chest welled with the desire to break out in praise for this glorious morning and all its splendor.

Just ahead, shadows took form, and his horse nickered, bouncing its head in an attempt to speed its pace. He chuckled. "All right, big fellow. Go ahead." He gave the horse his head, and the animal leaped forward.

Chris came to life, digging his heels into his horse's side. Together, they cantered noisily onto the ranch grounds. As they rounded the house, Chris suddenly pulled back on his reins and called, "Whoa!"

Instinctively, Geoffrey followed suit. "What is it?"

Chris pointed. "That rig. Doesn't it belong to Doc Stevens?"

Geoffrey frowned at the fringed, two-seat surrey parked right outside the kitchen door. "Yes, it does." Worry slammed him. Why would the doctor be at his house at this early hour?

Chris shot Geoffrey a nervous look. "You don't suppose Jim is sick again?"

Geoffrey forced a light chuckle. "Oh, I imagine the doctor just was out all night, delivering a baby or something for one of the neighbors, and saw our kitchen light. He probably stopped for a cup of Emmaline's tea."

Chris nodded slowly. "Yes. You're probably right."

Geoffrey slid from his horse. "Take the horses to the barn and get started quartering that deer. I'll check in with Emmaline and then come help."

With another nod, Chris took hold of the reins from Geoffrey's horse and headed toward the sheep barn.

Snatching off his hat, Geoffrey entered the kitchen. Expecting to see the doctor and Emmaline at the table, sharing a pot of tea, he was surprised to find a young girl with long yellow braids stirring something at the stove. He'd seen the girl in town, but he couldn't remember her name.

She looked up when he came in and wiped her hands on Emmaline's apron, which was tied around her waist. "Mr. Garrett?"

Geoffrey nodded.

"I'm Alice—Doc's daughter."

Why was she wearing Emmaline's apron and cooking at Emmaline's stove? "Where's Emmaline?" Dropping his hat on the counter, he headed toward the back of the house before the girl could answer.

The sitting room and spare sleeping room were empty. Geoffrey's confusion grew when he entered the parlor and spotted Jim slumped in Emmaline's rocker. The boy jumped to his feet. Without a word to Geoffrey, he dashed to the door of the main sleeping room and said, "Doc, Mr. Garrett is back."

Geoffrey looked through the doorway as the doctor rose from his perch on the edge of the bed. As Geoffrey's focus slid to the figure in the bed, his heart leaped into his throat. He burst through the doorway and stood at the bedside. Emmaline lay with her hair scattered across the pillow. Her flushed face told of a high fever. He reached for her but stopped short of actually touching her. He swung to face the doctor. "What happened to her?"

The doc removed his wire-rimmed spectacles. "According to young Jim here, she suffered a cut on her leg from some barbed wire in the tack room. I found the wound, and it's badly infected."

Emmaline had mentioned a little scratch. Geoffrey shook his head. "She's this sick from a scratch?"

"Now, Geoffrey," the doc said, rubbing the round lenses of his glasses with a white handkerchief, "infection is a funny thing. When it gets into the blood, as this one has done, it can wreak havoc on the person's entire system." He slid the springy earpieces over his ears and then pushed the glasses high on his nose. His watery eyes blinked. "This infection is wreaking havoc . . ."

From his spot near the doorway, Jim blurted, "Is she going to die?"

Geoffrey spun around. "Jim!"

The boy shrank back, and Geoffrey took a deep breath. Forcing an even tone, he said, "Go out and help your brother with the deer."

Jim hesitated for a moment, his gaze flicking between Emmaline and Geoffrey, but finally he nodded and slipped out of the room.

Doc Stevens gave Geoffrey a stern look. "Take it easy on the boy. If he hadn't come riding in for me like he did, we might have lost her. When I got here, she was unconscious. I lanced the site of the wound—"

Geoffrey's stomach clenched at the image his words painted.

"—drained it, and cauterized the area. Jim and I have spent the night trying to bring down her fever. Beyond that, there's not much else to do." He bent over and picked up his black leather bag. "Now that you're here, I'll let you take over."

As the doctor headed for the kitchen, Geoffrey trailed behind him, aghast. "You're leaving?"

Doc Stevens shot Geoffrey a firm look. "I just told you, fighting the fever is all that we can do. You can put cold rags on her head and spoon liquid into her as well as I can. I have to get back to town. I can leave Alice, though, if you'd like some extra help."

Geoffrey gaped. A mere child? What good would a child do?

The doctor put his hand on Geoffrey's shoulder. "If she should take a turn for the worse, have either Chris or Jim ride in for me. Just keep the wound clean. I left a roll of bandages and some salve in the bedroom. Get her to drink as much as you can, too."

Geoffrey swallowed. "When . . . when might I know if she's going to recover?"

The older man raised one shoulder in a shrug. "I can't put a time on it. Either the fever will abate or it'll worsen. If her muscles start to tighten up so she can't swallow, you come for me right away. But if it gets to that point, well . . . ." He shrugged again, his expression sorrowful. No other words were necessary. "Do you want Alice to stay and help?"

Geoffrey shook his head. "No. I'll care for her myself." He saw the doctor and Alice to the door and then started to return to the bedroom. But he remembered Doc saying Emmaline should drink, so he prepared a cup of tea for her with the hot water in the kettle. When he entered the bedroom, he discovered Emmaline's eyes open. He set the cup down on the bedside table and leaned over her.

"Emmaline? You're awake?"

"Geoffrey . . . you're back."

He had to strain to hear her whispered voice. His hands planted on the mattress, he nodded. "Yes. I'm back." Unnecessary words, but he wanted to talk to her, to reassure himself that she would be fine.

"I thought I was dreaming. . . ."

"No." He cleared his throat, battling a sting behind his nose. "I'm here. Do . . . do you want a drink?" He reached for the cup.

She shook her head, and her hand slipped from beneath the sheet to cup his wrist. "Geoffrey?"

Slowly he sat on the edge of the bed and turned his hand to clasp hers.

"You never said . . . if you read my samplers."

Tears pricked his eyes, and remorse smote him. He wanted to thank her for her work. But he couldn't find words.

She licked her lips, her glassy eyes searching his face. "Without faith, you're lost, Geoffrey. I want you to find your faith again. Did . . . did the verses help?"

He lifted her hand to his lips and kissed its back. "Don't worry about me. Think about yourself now. Think about getting well."

Wildly, she shook her head, her hair tangling. "I'm all right. But you . . . you can't go on this way, fighting against God. You need Him, Geoffrey. Tell me you'll seek Him again." Her fingers tightened on his hand; her head and shoulders lifted slightly from the pillow. "Tell me."

"Emmaline, please . . ."

Suddenly she relaxed, her eyes drifting shut once more.

Geoffrey released her hand and placed it under the covers. He sat for a long while, staring into her still face and listening to her labored breathing. *"Tell me you'll seek Him again."* Her words transported him to England and his grandmother's sitting room, where he sat in the evenings and listened to Grandmother read from the Bible. Grandmother had once told him something very similar: *"A wise man recognizes he has no strength on his own, my dear boy; a wise man leans on God."*

All of his life, he'd leaned on God. When his mother had left, he'd relied on prayer to ease the pain of rejection. When his father was harsh, he had soothed himself with the knowledge of a heavenly father's tender care. The early years in Kansas, while establishing this ranch, constant prayers—requesting strength, expressing appreciation—had hovered on his heart.

He rose from the bed and paced to the window, peering across the grounds of Chetwynd Valley. Emmaline was right. His faith was gone. When had he let it go? *Why* had he let it go?

A weak cough drew his attention. He hurried back to the bed and helped Emmaline sit up. When the coughing fit had passed, he held the cup so she could sip. With his encouragement, she drank nearly half the cup but then, exhausted, fell back asleep. Geoffrey pulled the rocking chair into the bedroom and spent the day at her side, alternately washing her face with cool water and spooning liquids into her mouth when she was too tired to sip.

Each time he changed the bandage on her leg, nausea attacked him, but, just like with the sheep, he did what needed to be done. He must see to Emmaline's needs.

At suppertime, Chris appeared in the doorway of the sleeping room. "I prepared some deer steaks and made a broth, as well, for Emmaline. Come and eat."

Tiredly, Geoffrey tugged the sheets across Emmaline's sleeping frame and placed a cool cloth across her forehead. Pleasant aromas greeted his nose when he entered the kitchen, but he had no appetite for food. His belly was filled with worry.

Midway through the meal, Jim dropped his fork onto his plate with a clatter and pinned Geoffrey with a fierce look. "You don't believe she will . . . *die* . . . do you?"

Geoffrey grimaced, but he answered truthfully. "She is very sick, Jim. While I hope she will live, we . . . we must face that possibility."

Chris shook his head. "We have had too much death. . . ."

Geoffrey agreed. He saw tears pool in Jim's eyes, but Jim quickly blinked them away. The boy stood from the table. "I must go out and . . . and . . ." He dashed out the door.

Chris started to rise and follow, but then he sank back down. His sad gaze met Geoffrey's. "It will be hard on Jim should Miss Emmaline die. He thinks a great deal of her. It will be like losing his mum all over again."

Geoffrey understood that all too well. He had lost his mum, too. The thought of losing Emmaline burned red-hot in his soul. His stomach rolled, and he felt as though he would be sick. He pushed to his feet. "Can you keep watch over Emmaline for a few minutes? I must . . . take a little walk."

Before Chris could answer, Geoffrey bolted to the yard. He stood in place for a moment, his hands on his knees, sucking in gasps of air that brought his queasiness under control. Then he looked around, uncertain what to do or where to go. This ranch, which had always been a place of security and solitude, now offered nothing that would soothe his troubled mind. Inside the house, Emmaline lay dying. His chest began to heave, each breath searing in its release. He needed to escape. But where?

His feet began to move almost of their own volition. He charged across the ground and found himself heading directly for the tack shed. No one would bother him in there. He broke into a stumbling run.

The shed was nearly black inside, an appropriate setting for his despondent mood. He closed himself in the small building and then stood in the middle of the floor, blinking, until his eyes adjusted. Murky shadows took shape—the work bench, a nail keg, tools hanging from pegs on the walls, a square whitish patch near the door. He frowned at the patch. What was that?

Slowly, he crossed to the odd item and leaned forward. Then he jerked back as if stung. One of Emmaline's samplers! He tipped his body toward the sampler and squinted.

The letters, carefully formed with tiny stitches of black thread, stood out against the white backdrop. *Thou wilt keep him in perfect peace, whose mind is stayed on thee: because he trusteth in thee."*

Geoffrey swung away from the sampler, covering his face with one hand. A sob nearly doubled him in two. Peace? He had no peace! He hadn't had peace for months. "Why, God? Why have You let everything fall apart?" The words tore from his soul. Pain seared his chest.

He dropped to his knees and cried in harsh, hiccupping

sobs—sounds the likes of which he hadn't known could pour from a man. The weeks of heartache, the pain of loss, the worry about Emmaline . . . everything spilled out in a rush. And when he'd spent his last tear, he turned to sit on the hard floor with legs bent, elbows on knees, and his head in his hands.

He released one last, shuddering sob, then fell quiet. The silence of the shed enveloped him, and the words from the sampler echoed through his soul. He slowly lifted his head and stared at the square of white.

" 'Thou wilt keep him in perfect peace, whose mind is stayed on thee: because he trusteth in thee.' " He whispered the words, and the truth pelted him like raindrops from heaven. God hadn't left him. Geoffrey had let his mind slip away from God, and the more he'd turned his mind from God, the harder it had been to trust Him. With the lack of trust, peace had disappeared.

If he were to reverse the process—if he were to turn his mind to God again—would peace return? Burying his face in his hands, Geoffrey groaned with the desire to once more bask in peace. To believe God was in control and would guide him, uphold him, protect him.

Seated on the floor of the tack shed, Geoffrey opened his soul to God and begged Him to draw near.

# THIRTY-FOUR

⁓

WITH HIS HANDS in his pockets, Geoffrey stepped from the tack shed and looked upward where stars peppered the sky. He breathed a heartfelt, "Thank you, Lord . . ." He was still concerned about the ranch, but he felt he had made the first step toward peace. Hope sat precariously on the precipice of his heart, and he trusted that its grip would gain strength as he continued to pray and seek God in the days to come.

As he approached the house, two shadowy figures—one two-legged and one four-legged—rounded the corner and stepped into his pathway. He gave a slow nod. "Jim . . . Have you and Miney thrown hay for the sheep this evening?"

Miney whined at the mention of his name and rose up, but Jim put his hand on the dog's head. The animal immediately sat back on his haunches and panted up at his master. "Yes, sir. I've seen to the evening chores."

"Good." Geoffrey started to step past him, but Jim held out a hand.

"I wanted to give this to you."

Geoffrey squinted. In the dim light cast from the lantern

behind the kitchen window, he couldn't quite make out the item in Jim's hand. Small and rectangular in shape, it could have been anything.

Jim shifted slightly, and the shaft of lantern light fell across the boy's hands. He carried a little tin box. Recognition exploded in Geoffrey's brain and he reached for it.

"I found it a while back, and I hid it," the boy said. "It has money in it. I planned to use it to take Emmaline and me to England in the spring, but . . ." Tears glittered in the boy's eyes. "If she dies, buy her one of those fancy carved coffins with the satin all lining the inside, like the undertaker has in his window in Moreland. Don't just put her in a . . . a pine box. She's too pretty for that. Then send her to England and let her be buried in your village there."

Bouncing the box slightly, Geoffrey said, "And what if she lives?"

Jim shrugged. "She can still have it. To go back to England, or to buy lots of flower seeds. I don't care. Whatever she wants . . ."

Geoffrey held the tin box in his hands. The amount in the box must have seemed a fortune to Jim, yet he was willing to part with it for Emmaline. He placed his hand on Jim's shoulder. "Thank you, Jim. I know Emmaline will be grateful, too."

The boy hung his head, and one tear slipped down his cheek. "I'm going to put Miney in the shed for the night. I . . . I'll be in later." Jim shuffled off with Miney at his side.

Once more, Geoffrey started to enter the kitchen, but the sound of horse hooves and wagon wheels approaching shifted his attention to the road. He hoped the visitor was Dr. Stevens, returning to check on Emmaline. But instead of a surrey, a wagon pulled into the lane. Two figures perched side by side on the seat.

He waited at the corner of the house for the wagon to draw near, and a familiar voice called, "Geoffrey Garrett, what for you standin' wit' your face all scrunched up 'stead o' sayin' howdy? Don't you got no better manners'n that?"

Geoffrey leaped forward as Ronald drew their mules to a halt in front of the porch. "Tildy! And Ronald!"

The pair beamed down at him, their smiles white in their dark faces. "Yessuh, it's us, shore as you live an' breathe," Tildy said in her gravelly voice. "We tried a-livin' in a town called Colby, but them folks was already used to their own smithy—Ronal' couldn't git 'nough business for us to have a decent livin'. So I tol' him, let's go back."

Ronald leaned forward. "Figure you's still willin' to let us live on that piece o' ground, an' we'll jus' rebuild our soddy an' I can git back to work. Ruther starve among frien's than feast among strangers."

"Of course you're welcome to stay! It's so good to see you again."

Tildy shifted her gaze to the house, her round face eager. "Where be Miss Emmalion? Shore am hankerin' to have a cup o' tea wit' that girl."

Geoffrey tucked the tin box beneath his arm and reached toward Tildy. "Come down from there, Tildy. I'll take you to Emmaline. I think you are going to be a very welcome sight."

After one look at Emmaline lying in the bed, Tildy took control of the household. She shuffled Jim to the bunkhouse with Chris and Geoffrey, instructing Ronald to sleep either with the bales of hay or in their wagon—made her no nevermind, but she would be claiming the bed in the spare sleeping room as her own. The men obeyed her directions to carry in her belongings, and while they stacked boxes next to the bed, she proclaimed, "I'll be a-carin' for Miss Emmalion. You men jus' scoot an' let me git that girl back on her feet. Mm-mmm, she'll be sprightly an' fine afore long or my name ain't Tildy Senger!"

Despite Tildy's command to scoot, Geoffrey couldn't bear to stay away. With Ronald helping with the sheep, he had the freedom to sit on the edge of the bed and keep vigil over Emmaline. When Tildy forced him from the room so she could give Emmaline a sponge bath or see to her wound, he tended Emmaline's flower boxes. To his delight, tiny green shoots had broken through the soil.

Tildy fussed at him frequently, accusing him of being underfoot. Her husky voice scolded, "Leave her be! Your gawkin' ain't gonna change nothin' in here." But he ignored her. For too many months he'd let Emmaline be, and his distance had created a barrier between them. He was determined to bridge that gap by showering her with attention now. He told Tildy, "My gawking might not change a thing, but my prayers can . . . and will." He clung to hope.

Watching Emmaline fight against the infection, he thought of Jonathan Bradford's claim that she was weak and in need of protection. Bradford didn't know his daughter very well. Emmaline had faced much in her short time in Kansas, and she had developed a source of strength that belied her small size and delicate nature.

Day by day she grew stronger, fortified by Tildy's meat broths and the tea poultices that drew the infection from her leg. On the third day after Tildy's arrival, Emmaline sat on the edge of the bed and Tildy washed her hair. Geoffrey was banished during the procedure, but Tildy allowed him to come in after she'd tucked Emmaline back beneath the covers. When he entered the room, Emmaline said, "Please be seated, Geoffrey," as formal as if she had asked him to join her for tea in the parlor.

Tildy stood watch from the corner, her arms crossed over her ample chest as Geoffrey sat on the edge of the bed. Emmaline offered her hand, and he took it, holding it between both of his. "You look so much better."

Her laughter trickled, and she tossed her head. Her long hair, still damp from its wash, tumbled over her shoulders in beguiling disarray. "And I no doubt smell better, too, thanks to Tildy."

Tildy's low chuckle rumbled, but Geoffrey kept his gaze pinned to Emmaline. "It is so wonderful to see you looking well. I am quite grateful to Tildy . . . and to God."

Emmaline's face lit. "Have you been praying, Geoffrey?"

He nodded, a lump filling his throat when tears flooded her dark eyes.

"Oh, I'm so glad. . . ."

"I am, too. I didn't realize how much I missed talking to God until I started it up again." He squeezed her hands. "Thank you, Emmaline, for helping me recover my faith. Hope lives again, in here." He pressed one hand to his chest. His heart beat in a steady thud beneath his palm.

A tear splashed down Emmaline's cheek, but her smile never wavered. For long moments, she held his gaze, her tear-filled eyes glowing with pleasure. Then suddenly she shifted, sitting up straight and folding her hands together in her lap. She tilted her head. "Tildy told me Ronald and some men from town have replaced the barn roof."

Surprised by the change in topic, Geoffrey merely nodded.

"And the same men who fixed the roof have promised to help Ronald rebuild his soddy."

Geoffrey shot Tildy a startled look. The woman's knowing smirk made him wonder what she was thinking.

"When their soddy is repaired, Tildy and Ronald will be able to move back into their own home."

"That's right."

Another chuckle sounded from the corner.

Emmaline continued in a conversational tone. "I assume

since the barn is repaired, the bales of hay that fill one side of the bunkhouse can be moved to the barn?"

Geoffrey blinked in confusion. He gave one slow bob of his head. "Yes."

Emmaline tapped her lips with one finger, her forehead pinched in thought. "With the bunkhouse free of bales, a person can once more take up residence in that side. . . ."

Geoffrey looked from Emmaline to Tildy. Tildy's apple cheeks were puffed, as if she held back laughter. Turning back to Emmaline, he said, "If you're referring to Jim, then . . . yes. He can return to the bunkhouse." With a frown, he asked, "Has his presence in the house been a bother?"

Emmaline's eyes grew wide. "Oh no! He's been no bother at all." An impish twinkle replaced the innocent look. "But his departure will make the house seem quite empty."

"Empty?"

"Yes. This house was not designed for me to reside here all alone, now, was it?"

Geoffrey searched Emmaline's face. Her brown-eyed gaze, warm and steady, held him captive.

Emmaline's voice was as soft and sweet as the gentle flow of the Solomon River. "Tildy says my daisies have broken through the soil."

Geoffrey cleared his throat. "Yes. I've been watering them."

"In the spring, I shall transplant them around the porch and along the pathway to the river. In time, they shall reseed themselves, and we shall have a veritable field of daisies. Will you pick me bouquets then, Geoffrey?"

"Y-yes." He swallowed. "I shall pick you as many bouquets as you like."

"Thank you. And I should like it very much if you would build me a little potting shed so I can grow more flowers. I would like my potting shed constructed of stone, just like the house. And it must have a window that looks out over the Solomon. I so love listening to the song of the Solomon. Will you do that for me, Geoffrey?"

He would do anything for her when she looked at him with that adoring gaze. "Of course. I shall start collecting rocks now. By spring, certainly I'll have enough."

Her lips curved into a sweet smile. "I can provide the first stone."

Tilting his head, he raised his eyebrows in silent query. A guffaw blasted from behind him. Geoffrey peeked over his shoulder at Tildy.

She shook her head at him, her eyes sparkling. "That girl done all but said the words. Cain't you read into what she's tryin' to tell you? She's a-plantin' her English rock in Kansas soil." When Geoffrey didn't reply fast enough, Tildy flung her hands outward and said, "She's wantin' to stay, foolish man! But don't seem proper to keep her here 'less you two gits yo'selves hitched."

# THIRTY-FIVE

SHO' 'NUFF SEEMS peculiar to see a handful o' daisies in your hand, it bein' Novembuh." Tildy shook her head, making the robin's wing sewn to the side of her black felt hat quiver. Outside, a wintry wind whistled, shaking the windowpanes of the little upstairs room in the pastor's home.

Emmaline lifted the cheery bouquet of daisies to her nose. Although the daisies carried a pungent rather than pleasing aroma, the scent brought back memories of happy times. "Peculiar or not, I'm thrilled to carry a wedding bouquet of daisies. If I had married in England, it's exactly what I would have chosen, no matter what the gardener had available in the flower pits."

Tildy fluffed the skirt of Emmaline's gown with her glove-covered hands. "Mm-mm-mmm, no mattuh what flowers you carry, you gots to be the purtiest bride evuh, Emmalion. Your mama would be right proud. Too bad she cain't be here. Seems like a girl oughtta have her mama close by when she gits herself married."

Emmaline touched the flurry of ruffles around her neck, picturing Mother's hands stitching the rows of delicate lace to the dress's ruffles. "She's with me in spirit, Tildy, and having you here means so much to me. You couldn't take better care of me if you were my mother."

Tildy flapped her hands. "Oh, chil', now don't be makin' me cry. I wants to see clearly when you an' Geoffrey exchange them vows!"

Emmaline laughed and embraced her friend. "Very well. Is it time?"

Tildy glanced at the little clock ticking on the dresser top. "Jus' a few more minutes." She scowled. "You feelin' all right? You's still spindly as a broom handle."

Although almost a month had passed, Emmaline hadn't regained all of the weight she'd lost during her sickness. The gown of yellow lawn—custom fit to her measurements prior to leaving England— hung loosely on her frame. Tildy chided her constantly about her hollow cheeks, but Emmaline had never felt better in her life.

"I feel wonderful, Tildy—very happy and content. And quite eager to become Mrs. Geoffrey Garrett." Her attitude about marriage had changed so much since her last time in this room. God had worked a miracle in her heart.

Tildy patted Emmaline's cheek with her thick palm. "You's done a lot o' growin' up, chil'."

Yes, Emmaline had done a great deal of growing. Sitting on the edge of the bed, she peered up at Tildy. "I've learned a lot. Hardships will either destroy you or make you stronger. The past months have been *so hard*, yet I wouldn't change them."

Tildy sat, too, her heavy bulk causing the mattress springs to protest. "You have had your troubles, mm–hmm. An' don' be thinkin' they's all done, neither. Every season has its heartaches, but you done learned the most 'portant lesson, an' that's that God gits you through. No matter what comes along—when you leans on Him, He gits you through."

Emmaline nodded. "Geoffrey and I will lean on God and on each other."

" 'Course you will, chil'." Tildy squeezed Emmaline's hand. "You's marryin' a fine man, an' he's gittin' hisself a dandy li'l bride." Tears formed in the woman's eyes, and she swished them away with an impatient flick of her fingers. "An' I'm thinkin' we best git you to the chapel right now afore you miss your own weddin'!"

At that moment, a voice called, "Tildy? Miss Emmalion? Preacher say it time to start. Git on down here!"

Tildy made a growling sound in the back of her throat. "Oh, dat man o' mine, always givin' orders."

Emmaline swallowed her giggle. Ronald was generally *taking* orders . . . from Tildy.

Emmaline sprang from the bed and skipped out the door with Tildy on her heels. Ronald stood at the bottom of the stairs in his new black suit. A satin ribbon tied beneath his clean-shaven chin set off the crisp white collar of his shirt. "You ready to walk that aisle, Miss Emmalion?"

Tildy nudged Emmaline with her elbow. "Don' Ronal' look fine? Never seen him so gussied up, but he's proud as proud can be, gittin' to hand you off to Geoffrey."

Both Tildy and Ronald sported fine new clothes for this celebratory occasion. "He is only as handsome as you are beautiful," Emmaline told Tildy.

Tildy snorted. "Oh, law, git on wit' you, chil'!" But her broad grin let Emmaline know she appreciated the compliment.

Emmaline flashed Tildy a smile before lifting her skirt slightly and descending the stairs. She slipped her hand into the bend of Ronald's arm. "I'm ready."

"Then let's go. Your groom's a-waitin'!"

*Six months later . . .*

Emmaline bent over and pulled out a weed that had dared to grow in her expanding flower patch. She tossed the errant green scrap aside and then pressed her hands to her lower back, arching her spine. With a giggle, she addressed her stomach. "If you are already getting in my way, what will I do as your arrival date nears?"

Geoffrey teased her for talking to their unborn child, but he always smiled when she did it. His excitement at the prospect of a baby was second only to her own. And wouldn't Mother and Father be delighted to know they would become grandparents in the late summer? Hopefully her letter had reached them by now.

A tiny niggle of disappointment wiggled down her spine as she thought of delivering this baby far away from Mother. She had expressed that regret shortly after discovering she was in a family way, and Geoffrey had asked, "Would you like me to send you to England for your confinement and delivery? You could return with the baby the next year." That he would make the offer touched her deeply, but she couldn't imagine leaving him. Kissing his lips, she had said, "You and I will welcome this child into our lives together right here in our own home. Mother and Father can come visit us next year!"

She crouched to loosen the soil around the delicate forget-me-nots, and then shifted over a few feet to thin out the section of daisies. Reaching to the base of the flower stems, her knuckles encountered something hard and immovable. She pushed the cheerful blooms aside and frowned at the large rock plopped right in the middle of the daisy patch.

Running her hand over the smooth stone, she gave a start. The rock was the same one she had carted from England! Why wasn't it in the growing pile that would soon become her promised potting shed? She cupped the cool stone with both hands, intending to put it back on the pile, but before she could lift it, someone said, "Emmaline, what do you think you are doing?"

She peeked over her shoulder. Geoffrey moved toward her, a curious expression on his face. Pushing a strand of hair from her eyes, she answered, "Moving my rock."

He caught her shoulders and guided her to her feet. "You shouldn't do any heavy lifting."

"Geoffrey Garrett." She plunked her dirty fists on her hips and sent him a scowl. "I carried that rock all across the countryside without any difficulties. Surely I can move it from one place to another."

He smirked and tapped the end of her nose. "That rock's traveling days are finished, my dear wife. Let it remain where I placed it."

"*You* put it there?"

"Yes, I did." Geoffrey gazed down at the rock, fondness curving his lips. "And there it shall stay."

"But why?"

Slowly he angled his head to meet her gaze. "Because every time I walk into the house, I'll see it there. It's a reminder of my birthplace, but it also reminds me that I am blessed. You chose to stay here with me. And together we're building our life on a firm foundation of faith." He caught her hands and lifted them to his lips. "A rock has permanence, Emmaline—just as our love is permanently grounded in God and in each other. So leave it there, hmm?"

She gazed down at the rock and smiled. Geoffrey was right—it belonged nestled amongst the daisies. Lifting her face, she tugged the brim of her bonnet forward to shade her eyes. "Will you remember to send Jim in so he and I can complete his arithmetic lesson?"

Even though the boy wasn't able to go in to Stetler each day for schooling, Emmaline had made it her duty to educate him as best she could. He soaked up knowledge like a sponge, and in another year or two he planned to leave the ranch to pursue a different kind of profession than sheep ranching.

"He won't let me forget." Geoffrey shook his head, feigning disgust. "If I don't send him, he'll come in on his own."

Emmaline ran her fingers down the line of Geoffrey's whiskers. "Do you mind?"

He shifted his head slightly to kiss her palm. "Of course not. He has a lot of catching up to do if he wants to go to a university." He chuckled. "But don't set a plate at the supper table for him. He's going in to Stetler."

"Ah. Alice's house again?"

"Again." Geoffrey crossed his arms. "They seem awfully young to be spending so much time together."

"Geoffrey!" Emmaline burst out laughing. "Alice is the same age I was when you began to woo me." She laughed again when he cleared his throat and frowned. "Besides, Dr. Stevens' daughter is as cute as could be. She and Jim would make a darling couple."

Geoffrey sighed, regret tingeing his features. "You know, if Chris chooses to leave when Jim goes to school, it will mean some changes around here. But"—the worried look drifted away as he raised his shoulders in a shrug—"I trust God will send the right workers along to replace them."

"He does meet our needs." Suddenly an abrupt kick inside her belly made her double over. "Oh!" She grasped Geoffrey's hand and held it against her rounded stomach. "Little Matilda is active today!"

"I believe you intended to say," Geoffrey said with a grin, his fingers firm and warm even through the layers of fabric, "*Chet* is making his presence known."

She laughed lightly, wrinkling her nose at her husband. Fixing him with a pensive look, she asked, "Will you be disappointed if this baby is Matilda instead of Chet?"

"Of course I won't be disappointed, because I *know* it's Chet." His eyes sparkled as he whispered, "But don't tell Tildy I said so."

They shared a laugh. Geoffrey looked toward the pasture. "I must get to work." He lifted his hand to caress her cheek. "Don't stay out in the sun too long, hmm? Sit on the porch in the shade and finish stitching that baby quilt instead. The flowers will survive without you wearing yourself out."

Without waiting for her reply, he leaned forward and delivered a kiss on her lips. Then he walked across the ground in his familiar long-legged stride toward the pasture where the sheep peacefully grazed beneath a sky of azure blue. Emmaline stood watching after him while the Solomon sang a peaceful lullaby, and her flowers—encouraged by a light spring breeze—swayed gently to the music.

Her mind drifted over the past year and all she and Geoffrey had weathered together. With an overflowing heart, she whispered a prayer of thankfulness for the blessings God had brought into their lives, even when they had turned their backs on Him. Just as His Word promised, He had given them the strength to triumph over challenges. The difficult times had even served a purpose—of growing their faith in God and in each other.

She touched her burgeoning belly and sighed with contentment. Each and every day of the past year, God had showered her and Geoffrey with His loving care, and they, like wild flowers fed by sunshine and rain, would continue to blossom in this land called Kansas.

# ACKNOWLEDGMENTS

To my family—thank you for your endless support. I couldn't meet the challenges of this ministry without it.

To ACFW Crit14, Ramona, and Judy—Thank you for your suggestions, encouragement, and friendship. You are all very special to me.

A wink and a smile to Elise Johansen for "boycotting" my books until I got this story written. What a motivator!

To my prayer warriors—your petitions on my behalf are a blessing beyond description. May God bless you as richly as you have blessed me.

To Kathy H. and Kathy A.—your friendship, your willingness to share with me through both tears and laughter, is a priceless gift. Thank you.

To my agent, Tamela—thank you for your continued belief in me.

To the wonderful staff at Bethany House—your efforts to create a quality book are always exemplary. Thank you so much for all you do. I so enjoy being a part of your "family."

And most importantly, to God—You always keep Your promises, and I am forever grateful for Your steadfast presence in my life. May any praise or glory be reflected directly back to You.

# ABOUT THE AUTHOR

KIM VOGEL SAWYER is fond of C words like children, cats, and chocolate. She is the author of 12 novels, including the bestsellers *Waiting for Summer's Return and My Heart Remembers*. She is active in her church, where she teaches adult Sunday school and participates in both voice and bell choirs. In her spare time, she enjoys drama, quilting, and calligraphy. Kim and her husband, Don, reside in Kansas and have 3 daughters and 6 grandchildren.

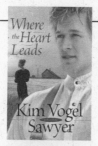